'Morpuss overlays sci-fi concepts on the conventions of vintage crime fiction [and] arrives at a satisfying destination'
Financial Times

'An intriguing take on an Agatha Christie-type locked-room mystery'
Irish Independent

'A delicious, sophisticated puzzle you'll want to take your time to solve. It gripped me for a week. Incredible'
Janice Hallett, author of *The Twyford Code*

'A very enjoyable read. An endlessly inventive murder mystery – gripping from the first page'
Alex Pavesi, author of *Eight Detectives*

'Guy Morpuss is quickly establishing himself as a key player in the speculative fiction genre. A very clever and brilliantly imagined locked room mystery'
Victoria Selman, author of *Truly, Darkly, Deeply*

'Dizzyingly brilliant ... had me gripped from the start. If you like your crime stories to dazzle with unique settings, genius plotting, great characterisation and sublime speculative twists, this is the book for you'
Philippa East, author of *Little White Lies*

BLACK LAKE MANOR

Also from Guy Morpuss and Viper
Five Minds

BLACK LAKE MANOR

GUY MORPUSS

 VIPER

This paperback edition first published in 2023
First published in Great Britain in 2022 by
VIPER, part of Serpent's Tail,
an imprint of Profile Books Ltd
29 Cloth Fair
London
ECIA 7JQ
www.serpentstail.com

Text design by Crow Books

1 3 5 7 9 10 8 6 4 2

Printed and bound in Great Britain by
CPI Group (UK) Ltd, Croydon, CR0 4YY

A CIP catalogue record for this book is available from the British Library.

ISBN 978 1 78816 5716
eISBN 978 1 78283 7275

To Omi

The Wolf That Eats Time
From the Oral Traditions of the Akaht

Only one who is Hamatsa may summon the Wolf
The Wolf will eat no more than one quarter of one Day
Only the Hamatsa and any who pass to the Night will remember
The Wolf will heed the call of each Hamatsa only once

1804

1804

1

THE WRECK OF
THE *WHITBY*

Maquina, chief of the Mowachaht, watched impassively as the *Pride of Whitby* broke her back.

He and a companion had scrambled up the rocky path that led to the clifftops surrounding Pachena Bay, leaving the rest of the whaling party below. On seeing lights near the entrance to the bay Maquina had been curious to know who it was that had braved the first storm of winter.

This was not a night for venturing out in a cedar log canoe. Far safer to do as Maquina had done: wait onshore for the storm to blow a drift whale into the bay. As he had predicted, a carcass had been washed ashore, and he had left his men butchering it while he investigated the lights.

Once they climbed the cliffs it was swiftly apparent that the vessel was no canoe. Maquina lowered his stolen telescope, tucking the precious instrument back into his cloak, away from the driving rain.

'There are three masts, so she's one of yours,' he said to his companion.

The other man nodded. 'What the devil do they think they're doing? They'll be on the reefs any minute.'

'Perhaps they think this is Friendly Cove. It's an easy enough mistake to make in the dark, especially on a night like this.'

The two men watched in silence, squinting into the rain. As the ship was driven closer in they didn't need the telescope to see figures scurrying between pools of light on deck. Some seemed to be trying to trim the sails, pulling on lines. Others were gathering near a lifeboat stowed at the rear of the ship, perhaps already looking for an escape. A tall man stood in the centre of the chaos, shouting and gesturing to the crew. He appeared to be the captain but his orders were either being ignored or drowned out by the roar of the wind.

He gave up, striding aft, elbowing a crewman out of his way. As the man fell to the deck, the captain grabbed the ship's wheel, and turned it hard. For a moment nothing happened, then the bow began to point further into the bay. Towards safety.

At first Maquina thought they might make it, that they would clear the reefs that guarded the narrow entrance.

Then the inevitable happened.

The ship stopped dead. One of the masts cracked, and toppled forward. The captain stumbled, joining his crewman on the deck.

The ship's bow was held firm on the reef, but the stern continued to be battered by the waves. She was twisted round, timbers cracking, until she was side on to the watchers. And worse, side on to the waves.

'Hell,' muttered Maquina's companion. 'We have to do something.'

'We do nothing.'

'They are all going to die! We have to help them.'

Maquina turned to look at the other man. 'Of course they will die, and I will have none of my people die with them.'

The other turned back towards the path. 'Then I will go alone,' he said angrily. 'We can't just stand here and watch.'

'No you won't,' said Maquina firmly. 'Don't forget, Jewitt, that you are my property, and I'll not see it destroyed. If I want that, I'll destroy it myself.' He touched the telescope through the folds of his cloak. 'I put your master's head on a stake after I took this from him, and another twenty-four heads next to his. It won't hurt me to add one more.'

Jewitt muttered something that was carried away by the wind. He turned back to the stricken ship, scowling.

Maquina felt nothing for these strangers who had journeyed halfway across the world to die on the shores of his island. He reached for the telescope again.

Several men were now in the water round the ship, flung overboard by the impact with the reef. None would survive for long. On deck, where the mast had fallen, was a tangled mess of lines and canvas. Anyone trapped under that was probably dead already, or soon would be.

The waves were starting to break over the side of the ship, washing across the deck as she settled lower.

Maquina swung the telescope aft. The only activity now was around the lifeboat. The captain had got back to his feet, and was shouting orders to those who remained. This time they appeared to be paying some attention, perhaps because they saw that their lives depended on it. Some were untying a canvas that had been covering the boat. Others were hauling on ropes, raising it up off the deck.

Maquina counted. Apart from the captain, there were six men left. Perhaps that was enough to row to shore, but it seemed unlikely. Odds were that even if they managed to launch the boat, they would quickly be swamped.

He snapped the telescope shut and put it away again.

'We head back down,' he said. 'And then home. We need to get the meat to our people.'

'What about the crew?' asked Jewitt. 'We should wait in case they get to the shore. It won't cost us anything to help them then.'

'They won't get here,' said Maquina. 'And if they do, you know we don't have food to keep them all alive till spring. Will you let your wife die so some stranger can live?'

'They aren't strangers to me.'

'These aren't your people any more,' said Maquina. 'The storm is going to blow itself out late tomorrow, so we'll return then, to salvage what we can. There should be metal, which will give you something to do through the winter.'

He turned his back on the ship, heading for the path to the beach.

Jewitt cast a last glance at the *Pride of Whitby*. The crew were still battling with the lifeboat, one end now higher than the other, as their ship sank ever lower into the water.

Jewitt cursed.

Then he too turned away, and followed his chief back into the night.

2025

2

MURDER AT
THE GRANGE

Throughout his life the 8th Duke of Ombersley had found the lessons contained in *Debrett's Correct Form* to be more than adequate for coping with unfamiliar situations. As a young boy those lessons had, on occasion, literally been beaten into him. And while they might not precisely cover every circumstance, there was usually some guidance on which he could draw.

But for once his youthful learning was of limited value.

He seemed to recall that *Debrett's* included a passage on how to deal with the house guest who overstayed his welcome. Also, he was pretty sure that there was something about smoothing your guest's departure when it was time to leave.

Yet, much as he wanted this particular guest to leave, and swiftly, neither piece of advice seemed particularly apposite for someone who was pointing a pistol at the duke's stomach.

He fell back on ingrained good manners. 'Come on, old

chap, is that really necessary? Let me get you a drink and we can talk about this.'

The duke hadn't wanted this meeting in the first place. It seemed a little grubby to be selling off his heritage to a man whose family had until recently been living in tents in the desert and herding goats. And it was taking the duke away from the tournament that he had spent six months organising.

But needs must. It didn't come cheap to bring four of the world's top ten grandmasters to your home, even when you threw in the venue for free.

So, despite his irritation at the sheikh being almost half an hour late, the duke had put on his best smile as he walked down the front steps to greet his visitor. The silver Rolls-Royce Phantom that crunched to a halt at the end of the long gravel driveway was rather too flashy for the duke's taste. He preferred the Bentley Continental that he had inherited along with the Grange. Still, it was at least a nod to tradition.

The man who emerged was dressed in a smart grey suit, paired with a plain white keffiyeh headdress. His face was half hidden, but from what the duke could see he looked younger than expected. That should, perhaps, have been the first clue. There were beads of sweat on his forehead. Which, with hindsight, was the second clue.

But it was not in the duke's nature to doubt or judge his guests. Trust was important; besides, he knew the sheikh's father.

The duke stepped forward, holding out his hand. 'Sheikh al-Katoun. It is a pleasure finally to meet in person.'

The man's handshake was brief. He offered no apology for

being late. 'Please, call me Naz,' he said, looking around him. 'Cool place.'

The duke shrugged modestly. 'It suits us.'

He turned as a young man descended the steps from the front door. 'Sheikh al-Katoun, this is my personal secretary, Lincoln Shan. He will show your driver where he can wait, and will join us to sort out the paperwork.'

The sheikh shook his head. 'No need,' he said shortly. 'We won't be long, so my man can wait with the car. And I'd rather speak with you alone.'

For a moment the duke looked nonplussed. 'I'm sorry. I thought the plan was for you to stay for the tournament final and then dinner. Your father told me you are a keen follower of speed chess.'

'That is true, but something has cropped up in London with the family interests so I need to get back tonight.'

The duke grimaced. 'Personally, I go to the City as little as possible, and I leave my business there for others to manage. It's a real shame that you can't stay. I'm hoping that the final will be between Hagen and Petrov, which would be a fine match.'

'Sadly not,' said the sheikh. He looked pointedly up the steps. 'Shall we?'

'Of course.' The duke guided him to the front door.

They entered a high-ceilinged hallway which ended in a grand double staircase. To their right tall wooden doors were open, giving a glimpse into a reception room from which a murmur of voices emerged.

'The diamond is in my study,' said the duke, gesturing to a closed door on the other side of the hall.

'We go alone,' said the sheikh, looking at Lincoln.

The duke turned to his secretary. 'Wait here. Or better still, see how the tournament is going. They're about to start the semi-finals, and Xi versus Hagen will be interesting, a real contrast of styles.'

Lincoln smiled. 'I fear the subtleties will be lost on me, sir, as I'm not much of a player.'

'Well go and see who wins, and then come and join us in ...' He turned to his guest. 'Ten minutes? I'll need Lincoln to sort out the contract: that's all a bit beyond me.'

'Make it fifteen,' said the sheikh.

Lincoln bowed slightly, glancing at his watch. 'Very well, sir.'

As the two men turned towards the study, the lights in the tournament room dimmed, then began to flash. Booming music emerged from the room, bouncing off the walls of the entrance hall: '*Ich bin ein Pandabär, Ich bin ein Pandabär ...*'

The sheikh jerked round, staring behind him. 'What the hell is that?'

The duke smiled weakly. 'That'll be Xi making his entrance.'

The sheikh looked at him blankly. Which should have been the third clue. 'What?'

'Xi Liang,' said the duke. 'The world Number Five. Or, as I'm told we are now meant to call him, "The Panda from Anda".' He shuddered. 'Apparently this is the way to bring chess to the younger generation: flashy lights and music, and they introduce the players like boxers. Personally, I think it's all a bit gauche, but I suppose they know better than I do what works. Come on.'

As the music faded, the duke opened the door to his study, and ushered his guest inside. The room was dominated by an oak desk the size of a snooker table. There were two leather armchairs in front of it, and the walls were lined with books.

He shut the door, and gestured to a drinks trolley in one corner. 'Can I get you something?'

'No, thanks. I just want to see the diamond.'

The duke walked over to a bookshelf, pulled a hidden lever, and two shelves of books swung out, revealing a keypad. He looked over his shoulder. 'Sometimes the old ways are the best.'

The sheikh nodded impatiently.

The duke typed in a code, and reached inside the safe to extract a small wooden box. He walked to the desk, put it down, and carefully opened the lid. Nestled in velvet was a rectangular cut stone of the deepest blue.

'Here it is: the Ellora Blue. It once graced the forehead of a maharani, and has been in our family for more than two hundred years. It's said to be cursed, but I don't believe in that stuff, do you?'

The sheikh stepped over to the desk, glanced briefly at the stone, then shut the box.

The duke frowned. 'What's wrong, don't you want to inspect it?'

'No need. I trust you.'

'That was quick. You have the bonds? Shall I call Lincoln to bring the contract, then?'

'Again, no need.' The sheikh tucked the wooden box under one arm, and with his other hand reached inside his jacket. He produced a pistol, which he pointed at the duke. 'Perhaps you should have paid more attention to the curse.'

'Oh dear.' The duke looked his guest up and down. 'You're not really Sheikh al-Katoun, are you?'

The man smiled. 'No. We picked him up on his way here, and he's being held close by. Once this is over we'll stage a car crash with him in it, which should cause enough confusion while we get out of the country with his bearer bonds and the diamond. Apart from you, the only person to see me here is your secretary. I don't imagine he'll remember much beyond the headdress.'

The duke was studying him closely. 'I will remember you.'

The other man smiled thinly. 'Sadly, yes. And that's not a risk I can afford.' He raised the gun. 'This pistol belongs to the sheikh, and I'll leave it here to be found by the police.'

The duke took a step back. 'Come on, old chap, is that really necessary? Let me get you a drink and we can talk about this.'

The man merely stared at him in response.

The duke squared his shoulders. In 1944 his grandfather, the 6th Duke of Ombersley, had marched towards the German guns at Sword Beach armed with nothing more than his Webley service revolver, a swagger stick and a stiff upper lip. So the duke supposed that he ought to be able to face down one man with a pistol.

Nevertheless, he swallowed. 'Let's—'

The man shook his head. And pulled the trigger.

Twice.

Lincoln watched as his employer followed the sheikh into the study and shut the door behind them. Their guest was an odd one; he seemed ill at ease, and had a sweat stain on the back of his expensive jacket.

But the duke knew the sheikh's father, and apparently trusted the man.

Lincoln shrugged. So today he was a 'personal secretary'. The duke hadn't wanted a bodyguard, and Lincoln had been forced on him by investors, nervous about the duke's high profile and low security. Amiable though he was, he still tended to dismiss Lincoln at every opportunity.

Although perhaps that didn't really matter, since Lincoln wasn't that sort of bodyguard. He didn't even carry a weapon.

He walked through the double doors into the tournament room. The lights had dimmed, but at the far end of the room he could make out a stage with a table in the centre, and a screen behind displaying a chessboard. A man was settling himself into a chair next to the table. Lincoln cared nothing for chess, but he assumed that must be Xi Liang.

There was scattered applause from the spectators occupying the rows of seats between Lincoln and the stage.

A voice came over the speakers: 'And now we welcome the third seed at today's tournament, and World Number Six, from Oslo, Norway, here to blow your mind ... it's ... Inger Hagen!'

The voice was replaced by music, and the lights flashed again. The opening lines to 'Killer Queen' echoed round the room.

Lincoln supposed that he was the demographic at which this new approach was targeted, but it wasn't doing much for him. Maybe it helped to have some interest in chess to start with. So far he had managed to avoid the duke's efforts to get him to watch. He might just about be able to work out who had won, but the rest would be lost on him.

Inger Hagen received a rapturous welcome as she made her way on stage. Someone stood up and shouted, 'Crush him,

Inger!'

Lincoln lost interest. As the lights came back up he turned to the tables against the back wall of the room. Most were covered with stacks of books and other chess-related merchandise. He was surprised the duke had allowed it at the Grange, but then the whole thing seemed a bit tacky to Lincoln's eyes.

There was one display that was different. In the far corner, squeezed between the wall and a table, was a waist-high black plinth, topped with something shiny that caught the light. As Lincoln walked over he realised that it was a chessboard, each of the chess pieces made of glass. He reached out to touch one of them, but then noticed that someone was half-way through a game, with several pieces missing. He'd better not disturb it.

'Go ahead,' said a soft voice from behind him. 'It's fine to pick them up.'

Lincoln looked round in surprise. The speaker was a young girl who'd been sitting in the back row of the audience. She had straggly red hair which looked as though it was never brushed, and thick-lensed black-framed glasses. Lincoln wasn't good on ages, but she looked to him to be no more than fourteen or fifteen. She had a gentle accent that he couldn't place.

'This is yours?' he asked.

'Well, it's my father's really, but he's up there watching the match. He told me to keep an eye on things.'

Lincoln looked past her to the stage. At first he'd been concerned about talking, as he'd assumed the chess match would be conducted in hushed tones, but it was far from quiet. Hagen was on her feet, striding around the stage and occasionally returning to the board. The audience was loudly discussing – and sometimes cheering – each move.

The girl walked round to the other side of the plinth. 'Try it. Come on, play me.'

Lincoln looked down at the board. 'I don't really know what to do.'

'It's easy. Take your knight – you know which one that is?'

Lincoln nodded, and picked up the glass piece. It felt strangely slippery, almost liquid. 'What do I do with it?'

'It can capture my rook, here.' She pointed to a piece on her side of the board. 'Touch the rook with the knight.'

Lincoln did as she said.

The pieces felt solid as they touched, but then the rook vanished.

Lincoln stared. 'What the hell just happened?'

The girl laughed. 'Isn't it clever? Let me show you again. Put your knight where the rook was.' Lincoln complied, and she moved a bishop across the board, tapping the knight.

Which itself vanished.

The girl smiled at Lincoln, and reached across the board, holding out her hand. 'Hi, I'm Rebecca. It's pretty cool, isn't it?'

Lincoln shook her hand. 'How did you do that without me seeing? You weren't even touching the pieces when I moved them.'

'It's not a trick,' said the girl. 'Not really. It's done with hard light. You must have heard of that – it looks and feels like glass, but it's made out of light. There's a projector in here that generates the pieces.' She touched the plinth.

'It's fantastic. How do I buy one?' asked Lincoln.

'I thought you didn't know how to play.'

'I don't care about the game. It's the tech that interests me.'

'Talk to my father when they're finished,' said Rebecca. 'This isn't really for sale yet, although he is looking for investors. He's been offering prototypes for half a million.'

Lincoln gaped. 'Pounds? That's crazy!'

The girl looked confused. 'I thought you were here with them.' She gestured to the audience. 'Judging by the cars parked outside they all have loads of money, and it's cutting edge.'

Lincoln laughed. 'I just work here. Thanks for the demonstration but I don't think I'll be buying one.'

As he turned away from her there was a loud cheer from the audience, and clapping. Xi stood up, briefly shook his opponent's hand, and stalked off the stage. Hagen turned to the audience, raising her arms in triumph. 'Killer Queen' blared through the speakers again.

But then, over the sound of the music, Lincoln heard something else, like a door slamming loudly. Twice.

Had the sheikh left already? Had something gone wrong with the negotiations?

He moved quickly back into the hallway, but it was empty. The door to the duke's study was still shut. Lincoln had been told to stay away for fifteen minutes, but something felt wrong. Hesitantly he crossed the hallway, and put his ear to the door. He could hear nothing, not even voices.

As he put a hand to the door handle, Lincoln heard the roar of a car engine, and the crunch of tyres on gravel.

He ran to the front door and flung it open.

The Rolls-Royce was leaving fast, kicking up a spray of stones behind it.

He couldn't catch them, and besides, the duke was his priority. Lincoln ran back to the study.

The first thing that struck him was the smell. A harsh combination of something acrid and salty. That was quickly forgotten when he saw the duke, lying on his back by an armchair, blood staining his pristine white shirt.

Lincoln ran over and knelt beside him. The duke's eyes were shut, his chest rising and falling rapidly, breath rasping, blood bubbling on his lips.

Lincoln's first instinct was to run for help. Then he stopped, and looked behind him at the open door of the study. The rest of the Grange's staff were busy with the tournament, and no one seemed to have noticed anything untoward. Yet.

Perhaps it would be better to let the duke die. Unconscious he was no use to anyone.

Lincoln grabbed the duke's hand, squeezing hard. There was no response.

He needed to think. He got up and pushed the door shut, then stood over the duke, chewing on his lip, trying to work things out.

If the duke died quickly there was no problem. But what if he didn't? What if he stayed unconscious for days, and never woke up? That would be a disaster for all of them, particularly Lincoln.

He walked around the body. The flow of blood seemed to be easing, but the duke was still breathing. Was that a good sign?

Did he want him to live?

On his second circuit Lincoln noticed the gun left on the desk. He reached out a hand. He could use that right now to solve everything. Did he dare?

But maybe the duke would recover.

Lincoln hesitated, then lost his courage. He pulled out his phone, and dialled 999.

'I need an ambulance at Ombersley Grange. It's urgent.'

Lincoln perched on the edge of the desk as the green-suited paramedics worked on the duke.

In the ten minutes it had taken them to reach the Grange he had picked up the gun three times, wondering whether to end it all. Eventually, though, he had hidden it on one of the bookshelves.

There were two paramedics, a man and a woman. They had told him to leave, but then ignored him when he failed to comply. They were knelt over the duke, who was rapidly disappearing under a pile of medical equipment, the purpose of which Lincoln could not discern.

He had closed and locked the study door in the face of the staff and guests who had emerged from the tournament room on the arrival of the ambulance. He had belatedly noticed the open window through which the duke's attacker must have fled. So far, though, no one had come into the garden to peer through.

The female paramedic paused from her efforts for a moment, and looked up at Lincoln. 'You're the one who called this in?'

Lincoln nodded.

'Who shot him? How long till the police get here?'

'They're on their way,' said Lincoln. 'He was shot by a burglar who left through the window.' He gestured to his right.

The paramedic looked down again, seemingly accepting, at least for now, that she was not sharing a room with a potential murderer.

'Is he going to live?' asked Lincoln.

She ignored him, so he repeated the question.

She hesitated, then looked up. 'Hopefully, if we can get him to hospital quickly, but he's lost a lot of blood already. Are you family?'

Lincoln shook his head. 'I just work here. If he dies, will it be soon?'

'I really don't know,' said the woman. 'Look, I realise you're in shock, but we need to get on and stabilise him fast. I can tell you more when we've done that.'

'It's important,' Lincoln insisted. 'Could he be unconscious and then die? Could he die after more than' – he looked at his watch – 'say, five and a half hours?'

'What?' The woman looked up at him sharply. 'I just don't know.'

'Are you saying he could be unconscious for the next six hours, and then die without ever waking?' asked Lincoln.

'Of course it's possible,' said the woman. 'Please, just let us get him to hospital and then I'll answer any questions you've got.' She went back to working on the duke.

Lincoln breathed out heavily. 'Fuck,' he muttered under his breath.

His choices had narrowed to one.

Wearily he pushed himself off the desk, and walked over to the bookshelf. This hadn't been in the job description.

He retrieved the gun.

The woman saw him first. She glanced up, then down, then quickly up again, and scrambled backwards, falling over, ending up sitting on the floor. 'Shit! What are you doing?'

The man had his back to Lincoln, so was slower to catch on. Then he turned, and stood, facing Lincoln, his palms raised.

'Calm down, sir. Put the gun away. I don't know what's going on here, but this isn't going to make things better.'

Lincoln brought the gun up, holding it with both hands. They were shaking, the barrel jerking up and down.

'Step away,' he said, gesturing with the gun. As the man hesitated, Lincoln shouted: 'Now! I mean it.'

The paramedic took a step back towards the door. His colleague remained sitting on the floor, watching.

Lincoln knelt next to the duke. He put the barrel of the gun to the duke's head. He was struggling to hold the gun still, and wasn't sure where the bullet would go. And could he really do this? He moved the gun lower, pointing it at where he thought the heart would be. The medics would know, but they were hardly going to tell him.

As he tightened his grip on the gun Lincoln sensed movement. Realising what he was about to do, the female paramedic was lunging for him.

Before she could get close, Lincoln shut his eyes, and pulled the trigger.

He was deafened by the first shot, and wasn't sure how many more times he fired before the woman crashed into him.

Lincoln was face down on the floor when he felt a second person land on his back. A hand grabbed for the gun. He let it go.

'Is he dead?' he shouted. 'Tell me! Is he dead?'

He felt the weight on his body ease slightly, and twisted his head to look at the duke. The female paramedic was bent over him again, a hand to his neck. After a moment she turned to her colleague, her face white.

'He's gone.' She reached into her pocket. 'Hold him while I call for help.'

For the first time in what seemed forever, Lincoln relaxed. His ears were still ringing, and his body shaking. But it was over.

'I can't breathe,' he gasped. 'Can I sit up?'

'Stay on the floor,' said the man. He stood, stepping away from Lincoln.

As he rolled over Lincoln could see that the man was holding the gun, pointed at him.

Lincoln sat up carefully, arms crossed over his knees. He twisted his right arm, looking at the black ink tattoo on the inside of his wrist. A circle enclosing the head of a howling wolf. He moved the fingers of his left hand to touch the wolf.

'What are you doing?' said the paramedic. 'Stop it.'

Lincoln smiled up at him. If this didn't work he was in all sorts of shit.

'*Kuwitap*,' he said softly.

And the wolf ate time.

3

THE PAYOFF

'Young man,' said the Duke of Ombersley, 'I really didn't think that would work.'

'What do you remember?' Lincoln asked urgently. 'Do you remember that I saved your life?'

The duke paused before answering. It seemed that even death had not managed to disturb his sangfroid. He looked at his watch, then pulled his jacket sleeve straight to cover it. Although Lincoln noticed that his fingers brushed lightly over his chest, as though checking that the bullet holes were gone.

They were seated across from one another in matching armchairs in the duke's study. There was no gun, no blood, and no paramedics. No bullet holes. There never would be now.

But Lincoln was still shaking. To him it had been real. It had happened. He stood quickly, and walked over to the drinks trolley. 'Do you mind? Do you want one?'

The duke raised an eyebrow. 'Not for me, thank you, but if you feel the need then do go ahead.'

Lincoln poured himself a large measure of single malt. He went back to his chair and emptied the glass in one gulp.

The duke studied him. 'The grandmasters will be arriving soon, and I need to be there to greet them, so you need to sort out the sheikh. Make sure the real one gets here safely this time. According to what our guest said before ...' He paused, and swallowed. 'Before he shot me, he and his confederates kidnapped the real sheikh from somewhere nearby. You need to get in touch with him before that happens. It would perhaps be best if we cancel the meeting and see him in London later in the week. I'll leave you to sort it out.'

'I can do that,' said Lincoln. 'But there's no point in me coming to London with you. Consider this my one week's notice. I'm no use to you as a secretary, nor as a bodyguard now.'

The duke inclined his head. 'You can never do it again?'

'No. I can only summon the wolf once, and that's why the price is so high.' He coughed. 'Talking of which ...'

'The five million dollars will be with you this week. My investors will consider it cheap at the price.' He paused, and smiled. 'As do I.'

'What exactly do you remember?'

'I remember that ... that gentleman I invited into my house shooting me. Very bad form, that. Then nothing, until I was back here with you, just now. I assume he killed me?'

Lincoln hesitated. 'It was a bit more complicated than that, but in broad terms, yes.' He didn't think that his employer needed to know the details of how he had died, or why it had been necessary. Lincoln's fear had been that the duke might linger for days without waking up, and then die. Bringing the

27

duke back to a time when he was unconscious would have been pointless.

Lincoln idly rubbed the wolf tattoo on his wrist. It had worked, but he could sense now that his power was gone.

'As a matter of interest,' said the duke, 'who won the match?'

'If you're hoping to bet on the result, don't bother.'

'Absolutely not!' The duke looked shocked at the idea. 'How can you suggest that? I was just curious.'

'Sorry, but people have tried that in the past,' said Lincoln. 'It doesn't work. Things that depend on human decisions or interactions don't always play out the same way second time round.'

'It's probably better not to spoil it anyway,' said the duke. 'So what are you going to do? Is there anything I can help with? It goes without saying that I am of course most grateful.'

'I'm going home. You'll be contacted, and if you want a replacement for me, I'm sure that can be arranged.'

'I won't forget you, Lincoln. You're only, what, nineteen?'

'I'm twenty this year.'

'That's a hell of a lot of money to have at your age. Do be careful with it, dear boy, and don't tell anyone, or you'll have so many friends that you'll never know who they are until it's all gone. If you want I can get my man at Coutts to give you some advice on investments. I'll find you his card.'

'No thanks,' said Lincoln. 'I've got plans for the money. I'm going back to the island.' Then he smiled. 'But first I need to see a girl about a chess set.'

2045

4

THE RELUCTANT GUEST

I was going to be late for the party, and my octopus was sulking.

Scarlett had sunk to the bottom of her tank, her red mantle turned black, and was balefully regarding me out of one eye. I wasn't sure if she could sense the weather front pushing in over the Juan de Fuca Strait, or if she was cross that I was going out for the night.

Almost certainly the latter.

For the first time in ages I wasn't planning a girls' night in with a glass of Sauvignon Blanc and a Pacific Red Octopus for company.

With one arm Scarlett was listlessly toying with the lid of the jar that had contained the live crab she'd just eaten. I'd hoped to leave while she retreated into her cave and worked out how to open the jar, but she was getting too quick for me. All that remained of the crab was a neat pile of shell fragments by the cave entrance. Then she'd spotted the frozen shrimp sitting in the auto-timer at the top of her tank. She knew what that meant. She liked her prey to fight back.

A bit like me.

I sighed. Maybe I could use Scarlett as an excuse for not staying over. The road to Black Lake was treacherous but short. I'd watch what I drank, and it wasn't as though anyone was going to stop me on the way home. I was the closest thing to law enforcement in a fifty-kilometre radius, and I worked part time. I could have the night off.

'Call Koji,' I said.

The face that appeared on the screen next to Scarlett's tank was mostly obscured by a tightly drawn orange hood. But I'd have recognised those striking green eyes anywhere.

'Ella?' he shouted.

I could barely hear him over the roar of the wind. Rain was dripping off the hood on to his bushy, black moustache.

'Where are you, Koji-Na?' I shouted back.

'Hang on, I can't hear you.'

He disappeared as the picture wobbled, and I had a brief glimpse of trees, and then a sky filled with dark clouds. The roar of the wind dropped a little, and his face reappeared. He was pushing back his hood with one hand, and wiping water from his moustache.

'What are you doing on the roof?' I asked. 'It doesn't look safe up there.'

Koji grinned. 'Of course it isn't, but when has that ever stopped me? It's blowing like mad up here. Crazy to think this is where we were going to have the party.'

'What are you doing?' I asked again.

The picture changed and I was looking out across a windswept roof garden, potted fir and cedar trees lining either side. They were bent and shaking in the wind, and looked in danger of being blown over at any moment. In the distance, on a metal walkway next to a large, black satellite dish, a figure was hunched over.

'I've been up here with Yahl, adding some strapping to the trees,' Koji said. 'This is the worst storm we've seen since we brought them up here, and I don't want them going over the side during the night. It's getting worse, so I'm worried about the satellite dish as well. It's like a giant sail, but the boss is insisting we keep it up. I've got Yahl trying to tighten everything.'

'Leave that to Yahl,' I said. 'You're getting too old to be playing around up there in a storm.'

The image on the screen switched back to Koji. 'I'll be fine. Anyway, why did you call? I know you hate parties but please don't tell me you're cancelling. If you don't leave soon you won't make it.'

'I'm not cancelling. I've got no choice but to come. But I was hoping I might get back tonight. What's the road looking like up there? Scarlett's in a mood with me, so I'd really rather not stay.'

'Not a chance. You'll be OK for the next hour or so, but the forecast is for it to get worse after that, potentially peaking at Force Twelve. You won't be able to see a thing. If you don't get blown over the cliffs you'll probably just drive off the road in the dark.'

I sighed. 'I guess Scarlett's just going to have to suck it up and live with the frozen stuff for one night. I'll leave soon.' I paused. 'If it's getting worse you shouldn't be up there. Can't you get the younger guys to do it?'

'There's no one else left. I've sent them all back to the village

33

as it won't be safe for them later. But don't worry, we've done all we can; we're almost finished.'

'Just get down from there,' I said. 'Your life isn't worth a couple of plants.'

He snapped a mock salute, grinning at me. 'Yes, Commander.'

'Fine, don't listen to me.' I was about to hang up, when he raised a hand.

'El,' he said. Then hesitated. 'Look, I probably shouldn't say this, but I know you haven't been here in a while. He's still hurting, so be careful what you say. Things could be awkward.'

I frowned. 'I don't see why. I'll be there professionally, representing the Marine Centre. He's the one who insisted I come.'

Koji looked away. 'Just be careful. Not everyone's as good as you are at compartmentalising their life.'

'Fine.' I shrugged. 'I'll deal with it. Got to go.'

I cut the call.

I knew I needed to leave, but talking to Koji had made me realise just how much I didn't want to go to the party. A blackness was seeping into my brain.

I walked over to Scarlett's tank and unclipped the feeding hatch. For a moment she stayed where she was, but then her desire to play overcame her bad mood. Her whole body turned red with excitement and she shot towards the top of the tank. I plunged one arm into the water. It was instantly enveloped in a foaming mass of suckers, touching, feeling, tasting me. I stroked her in return, and her skin turned white at my touch. She was calm again, relaxed.

As was I. My eyes closed, I let Scarlett draw away my stress. A few minutes with her was better than any therapy.

I could have stayed there for hours, but I knew that I needed to leave. Even Koji wouldn't accept cuddling with an octopus as an excuse for missing the party.

Reluctantly I pulled myself free, suckers popping as Scarlett let go. Often it would be a battle to get away as she tried to climb up my arms and escape. On this occasion, though, she seemed to sense that I had to go. She'd given me what I needed.

She sank back to the bottom of her tank, her mantle turned white, content.

If only people were as easy to read.

The road from Bamfield to Black Lake was worse than I remembered. Over recent years tens of millions of dollars had been poured into turning the former mining town by the lake into an exclusive eco resort. There were only ten high-spec lodges nestled in the woods running down to Pachena Bay. But one week in a lodge cost more than I paid in rent for a year. So the guests it attracted either arrived by seaplane or moored their yachts at the newly built pier. The locals were waiting with grim expectation for one of the captains to fall foul of the unfamiliar reefs and currents. It was with good reason that the west coast of Vancouver Island was known as the Graveyard of the Pacific.

Because no guests ever arrived by car, not a single cent had been spent on repairing the road that had been torn apart by construction traffic and winter storms. I struggled to keep moving in a straight line, and wouldn't have fancied taking the route in the dark even without a storm.

The mist that had shrouded the coast for most of the day had blown off, to be replaced by heavy black clouds. As I rounded the high point of the road, cliffs falling away on my right to the ocean a hundred metres below, my jeep was shaken by a blast of wind. The waves were breaking fiercely in Pachena Bay, the pier deserted. Whatever yachts might have been tied up there earlier would long since have fled south to the safety of Victoria Harbour.

The road improved slightly as I crossed the creek next to what had, until the previous year, been the site of the First Nations village of the Akaht people. I'd spent hours playing there as a child, but now it was abandoned. The ancient longhouse had been taken apart and rebuilt next to the lake. It was part of a reconstructed village that offered the authentic experience that guests expected, but with easy access via boardwalks from the log cabins. Even the historic totem pole had been relocated. Quite what the raven god who topped the pole thought of this was unknown.

I'm not Akaht. Although I grew up in Black Lake, I'm descended from European goldminers. Still, I found this desecration of their heritage depressing, particularly as it had been done with their connivance. Money talked. And more money had been thrown at the Akaht than they might ever have expected to see in their lifetimes. The absence of their chief for twenty long years probably hadn't helped.

Not that my part of town had fared much better. My childhood home on the east side of the lake was gone. Where it had been was now a neat row of log cabins for those who had been displaced and worked in the eco village. The only bits of the old town that remained were a few buildings around the entrance to a mineshaft that stretched a hundred or so metres into the hill to the south of the lake. That part of the mine had been restored carefully and made safe. As I knew to my cost, the real mines went far beyond that, and were anything but safe.

The guests would never see those parts. Their wilderness experience was carefully controlled to ensure that they got what they paid for, and nothing more dangerous.

As the road dropped, the woods opened out ahead of me, providing the first glimpse of the lake itself. Most of the year it was an inviting blue, reflecting the wooded slopes beyond. In the fall it was a stunning vision of gold and red. Kayakers and windsurfers would be skimming across its surface. Perhaps the occasional waterskier. But today it lived up to its name, black waters whipped up by the approaching storm, whitecaps beginning to break. No one would be out in that.

And above it, on the southern shore, loomed the colossus that had usurped not only the name of the lake, but the surrounding landscape as well. A solid hulk of glass and granite, crowbarred on to the peak above the water. Like the fortresses built by conquerors of old, it was a statement by one man of his ability to bend nature to his will.

Or, as he would have said, a modernist sculpture, with picture windows framing majestic views out across the North Pacific.

It projected power.

Black Lake Manor.

I knew it well. I'd been inside it more than most.

When the road split near the shore I turned left and followed the eastern path. It was the longer way round, but I wanted time to prepare myself. I slowed. I was in no rush to retrace this familiar route. I let the AI drive, and checked my make-up.

I probably looked a little more windswept than the usual visitors to the Manor, my blonde hair bleached by a life spent outdoors instead of drifting round cocktail parties in Vancouver and Victoria. But my red pantsuit fitted me well. I looked, and felt, lean and strong. I told myself I was looking good for forty.

I needed to think that.

I needed to be ready to face Lincoln for the first time in a year.

5

A LESSON
IN LOYALTY

Lincoln was waiting for me as I stepped out of the funicular. Dressed in a plain black Nehru-style suit, no tie, his black shoulder-length hair being blown about in the wind.

I kept my features impassive but tried to analyse what I was feeling. Regret? Desire? Fear? Anger perhaps, although I've never seen the point of that.

Lincoln Shan. Technology genius. Friend of world leaders. Self-proclaimed eco-warrior.

Hypocrite.

A man whose company, Orcus Technology, owned half of British Columbia and more oil rigs than most small nations. Clinging to old industries for as long as they turned a profit.

A man whose vision had transformed Black Lake from a run-down mining town into one of the most exclusive celebrity retreats in North America.

My childhood friend.

My ex-fiancé.

I couldn't tell what he was thinking. I'd always found Lincoln easier to read than most, but that wasn't saying much. And there usually wasn't a lot to see. He hid behind a facade of charm.

He smiled, and stepped forward. 'El, you look great.' He hesitated, then kissed me lightly on one cheek.

I pulled away. Lincoln used to be one of the few people whose touch didn't make me recoil. Now, though, it felt different. I could feel my heart starting to race. Instead of Lincoln's kiss, I imagined Scarlett gently caressing my arm and I tapped my thumb and forefinger together eight times. It helps.

I made myself look him in the eye. 'I'd like to say I've missed you, Linc, but I haven't. I'm only here because I was told you'd pull our funding if I didn't come to the launch.'

His smile faded slightly. 'I see that time away hasn't dulled your edges. I'd hoped we might at least still be friends.'

'Fuck you, Linc,' I said. 'You force me to work for your company for a year, for God knows what purpose. Then you make me come up here to sweet-talk your clients.' I shook my head. 'That's not what friends do to one another. You ought to know by now that I don't respond well to being bullied.'

He met my gaze for a moment, then looked away. 'Come on, let's go inside. I thought we could at least be civil to one another.'

'Don't worry,' I said, 'I know my place. I'll be your little performing monkey for your guests tonight. It was made quite clear to me that you're worth a lot more to the Marine Centre than I am. But that's it. Don't expect me to pretend I'm enjoying it.'

An awkward silence was broken by the elevator doors behind Lincoln sliding open.

Koji emerged. His smile was wide, and unlike Lincoln's it didn't come with any strings attached. He had discarded the orange jacket and dried off since I'd last seen him.

'Ella!' he exclaimed. 'We've missed you here. It's been too long.'

He stepped forward and held out a hand for my bag. Instead, I gave him the hug that I had denied Lincoln. A short, stocky man, his moustache tickled my neck, bringing back memories. He didn't have suckers, but his touch was comforting.

As usual he seemed to be reading my mind. 'How's Scarlett coping on her own?'

'She'd calmed down by the time I left, but she'll be sulky when I get back tomorrow.'

'Who's Scarlett?' Lincoln asked quickly. He hated the idea of people having secrets from him.

I grinned. 'It didn't take me long to replace you.'

He raised an eyebrow. 'Scarlett? Interesting. You should have brought her along.'

'Hardly,' I said. 'While you think you have nine brains and blue blood, she really does. Scarlett's a Pacific Red. She got brought into the centre a few months ago after losing an arm. I nursed her back to health and now she lives with me. And she's guaranteed to be dead within two years so no messy break-ups to worry about.'

'It sounds as though you haven't got over me at all,' Lincoln said. Then he frowned. 'How did Koji know about her, when I didn't?'

'You don't get to choose who I speak to,' I said. 'Koji's one of my oldest friends.'

'Of course,' said Lincoln. 'Uncle Koji. Koji-Na.' He glanced sideways at the man who had been a constant presence in our childhood and was now Lincoln's general dogsbody and fixer.

'Shall we get inside?' said Koji. I guessed he was worried that I might let it slip that we still met up once or twice a month when he came into Bamfield. Lincoln wouldn't approve, as he prized loyalty above all else. Loyalty to him, at least.

For Koji's sake I moved the conversation on. 'Where am I staying? In one of the lodges?'

'Sorry, no,' Koji said. 'We had put you in one but with the storm coming in it's going to be too dangerous to get to them later. We're going to have to shut the funicular, so everyone's staying in the Manor.'

'Everyone?' I turned to Lincoln. 'It's not going to be much of a party, then. How many are here?'

'I'll leave you to work that out. We've got a hundred guests, so you tell me which ones are staying over.'

I bit back a retort that I wasn't there to play games. It was going to be a long night, and it would be better if we didn't spend the whole of it bickering.

Lincoln turned to Koji. 'Put Ella's bag in her room, and then get back up to the roof. I need you and Yahl ready to go by eight, so check that the camera link is working.'

Koji nodded and headed for the stairwell.

'I'd been hoping we'd be on the roof terrace tonight, but that's not going to work,' said Lincoln. 'They say it's going to be the worst storm in a generation.'

'What are Koji and Yahl doing up there? It's dangerous in this.'

Lincoln smiled. 'That's my surprise, and I don't want to spoil it for you. Don't worry, I'm protecting your precious Koji. He's just there to film Yahl, who'll be doing the dirty work. And there's no danger to Yahl either. I don't think Koji would be happy with me risking his grandson's life.'

'Fine, keep your secrets,' I said. 'What's Yahl doing back here anyway? The last I heard Koji had got him a job on one of your oil rigs. He said Yahl had finally found something he enjoyed.'

Lincoln grimaced. 'That didn't end well. He got into one too many bar fights, which is quite something by roughneck standards. My foreman kicked him off the rig after some trouble with the police so he's been doing work for me at Iona Island. I try to look after fellow Akaht, but it's always been a struggle with Yahl. Rebecca brought him up here for a few days to help out with the launch.'

Lincoln reached for the elevator call button.

As he did so I noticed a flash of black under his left sleeve, a battered watch with a black strap and a white face.

'Is that what I think it is?' I asked.

Lincoln raised his arm and showed me the Seiko Chariot watch he was wearing. 'I wasn't sure you'd bring me a present this year so I picked this one up from my last birthday. You left it behind – along with your engagement ring,' he added pointedly.

I looked at it more closely. 'You've broken it. It's showing two o'clock.'

'Ah, yes,' said Lincoln. 'I've made some modifications to it, and I guess it needs a new battery now.' He slid his sleeve down to hide it.

We stepped into the elevator. 'Level Two,' he said.

Lincoln had named the eight floors of the Manor in typically eccentric fashion, starting with the roof garden as Level One, and working down. I liked the fact that there were eight levels. I didn't like the fact that they were the wrong way round. Level Two was a vast reception room that occupied the entirety of the floor. Level Three was Lincoln's bedroom suite. Level Four the kitchen and dining rooms. Level Five the guest suites. Level Six his office and work space. Level Seven the staff quarters. Level Eight was where we were: the basement, machine rooms and funicular station.

As we travelled up Lincoln said: 'I know you hate all this but I'm glad you came. I do realise the struggle you have to calm things down inside your head.'

'The struggle isn't to make things calm,' I said. 'They never are no matter what I do. The struggle is to find somewhere quiet that I can hide in the midst of all the noise.' The elevator doors opened and a babble of voices enveloped us. 'This really doesn't help.'

That said, emerging into the reception room I couldn't help but admire the view. Whatever one might think of the Manor's brutal outer shell, from within it was breathtaking. Perched on top of the hill, it offered a 360-degree panorama of all that was best about Vancouver Island. To the east the peaks of the Somerset Range disappeared inland. To the west were the eco lodges hidden in the forest, and beyond them the vast expanse of the North Pacific. Look north, beyond the dark lake, and I would just be able to make out my house in Bamfield and the Broken Islands Group beyond. To the south the coast stretched away towards Port Renfrew.

Above us was the roof garden where Koji and his grandson had been sent for some mysterious purpose. One half was the roof garden itself. The other half, nearest the ocean, was glazed. On a clear night you could lie back, staring up at the distant Milky Way, and almost imagine you were floating in space. I glanced up, but today could see only dark clouds.

Still, I wasn't there for the view.

The one hundred guests had comfortably been swallowed up in the vast room. Many were gathered near the windows on the far side, staring out at the storm.

In the centre of the room, where the roof garden and glass roof met, was something new. It seemed to be a sculpture made up of various lengths of glowing crystal, each pulsing a different colour, haphazardly thrown together in a pile that almost reached the ceiling. The colours of the crystals kept changing.

I didn't like it. The discordant colours were too close to how I felt inside.

'What's that?' I asked.

'That was part of my birthday present to myself. It's a light sculpture, called *The Cage*, by Isabella Richter. I had it specially commissioned, at a cost of four million dollars.' He paused. 'It's got a present hidden inside.'

He wanted me to ask what the present was, so I ignored him, and looked around the room. It seemed like a normal party. Guests mingling, champagne flutes in hand, waiters circulating discreetly with trays of canapés. The buzz of voices pressed at me from all sides. Hurting me.

I needed to find one person to focus on. 'So, who should I be talking to?'

Lincoln shook his head. 'I told you, you're going to need to work it out.' He gave me his irritating, patronising smile. 'I tell you what, for every guest you can identify who's here, you can have a kiss at midnight.'

'For fuck's sake, Linc, I'm not playing your stupid games. Especially if that's the prize. Besides, aren't you fucking Rebecca?'

His nostrils flared, which I'd learned was a sign of strong emotion in him. He'd never liked my refusal to sugar-coat things. 'Rebecca? Koji never could keep his mouth shut. She's just a bit of fun, she's not you. She's been chasing after me for years, and I finally gave in. But if you don't fancy that prize I'll make you an offer you will like. For every one you identify I'll give you ten thousand dollars.'

'How many times do you want me to tell you to fuck off tonight? I don't want your money.'

He shook his head and pinched the bridge of his nose, sighing. I knew that meant he was trying to stop himself saying something. He breathed out heavily. 'Fine. Let's go and find someone to talk to.'

He snatched two glasses of champagne from a passing waiter, and handed me one. He seemed upset, but I couldn't see why. He was the one being a dickhead.

I took a long drink. It was a good thing that the storm was going to stop me driving back. This was promising to be a difficult evening, and alcohol was probably the only way I was going to get through it.

He took me over to a group of three people standing next to one of the picture windows, two men and a woman.

I knew only one of them. Rebecca Murray, vice-president of intelligence at Orcus Technology. Tall and slim, her shoulder-length red hair contrasted with the simple black dress that she wore with an understated elegance that I was never going to match. The last time Koji and I had met up for a coffee in Bamfield he'd let slip that Rebecca had become a regular visitor to the Manor. It hardly surprised me. Lincoln hated his own company, and always needed someone around to worship him. It was bound to be a breach of Orcus's code of conduct for the CEO to be dating an employee, even such a senior one, but Lincoln never thought that rules applied to him.

He slipped an arm round Rebecca's waist, pulling her close.

She stiffened and seemed about to say something. Then her gaze turned to me, a smile lighting up her hazel eyes.

'Ella, it's been ages since we met for real.' There was a faint lilt to her words, a hangover of her Glaswegian upbringing. Her Gaelic ancestry was doubtless the reason for her striking mane of red hair. She could have had pretty much anyone she wanted, so why she'd waited so long for Lincoln to choose her I didn't understand.

I offered her my hand but instead she slipped free of Lincoln and enveloped me in a hug. I responded stiffly with one arm, trying not to spill champagne down her back.

I pulled away. 'Rebecca, you look amazing.'

Lincoln turned to the two men. 'Let me introduce you all.

This is Ella Manning, my ...' He looked at me thoughtfully. 'My second oldest friend. She works here in Bamfield at the Marine Centre, and she and Rebecca have been collaborating on one of my newest projects. She's also our local cop, so I'm not sure what she calls herself these days. Dr Manning? Constable? Or are you still Lieutenant Commander Manning?'

'Ella will do,' I said.

He nodded and turned to one of the men, grey-haired, red-faced, and a good ten years older than me. 'This is Paul Kleber, my lawyer.' Lincoln patted him lightly on the back. 'Paul's the man I can't do without, as he knows where all the bodies are buried.'

Kleber coughed, and pulled a face. 'I can't disagree with my client, since he's paying my bills. But let me make clear first, that there are no bodies, second, that any bodies that may be discovered are nothing to do with Orcus, and, third, that I know nothing about the location of any such bodies.'

The others chuckled. Perhaps it was meant as a joke, but it didn't seem terribly funny.

Kleber. What did that sound like? Crab. With his greying hair I imagined his face on a Dungeness crab. I'd remember him now. It was one less thing to stress about.

I turned to the other man. He was younger than me, improbably handsome, designer stubble on his chin. He seemed too perfect. I looked from him to Lincoln.

'Is he ...?' I asked.

'Is he what?' Lincoln asked innocently. 'I thought you said you weren't playing.'

'I'm not.'

'Ella,' said Lincoln, 'this is Terry Vance. He's a journalist with the *Vancouver Courier*, and here to cover today's launch.'

Vance. Dance. I pictured him dancing with an octopus in the bottom of a tank. Not Scarlett. I didn't know him well enough for that.

'I'm intrigued to know what you think I might be,' he said.

'It's nothing,' I said. 'Just a game of Lincoln's.'

Vance shrugged. 'You seem to have a lot of titles. Where does Lieutenant Commander come from?'

'I was in the navy for a while, but I can't use that title any more.'

Lincoln interrupted. 'I'm going to leave you lot to it. It's almost eight and I need to get the show on the road.'

He glanced at me, raising one eyebrow. It had always been his way of checking if I was all right in social situations before leaving me alone. I nodded.

'Before you go, I'm curious,' I said. 'I'm only your second oldest friend. Who is it that beats me to first place? Koji?'

He looked surprised. 'Not Koji. Noah, obviously. I met him before I met you.'

'Seriously? The last I heard he was calling you the biggest threat to the environment in a generation, and he's on trial for inciting members of GreenWar to blow up one of your oil rigs. I understood you'd got him put in jail in Vancouver.'

Lincoln grinned. 'You know what it's like with friends, sometimes you go through a rough patch. Actually, we're much closer than you think.' He chuckled to himself at some private joke, then nodded to the others. 'We'll speak later.'

As he left, I managed to grab some canapés from a passing waiter.

49

When I turned back Rebecca was talking to the lawyer. I was left with the journalist. I tapped my thumb against my forefinger eight times.

'So,' I asked, 'did you watch the game last night?'

'What?'

'Did you watch the Stanley Cup?'

'I missed it,' said Vance. 'You're a Canucks fan, then?'

'Of course.'

In truth, I had no interest at all in ice hockey. I'd never understood why anyone would make their own self-worth depend upon the actions of a bunch of people they didn't know or control. I'd found it was a good conversation starter, though. It helped me blend in. Scarlett has her camouflage. I have my prepared conversations.

I tried with a different one. 'I work with octopuses. People find that either repulsive or pretty cool.'

'I'm definitely in the cool camp,' said Vance. 'Is it true they have more than one brain?'

'Nine.' It was one of the things that had first drawn me to them. Like an octopus I often feel as though I have brains in every limb, taking in too much information, overwhelming me.

'That's weird,' he said. 'Cool, but weird.'

'It gets much weirder than that. The thing that most people find surprising is that octopuses only mate towards the end of their lives, sometimes only once. The male usually dies soon after. And sometimes the female will kill and eat him after mating.'

'Gross,' he said. 'You'd have thought that would put the males off ever wanting sex.'

'It has. To avoid being eaten one species has developed a detachable penis. It swims over to the female who keeps it in her mantle until she wants to fertilise her eggs. Some will have several in there at the same time.'

'Now you're just messing with me. An octopus orgy with detachable dicks? That can't be true.'

'I never lie,' I said. 'It's called the argonaut. Look it up if you don't believe me.'

He looked at me oddly.

Then Rebecca grabbed my arm, pulling me towards her, leaving Vance to talk to the lawyer.

'This is so wild,' she said. 'We've got them all here, walking and talking among us, and no one knows a thing.'

I eased my arm free from her grip. 'It's really working? No one's guessed anything?'

'No. It's perfect.' She looked away for a moment. 'It's such a shame my dad isn't here to see this. It was his vision more than anyone's, more even than Linc's. He wouldn't have believed what we've achieved in the last ten years. The first time I met Linc we were at a chess tournament with Dad's prototype set, and now the ghosts make his original ideas look timid.'

'I'm sure he'd have been proud of you.'

She nodded, and gave me a thin smile. 'I think Linc has got some sort of tribute to him planned for later. He's doing his big announcement, and then he told me he's got a second one, something much more personal, but he wouldn't tell me what it was.'

'That's sweet,' I said.

'Who'd have thought that a run-down workshop in Barlanark

could have led to this? Me drinking champagne with the high and mighty. Of course, Dad would have hated it, and no one would have understood his accent. They struggle enough with me.' She shook her head. 'I'll have to try not to cry.'

Giving comfort is not one of my strengths, so I changed the subject. 'You need to tell me who's who.'

'That would be cheating,' said Rebecca. 'This is the real test, because if *you* can't tell the difference, no one else will.'

Then she looked over my shoulder and I was suddenly aware that the room had gone quiet. Everyone was turning to look behind me. I followed their gaze, and saw that Lincoln had climbed on to a low table, and was holding up his hands for silence.

For the first time I could hear the wind and rain battering against the windows. A particularly violent gust seemed to shake the entire building. A few guests cast each other nervous glances.

'Please don't worry about what's going on outside,' said Lincoln. 'As someone else once said before me, this place was built to last a thousand years. I'm not going to emulate him, as it all ended rather badly. And, unlike him, I'm not a great one for speeches, but I would ask you to bear with me while I say a few words. Today is my fortieth birthday, and that is the reason I have invited you to Black Lake Manor.

'However, this is more than just a birthday celebration, because I want to show you something. And not just those of you who are here. As of eight o'clock this party is being live streamed to Orcus subscribers and technology journalists worldwide. Welcome to you all.

'I want to begin with a demonstration, and a story about another fortieth birthday party that took place many years ago, a long way from here. Please, look behind you.'

We turned as one to see that a section of the vast picture window looking out over the ocean had dimmed, and was now a screen. The image displayed was of the roof garden above us. I guessed from what Lincoln had said that it was Koji holding the camera, and he was struggling in the wind, the picture bouncing around. In the centre of the screen, his back to us, was Koji's grandson, Yahl.

He looked over his shoulder at the camera, squinting through the rain, and gave a thumbs-up.

Lincoln's voice came from behind us. 'The birthday celebration I want to tell you about took place in July 1827, in southern Africa. The precise date is lost to history, but it is believed that it was the fortieth birthday of Shaka kaSenzangakhona, better known as Shaka Zulu. He, his wives, his warriors and certain local chiefs had gathered for a feast on cliffs high above the Tugela River.'

As Lincoln spoke Yahl started to walk away from the camera. It was clearly hard work heading straight into the storm. Koji followed, the erratic camera movements becoming more pronounced. When Yahl reached the low wall that separated the roof garden from the glass roof, he stepped across it, cautiously testing the glass for grip. I looked up, and could see him appear above us as well as on the screen.

Lincoln continued. 'The celebrations for Shaka's birthday went on all day, and no doubt a lot of maize beer had been consumed by the time the chiefs got into a heated discussion about loyalty. Each insisted that his impis – his warriors – were the most loyal. Shaka was determined to prove them wrong.'

Yahl continued his slow walk across the glass roof. It was harder now, and he was slipping, leaning into the wind. Koji hadn't followed him on to the glass, so Yahl was becoming smaller on the screen, but he was now easily visible in person above us, a dark figure against dark clouds, his coat flapping in the wind.

'Shaka called over one of his soldiers, and ordered him to walk to the edge of the cliffs, and jump. The soldier merely nodded, did as he was commanded, and jumped unhesitatingly to his death. Shaka had proved his point and the other chiefs conceded that his impis were the most loyal.'

The room went silent. Yahl had reached the edge of the roof. Below were cliffs, and a sheer drop of over a hundred metres.

Yahl paused for a moment, then raised his arms above his head, leaned into the wind, and dived off the roof.

His body flashed past the window in front of us, then disappeared.

Somebody screamed.

1804

6

THE KNIFE

The bosun was woken by the scrape of iron on stone.

In one way it was pleasant, a change from the pounding of the ocean which had been the backdrop to their lives for the past few weeks. But in other ways it was not. Sleep, however fitful, had been some respite from the constant hunger and cold that gripped them.

Worse. The rasping echo was a reminder that they were trapped.

The storm that had sunk the *Pride of Whitby* had driven their lifeboat into the mouth of the cave that was now their entire world. At first it had seemed fortuitous – a miracle that seven of them still lived. They'd had no real control over the boat's course, and twenty yards to either side she would have been dashed against the cliffs, drowning them all.

But the same storm that had saved them had added a cruel

twist. As they sat on the shingle beach at the cave entrance, grimly contemplating the meagre provisions that they had been able to salvage, a roar from overhead had heralded the collapse of the cliff face.

Those directly below had stood no chance. Two sailors had died instantly. Two had lasted a little longer. Seaman Blanchard, coughing up blood from a staved-in chest, survived for a few minutes. The carpenter, both legs broken and bleeding heavily, had groaned through the night. It had been a relief to the others when, come morning, his moans had died with him.

A small cairn of rocks marked their remains.

The three who remained alive were little better off. The collapse of the cliff had sealed shut the entrance to the cave.

The bosun pushed himself up on to one elbow and looked around.

The fire was almost out, and with it their only light. They needed to conserve the driftwood scattered towards the rear of the cave. There was little enough left, and what remained was damp and increasingly hard to light with their single flint.

The bosun could dimly make out Seaman Cooper curled up on the other side of the fire. He had not spoken for days now, and could barely be persuaded to drink from the freshwater stream running down the back wall of the cave.

He would not be with them much longer.

Captain Ross was seated further away, patiently scraping a piece of metal on rock.

The bosun got unsteadily to his feet, and staggered over to him. 'What?' he asked through cracked lips.

Ross stared at him, then held up the strip of metal he was

working. 'It's the nameplate from the lifeboat,' he said, his voice as hoarse as the bosun's. 'We're dying. We can't live on water alone. We need to eat, so I'm making a knife.'

The bosun nodded slowly. He looked across at the rocks hiding the remains of Seaman Blanchard and the carpenter. Then back at the captain.

Questioning.

'No,' said Ross. 'They've been dead for too long. They'll poison us. We need fresh meat.'

The bosun took a step back, eyes wide, looking at the sleeping seaman by the fire. 'No!'

'We haven't any choice,' said Ross harshly. 'You and I have one last chance. We eat, and then we find a way out of here. Or we all die.' He tested the point of his makeshift knife against his thumb. 'It'll do. Are you with me?'

The bosun took a long breath as he met his captain's fierce gaze. A wave of revulsion rolled through him. If they did this their souls would be damned for ever.

Yet if they did nothing they would soon be dead.

Eventually the bosun nodded.

'Good,' grunted Ross. 'We do it now, before he wakes. You hold him down and I'll make it quick.'

2045

7

GHOST DANCERS

As the guest's scream died away there was silence. Then everyone turned back to Lincoln.

I shook my head. Typical. Why couldn't he just do a product announcement like anyone else? Even I'd been fooled for a moment.

Lincoln was grinning wildly, delighted at the stunned reaction. However much he might deny it, he liked nothing better than being the centre of attention. It still surprised me sometimes how the geeky teenager I'd known had turned himself into the tech guru whose word could make or break new products. Who'd become the most eligible bachelor in North America.

Whom I'd dumped.

He held up his hands. 'Please, let me assure you that no one has died. Unlike Shaka, I don't require that level of loyalty from my staff. Yahl is fine.'

Lincoln turned to the elevator behind him as the doors opened and Yahl stepped through. He was dry, although Koji, who followed him, was dripping water on to the wooden floor. Yahl raised a hand in acknowledgement. He had dark goggles pushed up on to his forehead, and a pair of long black gloves tucked under one arm.

'What you have just witnessed is the demonstration of a completely new technology,' said Lincoln. 'It's not magic, and nor was it CGI or camera trickery. What you saw really happened. Some of you here might be starting to work it out, but for those who haven't, or for those watching the live stream, let me explain.

'This year is not just when I turn forty. More importantly, it's twenty years since I founded Orcus. People thought I was crazy. This kid from the backwoods of the island setting up a technology company in an abandoned sewage works in the most unfashionable part of Vancouver. They thought I'd be gone in a matter of months, those that even bothered to notice. When we started in the corner of a run-down warehouse there was just me and my dog. And that's because Kun was the only one I could afford to pay. But that same business is now the biggest employer in British Columbia. Last year Orcus's capitalisation topped eight billion dollars. Iona Island, which locals once had to avoid during the all-too-frequent sewage emissions, is now a thriving community. We've built houses, businesses and a college, and we now command the highest rents in the entire city.'

The bit about one man and his dog wasn't entirely accurate. It was true that Lincoln had purchased half of Iona Island when the city had finally succumbed to pressure to stop discharging sewage into the Fraser River. It was said that he'd bought it for one dollar, because the clean-up costs were so high that no one else wanted it. But Kun had been dead for several years by then. And he'd been my dog, not Lincoln's. As usual, there was a fair amount of reinvention. Lincoln tended to remember things as he wanted them to appear. And the bit about the run-down warehouse was entirely made up. When I'd visited as a freshly minted marine biologist from the University of Victoria, on the promise of a job offer, there had been a shiny new research lab with a staff of twenty. Even at that age Lincoln had somehow persuaded investors to pour millions into his vision.

I'd turned him down, troubled by how uncertain it all was, and gone off to join the navy and play with dolphins. Until that all went wrong, and I came home, tail between my legs.

'The success of Orcus is based on two things,' Lincoln said. 'Our foresight, and our people. Some of you are here tonight, and I thank you, as without you we would be nothing.'

I glanced across at Rebecca, who was gazing up at him, transfixed. The cult of Lincoln was working its magic.

'I say that "some of you are here", and there is a good reason why I phrased it that way. Look around you. If you took the time to count, you would know that there are precisely one hundred guests in this room. Those guests have been talking to one another, interacting, eating, drinking, touching one another. And it will have seemed real. But it isn't. In fact, I can tell you that there are only six people present here tonight.'

Lincoln paused as the guests looked at one another. There was a low murmur of voices. Someone laughed. Lincoln held up a hand. 'Bear with me a moment longer. As you know, since it was established twenty years ago Orcus has been at the forefront of hard light research. It's always been a passion of mine. We've sunk tens of millions of dollars into it. Or, as my investors would probably say, wasted tens of millions of dollars. Because historically it's been seen as a non-starter. There has always been one major problem with hard light – the ridiculous amounts of power required to turn photons into something solid.'

He gestured to the light sculpture in the centre of the room. 'I hope you have all been admiring my latest acquisition: *The Cage* by Isabella Richter. It's a tribute to her uncle, and some of his most iconic paintings. It looks and feels real, so real that you could stand on top of it.' He paused, and grinned. 'Although I'd rather you didn't. But at the push of a button it would all disappear. It's ephemeral, made of nothing more than light. Yet, impressive though it is, it needs a battery pack the size of a small car if I want to take it anywhere. That means that hard light is essentially a static medium. There is no portable power source that is both small enough and capable of generating the energy required.' He paused, and looked around the room with a satisfied smile.

'Until now.' He reached into his pocket and with a dramatic flourish produced a small white disc about the size of a quarter. 'We at Orcus have solved hard light. We have made it truly portable. Now, thanks to Orcus's research, this' – he held up the disc – 'is all you need to produce that.' He pointed to *The Cage*.

'This is revolutionary, and most companies would have announced it with a fanfare when we developed the technology two years ago. However, that's not how we do things at Orcus. Instead, we asked ourselves what we could create with the new technology. How could we use it to produce something that would benefit humankind?

'So we created ghost dancers. And they are going to change your lives. What are they? Let me show you.' Lincoln bent down and carefully placed the disc on the table next to him. He stepped away from it, and looked behind him. 'Yahl, if you would.'

Yahl pulled the dark-lensed goggles over his eyes and put on the black gloves. He twitched his fingers, and another, life-sized, version of him sprang to life on the table next to Lincoln where the disc had been.

'So he's back,' said Lincoln. 'No one actually jumped off the roof. All that I lost was one of these.' He was holding another of the white discs between his fingers. 'They cost me five cents to make. They are so small – and so light – that the ghost dancer carries the disc around within itself. This makes them truly independent. No cables, no bulky battery packs, no external projectors. They can go wherever they want.' He gestured to the copy of Yahl next to him. 'See.'

The ghost Yahl jumped down from the table, threaded its way silently through the crowd to the elevator, and pressed the call button. When the lift doors opened, it stepped inside. The doors closed, and it disappeared.

Lincoln continued. 'I apologise if I shocked anyone, but there's no need to call for the Mounties. As you can see, I didn't kill Yahl. What I hope I have done is demonstrate to you the value of this new technology. Those of you who are invited guests have all been very patient with me, because in fact you knew this already. In the past couple of weeks each of you was taken to Orcus's headquarters on Iona Island and subjected to a detailed scan from which we have produced a replica. I'm afraid that each of you was misled. You were made to sign a strict non-disclosure agreement, provided with a tactile kit – goggles and gloves – and told that you were the only one who was going to attend the party from the comfort of your own home. That last part was untrue, but we wanted to give the technology its ultimate test. We wanted to see if you would fool one another into thinking that each of you was real. I'm pleased to say that the experiment has been a resounding success.' He paused, and looked around.

'So, ladies and gentlemen, welcome to a brave new world – the world of the ghost dancer. The name is a nod to my Akaht heritage. They will be on sale from midnight tonight – prices, specs and options can all be found online, as well as technical details for those journalists wanting to write them up. I should make it clear that although I said the discs cost five cents to manufacture, that's not what we'll be selling them for. There's a lot of research and development gone into the ghosts, over many years. So you'll need to pay an initial licence fee when you get scanned for the ghost. The one restriction at present is the need for a one-off full-body scan, which presently can only be done at Orcus's headquarters. But from next month this will be available in Montreal, New York and London and we'll roll out more worldwide as the year goes on.

'I'm going to stop there for now. I do have another surprise for you all, but it's much more personal, and before I reveal it I'm willing to take some questions about the ghost dancers.'

He looked around the faces below him, then pointed to an upraised arm.

'Terry Vance, *Vancouver Courier*.' It was the journalist who hadn't believed me about detachable penises. 'Your demonstration was quite dramatic, but what is the point of these ... these ghost dancers? You said they are going to change our lives for ever. How? I've got no desire to pretend to jump off a roof.'

'Great question, Terry. We see a lot of uses for them. Let's say you want to visit London for the day, but you don't like flying, or you haven't got the time. Or you want to have lunch next to the Eiffel Tower and be home in time for dinner. Now it's possible. You log on, put on your tactile kit, and choose where to go. Soon every big city will have machines filled with discs, ready to vend ghosts. You'll step out, do your thing, and then just log off when you're done. You'll be experiencing it as though you're actually there, but with none of the cost, waste of time, jet lag or environmental damage.

'We also see big uses for ghost dancers in industry, in dangerous jobs. Instead of using workers you send in a ghost, and if anything goes wrong it's the same as with Yahl – all you've lost is a disc.'

Vance waved his hand again. 'Virtual holidays and remote workers are all very well, but it seems rather trivial. How does this really benefit humanity in things that matter?'

Lincoln looked slightly stung by the lack of enthusiasm. 'I don't think it's fair to call them trivial, Terry. They're going to change the way we interact with the world and one another. If you want something more serious, though, do you know what the third biggest cause of death was last year in North America? Medical negligence. And a large part of that was surgery gone wrong. However highly you train a surgeon, they're human, so they get tired and they make mistakes. We've started a trial with Victoria General Hospital to change that. Obviously we can't replace surgeons, but it is possible to take away the need for them to perform many routine tasks. We're using hard light to create miniature ghosts for specialised functions, to assist in operations. This technology is going to save people's lives.'

'Mr Shan,' a woman near the front of the crowd shouted. 'Jo Bright, *Toronto Star*. Why are you just making remote-control ghosts? Surely it wouldn't be difficult to program them, make them autonomous, and then you could do so much more. If all you need is one of these discs, you'd be carrying someone round with you, ready to pull out when you needed them. A driver, personal assistant, chef ...' She grinned. 'A lover, even. They appear when you want, do what you need, and then you switch them off. It sounds like the perfect man. You could call them ... I don't know ... how about key-chain ghosts?'

Lincoln smiled, but shook his head. 'I love the way you're thinking, Jo, and it's something we've thought about ourselves, but we're not ready for it yet. Have you heard of Kenji Urada?'

The journalist shook her head.

'There's some debate as to whether he was the first person to be killed by a robot, but there is no question that he was stabbed in the back by a robot doing what it had been programmed to do. I'm told that we're still one or two decades away from having the sort of AI we'd need for your key-chain lovers. That's why, at Orcus, we've focused on what's achievable. I'm sure you'll be right at some point in the future, and it will be great, but we're just not there yet, Jo.'

'Hang on,' she responded, 'doesn't that contradict what you

said about your micro-surgeons? They must be running AI of some sort. What if that goes wrong? The consequences could be deadly.'

'Not at all,' said Lincoln. 'They aren't using AI. They're just pre-programmed tools, each for a particular task. It will be like carrying a set of wrenches round with you. Surgeons will have a box of mini-ghosts to take with them, each designed to perform a particular task, the sort of tasks that real surgeons get wrong precisely because they're routine. The mini-ghosts are similar to the robots surgeons already use in operations, but so much more versatile, and easily portable.'

Lincoln glanced around. 'Terry – you've got another follow-up?'

'Yes, Mr Shan. Surely these ghosts pose a danger to people? Say I ... what's a good example? Say I want to steal someone's phone. Instead of doing it myself I use a ghost. If it all goes horribly wrong I'm far away – the real me is – when the cops show up. It seems like you've created risk-free crime.'

Lincoln shook his head. 'I doubt your average street mugger could afford a ghost, Terry. But in any event, let me show you.'

Lincoln jumped down from the table, and grabbed a bottle of champagne from a waiter. He walked over to the journalist, and handed him the bottle. 'Come at me, Terry. You're here as a ghost. I'm real. Pretend you're going to hit me with that.'

Vance looked dubious. 'Seriously?'

'Trust me, you can't hurt me.'

'All right. I suppose this will make a good story either way.' He gripped the bottle in one hand, hesitated a moment, then swung it hard at Lincoln's head.

He failed to make contact. As the bottle was about to connect the journalist's arm froze.

Lincoln laughed, and reached up to take the bottle from him. He pushed Vance's arm down to his side, then returned to stand on the table.

'We aren't complete idiots,' he said. 'We had thought of that. Besides, although we've developed ghosts in secret, we are still obliged to comply with all Health Canada safety standards. It was one of the first things they required, that we build in a constraint that prevents ghosts being used to harm humans. It's a bit like Asimov's first law for those of you who can remember that far back, and it's hard written into the discs. Not even I can change it. The reason it was required was because the regulators recognised just how revolutionary ghosts are going to be.'

A young woman elbowed her way past me, hand waving. 'Mr Shan,' she shouted, 'you say that for people using ghosts it will be as though they're really there, but we all know from tonight that that's not true. Yes, we can see and hear as though we are in your mansion, and we can feel things through the gloves. But we can't smell, or taste. We can pretend to eat or drink, but we don't feel any of that. You've actually only got some of the senses working.'

'It's early days, Ms …?' said Lincoln. 'I'm not sure I know who you're with.'

'Hayley Green, *Victoria Times*.'

'Well, Ms Green, it's true that we can't give you a one hundred per cent experience yet, but we're getting close. To have taste and smell would probably require some sort of brain implant. But people have been playing virtual reality games for years, and having no problem with the lack of some senses. What we are offering here is something a hundred times more immersive than that, and in time – pretty soon – I'm sure it will be the complete sensory experience.'

Before Lincoln had the chance to look elsewhere, she threw another question at him. 'You say that this technology was created by Orcus, but that's not true, is it? In fact, Dr Ella Manning, of Bamfield Marine Science Centre, has been acting as a consultant on the project, and taking time from her government-funded work to do that. Dr Manning, who was your fiancée. How do you justify spending government money on private research?'

I went cold and took a step back, trying to shrink into the darkness. I hate being the centre of attention. Rebecca turned to look at me, and a couple of other heads followed. But most people at the party didn't know me. I wasn't certain the journalist even realised who I was, as she had pushed past me with no sign of recognition.

Lincoln frowned down at her. He answered slowly. 'Three things you should know, Ms Green. First, the fact that Dr Manning was engaged to me is of no relevance at all. She only became a consultant after our personal relationship was over. Orcus has retained her because she has skills that others don't. Second, it is true that Dr Manning has been assisting Orcus in studying parallels between multiple octopus brains and some early attempts at ghost AI. None of that is close to being ready for production, so our payment obligations to the Marine Centre haven't kicked in yet. In any event, though, Orcus is one of the principal private funders of the Marine Centre, so there is no reason why it cannot call on Dr Manning for advice. Third ...'

Lincoln paused, and jumped down from the table, walking through the crowd to the journalist. He lowered his voice, so that only those of us nearby could hear him. 'Third, Ms Green, I will of course be sure to mention your skill and persistence as a reporter when I next meet your editor-in-chief for a round of golf at the Victoria Country Club. He's a personal friend of mine.'

She seemed undeterred by the threat. 'Mr Shan, how do you respond to the allegations being made in the GreenWar trial that Orcus Oil secretly funded protests against its own oil rigs, a protest in which two people died?'

Lincoln ignored her. He turned instead to look over his shoulder, to where Koji and Yahl were standing in the shadows. Lincoln caught Koji's eye, then drew a finger across his throat. I saw Koji pull out his phone.

'What do you say to—' the reporter began.

And disappeared.

One moment she was there in the room. The next a white disc was fluttering to the wooden floor. I stepped back as it landed amidst a splash of champagne and half-chewed canapés. She had been right that the ghosts didn't enable people to sense what they were eating or drinking, or digest it. That was just pretend.

As Lincoln turned away he stamped hard on the disc where it had landed, crushing it. Then he hopped back up on to the table. 'Oh dear, we seem to have lost communication with the inquisitive Ms Green. How unfortunate, as she had such interesting questions. I suspect that is a good time to move on, though. Any follow-up queries can be sent to Orcus's press office. Questions about the ghosts *only*.

'Now I told you that I had a second thing to announce, which is rather more personal.'

I looked across at Rebecca. She straightened up, waiting for what was to come.

'I realise that the downside to having most of my guests attend remotely is that it dramatically reduced the number of birthday presents I got.' There was laughter round the room. 'I'm sure that's a relief to most of you. I'm not an easy person to buy for. So I've bought myself a present.' He pointed to the glass sculpture in the centre of the room. 'It's hidden inside *The Cage*. Or perhaps I should say "he" is hidden there, our special guest for the night.'

The lights of the sculpture suddenly flared white, then red, purple, fading to black, and the crystals became clear. It took a few seconds for my eyes to adjust. As they did so I could see a figure sitting cross-legged inside *The Cage*, back towards me. Had he been there all along? A spotlight was switched on at the top of the sculpture, shining straight down, illuminating him.

He was wearing an orange hoodie with the words 'Clark County Jail' on the back. The hood was up, so from where I was standing it was impossible to identify him.

But I had a bad feeling about this.

The guests moved towards *The Cage*, crowding round it. I hung back. As did Rebecca. She was looking at Lincoln, a puzzled frown changing to something else I found hard to read. Anger?

Then someone gasped. Followed by others.

'Ladies and gentlemen,' said Lincoln, 'I present to you our final ghost for the evening. Straight from his jail cell in Vancouver, I give you Maquina, chief of the Akaht.'

What the hell was Lincoln up to?

Maquina.

The man I'd known as Noah Diaz.

The third member of our childhood gang.

2023

8

THREE FRIENDS

I was seventeen years old the day Kun went missing.

It was my fault.

It was one of those balmy summer days that make you forget that for half the year Bamfield is known as the storm-watching capital of Vancouver Island. It had surprised me to learn that that was a thing. People would come to Bamfield, pay an exorbitant sum to rent a cabin near the shore from a bemused local, and then sit inside and watch the storms roll in. Or occasionally venture out. Sometimes with fatal consequences. Almost every year there would be some tourist who decided that posing on the rocks at Aguilar Point would look good on their social media. A little while later the person taking the photo would be knocking on the nearest door, tearful, breathless and wet, saying that a rogue wave had swept their friend, lover or family member into the ocean, and could the coastguard please go out to save them.

That was usually the end of the matter. Occasionally, if they were lucky, days or even weeks later a body would wash up somewhere along the coast. Often with bits nibbled away by the black claw crabs. But usually the North Pacific claimed them for its own.

Pachena Bay in the summer is quite different. A long stretch of curving white sand where the Pachena River meets the ocean, sheltered from the worst of the weather by woods on either side.

We'd got there early. It was never busy, but by midday there could be an influx of walkers starting, or ending, the West Coast Trail, a rugged seven-day hike between Bamfield and Port Renfrew.

We preferred to have the place to ourselves. The bay was only a kilometre from Black Lake, but it was a tough walk through the woods over little-used trails. By the time we got there we were sweating. Noah dropped his shoes, bag and shirt in a heap, and charged off into the water, Kun chasing after him. Lincoln and I found a spot in the shade, backs to an old tree trunk that had been hurled up the beach by the winter storms.

The morning fog had long since burned off, and there was no one else in sight. Not even the seals or black bears that we sometimes encountered. The seals were no doubt out in the ocean searching for breakfast. And at that time of year the bears tended to be further south, by the rockpools, teaching their cubs the delicate business of cracking open and eating mussels. Fortunately they preferred them to humans. There was a dark patch of something near the shoreline, but it looked more like kelp than the drift whales that we sometimes found. The Akaht had traditionally been known as whalers. While that some-times involved venturing out on to the ocean in their cedar log canoes, more often it would mean gathering on the beach waiting for the body of a whale to be blown in. The standing of the chief had often depended upon his ability to predict which storms would produce a carcass, and where.

Lincoln and I sat in silence, getting our breath back, watching Noah messing around with Kun. I'd found the dog five years before, an unwanted stray. He was some sort of terrier cross-breed, with a lot of mongrel, white, but with an odd black patch on his forehead that looked like a whale. That was how he had got his name: Kun was whale in the Nuu-chah-nulth language.

His size meant he was well suited for exploring the mines around Black Lake, which had been our passion that summer. Or at least for two of us. We'd discovered fairly quickly that Lincoln didn't like being underground. He'd rarely come more than a few metres into the mines before turning round, saying he'd wait for us outside. One time when he did try to go further he panicked, and I had to drag him back to the surface scream-ing and gasping. He'd hated that. Lincoln didn't like failing at anything.

He also didn't like the fact that Noah and I were spending so much time together. Things were changing. We were changing. My two oldest friends, but now they looked at me differently. Treated me differently. Linc seemed to resent it when I spent time with Noah.

I wasn't entirely sure how comfortable Noah was under-ground either. Sometimes I had the impression that he just put up with it to be with me.

This was going to be our last summer together. I was off to university in September. Linc said he was going travelling. Noah had no choice but to stay in Black Lake. He was being groomed to take over as chief of the Akaht when his father – who was seldom in the best of health – died. I'd always envied Noah, having a purpose, knowing what he was going to do with his life. But he didn't see it that way. He felt that he was shackled to the land by his heritage.

'Are you taking Kun with you to Victoria?' Lincoln asked.

'Of course. Why? Are you hoping I'll let you have him?'

'No, I can't take him round Europe with me. I thought maybe you'd leave him here with Noah. He's going to be pretty miserable when we've both left.'

'Definitely not.' I hesitated, looking down at my fingers. How much to share? 'It's going to be scary meeting lots of new people and losing my two best friends – I'll need someone I know. Having Kun there will help.'

Lincoln went quiet for a while. Eventually I glanced up at him. His gaze met mine and I looked away quickly. I always feel as though my eyes give too much away, putting all my fears on display.

Lincoln reached over to take my hand, but I pulled back.

'Ella,' he said, 'I've been wanting to ask you something. Are you sure you won't come round Europe with me? Having a gap year won't make any difference to you long term, and it would be fun.'

I shook my head. 'No, Linc. You know I've got a place in Victoria now, and anyway I can't afford to take a year out. Come there with me instead. I'd love to have a friend, and with your grades you'd walk on to any course, even this late.'

'No. It's not my thing. I'm tired of being told what to do, how to think. I need to go away and free my brain. You sure? If it's just about the money I could help you out with that.'

'I'm sure,' I said. 'I'm not having you pay for me to come round Europe with you. That ... that doesn't feel right. Look, you'll find some sexy French girl, fall in love, and forget all about me.'

He looked down, but said nothing.

An awkward silence was broken by Kun running up and shaking cold seawater all over us. We both jumped to our feet.

'Thanks, Noah,' I said, as he followed the dog up the beach. 'I didn't want to go swimming yet.'

Noah was laughing at us, as Kun jumped around barking. 'It's a great way to wake up.' He reached into his backpack and pulled out a towel. As he dried himself I couldn't help notice how much he and Kun resembled one another. The scrawny boy and the scrawny mongrel, neither of whom ever sat still.

'So, what's the plan today?' he asked.

'I know what I'm doing,' I said. I pointed to my pack. 'It's why I brought all this.'

Lincoln groaned. 'Not the mines again, you two. It's going to be a beautiful day and you want to waste it crawling underground like moles.'

'This could be our last chance,' I said. 'You know we can only do this when the water levels are low, and it hasn't rained in two weeks now. I want to see if we can find out what's beyond the gap.'

'Suits me,' said Noah. 'I'm not going to be able to go once you've left, El. I don't know the mines the way you and Kun do.'

That was true. Kun and I had been venturing into the mines for a couple of years before I shared my secret with the others.

Lincoln sighed. 'All right, you two go off and explore, or whatever it is you do down there.'

Noah regarded him sideways, but said nothing. He started to get dressed.

'You're lucky I've got someone better to keep me company,' said Lincoln. He reached into his bag and showed me a book. The cover photo was of a man in a black turtleneck and rimless glasses. The title read: *Steve Jobs: The Man Who Thought Different*.

'Not another one,' I said. 'You must have read every book written about him. He's still dead, you know.'

'I can't see why you idolise him,' Noah said. 'You know that the gold in his phones came from places like this.' He gestured to the forest that surrounded us. 'It may look beautiful now, but there are slag heaps hidden away that are toxic, and they're leaking poison into our water system. That's what you're drinking every day.'

Lincoln sighed heavily. 'Give it a rest, Noah. Progress always comes at a price.'

'Have you seen my dad recently?' Noah asked. 'He's paid the price, and he's getting worse. The shakes come more often, and his memory is full of holes now. He refuses to accept that it was twenty years of exposure to mercury and cyanide in the mines. But I know the truth. We've got to do something to stop it before it's too late.'

Lincoln opened his book and waved us away. 'Go on, El, you go and explore the mine with your two lapdogs.'

Noah stared at him, then shouldered his backpack. 'Let's go. We should give Linc some alone time with his toxic crush.'

9

SIX SKELETONS

We couldn't use any of the entrances near town for fear of being spotted. The mineshafts were regarded as dangerous and strictly off-limits, and not just for the reasons that Noah had given. Rockfalls and unprotected drops would kill you much more quickly than mercury poisoning. Or you could just get lost and never find your way out.

When I'd first gone into the mines my concern had been that my parents might find out. That was no longer an issue. The day after my seventeenth birthday my mother had sat me down and told me that she was leaving my father and moving back to Toronto. She seemed to feel that her obligations to me were fulfilled, and I wasn't invited to go with her. My father's response had been to become increasingly withdrawn, his logging trips inland getting longer and longer. It had been weeks now since I'd seen him.

But that didn't mean that I was free from scrutiny. Koji had been their oldest friend for as long as I could remember. To a non-Akaht child he'd appeared mysterious, glamorous even, and had become Koji-Na – Uncle Koji – to me. With my parents gone he'd been keeping a close eye on me. I knew I'd never hear the last of it if he found out I'd been in the mines.

So we used as our entrance an old ventilation shaft hidden in the woods near the beach. It had been sealed with a wooden lid that was so rotten you could push your fingers through. The shaft dropped vertically for a good five metres before emerging into the roof of a mine. The tunnel sloped downwards towards the ocean, probably to what had been the original entrance, but it was blocked by a cave-in after a few metres. In the other direction it joined up with the maze of mineshafts below Black Lake.

We'd fashioned our own rope ladder, fastened securely to a tree next to the entrance. That was one knot I always double-checked, as it was our only way out. I tied another rope to the tree, just in case, and dropped it down next to the ladder. We got out our headtorches and flashlights. We each had spare batteries, glow-sticks and, if the worst happened, our phones. It was pitch black in the mines, so we carried at least three different forms of light.

I hadn't told the others, but the reason I'd got interested in the mines was when a hiker, clearing out his bag at the campsite near the beach, had given me a battered paperback. The title was *Trapped! The Story of Floyd Collins*. It was the exclamation mark that had made fourteen-year-old me decide to take a look. It was a miserable tale from more than one hundred years before. Collins was an experienced caver who'd got trapped when a rock fell on his leg as he was squeezing through a narrow passage underground.

86

It had taken him more than a week to die, and his suffering had been front-page news. After death he had suffered the indignity of having his body displayed in a cave in a glass-topped coffin, then stolen, and eventually recovered with one leg missing.

I suppose all that should have put me off ever going underground, but it did the opposite. I was intrigued to know what it was that had gripped Collins sufficiently to make him risk his life in that way.

But it did make me careful.

Noah had zipped up his fleece and was ready to go. I picked up Kun and put him in the sling round my neck that we'd made for this purpose. The first time I'd gone into the mines I hadn't taken him with me. But he'd run around the edge of the shaft and made so much noise that I'd been worried he was going to fall in or attract someone's attention. So I'd given in. He seemed to like it down there even more than I did.

'I'll go first, and steady the ladder for you,' said Noah. He shuffled cautiously over the edge and disappeared from sight. Then he shouted up and I followed. With a backpack and a dog it wasn't easy, but I made it down safely if not gracefully.

I put Kun on the floor and he sniffed around, staying nearby. It'd been over a month since we'd been down, but nothing seemed to have changed. The walls looked pretty dry, which was always my first concern. There'd been a heavy storm three weeks earlier, which had stopped us coming back for a while.

'Are we going straight to the gap?' asked Noah.

'Yes. This could be our last chance to see what's on the other side.'

Sometimes the shafts that had been hewn by the miners more than a hundred years before broke through into natural underground caves. When they did so it was important to orient yourself, to mark the shaft so as to find your way out again. Some of the caves were sizeable, as high as our headtorches could reach.

The last time we'd been down we'd found such a cave. Usually where there was an entrance there was an exit. If the miners had burrowed in at one end they would generally dig a tunnel out at the other. But on this occasion we'd found nothing. It wasn't a particularly large cave – no more than ten metres across – so we didn't see how we could be missing an exit. Then Noah had boosted me up on to a ledge at head height, and I'd immediately felt a strong breeze. I knew that there must be a passage somewhere. Lying on the ledge I could see that there was a gap in the rock face next to it, little more than twenty centimetres high and about as long as I was tall. It would be tight, like squeezing into a coffin under hundreds of metres of stone, but I could probably make it. I'd reached in, shining my flashlight as far as I could. It was hard to see much, but it looked as though the gap opened out further on.

Then I'd heard the noise. It was a grinding, as though of stones on stones as the tide went in or out. Could we be breaking through into one of the caves lining the ocean?

I'd wanted to push through, but Noah had refused. We'd already been underground for more than four hours, and had to swap out our batteries once. I'd been annoyed at the time, but he was right. He'd promised me that we'd come back and investigate properly.

Although it was always slow going underground I reckoned that we could get back to the cave in about two hours. We wouldn't take any diversions this time. That would give us plenty of time to explore. We wouldn't be missed in town till evening, by which time we'd need to be out anyway.

We set as fast a pace as we could. At first the tunnel sloped up, then it joined a larger tunnel. I knew that if we went left it soon came to a collapsed roof, with no way past. So although that was the direction we wanted, we had first to head right and then circle back round. Fortunately I knew this part of the mines intimately. Even if our lights had failed I could probably have got us out of this section in pitch dark. Not that that was a boast I wanted to put to the test.

Kun bounced around at our feet, rarely going further than the light of our headtorches.

An hour in we stopped briefly to gather our breath and have a drink.

'How are we doing?' asked Noah. 'We're getting to bits I don't remember well.'

'We're making good time. Probably halfway there. These parts I still know. It's only the last couple of passages that were new to me.'

We pressed on until we broke out into a large cavern. This was one of my favourites. There was some sort of crystal in the walls, and if you caught it at the right angle it shone back. The first time I'd been spooked, thinking there were hundreds of tiny eyes staring at me. But once I knew what it was I found it stunning.

We paused in the middle of the cavern, sitting for a moment on a flat rock. I gave Kun some nuts. From here on we were in tunnels I'd only ever travelled once.

But it wasn't far now.

We scrambled up a slope of loose rock at the other end of the cavern, ducked through a low arch, and emerged into a tunnel that seemed much older than the others. It was narrow, our shoulders sometimes brushing against both sides, and barely taller than me. I was just about all right, but Noah caught his headtorch on the roof a couple of times. Kun had to stop his habit of racing back and forth as there wasn't space for him to squeeze past us.

The tunnel ended in what at first looked like a solid wall. However, I'd learned the last time that by sitting on the floor it was possible to drop into a narrow void below, and then crawl forward on all fours to emerge in the final cave.

I was dusty and out of breath by the time I stood up again. We'd made it. I looked at my watch. Just over two hours. Good going.

Noah and Kun followed me into the cave.

'Is this it?' asked Noah. 'I seem to remember that drop at the end of the last shaft.'

'Yes. We're here. Now to see if we can get through.'

'Fine.' He hesitated. 'I know you're excited about this, El, but let's agree now we go no more than an hour past here. If we can get through. It's a long way back. I know you. You get fixated on the goal and forget the danger.'

'Always trying to spoil my fun, Noah.'

'Seriously? Most friends would have turned back five minutes in. I don't see Linc down here, do you?'

'True,' I said. 'Fine. We go for an hour. No further. Give me a boost-up.'

Once I was on the ledge I removed my backpack and held my headtorch in one hand – there wasn't enough space to wear it through. I turned my head sideways. The gap seemed narrower than I remembered. The breeze was still there, but I couldn't hear the grinding of stones. Maybe the tide was different from the last time we'd been down.

'Here goes.' I took a deep breath, then exhaled fully, and squeezed into the gap, ears scraping against the ground and roof. There really wasn't much clearance. There was a little more space over my stomach and legs, so I managed a shallow breath.

I slid further in, hand out to my side, holding the headtorch. I could see about a metre ahead, and the gap didn't seem to be getting any wider. I'd never had a problem with confined spaces, but this was unpleasant. If it got any narrower I was going to struggle to get out. My head was twisted the wrong way, so I'd be going back blind. Too late it occurred to me that I should have tied a rope round my waist so that Noah could pull me out if necessary.

'How is it?' he shouted.

I couldn't reply. I grunted something and squeezed on.

Just as I was beginning to wonder if I should turn back, the gap seemed to open slightly. I was aware that my right ear was no longer scraping the roof. I stopped, breathing hard, and twisted the headtorch around to try to see ahead. The gap was definitely opening out. Encouraged, I crabbed sideways. Another minute and there was enough space for me to roll on to my front, relieving my cramped shoulders and thighs. I was through.

I scuttled forwards on all fours, and soon could crouch, and then stand.

Before I could look at where I'd come out I heard a worried shout from Noah. 'Ella! Are you all right? Talk to me.' He sounded distant.

I turned back to the gap, and shouted into it. 'I'm through. It's a tight squeeze but then it opens up.'

There was a pause. 'Will I fit through?'

Good question. Noah was a bit taller than me, but he was slim. And I knew that if he didn't get through he wasn't going to let me go any further. So there was only one answer I could give.

'You'll be fine,' I shouted. 'It's tight, but if I can make it you will. Send Kun first.' Then I realised that I'd left my backpack on the ledge. I'd intended to drag it along behind, but had got too focused on getting through. 'And tie a rope to our packs so that we can pull them after you.'

'All right. Here comes Kun.'

It was easier for the dog. He must have had to crawl the first bit on his belly, but what had taken me at least ten minutes Kun managed in a fraction of the time.

Then I had to wait. All I could hear was scraping and occasional muttering. I kept quiet, and shone my flashlight into the gap so that Noah could at least see where he was going. All the while I could feel the breeze in my face.

And then it died down. Despite that, the tunnel seemed to have got colder. I thought I heard a scraping on the rocks behind me, and what felt like a breath on the back of my neck. Kun growled.

I whirled round, scared for the first time. My light bounced around, from rock to rock. There was nothing there. Just an overactive imagination. I breathed out again.

'Hey!' Noah was shouting.

'Sorry.' I turned back, shining the light for him again. But I was listening carefully to what might be behind me in the darkness. Heart still racing.

Noah was no quicker than I'd been, but he made it. He

scrambled towards me, straightening up. The beam from my headtorch caught him in the eyes. He looked like a frightened animal.

'Fuck, that was horrible,' he said. 'I'd like to see you get Linc through there. I'm not looking forward to the return trip.' He turned back towards the gap, pulling on the rope and dragging our packs through.

'Let's see if it was worth it,' I said, relieved to have him there.

We were in a short tunnel that was opening out into what was clearly a cave. The tunnel didn't look man-made, the walls smooth as though carved by the ocean. The floor sloped down until it ended at a low drop.

We walked to the end of the tunnel and looked around.

We were standing on a ledge halfway up the back wall of a cave a good hundred metres or so across. The floor looked to be a shingle beach. It was wet, our lights reflecting off it. That had to be what I'd heard from the other side of the gap last time – the tide rolling the stones around. It stank of rotting seaweed, which was piled up around the edges of the cave. I could hear the occasional rumble of waves crashing against rocks.

'El, turn off your light,' Noah said.

'What? Why?'

'Just do it.' There was an unusual urgency to his voice. Almost an order. I didn't like it.

'All right. Chill.' I reached up and turned off my headtorch.

It took a moment for my eyes to adjust to the dark. I'd done this many times before in the mines. In fact I'd insisted on doing it with Noah the first time he came down, to show him what it was like without light. Underground, light was life. I'd

93

wanted him to know that without it he would almost certainly die. When you turn off the light it's the purest black you'll ever see. Or not see. You hold up your hand in front of you and your brain imagines it can detect your fingers moving. But it can't.

This time it was different. I began to see light, high up in the corner of the opposite wall. I realised it must be a passage through to the open air. We couldn't see the sky, but there was enough light trickling through to know that it was there – just out of sight.

'I thought I saw light,' said Noah softly. 'I know this place.'

What?

'Quick,' said Noah. 'We need to get down.'

'Why? How can you possibly know this cave? Have you been here before?'

'No. But we need to get down there. We need to look for a boat.'

'A boat?' I asked.

'Yes,' replied Noah. 'And six skeletons.'

10

THE LIFEBOAT

Noah refused to answer any more of my questions. 'Just help me look,' he said impatiently. 'I'll tell you later. At least what I can.'

The descent wasn't easy, but we made it to the floor of the cave. I hoped we could get back up again.

'What sort of boat am I looking for?' I asked. 'And how would it have got in here?'

'There used to be a way in from the sea,' Noah said. He shone his flashlight across a narrow strip of water, which ended in a rock wall. 'If we're where I think we are the entrance collapsed a long time ago, sealing the cave. You're looking for an old wooden lifeboat.'

He walked off to the right, following the edge of the water. I went in the other direction, with Kun, who jumped into the water, probably trying to catch a fish.

I wasn't sure what exactly I was looking for, or why.

Then Noah shouted. 'Ella, quick, over here.'

Kun ran ahead of me to where Noah was standing in the water, pulling up pieces of rotten seaweed and throwing them behind him. Kun thought it was a game. He was jumping at the pieces as they flew past him, barking. The noise echoed round the cave.

'Shut up, Kun!' Noah shouted. He was normally more patient with the dog. Then he saw me. 'Help me clear this.'

I joined in reluctantly. The seaweed stank and fell apart in my hands. But we were uncovering something half submerged in the shallow water.

'This is it,' said Noah excitedly. 'I can't believe we've stumbled in here. I thought this place was lost.'

'What are you talking about?' I asked. He was irritating me with his man-of-mystery attitude.

'I'll tell you in a minute,' he said. 'Just help me uncover it.'

I continued, grumbling under my breath.

After five minutes' hard work we stood back.

It didn't look much to me. The boat was about four metres long, dark wood with a few flecks of white paint. The sides were rotting and falling apart. The back end was flooded, the front filled with bits of seaweed and rubbish. It reminded me of the half-submerged hulks you'd see every fall in Bamfield harbour, which remained there through the winter, frozen in, abandoned, until next spring the harbourmaster had to pay someone to clear them away.

But Noah was entranced. He stared at it, silent, almost reverent.

'What—' I began, but he held up a hand, not looking at me.

'Quiet, El. I need to see if there are any bones.'

'Why are we looking for bones?' I asked. 'Who's died in here?'

I got no answer. He turned away from me and started rummaging around inside the boat, tossing out bits of rotten wood.

I didn't know what had got into him, but he clearly wasn't going to tell me anything until he was ready to. It was annoying. Usually he did what I told him.

I peered into the boat, shining my headtorch along its length. Near the bow something reflected the light back at me. I leaned in, reaching for it. A piece of seaweed moved, brushing over my hand. I tried to flick it away, but it stuck to me.

And suddenly started pulling me into the boat!

I screamed, stumbling backwards. With a loud popping sound my hand came free.

The next thing I knew I was soaked in a blast of water.

'What the hell?' I spluttered.

Noah was laughing. 'You grabbed on to an octopus. It must have been living in the boat. It swam off.'

'It sprayed me!'

'They do that when they're scared,' he said. 'I've not seen one that close before. It was incredible.'

'You're welcome to it,' I said. 'I need to get dry.'

I went back to where we'd left our packs, and dug out a clean shirt and fleece. I glanced over at Noah, but he was still absorbed in searching the boat, so I quickly stripped off and changed.

Kun had got bored with the boat and came over to join me, nuzzling at my feet. I found a small rock where we could sit, and poured some of our water into my hand for him. He lapped it up greedily.

I looked at my watch. We'd been in the mines now for well over three hours. We had power to last at least another five, but I always liked to leave a good margin of error. How long was Noah going to want to be here? For me the trip was a disappointment. I'd been hoping we'd find more tunnels beyond the gap. Instead we'd found a dead-end cave with a rotten boat. It hadn't been worth the difficult crawl.

I decided I'd give Noah the time it took me to eat my lunch, and then we were leaving. While I ate I could see his headtorch bobbing about near the boat.

I was just finishing up, sharing the last of my cheese sandwich with Kun, when Noah came over. He sat down next to me, pulling out his water bottle and taking a long swig.

'What's going on?' I asked. 'Why are you so excited about a mouldy old boat and a grumpy octopus?'

'I wish I could tell, but I can't.'

'Christ, Noah, without me you'd never have even found this place. What's so special about it? You said you knew the cave. Have you climbed in through the hole up there before? And what's all this stuff about skeletons, or was that just to scare me?'

'It's real,' he said. 'And no, I've not been here before – no one has for well over two hundred years.' He paused. 'Look, I'll tell you what I can, but it's not much. That hole up there was dug by Royal Marines from *HMS Carlisle* in the summer of 1806. They'd found a passage from the surface, and enlarged it to get through. Who knows what they were looking for. Maybe they were just exploring, the British did a lot of that. Maybe they'd heard the story about the wreck and the boat from the Mowachaht, and were looking for it. Whatever the reason, they found a boat – that lifeboat – and six skeletons. The skeletons aren't here any more so they must have buried them.' He looked around him. 'Maybe in the cave somewhere.'

Shit! We were sitting in an underground graveyard? I recalled when I thought I'd heard a sound, and felt someone's breath on my neck.

'How do you know all this?'

'I ... I can't tell you much more,' he said. 'It's part of my people's history. Perhaps their biggest secret.'

'Where's the boat from?'

Noah hesitated. Then he reached into his pocket and handed me something.

It was a thin strip of metal, about the length of my forearm, pointed at one end. I could just about make out raised letters, but they were difficult to read. It was caked with black seaweed and dirt.

'What is this?'

Noah took it back. 'It's the nameplate from the lifeboat. It seems to have been used as a knife, which fits with the stories I've heard. I can't read it properly, but I'm pretty certain that if we clean it up it will say *Pride of Whitby*. It's one of the ships that sank off the coast over the years. In 1804 she struck a reef in the middle of a storm. Only one lifeboat got away, with seven crew on board. This was it.'

'So the skeletons were the survivors?'

'Sort of.'

'You said the marines found six skeletons, but you just told me that seven crew got away. What happened to the other one?'

He sighed. 'Sorry, I've told you too much already. There are some things even other Akaht don't know. I only know because of my dad.'

He was irritating me, and I'd had enough of the cave. 'Is this part of the Akaht legend about turning back time? I know all about that. Everyone in town does, even if they don't talk about it.'

'It's not a legend, it's real. Don't you believe it?'

'There's lots of strange shit goes on here. Everyone seems to think it's real.'

'It is,' Noah said firmly. 'There's no question. And, yes, this cave has something to do with that. Everything, in fact, but I really can't tell you more.'

'Fine,' I said. 'If you're going to be so fucking mysterious then don't ask for my help. Let's head back.'

'No,' he said. 'I want to see if we can get up to the hole. This place has been lost for two hundred years. I want to know where that passage comes out on the surface. And if we can get up there it'll be a much quicker route out as we won't need to go back through the tunnels.'

'For all we know it comes out halfway up a cliff face. There's probably a good reason no one's found it in two hundred years.'

Noah turned to me and grabbed one of my hands, squeezing tight. Forgetting.

I pulled away.

'Sorry,' he said. 'Please help me. This is really important. I can't tell you more, but we may never come back here again. There's no way I could get through the tunnels without you.'

*

We wasted almost an hour trying to get to the hole. The first few metres were an easy scramble, but then it became vertical. We could get halfway up that bit with one of us boosting the other but then it turned into an overhang. There was nowhere to tie a rope. We tried repeatedly to throw a loop of rope up into the hole, hoping it would catch on something strong enough to hold our weight. Occasionally it would snag, but the moment we pulled it fell back down.

Eventually I'd had enough. I looked at my watch: it was almost three o'clock.

'We've got to go,' I said. 'Those marines must have tied off above and got in and out on ropes. We just can't do it from down here.'

Noah ignored me, staring up in frustration.

'Noah, I'm going. Come with me or don't, but you'll never get out on your own.'

He finally looked across at me and gave a scream of frustration that echoed round the cave. For a moment I was scared, it sounded so primal. But then he nodded, and started coiling the rope over one arm.

'You're right,' he said. 'It's hopeless.'

The crawl back through the gap was every bit as unpleasant as the way in. This time Noah went first, then Kun, then he pulled the backpacks through and I followed.

I didn't enjoy the ten minutes or so I was left alone on the wrong side of the gap. Alone with the six skeletons buried somewhere behind me. And the missing seventh sailor.

Noah was silent on the way back, and I didn't feel like talking. I was unsettled by what we'd seen in the cave, and what he'd told me. And hadn't told me. The caves no longer felt safe, my place to hide from the world. Instead, I felt as though I was being watched by something from the darkness.

We'd just passed through the crystal cave and entered the next tunnel when I stumbled. I put a hand on Noah's back to steady myself.

He turned sharply. 'What was that?'

Kun barked.

Then it happened again. The entire tunnel shook. Small stones rained down from overhead.

It took me a moment to realise. 'Fuck, it's a quake!'

Vancouver Island is part of the Pacific Ring of Fire, one of the most seismically active areas in the world, stretching from New Zealand to Japan to Alaska, and then all the way down to Peru. Tourists in Bamfield take smiling photos of themselves next to the signs saying 'Tsunami Evacuation Route'. But it's no joke. We'd been taught at school how the Juan de Fuca Plate was being pushed under the island, how the pressure would one day release in a violent earthquake.

'What do we do?' said Noah, his voice squeaking.

I felt strangely calm. The ground was still again. 'We go on,' I said. 'It may have passed. There's nothing we can do except get out as quickly as possible.'

Noah stood there, unmoving.

I stepped round him, and carried on up the tunnel, but I couldn't hear him following.

When I turned round he was frozen in place, ten metres

back. Kun was halfway between us. My headtorch caught Noah's eyes staring wildly at me. 'Come on, Noah, you're in a bad place there. You've got to move, now!'

I didn't like the fact that pebbles had fallen on us with the last tremor. It suggested that there was loose rock above.

'I can't,' Noah said hoarsely. 'I can't move.'

'For fuck's sake, Noah, we can't stay here. Staying where you are is the worst possible option.'

He still didn't move.

I couldn't leave him. Cursing under my breath, I started back down the tunnel towards him.

Which was a mistake.

If I'd stayed where I was I wouldn't have been standing under loose rock when the next tremor struck.

11

LOST

I woke to the sound of someone crying.

It was dark.

My head ached.

I was lying on my back on a rocky surface.

I rolled on to my side, feeling for my headtorch. It was gone.

The crying stopped. Followed by a sniff.

'El? Are you awake?' It was Noah. He switched on a light, blinding me.

I struggled to sit up. I felt sick and my throat was parched.

'Noah?' I croaked. 'Can you give me a drink?' He handed me a bottle and I took a long swig. 'What happened?'

'Don't you remember? There was a quake. Half the roof fell in. Luckily I was behind you, but you got hit. I've been carrying you round these tunnels, trying to find a way out.' He paused, his voice breaking. 'Now we're completely lost. We're never going to get out.'

As the water hit my stomach it had entirely the wrong effect. I turned away from Noah and threw up until there was nothing left. My throat ached.

'Come on,' I said hoarsely. 'I'm sure I can get us out of here.'

'But we're lost. We're going to die down here.'

'For fuck's sake.' Maybe he was frightened, but this wasn't helping. My head was throbbing and I was struggling not to throw up again. 'Stop being so pathetic. First you're all mysterious about that stupid boat, and now you want to lie down and die. Grow a pair.'

Noah was silent for a moment. 'Don't be so mean, El.' He sounded as though he was going to burst into tears again. That was all I needed.

I pulled my flashlight out of my pocket. Fortunately it was still working, and I shone it up and down the tunnel. One way the light was swallowed up by the darkness. The other I could just make out a junction in the distance.

I looked for my watch, but it was gone. For some reason that annoyed me most of all, as it had been a present from my mother. Not that she would ever notice I'd lost it.

'What time is it?' I asked.

Noah didn't answer, so I dug out my phone.

16:53. I hadn't been unconscious for long.

I turned back to Noah. He was huddled against the tunnel wall, legs drawn up to his chest. He blinked at me, eyes wet. He was shaking, breathing hard. I knew that I ought to be patient, but it wasn't easy. It was his fault that we were in this mess, because he'd been too scared to move after the first quake. If I hadn't had to turn back for him I'd have been fine.

But I needed to try to understand what he was thinking.

I crouched beside him and put a hand on his shoulder, looking into his eyes. 'Noah, listen to me. We've got to stay calm if we're going to get out of here alive. I can find the way out, but you've got to stop panicking. You're useless to me if you panic. Man up.'

He was silent. His breathing slowed. Then he spoke again, more assured. 'Don't be such a bitch. I'm not your lapdog. I saved you.'

My patience was short-lived. 'You dragged me out from under a rock and then got us lost. And I was only under the rock because you hadn't got the guts to carry on walking. Just pull yourself together and let's get out of here.'

'No. You're as bad as Linc. You two always gang up on me, acting like I'm still a child.'

'We don't have time for this. I'm going to find my way out, and you can come or not, it's up to you.' Then I realised something was missing. 'Where's Kun?'

'You care more for that fucking dog than you do for me,' Noah said. 'He ran off.'

'I'm going to find him then. He's worth ten of you.'

As I turned away Noah grabbed me by the arm.

I pulled away.

'You don't understand, do you, El? I saved your life.' He swallowed hard. 'You were dead and I turned back time and saved your life. I only get to do it once, and I wasted it on you. Show some fucking gratitude.'

What? What the hell was he going on about?

Noah was babbling. 'After the rockfall you were breathing

but unconscious. I've been carrying you round these stupid tunnels for hours. Eventually I gave up, and then I realised you'd stopped breathing. And I knew then that I would be dead soon, because there was no chance I'd find my way out without you. So I did the only thing I could. I used my power to summon the wolf, to go back before we reached the cave with the lifeboat, before the rockfall. But even then you were still unconscious. I don't know why. So I started all over again, carrying you through the tunnels trying to find a way out. I'd just about given up, thinking that you were never going to wake, and that I was going to die too.'

He stopped and stared at me, as though willing me to believe him.

It sounded crazy.

'But I can remember it all,' I said. 'The cave, the lifeboat, the octopus. If you'd really turned back time it never happened.'

'No. You died, so you remember. To you it's still part of your timeline. I don't know why, but that's the way it works.'

I felt as though I'd suddenly been cut loose. This couldn't be true. None of it made any sense.

'That can't be right,' I said. I put a hand to my head, where it hurt. Where the rock must have struck it. I could still feel the bruise. 'I was knocked out. If you're right, then that never happened.'

Noah shook his head. 'You're missing the point. Just because I turned back time doesn't stop things happening. There was always going to be an earthquake here this afternoon so it happened again. I was walking still at that point and I'm sorry I ... I dropped you. I guess that's where you got the bruise. That's not why your head hurts, though. That's because of the shift in time. The closer you are the worse it is. My head feels as though someone has driven a spike through it.'

I wasn't sure I believed anything he was telling me, but it was too much to process just then. Everything was changing. The mines were different. Noah was different. I needed to get things back to normal.

'Forget it,' I said. 'We need to find Kun. Then we need to get out of here.'

Getting out was easy. Finding Kun was not.

After walking for five minutes I knew where we were. We came to a junction that even Noah should have recognised.

Finding my dog was more difficult. I called, shining my flashlight up and down the tunnels. Nothing.

Noah wasn't much help. He followed silently behind, staying close. I wasn't sure if he was in shock or sulking from what I'd said to him. I didn't really care. I needed to find Kun.

I don't know how long I spent looking. I lost track of time. But eventually Noah spoke. 'El, we know he's not here, so we've got to get out. Our lights won't last for ever and if we leave it much longer people will be looking for us.'

Logically he was right. I'd always had strict rules on how long we spent in the mines. This was an emergency, but we were breaking the rules.

And in truth I knew that however long I spent down there I wasn't going to find Kun alive. Something had happened to him. He never normally ran much beyond our lights. I hated to think of him having fallen down somewhere, trapped, waiting for me to come and find him. But I knew that if he was alive he'd have barked, and noise echoed for ever in the mines. He was gone.

As we turned towards the exit it felt as though something had clutched at my gut. For a moment I doubled over in pain, as though I was going to throw up again. But this wasn't physical. Was it grief?

Normally I'd have asked myself how Kun would have reacted. But that made no sense.

Whatever it was I shrugged it off and walked on. I needed to deal with this alone, and to be alone I needed to get out of the mines.

Lincoln was waiting for us by the exit, shouting down into the ventilation shaft. He sounded desperate, and said he'd been there for over an hour, calling and wondering when he should head back to town and tell Koji. He'd felt the quake too, and had feared the worst.

We scrambled up the rope ladder and collapsed on to the grass, staring up at the fading sunlight.

'God, you two smell like a rotten whale,' Lincoln said. Then he looked around, puzzled. 'Where's Kun?'

I shook my head. 'Kun's gone.'

12

THE END OF SUMMER

By finding the lifeboat I not only lost my dog, but also my childhood friends.

The first loss was obvious. It took me a while to notice the second.

I didn't go into the mines again that summer.

Before we left, Lincoln had insisted on going down the rope ladder to look for Kun. He hadn't gone far, but given his fear of the mines I'd been surprised. He must have been fonder of Kun than I'd realised. Or of me.

After he gave up, and as we trudged back to town, the fine weather broke. It rained for the next week. We'd been in the lower passages, where the mineshafts dropped down towards the ocean. I told myself that most of where we'd been would be flooded, impassable now. But the truth was that I didn't want to go back in, even for Kun. After the discovery of the lifeboat something had changed for me. My caving days were over.

I'd felt pretty sick for the first day. I wasn't sure if that was the knock on my head or something to do with Noah's crazy story about turning back time. It was only later that I realised I probably ought to have been checked out for concussion.

In the days that followed I felt flat. Sometimes I'd forget, reach out a hand for Kun, or call him. But he was gone for good.

I avoided Lincoln and Noah. Whatever I was feeling I didn't want to discuss it. I didn't want to know how they felt about Kun's death. He had been my dog, not theirs. Once I had decided how to react I could talk to them again.

But I couldn't avoid them for ever.

Noah came round on the third morning, and stood outside the house in the rain, knocking on the door.

'I know you're there, El,' he shouted. 'Let me in.'

Eventually I did. He dripped water all the way to my room, then sat on a chair quietly steaming. I was cross-legged on the bed, still in the shorts and T-shirt I'd slept in.

I'd expected him to want to talk about what had happened to us, about him saving my life, but he seemed to have moved on from that already.

'El,' he said, looking at me intensely, 'it was amazing finding the cave. I'm sure now that we were meant to be the first to see the lifeboat in two hundred years. It was a mystical experience, and it made me realise what I need to do.'

I was rather thrown by that. 'What?'

'We can't carry on as we are. We've got to connect with the spirits that live around us, in the caves, in the woods, in the water. We've got to connect more with the planet, before we destroy it. Being down there made me understand what I'm meant to do. Don't you see it? Our parents have destroyed this place, and themselves with it. The whole of Black Lake is riddled with tunnels that they dug grubbing around for money. It looks beautiful, but just under the surface it's all tainted. Everything here is sordid. It's too late for us to stop what's happened here, but we need to stop it in other places.'

His blue eyes pierced impatiently into mine. I wasn't sure how to respond. Finding the cave had killed my dog but seemed to have given Noah some sort of Messiah complex.

'Don't you see it, El?' He leaned forward. 'What we found in the cave was a message to us, to me.' He paused for a moment. 'I've made a decision, and you're the first to know. From now on I want to be known as Maquina.'

'What?'

'Maquina,' he repeated, looking at me expectantly.

I shrugged. 'Who the fuck is Maquina?'

'You've never heard of him? He was the chief of the Mowachaht two hundred years ago, and the greatest ever of the chiefs on the island. He was the first to trade with the Spanish, and he was friends with Captain Cook. He killed the crew of an entire ship and the British still forgave him. He saw the *Pride of Whitby* sink. I can't believe you've never heard of him. Lots of later chiefs have taken his name, to honour him. I'm going to do the same, to mark my connection to the spirits. To mark my new quest in life.'

I stared at him. 'For fuck's sake, Noah. Your stupid cave killed Kun, and apparently killed me too. And you think it was sending us some sort of message? What's it possibly got to do with the spirits or the world? What have you been smoking?'

This was too much on top of everything else. I put my head in my hands and the tears that I'd been holding back for days finally came.

'Go away!' I said between sobs. Whatever this was I didn't want to share it. I wanted Noah to leave.

Instead I felt the bed shift as he sat next to me, holding me. I wept on to his shoulder. Like some stupid, fucking cliché.

He whispered into my ear. 'You're alive, El, that's what matters.' Gently stroking my hair. 'I'd like you to come with me on this journey,' he whispered. 'Together we can change the world.' His hands moved to my shoulders, and I looked up. He was staring into my eyes, leaning in. Closer than we'd ever been.

No!

I pushed him away and jumped up. 'Fuck off! I'm not coming on some mystical quest with you. It sounds nuts. What's got into you?'

He sat back on the bed, hurt in his eyes, then got to his feet. 'Fine!' he said angrily. 'I'll go on my own, and it'll be your loss. I'll show you.'

He stormed out, slamming the front door behind him.

I'd barely got rid of him when there was another knock on the door. I assumed he'd come back. To try again? To apologise?

'Go away, Noah,' I shouted.

'Ella, we need to talk.'

It wasn't Noah.

It was someone else I'd been avoiding. Koji. I knew it wouldn't take him long to notice that Kun was missing.

'Koji-Na,' I called back. 'Give me a minute. I'm not dressed.'

When I opened the front door Koji was standing with his back to it, looking out over the lake. The rain had stopped, damp hanging in the air. He was smoking one of his foul cheroots.

'Please, put that out,' I said, waving away the smoke. 'You're going to kill both of us.'

Normally he'd have smiled at that, but his face was grim as he turned to me. 'It's less likely to kill you than going in the mines. Or at least it'll be slower.'

Shit! I stiffened. Someone had talked.

'What do you mean, Uncle?' I asked, as innocently as I could.

He threw his stub into the bushes. Which showed what mood he was in. I'd had more than one lecture from him on the dangers of unattended campfires.

'Don't give me that crap,' he said. 'I know where you've been. Where's Kun?'

I looked away. 'Kun's dead, but I guess you know that anyway. Which one of them talked?'

'Lincoln. He told me you and Noah went into the mines with Kun, and only two of you came out.' He turned to me.

Even I could see the pain in his eyes. I looked away.

'I know you're bored here,' he said, 'but what were you thinking? It's madness to go down there.'

I hesitated. He didn't know everything, because only Noah knew what had really happened. What to tell him? I couldn't make it any worse. And I did want to know if there was any truth to Noah's crazy story about saving my life.

'I'm sorry, Uncle,' I said. 'Can we go for a walk?'

He nodded, and we took the path round the lake, away from

town. There was a low mist hanging on the lake, and soon it felt as though we were the only two people left in the world.

I liked that.

As we walked I gave him a carefully edited version of my adventure. I didn't tell him how many other times Noah and I had been into the mines. Or about the cave with the lifeboat and the skeletons. I didn't want him to know how far we'd gone, or how long we'd been down there.

I did tell him about the earthquake. And Kun disappearing. And Noah's story about turning back time.

'Could that be real?' I asked. 'I've heard stories about it, growing up, but could Noah have really done that? For me?'

'It's possible. It's definitely happened in the past, so I know that the power is real. It's one of our oldest legends, and the one thing that marks us out from the other Aht, from the other bands on the island.' He stopped walking, and rolled up the sleeve of his right arm, showing me his wrist. 'You see this?' It was a black ink tattoo, a wolf's head inside a circle. 'Those of us who have the power of the wolf, we all have the same tattoo.'

I stared at him, wide-eyed. 'Are you saying you've done this?'

He shook his head. 'No. I'm saying I could. But I've never had the need.'

'So could Noah?'

'Yes. As the chief's son he knows more of our secrets that anyone. He has the power, but whether he used it to call the wolf, I don't know.'

'He sounded cross about it, said he'd wasted his one chance to use it just to save my life.'

Koji smiled. 'Don't feel guilty. There are two things you should remember. First, don't say "just" to save your life. That's more important than anything. But second, from what you've told me it doesn't sound as though it was just for you. He was lost, and the only way he was getting out of the mines again was if you showed him the way. He needed you alive as much as you needed him.'

We walked on in silence for a while. Then Koji stopped again. He turned to me. 'I won't tell your father this. It would be too much for him on top of everything else. In return, though, you need to promise me one thing. Promise that you'll never go back to the mines again.'

That was an easy promise to make. I had no desire to go back. I stepped up to Koji and gave him a hug. 'I promise, Uncle.'

It was a promise I kept for more than twenty years. And it was Koji who made me break it.

The rest of that summer went quickly. Noah was focused on his new obsession with the environment so I didn't see much of him. He spent a lot of time digging around in the overgrown slag heaps in the abandoned parts of the forest, returning with jars full of soil. I'd no idea what he was doing with them.

I was finally looking forward to getting to university in Victoria. It was change, but I could establish new routines. The old ones were ruined. There wasn't anything left for me at Black Lake.

Lincoln seemed to have realised that something had happened between Noah and me. Maybe he got the wrong idea, or maybe Noah told him things that weren't true. So we drifted apart. True, we stayed vaguely in touch, and a few years later he even offered me a job. But it wasn't the same. It was only when I returned to Bamfield that we got close again.

Noah became ever more obsessed as the summer went on. He said that our parents and grandparents had betrayed our generation and been ripped off by the mining companies in the process. He fell out with his father over it.

I partly agreed with him, but I didn't see the point of wallowing in regret. What was done was done.

I refused to call him Maquina. It was just too odd. Eventually I compromised on 'Maq'. Lincoln, on the other hand, seemed to have no problem with the idea of reinventing yourself as someone else.

I heard that Noah only stayed a couple more years at Black Lake. Then he abandoned his heritage to go off and tilt at windmills. The spiritual awakening that had started in the cave had turned into a full-blown crusade. I'd read about his exploits as a self-proclaimed eco-terrorist. The man who rejected other climate protestors as insufficiently militant. He founded his own organisation, GreenWar, which embraced violence to save the planet.

But I hadn't seen him again since that summer.

Until now.

2045

13

WHEN THE PARTY'S OVER

Lincoln always loved the grand gesture, the dramatic flourish that made everyone gasp.

His revelation of the ghost Maq had had the desired effect. Lincoln himself was forgotten, and people were crowding around *The Cage*. Some were even trying to reach through the bars and touch its occupant. There was a buzz in the room that drowned out the noise of the rain being driven against the windows.

But not everyone was happy.

While the guests had moved towards *The Cage*, Koji and Yahl had stayed where they were. Koji was arguing with Yahl, who was gesturing angrily towards *The Cage*. Koji put a hand on his shoulder, as though to calm him. Yahl flung it off.

Then someone grabbed me hard by the arm, pulling me round. It was Rebecca. She was in tears, and not for the reasons she'd expected. 'The fucking scrote,' she sobbed. 'Why's he such a dick? He didn't even mention Dad. It's all just about him.'

I led her towards a darker corner of the room, away from the other guests. I grabbed a napkin from a table, and passed it to her. She dabbed at her eyes, shoulders heaving.

'He's such a selfish bastard,' she said between sobs. 'Never thinks of anyone but himself. This whole thing was just about him.'

It was hard to disagree with that assessment. 'He knows where it all came from,' I said. 'I'm sure he remembers, even if he's not good at acknowledging it. You know what he's like, he tends to look to the future, not the past.'

'I do, but just once you'd like to think he might realise it's not all about his fucking genius. Why do I bother? I spent ages updating Dad's work, thinking that was what he was going to use tonight, and it didn't even get a mention. What a dick!'

'Ella,' came a voice from behind me, 'We need to talk.'

What now?

It was Koji. 'Ella, you need to stop this.'

'I'm kind of busy,' I said, gesturing to Rebecca.

'I'm sorry, but this is more important,' he said. 'You need to stop him, now.'

'Look—' I began, but Rebecca interrupted me.

'I need to get cleaned up,' she said. 'You sort out Koji, and we'll speak later.' She paused, then added, 'If I haven't pushed Linc off the roof by then.'

She stormed off, leaving me with Koji.

'Is this about Maq?' I asked. 'What do you expect me to do? Lincoln won't pay any attention to what I say. You've got more chance.'

'He will.' There was an urgency to Koji that I'd never seen before. 'Ella ...' he began, then stopped. He bit his lip for a moment. 'I don't want to seem disloyal to Lincoln, but this is all wrong. Maquina may not have been a great chief to us, too focused on righting the wrongs of others, and forgetting his people, but he's still our chief. This will cause trouble when word gets out. Please tell Lincoln to stop before things get worse.'

'Why does it matter?' I asked. 'Maq isn't really here, he's sitting in a cell in Vancouver.'

'Don't you understand? This is humiliating, using our chief as some sort of party piece. A hundred years ago the British were parading us round music halls so that we could show off our quaint native dances to civilised society. This is no better, putting our chief in prison, and then displaying him in a cage. It's as though we're animals. It was despicable what they did to us then, and what Lincoln is doing now is just as bad. I guess he cares more for his fancy friends than he does for his own people.'

'Look, I'll try,' I said. 'But you know Lincoln as well as I do, he'll do what he wants. I'm no happier about this than you are. Whatever he has become, Maq was once my friend.'

'Please speak to him, and quickly. It's a good job I'd sent the younger members of staff home. Yahl is bound to tell them, though, whatever I say, and he's not the only one with a temper. I hope by tomorrow things will have calmed down a bit, but Yahl was ready to go over and punch Lincoln, and that would be a disaster for all of us.'

'I'll try,' I said again, looking round for Lincoln.

I found him standing back from the crowd, a glass of champagne in hand, enjoying watching the stir that he had created. Smiling to himself.

How to approach this? Could I in my role as RCMP constable order him to stop? On what grounds? It hardly counted as a jailbreak as Maq was still sitting in his cell in downtown Vancouver. Maybe there was some law being broken, but without speaking to my superiors in Victoria I wasn't sure what. I was better off trying to prevail on Lincoln as a friend.

I grabbed a glass of champagne, took a gulp, and walked over to him.

'So,' I said, 'was this what you meant when you said you and Maq were close? It's a strange birthday present.'

Lincoln grinned. 'Koji's pissed off with me, as is Paul. Which of them told you to come and tell me off?'

'Koji thinks that you're insulting his chief and your people. Maq's your chief too, and was once your friend. Your oldest friend, apparently.'

Lincoln shrugged. 'It's all just a bit of fun. After what Maq's done the Akaht should have got rid of him years ago, so I don't know why Koji's so fussed.'

'Seeing your chief for the first time in twenty years, humiliated like this, can't be good.'

'It's not the first time they're seeing him. Maq has been back a couple of times. You weren't here when he came to protest about my building this place, a good fifteen years ago now. Actually, before he pulled his oil rig stunt I was thinking of getting him on board as Orcus's vice-president of environmental studies, or something like that. What was it President Johnson said about Hoover? Better to have him inside the tent pissing out, than outside the tent pissing in. It would have been a great PR coup, and would have neutered Maq. Destroyed his credibility with his followers, and made me look like I was doing something about the environment.'

'Rebecca is cross with you too,' I said.

'What does she care about Maq?'

'She doesn't, but she'd thought your personal announcement was going to be a moving tribute to her father and his contribution to the ghost dancers. Instead of which, he didn't even get a mention.'

Lincoln sighed. 'For God's sake, I paid her father millions for nothing more than a few chess pieces, and she'll get royalties on every ghost we sell. What more does she want? Women!' he exclaimed. 'You were never like this, El, you understood me.'

'No I didn't, I just tolerated you better. My needs are different from most people. What's the point of this stuff with Maq anyway? He's just sitting there doing nothing.'

'I don't think you realise just how bored I get sometimes, especially after you left. I've got to do something to keep things exciting.' He turned to me. 'Come back, El, I've missed you.'

'And you'd just toss Rebecca aside like that?'

'I told you, Rebecca's fun, but she's not you.'

I shook my head. 'No, Linc. She's wanted you as long as I can remember, and she's much better for you than I am. You want me to change. It's like with Maq, you'd rather I was inside the tent so you can neuter me.'

He grinned. 'There's lots of things I want to do to you, El, but neutering's not one of them. Just think about it. You know I'd give you a job tomorrow, with no strings attached. You're wasting your life hiding in Bamfield and playing with octopuses when you could be heading up a research lab. I could get you a professorship at the university tomorrow. We're not getting any younger, and there's going to come a time soon when you won't want to be jumping into the icy water to chase after your eight-legged friends.'

I started to protest, but he stepped closer, and reached up as though about to put a finger to my lips.

I stepped back quickly.

His hand dropped. 'Sorry. Don't answer me now. Just think about it.'

I bit back my response. 'Look, I'll think about it, but just the job, nothing else. Have some respect for Rebecca, and go and find her and say sorry. But first you need to stop this theatre with Maq.'

'Fine. I wasn't going to let it go on much longer anyway. He'll sit there in stubborn silence and everyone will get bored. I want people to get back to talking about my ghosts. It's already created quite a buzz with our stock rising more than four per cent in the last hour.'

'Great,' I said. 'Because poor little you really needed another billion dollars.'

'It's not about the money any more, it's about what it represents. Come on, let's go and talk to Koji and I'll end this.'

I hesitated. 'Before you do, I've not seen Maq in twenty years. Can I go and say hello?'

'You can try. You remember how he went all moody and contemplative the last summer we were here? He got into all that Buddhist bullshit with transcendental meditation or whatever it was. Well, he's got worse, and never uses five words where one would do.'

'I'd still like to see him.'

Lincoln shrugged. 'OK.'

We threaded our way through the guests towards *The Cage*. People had begun to drift away from it, no doubt disappointed that Maq wasn't doing anything. Many had returned to the windows looking out over the ocean. The storm was worse than ever, and they seemed fascinated by it. Another huge gust shook the building. Several people jumped, and someone screamed, even though they were in no danger. They were safely tucked away in their homes in Vancouver, or Victoria, or wherever. Their fear proved that the technology worked. It was truly immersive.

Maq was continuing to stare straight ahead. He looked like a resting Buddha, eyes half shut, seemingly oblivious to the bustle around him. But he blinked as we stepped into his field of vision, and I saw his eyes widen slightly.

I went up to the crystal bars.

He raised his hands slowly and pushed back his hood.

It felt strange to see him again after so long. I supposed I owed my life to him. And my death. So we were even.

His face was more worn. Harder. He'd lost all his hair, whether through nature or choice I wasn't sure, the light reflecting off his shiny skull. There was a poorly healed scar under his chin. He'd bulked up since the last time I'd seen him. It was easy to forget that this wasn't Maq at all, just a copy woven together from beams of light.

I put my hands on the bars, getting as close as I could.

He smiled, and tilted his head in the way I still remembered. His piercing blue eyes were fixed on me.

'*Et tu*, Ella?' he said. 'Has Linc managed to tame even the great Dr Manning?'

'Fuck off, Maq,' I said. 'I'm nobody's pet.'

'I'm surprised you let him use your beloved Kun in one of his cheap fairy tales.'

I'd forgotten about Kun. I was still cross with Lincoln about that.

'I don't control what Linc does.'

'I thought you two were ... you know.' He tapped his ring finger. 'I'm sure I saw it in some gossip rag somewhere.'

I glanced to the side, where Lincoln was standing, silently watching us.

'Linc didn't tell you? He and I split up last year.'

'Good move, El.'

'How do you know I dumped him?'

'Of course you did. We both know Linc. No one can stand him for any length of time.'

That wasn't entirely fair but I wasn't going to argue. Lincoln, to my surprise, stayed silent.

'So,' said Maq. 'What did you come here for? Or do you just want to gloat at my misery?'

'Of course not,' I said. 'I—'

Then the entire house shook again. But worse than the first time. For a moment I thought it was a quake.

It was the storm reaching new heights.

'It's all fine,' Lincoln said. 'It's a bit gusty out there, but the Manor is built to withstand much worse than this.'

Koji was walking towards us, fast. 'Boss,' he said urgently, 'the satellite dish isn't going to stand much more of this. We've got to—'

He was talking loudly over the noise of the wind and rain battering the house, but then even that was drowned out by something louder: the high-pitched scream of metal being torn apart.

The lights flickered.

Everyone vanished.

One moment we were surrounded by a hundred party guests. The next, all that was left were champagne flutes and wine glasses crashing to the floor, followed by a flutter of white discs.

We had lost our link to the outside world.

Something crashed into the glass roof above us.

I looked up.

The glass had become opaque, with cracks spreading out across it.

'It's the satellite dish!' Koji shouted. 'It's fallen. We need to get out of here.'

'We need Maq!' Lincoln shouted back. He was fumbling in his jacket as he backed away from under the glass roof. He pulled something out of a pocket and pressed a button.

The Cage disappeared.

The crystal bars to which I had been clinging were gone, and I fell forward into Maq's arms. He looked as surprised as I was. Then he pushed me away and ran for the elevator.

Lincoln grabbed my arm, stopping me falling.

There was a loud creaking above us. The glass sounded as though it might fail at any moment.

'Let's get out!' I shouted.

As we ran towards the elevator the doors closed on Maq.

The ghost was gone.

14

LIES

'What the hell just happened?' I asked.

We had gathered in Lincoln's office, four floors down. This one room was bigger than my entire house in Bamfield. Lincoln was sitting in a wingback chair behind a large wooden desk.

There were five of us. Paul Kleber and Koji were sunk into leather chairs in front of the desk. Rebecca was on a matching couch to one side. I was perched on the arm of the couch.

Was there a reason Yahl wasn't there? Was Koji trying to keep him away from Lincoln, worried about what might happen?

I'd never liked Lincoln's office. It was stark, masculine, and in his usual way devoid of almost any decoration. What little there was had been put there to make a statement. On the left-hand wall was a short-handled Akaht war axe with a dark black blade. On the opposite wall a black wooden mask of the raven god.

One thing was new. On a table below the mask was a large chessboard. It was half a metre or so across, with carved pieces around ten centimetres tall. It looked impressive, but I'd never known Lincoln play a game of chess in his life. He thought all games were a waste of time.

'The satellite dish got blown over, and we've lost communication,' said Lincoln. 'It must have acted like a sail up there and caught the wind.'

'As I'd warned,' said Koji. 'We should have cancelled the party.'

Lincoln looked at him sharply. 'It's not a big problem and no one got hurt. The ghosts will have got severed rather abruptly but they'll get over it. Can't you just imagine the headlines, since no one can communicate with us, and they won't know if we're even still alive? They might think that the whole house has collapsed into the lake. You couldn't pay for this publicity. Hell, maybe I'll even get to read my own obituary.'

'Surely our phones will work,' said Kleber, digging his out.

'No,' said Lincoln. 'This is the highest point around, and the local signal comes through here. You'd need to be halfway to Port Alberni before you could pick up another transmitter.'

The lawyer was staring at his phone. He grunted.

'When I asked what happened I didn't mean about the satellite dish,' I said. 'I meant about Maq. He was supposed to be a ghost like the others, but he didn't blink out when they did. I was talking to him when the link went down, but he stayed there and I touched him. He was real, not some ghost.'

'Ah ... that.' Lincoln looked away. 'Maq was different. He wasn't a ghost in the same way as the others. What I said up there about the ghosts wasn't entirely true.'

'In what way?' I asked.

'We aren't ready to go public with this yet, but the truth is that we are a lot further down the AI road than I let on. I don't want our competitors to know about it, though. Rebecca and her team have been building on some of the advice you gave us, Ella, about the interaction between an octopus's central and subsidiary brains. We're making big progress, but there are still lots of flaws. We know—'

Rebecca interrupted him. 'All very interesting, Linc, but those flaws are the reason we haven't tried to use AI in a ghost outside strict laboratory conditions. What the hell were you thinking bringing a copy of Maquina here that's run by AI? What was wrong with having him in his jail cell controlling the ghost?'

'I wasn't sure what he'd get up to. I didn't know if we could trust him to behave himself, so I thought it was safer just to have a copy of him that was programmed to sit there and say as little as possible.'

'And this is so much safer,' Rebecca snapped. 'You've now got an autonomous copy of Maquina running round the Manor, and who knows what he'll get up to? Why didn't you ask me about this first?'

'You'd have told me not to do it, and the idea was to keep him locked in his cage so he couldn't do anything. I'd have turned him off soon anyway.'

Rebecca sat back, arms folded. 'Why do you always have to push things too far? Why can't you just be happy with what you've got? You didn't need Maquina here at all. I spent ages building the chess set for you, so we should have just used that for the announcement instead. It's a great product.'

'I thought Maq was safe stuck in his cage. But it's really not a problem, since all we need to do is find him and shut him down. No one outside this room knows the truth, and once we've got the AI working properly people won't care about any rules we may have bent to get there. You saw how excited that reporter was about having a lover she can put on a key-chain.'

'Hang on,' I said. 'What do you mean about getting it working properly? Are you saying you've made a duplicate of Maq that's running round the Manor and may not be working right? Is this AI ghost subject to the same prohibition on hurting people – whatever you called it, a "no harm" constraint?'

'Of course. It'll be bound in the same way.'

'You can't possibly know that,' Rebecca said. 'We've never tested it with AI because we've always used that under laboratory conditions. This isn't something we've had to go to the regulators on yet because it's still just a concept, and we're not meant to be using it in the real world.'

'So the constraint might not apply?' I asked.

Lincoln shrugged. 'Who knows? But it probably does.' He didn't seem particularly troubled by the risk.

'Great,' I said. 'So why did you let him out of *The Cage* if you didn't know how he'd behave?'

'I thought the roof was going to fall in on him.'

'Why would that have mattered? You could just program another ghost. You said they only cost five cents.'

Lincoln looked away. 'I guess I wasn't thinking. It just goes to show how real they are, that I thought I needed to save him.'

'He can't have gone far,' I said. 'I need to find him and get him back into custody.'

'Why you?' Kleber snorted.

'It's my job,' I said.

'Of course, the community constable,' said Kleber. 'Are you actually entitled to arrest anyone? You aren't even allowed to carry a gun. I guess you don't need one to issue parking tickets to tourists. Besides, since the real Maquina is still in his cell in Vancouver, he hasn't actually escaped from custody. You don't have any jurisdiction here.'

'It's special constable,' I said. 'And I'm the only one among us with any jurisdiction. I'll arrest him and we'll sort out the legalities later.'

'This really isn't a problem,' said Lincoln. 'He can't leave the Manor in this weather, and Koji knows the security systems backwards. He can find the ghost and lock down the area it's in. Then we get to him and switch him off, problem solved. There's never going to be any question of arresting him.'

'Can you do that?' I asked Koji.

He nodded. 'I'm sure I can find him. It may take a while, but we can go through the door logs as well as the streams from the security cameras.'

'I'll come and help you,' I said.

Koji hesitated. 'Look, to be honest it will be a lot quicker without someone looking over my shoulder. It would be easiest if everyone went to their rooms, so I know that no one except the ghost is moving around the building. Once I've found him I can lock him down and come and get you. Besides, if there's any risk he might be dangerous it would be safest if you all stayed in your rooms.'

'Might he attack someone?' I asked Rebecca.

'Ask Linc, not me, this is his baby,' she said angrily. 'But if it's right that the constraint may not be working, and the AI is trying to mimic Maquina, then who knows what it might do? I doubt there's much risk to any of us, but it's probably safest to stay out of its way. And frankly, I could do with some alone time in my room right now.' She glowered at Lincoln.

I felt that I ought to be taking charge, but it did sound as though they would be quicker without me. And in fairness to Kleber, he was right that this was way above my pay grade as special constable. My job was essentially community liaison. If anything serious happened I wasn't meant to do anything more than hold the fort until the real police got there.

'All right,' I said. 'Let's do that. But, Koji, when you find him you need to come and get me straight away, so we can decide what to do.'

Koji nodded. 'I will.'

Lincoln stood. 'Koji, can you escort Paul and Rebecca to their rooms? Make sure they get there safely. I'll show Ella where she's sleeping.'

I saw Rebecca stiffen at that. Despite what she'd said about wanting alone time she clearly wasn't happy with Lincoln favouring me over her. She was already cross with him, and I didn't envy him the discussion they were going to have at some point. But she said nothing, and the others hung back as I followed Lincoln into the corridor.

We walked to the elevator, and went up one level.

'Why is nothing ever simple with you, Linc?' I asked.

'Simple is boring. You need to take risks if you want to achieve anything. Don't settle for what's comfortable, like living alone in Bamfield with your octopus. You can't hide away from people for ever.'

'Let's not start that again. We've got bigger things to worry about. We've got to catch this copy of Maq that you've created.'

He stopped at the door to one of the guest rooms.

'Here you are,' he said. 'Koji will have put your bag inside already. Lock the door and try to get some sleep.' He hesitated. 'And please, think about things, about us. I meant what I said.'

He leaned in closer, eyes locked on mine. I could smell the champagne on his breath. 'You know, in all the time we were together you never once told me that you loved me,' he said.

'Really? But you knew that anyway, why did I need to tell you?'

He sighed. 'You know I still love you and I want you back. Come and live here with me. I promise I won't try to change you this time. It doesn't even have to be here. For you I'll take a break from Orcus. They don't need me any more, and we can travel the world, go wherever you want, as remote as you want, for a year, two years, five. We can be together. Please.'

I didn't respond.

He put a hand on the back of my neck, and pulled me towards him. Our lips touched. For a moment I froze, startled. Then I pulled back. This wasn't right. Or sensible. I'd made my decision a year ago. For both of us.

I twisted away from him, slipping his grip.

Quickly I opened the door to my room and stepped inside, letting it shut in his face.

Then I crouched down on the other side, hugging my arms around myself, shaking. Trying to find calm amid the chaos.

1804

15

FOOD

With his eyes closed the bosun could imagine himself back in the Mayflower tavern in Rotherhithe. A warm hearth, food cooking, the smell of roasting pork filling the air.

All he needed was a good ale to go with it.

But when he opened his eyes the scene was very different.

The fire was blazing, sparks crackling. The captain had said there was no point in saving the driftwood now. Either they escaped once fed or they died. And it didn't matter whether they died in the light or the dark.

Seaman Cooper lay face down on the beach, the shingle stained black with the blood that had flowed from the hole in his throat. His breeches had been pulled halfway down his legs, strips of flesh cut away from his buttocks. The captain had carefully threaded them on to two thin pieces of wood, then put them over the fire to cook.

At the time the bosun had been revolted.

Yet now it smelled so good he was salivating.

Captain Ross removed one of the skewers from the fire. It burned his fingers and he hastily dropped it on to a piece of cloth, waiting for it to cool. He gingerly picked it up again and pulled a piece of flesh free. After a moment's hesitation he raised it to his mouth, biting a piece off, swallowing quickly.

He turned to the bosun. There was a light in his eyes that had not been there before.

'You need to eat,' he said. 'It's good.'

The bosun shook his head, taking a step back. There were tears running down his cheeks. 'I can't!'

'You eat or you die, and then his sacrifice was for nothing.' Ross gestured with the skewer to Cooper's body.

'No!' The bosun turned his back on the fire, instead watching his own shadow as it flickered across the wall of the cave. 'No!' he shouted into the darkness.

Ross shrugged and turned back to the fire.

As he chewed on a second piece of flesh he reached into the fire to retrieve the other skewer.

He was determined to escape, whatever the cost.

That night, for the first time, the captain heard the howling of the wolf.

2045

16

MURDER

It was getting light when I woke. I was surprised how deeply I'd slept after the events of the night before.

And that I hadn't been interrupted. I'd asked Koji to call me when they found Maq's ghost. Did this mean that it was still at large? Despite the weather, could it have escaped outside?

The guest rooms were on the ocean side of the Manor. The wind had died somewhat, but rain was still being driven against the glass. The clouds were black, large waves breaking in the bay beyond the woods. It wouldn't have been easy for the ghost to run far in that.

I'd only lain down on the bed to rest while waiting to hear from Koji, but the next thing I knew it was morning. I felt pretty rough. I didn't think I'd drunk all that much, but my head felt fuzzy. Most nights, if I got through one glass of wine that was good going.

I showered quickly and slipped on some clean clothes: jeans, a T-shirt and sneakers. As I finished dressing there was an urgent banging on the door. 'Ella!' shouted a familiar voice.

I flung the door open.

Koji stood outside, panting and sweating. His eyes were wide.

'Have you found him?' I asked.

'What?' Koji gulped.

'The ghost. Have you found him?'

'No ... Yes.' He seemed confused. 'You need to come. Someone's been killed.'

'Who? In the storm? Has there been an accident?'

'No. Someone's been attacked in Lincoln's office.'

'Who?' I asked again.

He hesitated. 'I'm not certain exactly, but you need to come and see. I've secured the scene as best I can, but you need to take charge.'

'Me?'

'You said it last night: you're the only one with any authority here. We've got no communication, and there's no way anyone's getting to Bamfield until the weather eases.'

Without waiting for me to respond he headed for the stairwell.

I followed him down to Lincoln's office.

When we reached it Koji paused outside the door. 'Do you want me to unlock it?'

'It's all right, I know Lincoln's code,' I said, stepping past him. In the early days of our relationship I don't think he'd wanted to acknowledge how big a part of his life I'd become. So instead of giving me my own code to get around the house he'd shared his. Typical CEO – he thought the rules didn't apply to him.

And he hadn't bothered to change it in a year. The door clicked open. I stepped through, holding it for Koji to follow, but then had second thoughts. 'Stay by the door,' I said. 'Don't come inside.'

My mind tends to work from the bottom up. I see the details first and then join them together to understand the bigger picture.

So what I saw were fragments.

The Akaht war axe that had been on the wall was now embedded in the surface of Lincoln's desk.

The black raven mask from the other wall was being worn by someone lying on the desk.

The raven's white eye seemed to be staring at me.

The black queen from the chess set was standing on the desk.

A white knight was on the floor, stained crimson.

Ropes trailed down the side of the desk to the legs at each corner.

Then the bigger picture sprang into focus.

There was a man's body lying on the desk, spreadeagled, wrists and ankles tied at the corners. The chest was bare, with a thick line running from throat to navel. At first I thought someone had drawn on him, but as I stepped closer I realised that it was dried blood, and his chest had been torn open. It looked like the scar of someone who had undergone open-heart surgery. Except that this was fresh, and no effort had been made to sew the skin back together.

The mask had prevented Koji from identifying the man – but I was pretty sure I knew who it was.

I'd never attended a crime scene before, let alone a murder. I knew that I shouldn't touch anything, so I took my phone out of my pocket, using it to tip the beak of the mask up. It rolled on to the floor.

My eyes tracked it, then flicked back to the face.

Lincoln's head was turned towards the door, lips twisted back, teeth exposed as though in a final scream.

I followed his sightless gaze to Koji, who was staring past me at his boss, shaking his head. 'No ...' he muttered, shoulders sagging.

I needed time. I needed to think how to react. I wanted to be on my own, not share this with anyone. Not even Koji. The first thing to do was to get rid of him. Then I could start to process what was happening.

'We've got to get out of here,' I said. 'Did you touch anything before you called me?'

'Nothing,' he said in a faint voice.

'We should seal the room until we can get a forensics team up from Victoria.'

Koji shook his head. 'That's not going to happen today. It's too dangerous to try to get to Bamfield, let alone Victoria.'

Shit!

'All right,' I said. 'But you can't come in here again. I'll come back, alone, with gloves, once I know more about what happened. I'll meet you ...' I thought for a moment. 'I'll meet you in the kitchen in ten minutes.'

Koji nodded and left.

As the door shut behind him I felt a sense of relief.

Despite myself, I found my gaze drawn again to Lincoln's twisted face. It was almost unrecognisable. Last night he'd been talking about wanting to rekindle our relationship, to give everything up to be with me. And now whatever it was that made him Lincoln was gone.

What was it I was feeling? Grief? Loss? Shock? What did any of that mean? And how did it help? None of it would bring Lincoln back.

He was gone to wherever his Akaht beliefs would take him. Where was that?

Years ago I'd read a book that ended with the protagonist in old age seamlessly moving from life to death, walking up a hill through tall grasses, throwing aside his walking stick, then starting to run, dropping the aches and pains of age, and being greeted by the friends who had gone before coming down to meet him. It had seemed almost joyous, the moment of his passing unseen.

I hoped that was how it had been for Lincoln, running through the woods near Black Lake, being welcomed by those he loved. Who would that be? Maybe Kun racing to meet him, barking. Linc had stolen my dog for his stories, so why not in death too? Or maybe it would be a thin man in a black turtleneck and rimless glasses. Linc might have thought that meeting really was worth dying for.

I realised that what I wanted most in that moment was Scarlett. I wanted to lean on the edge of her tank, let her fold her arms around me, wrap me up. Pull me into her tank where the water could close over me and shield me from the world.

I shut my eyes and counted to eight, imagining her touch drawing away my pain.

When I opened my eyes nothing had changed. But I knew what I had to do.

Lincoln was gone. Thinking about that wasn't going to help me or anyone else. But there was something I could do. Work out who had killed him.

I had a plan.

First, search the office. Second, find the ghost Maq. Third, speak to the other guests to find out what they knew.

Who could have done this to Lincoln? The most obvious suspect was Maq's ghost. It had been running free somewhere in the house, and Lincoln and Rebecca had been far from certain that it was limited by the 'no harm' constraint. If I'd insisted on finding it last night could this have been avoided?

But regrets weren't going to bring Lincoln back to life. All I could do for him now was try to solve his murder. And I needed to keep an open mind.

I couldn't touch anything until I'd found some gloves. I could still look, though.

The white knight was on the floor between the desk and the door. He was about ten centimetres tall, dressed in full armour, without a horse, a serrated broadsword dangling from his right hand. From the waist down he looked as though he had been dipped in blood, splashes of which covered the rest of his body.

The queen was slightly taller, standing upright on the desk next to Lincoln's right arm. She wore a curved scimitar sheathed on her left hip. She was pitch black, so it was harder to tell, but she appeared also to be covered in blood.

I turned next to the body. I didn't want to think of it as Lincoln any more. I needed to depersonalise it.

The body was lying on its back, limbs extended, spine slightly arched. The fists were clenched, fingers like claws, digging into the palms of the hands. The head was thrown back, twisted sideways.

The shirt and jacket looked to have been torn open, caked with blood that had flowed from the long cut that ran from throat to navel. Blood had also spattered the desktop.

The axe was sunk into the surface of the desk between the queen and the body. With its dark black blade it was hard to see the extent of any stains, but blood had pooled around it. It seemed the most likely murder weapon. I walked to the other side of the desk.

There, next to the body's left arm, I found the most curious object of all.

At first I thought it was a grey bowl, rough and misshapen. Then I realised what it really was: the top half of a skull, hollowed out and inverted. A skull cup.

I looked inside and the contents made me gag.

As a marine biologist human physiology is not my speciality. But even I can recognise a heart.

17

THE GHOST

My meeting with Koji was delayed by a visit to the nearest bathroom to throw up what little remained of the previous night's champagne and canapés.

I spent several long minutes leaning on the sink, staring at my haggard reflection in the mirror. I was glad of the time on my own. Soon I would need to speak to people about this. They would be looking at me, judging me, seeing how I reacted. Expecting me to react like them. Which I knew wouldn't happen.

Why hadn't I cried for Lincoln?

Yes I was sad. And I realised, despite everything, that I would miss him.

I felt hollow inside but nothing wanted to come out.

I'd cried for Kun, hadn't I, all those years ago, when he'd disappeared in the mines? But animals were less complicated, easier to train and predict. Easier to read.

Easier to mourn.

I remembered the medical report I'd been shown on my discharge from the navy: 'Lieutenant Commander Manning shows an unusually high empathy for animals but an unusually low empathy for people'.

I didn't have a problem with that.

I'd been sacked for trying to save the life of a dolphin that had been worth a hundred of the brainless admiral who'd killed him.

Still, why couldn't I cry for Lincoln? True, he could be the most colossal dick sometimes, but I'd loved him once. What was wrong with me? What would people think of me?

I stared at myself in the mirror for another long minute, then gave up. I got some handwash from the dispenser and rubbed a little into the corner of each eye, wincing at the pain.

That looked better.

Eyes moist and red, I headed up to the kitchen.

Like most rooms in the Manor the kitchen was built on a grand scale. Vast black granite worktops contrasted with plain white cedar.

This had always been the social hub of the building, a cosier place to meet than the giant reception room two floors up. The real kitchen, where the canapés for the party would have been prepared, was several floors down.

There was a long dining table in one corner, looking out over the ocean to the west and the lake to the north. Koji was standing there, his back to me, staring out at the rain. He turned as I entered.

He looked as though he had aged ten years overnight. 'Ella, I can't believe he's gone.'

I shook my head. 'I don't know what to say. It seems unreal.'

Did he expect me to collapse into his arms, in tears? That was hardly the behaviour of an investigating officer.

Should I tell him about finding Lincoln's heart?

No. I needed to do this properly. Stick to my plan. Having a routine was what would get me through this. Interview people, gather information, and treat everyone in the house as a suspect.

Even Koji.

My usual seat at the dining table was halfway down, looking out towards the ocean. I sat, and gestured for Koji to do the same.

My entire training with the RCMP had consisted of two weeks in the basement of a concrete block in Victoria, filing papers. Then they'd sent me back to Bamfield with a uniform, a badge and a book of incident forms. None of which included murder.

So I was going to have to work this out as I went along.

I placed my phone on the table between us and set it to record.

'We need to keep this formal,' I said. 'The time is 8:08 on 5 October 2045. This is Special Constable Ella Manning, of the Royal Canadian Mounted Police, investigating the mur ... the death of Lincoln Shan. I am interviewing Mr Koji Malak, an employee of Mr Shan, who found his body this morning. First, can you explain your role here?'

Koji sat up straighter. 'Formally, my title is Head of Security, but effectively I run the place. I control the local staff – all of whom are drawn from the Akaht band – and I do, or supervise, any jobs that are required. Head of Security makes it sound as though I've got a staff of guards who work for me, but it's actually a pretty meaningless title. Lincoln hated that side of things, so it's really just me and a decent security system.'

He produced a handheld screen from below the table, and offered it to me. 'There are some things I need to show you from the security cameras.'

'We'll get to that later. First, can you tell me in your own words how you found Mr Shan's…' I hesitated. 'Mr Shan's body.'

He nodded. 'Of course. After we parted last night I spent a while in the control room going through the streams from the cameras. Trying to work out where Maquina had run to.'

'To be precise, by Maquina you mean the copy of him that Mr Shan had created – what he called Maquina's ghost – that he said was being run by AI.'

'Yes.'

'Did you find him?' I asked.

'I found where he was. I could see that he'd fled into the lowest level of the house, where the storage rooms and machinery are. I guessed he was trying to hide in there somewhere. Most of the doors in the house log when they are opened or closed, so I was able to pin him down to a storeroom on that level. I told Lincoln and suggested getting you, and then the three of us, together with Yahl, could have gone down and caught him. Lincoln said to leave it till morning. He said now we knew where he was we should seal off that room and we'd find him in the morning. I thought it was odd, but he was the boss, so I did what he told me, and went to bed.'

'How did he get into the storeroom without knowing the door codes?'

'You don't need a code for those rooms. People are going in and out all the time to get things, so it's more trouble than it's worth. But I can still lock them remotely.'

'OK,' I said. 'But how did you know it was the AI ghost down there, not some member of staff?'

'He was the only one it could have been. I'd sent all the other staff home by then, apart from Yahl, but he was in his room.'

'What time did you stop the search?' I asked.

'A bit after ten. I can't recall precisely now.'

'So this ghost was locked in till morning?'

'No.' Koji looked confused. 'Or I don't know for sure. I think Lincoln must have let him out after he dismissed me. I know that now.'

'How?'

'While I was waiting for you I looked at the camera streams from last night.' He picked up the screen, fiddled with it briefly, then passed it over to me. 'See the time stamp. This was 22:58 last night. It's the corridor outside Lincoln's office.'

At first it was empty, but after a few seconds two figures appeared from the direction of the elevator. The first was Maq. He had discarded his orange top and was dressed in black trousers and a white shirt. The second was Lincoln, a pace behind him. Maq's head was turned over his shoulder as he walked, as though he was saying something. Lincoln replied. They paused briefly outside the door to his office, then went inside.

'What's that bottle in Lincoln's hand?' I asked.

'I'm pretty certain it's whisky. Lincoln had asked me to leave a bottle of Glenmorangie Pride – one of his best – in the kitchen before I went to bed. I'd thought maybe he was going to take it and try and make up with Rebecca after the way he'd treated her. But it seems not, as he took it into the office with him.'

'Is there a camera in the office?' I asked.

'No. Lincoln insisted on privacy there. They're only in a couple of the corridors, and by the main doors, for security. We used to have drones that patrolled the house but Lincoln got annoyed with them constantly in his face. Now all we have are static cameras.'

'Can we hear what they were saying?'

'No. I've tried, but this camera is at the end of the corridor, by the external door, so mostly all you can hear is the wind and rain. You can hear some other noise later – I'll show you in a minute – but not what they were saying.'

'So it appears that after sending you to bed Lincoln ... Mr Shan apprehended Maq's AI ghost and took him to his office. How did that turn into Mr Shan being tied to the desk and killed?'

'I don't know,' said Koji. 'I woke around seven this morning. It was seven thirty by the time I left my room. I wasn't sure if Lincoln was awake yet so I tried messaging him.'

'But the phones aren't working.'

'We can't call out but the internal network is functioning. I got no response. His phone was showing as being in his office so I went up there to find him. When he didn't answer the door something seemed wrong so I let myself in using my override code.'

'Was the door definitely locked when you got there?'

'Yes. His office is one of the doors that locks automatically, even when he's inside. Given the number of regulators it has to deal with, Orcus's Compliance Department insisted on that. Of course, that's rather pointless when, as I now know, he was sharing his code with you.' He looked down at his screen. 'There's a log. Here we go. It was unlocked using Lincoln's code at 22:59 last night, and would have re-locked immediately. That's when we saw him with Maquina on the stream.'

'I didn't see him typing any code in.'

'His code was linked to his phone,' said Koji. 'Provided he was carrying it the doors would unlock as he approached. The phone was reading his biosigns and wouldn't work with anyone else.'

'You said you unlocked the door with an override code. I assume that means you didn't have Lincoln's code?'

'No. As I said, I didn't even know he'd shared it with you. It's bad practice.'

'When you were in the office, did you touch the mask?'

'No. But I was pretty sure who it was. The clothes looked like his, and it looked the right size. My first thought was to come and find you.'

So that brought us up to date. I thought for a moment.

'You found Lincoln dead some time between seven thirty and eight?' I asked.

'Yes. I went in at 07:47 according to the door logs.'

'OK,' I said. 'We don't know when Lincoln died. Did you consider ...?' I wasn't sure how to put this. Did I want this question on the record, for the homicide detectives to hear? 'Did you consider doing what Maq did in the mines twenty years ago?'

Koji nodded. 'Of course. It was the first thing I thought of. But then I realised that he had been dead for too long.'

'How did you know that?'

'That's what I meant about noise on the stream. Let me show you.' He picked up the screen again, made some adjustments, then handed it to me. 'This starts at 23:15. I've turned the volume up as high as it will go and tried to screen out some of the background noise.'

I was staring at an empty corridor, and at first could hear nothing other than the wind. Then a low wailing started, an inhuman scream that continued for a good half-minute.

Koji reached over and paused the stream. 'I believe that's Lincoln you can hear. He must have been screaming very loudly to be heard through the closed door and over the sound of the wind. It continues for a minute or so, then goes quiet. I couldn't watch any further ...' His voice cracked and he swallowed. 'I guess ... I guess that's when Lincoln died. There didn't seem to be any point in ...' He made an unwinding gesture with his hand.

'Couldn't one of you ... and then another?'

'It doesn't work like that, because you can't stack them up. We've tried in the past, and it just doesn't work.'

I was wondering how I was going to explain these cryptic references when I gave the recording to the detectives from Victoria. They'd never believe the truth. No one would who hadn't grown up in Black Lake.

I'd deal with that later.

'It seems pretty obvious Maq did this,' I said. 'Or rather, his ghost. Maybe whatever AI Lincoln had stuck in it bore the same grudges as the original, sitting in his cell in Vancouver.' A thought struck me. 'There's no chance the real Maq did this, controlling his ghost?'

Koji shook his head. 'No. The satellite dish is a mess. As I said, we've got no communication with anyone.'

'OK. So Lincoln sends you to bed, then goes down and lets Maq's ghost out of the storeroom. They go up to Lincoln's office and something happens that leads to the ghost Maq killing Lincoln. Will there be a log of the storeroom door, the same as you showed me for the office? So we can see when Lincoln got him out?'

'Of course.' Koji picked the screen up from the table. After a moment he frowned. 'That's odd.' He jabbed at it again, shaking his head.

'What?'

'According to the logs the storeroom door hasn't been opened since 22:30 last night. That was when the ghost went in there. I locked it remotely behind him, and it hasn't been opened since.'

'So how did we see Maq's ghost on the stream with Lincoln half an hour later?'

'I don't know,' said Koji. 'According to this, it's still in the storeroom.'

'Could it have climbed out of a window?'

'No. The storerooms are at the back of the house, buried in the side of the hill, so the only way in or out is through the door.'

I stood up. 'Let's go and check. Get Yahl to join us in case the ghost tries to run away again.'

'All right.' Koji picked up his phone. 'Yahl ... I need you to meet me in the basement ... Yeah, we're going to flush out the ghost ... Right now ... Where are you? ... Get the gun from my room and we'll see you there.'

'He's got a gun?' I asked. 'Is that wise? Lincoln told me he'd been kicked off the rigs for fighting.'

'I trust Yahl,' said Koji. 'He's family. He just had some issues to work through.'

I wasn't sure I wanted anyone running round the house with a gun, particularly when I wasn't armed, even if Koji vouched for them. But if the ghost tried to fight his way out, having Yahl there with a gun might help. Although I was far from certain that a gun would have any effect on a ghost. The journalists had asked Lincoln about ghosts hurting humans, but not the reverse.

But we needed to get on and do this. 'Come on,' I said.

We took the elevator down to Level Eight.

Yahl was waiting for us. I didn't know him well, but he was a man cut from the same cloth as his grandfather, although not as stocky as Koji. Short and wiry, with a wispy moustache that seemed a feeble imitation of Koji's, he looked nervous, bouncing from one foot to the other with his right hand shoved into his jacket pocket.

'Be careful with that,' I said.

'Of course.'

'Come on,' said Koji. 'I'll show you the way.'

He led us down a concrete-walled corridor until we came to a halt outside a metal door with the number '12' stencilled on it.

We didn't need to open it to know that the ghost was inside. It must have heard our footsteps, because it started banging on the door and shouting: 'Help! Let me out!'

'Stand back,' I said to Yahl. 'Don't shoot unless I tell you to.'

Yahl nodded, drew the gun from his pocket, and stood with his back to the wall opposite the door.

'Open it,' I said to Koji.

He fiddled with his phone, and I heard the lock buzz. Before I had a chance to reach for the handle, it swung open.

Maq's ghost stood inside, looking at the three of us. Unlike on the stream Koji had shown me earlier, it was still wearing the orange prison hoodie.

Should I read it its rights? Could I even arrest a ghost?

It spoke first. 'Morning, Ella. I'm freezing. Any chance of a coffee?'

Which confirmed what I'd begun to suspect already. This wasn't a ghost standing in front of me. It was a man.

Maquina.

18

MAQUINA

'Lincoln was lying, wasn't he?' I said. 'He told us you were a ghost, but you're clearly not. You talked to me last night in a way that no AI could have, then you held me and pushed me away. A ghost couldn't have done that. And why would a ghost bother to escape if it was just a copy of something locked up in a cell in Vancouver? Now you want coffee.' I paused. 'You're Maquina, aren't you?'

He smiled, and nodded. 'I'd have thought that's obvious. Otherwise I'd have disappeared last night, along with all the ghosts.' He glanced at the gun in Yahl's hand. 'So you've got me. What happens now? You ship me back to Vancouver and get a gold star or something?'

'Things have got a bit more serious than that,' I said. 'You killed Lincoln last night.'

He flinched, and his eyes narrowed. 'I didn't. I've been locked in this freezing room all night. Is this some joke?'

'There's no point in denying it,' I said. 'We have a stream of

161

you going into Lincoln's office with him last night, and fifteen minutes later he was dead.'

He stared at me. 'Seriously? Linc's dead? How did it happen?'

'Someone ... you ... sliced him up with an axe. As you well know.'

He shook his head. 'I won't say he didn't deserve it but it wasn't me who killed him.'

'We need to do this properly,' I said. 'Let's go back up.'

We took him up to the kitchen. It seemed the most convenient interview room, and one that didn't have any obvious connection to the murder, so the odds of destroying evidence were low.

I took my usual seat and made him sit opposite me, where Koji had been before. Yahl was standing to one side, gun in hand. Koji had moved to the other end of the table, watching us. I placed my phone on the table, and set it to record.

'So how about that coffee?' Maq said, looking from me to Koji.

I ignored his request and held out my hand to Koji. 'Let me have the screen.' I passed it across the table. 'For the record, I am showing Maquina a stream of him entering Mr Shan's office at 22:59 last night, with Mr Shan.'

He looked at the screen, then slid it back across the table to me. 'That didn't happen. That's not me, and I know nothing about this. Is Linc really dead?'

'So where do you say that you were at 22:59 last night?'

'I was in the storeroom where you found me. I tried to get out of the house, but the weather was awful. So I thought I'd hide over-night, and make a run for it this morning in the light. I planned to take the old footpath through the woods to Bamfield, and then steal a car, or a boat, or something. Instead, I found I was locked in.'

'So how do you explain what we just saw on the screen?' I asked.

'Isn't it obvious? Parts of what Lincoln said at the party last night were true. Enough people in Vancouver owe Lincoln favours that he was able to get me taken to Iona Island for a day. He told them the plan was to do a scan so he could have me at the party as a ghost last night. But only the subject can be in the scanning room, so my guards had to wait outside. Instead of me walking out, my copy did. He said he'd run the copy for a day or two in jail, and then turn it off remotely. All that would have been left would be a white disc, which a guard had been paid to quietly sweep up with the trash. People might have been suspicious about the timing, but no one could have proved anything.'

'That explains how you got out of jail, not why you were seen going into Lincoln's office with him last night,' I said.

'I told you, it wasn't me. What you saw on the screen must have been a ghost.'

'Why?'

'How would I know? Lincoln did some crazy things. Like breaking me out of jail.'

'Why did he do that?' I asked.

'He said he was trying to save me spending twenty years in jail.' Maq smiled. 'I should have known he was lying, although I only learned the real reason last night.'

'Which was?'

'He wanted to eat my heart.'

I stared at him. I hadn't told anyone about Lincoln's heart being removed. Only his killer would have known that. But if Maq had killed Linc, why would he volunteer this information?

'Why would Lincoln have possibly wanted to eat your heart?' I asked.

Maq glanced left and right, at Koji and Yahl. 'Not with them here. There are things they're not allowed to know.'

'We are Hamatsa,' said Koji. 'We know the secrets of the Akaht.'

Maq smiled. 'Not all of them. There are things that only I know, from my father. I need to speak with Ella alone.' He paused, then looked across at me. 'Not to teach you your job, but they shouldn't be here anyway. If Linc is dead they're just as much suspects as I am.'

There was some truth in that, although I'd wanted them as protection more than anything.

But that had been when I'd thought Maq was a ghost being run by unstable AI. I doubted whether the real Maq could hurt me. And why would he try? There was nowhere he could run.

'All right,' I said. 'Koji, Yahl, leave us, but make sure at least one of you stays outside.'

Koji nodded and stood up slowly. He seemed reluctant. Yahl followed him to the door. As they reached it Koji turned back to me. 'Be careful. Shout if you need us.'

I smiled, looking Maq up and down. 'I think I can take him.'

As the door closed I turned back to Maq. 'So, tell me, why the fuck would Lincoln want to eat your heart?'

He sat back in his chair. 'There are a few things I need to tell you about the Akaht. Have you heard of the Hamatsa?'

I was surprised he hadn't asked me to pause my recording. He caught my glance at my phone, and laughed. 'You'll be erasing that by the end of this, or your bosses will think you're mad.'

I doubted he was right, but I was happy to go along with it.

'I've not heard of the Hamatsa,' I said. 'That's what Koji just mentioned, isn't it?'

'Yes. It's a secret society of my people. The most secret. It's open only to the high-ranking Akaht children. Unusually, among the First Nations bands, we allow both boys and girls to become Hamatsa. At around the age of seventeen a child will disappear into the woods, kidnapped by a spirit that lures them away. They spend four days with the spirit, being given special powers. Early on the morning of the fourth day the village will gather in the longhouse. The ghost dancer, one of the Hamatsa, will appear at the door and announce the return of the novice.'

'The ghost dancer? Is that where Lincoln got the name?'

'Yes. Yet another example of him raping our heritage to make a profit. The real ghost dancer is part of the Hamatsa ceremony. He appears, and then the other Hamatsa drop down from the rafters of the long house, where they've been waiting, shouting "*hap, hap, hap*". It means "eat, eat, eat". The novice will enter through a hole in the roof, gnashing their teeth and moaning, running around and biting people. Then the kinqalalala will appear, the novice's closest childhood companion, dancing to try to lure them home. But the novice will ignore the kinqalalala, because what they desire is flesh. They climb a cannibal pole outside the long house, a special form of totem pole, starting with the man at the top, then the raven, then man again, then the Tsonoqua, giant hairy women who live in the woods. The novice squeezes through a hole in the bottom of the pole, symbolising their rebirth, then runs around the long house, biting people's arms, chewing on the severed arm of a corpse offered to him by the kinqalalala. And then they collapse, spent, and are no longer a novice. They are Hamatsa.'

Maq paused. Looking at me. Trying to see what effect this story had had on me.

'So what does this have to do with what happened to Lincoln? Are you saying his death was part of some Akaht ritual? Was he Hamatsa?'

'He was,' said Maq. 'You remember the day in the mines, when we found the lifeboat?'

'Of course,' I said. 'The day Kun disappeared. And ... other things ...'

He nodded. 'The power I used that day can only be used by the Hamatsa. The shipwreck ...' he began, then hesitated. 'No, you don't need to know that. Do you remember what I told you about the power? It erases everything that happened in the last six hours.'

'That can't be right,' I said. 'I remember going to the cave, finding the boat, crawling through the gap with Kun. All that happened in the missing six hours.'

'I tried to explain it to you at the time. The reason that you remember is because you died. Everything that happened in your timeline up to the moment of death was preserved in your mind. Because you had stepped outside the living world, when time was unwound and you re-entered this world your memories stayed with you. Anyone else affected by it – if Linc had been with us, for example – would have remembered nothing of the missing six hours. I remembered it because I was the one who invoked the power. But just you and me. No one else would.'

'How many of you have this power?' I asked.

'Not many. You need to be descended from the founder of the Akaht and to have been inducted into the Hamatsa.'

'Inducted by eating human flesh,' I said. 'Did you do that? I thought cannibalism on the island was just a myth.'

'It doesn't happen any more. And even in the past, not for

food. That's always been a myth. Captain Cook and the other early explorers told stories of being offered arms and legs to eat by the Nootka. But that was just Western propaganda. Demonise the natives and then you can kill or brutalise them as you see fit, and your god will approve. We never ate one another for food. Ritual cannibalism is different, though. A few bites on a dried enemy's corpse to gain power, or chunks bitten out of the arms and legs of the living during a ceremony. Those who got bitten regarded it as an honour.'

He could see the look on my face.

'Don't seem so disgusted with us, Ella. You belong to a religion whose central ceremony is the eating and drinking of your god. Your god told his disciples that if you eat his flesh and drink his blood you will have eternal life. Your Bible says that many of his followers grumbled and deserted their messiah after he told them to eat his flesh and drink his blood. They turned back and no longer followed him. He was left with just his twelve disciples. They were your Hamatsa, the inner cabal who were prepared to eat their messiah's flesh when no others would. Yet now you think it's normal. For many it's forbidden, on pain of excommunication, to deny the power of the priesthood to turn bread and wine into the body and blood of your Christ.' His voice had risen, and he leaned across the table towards me. 'Don't mock us as savages, Ella, when millions of your people do this every Sunday. At least we stopped doing it.'

I shrugged. I hadn't been to church in years. I wasn't going to start arguing about which of our belief systems was more cannibalistic.

Maq sat back and took a deep breath. 'Look, the point is

that Linc used his power years ago, when he was travelling in Europe. He saved someone's life and was well rewarded for it. That's where he got the seed money to start his business.'

'I heard he got some bank to back him. Someone who shared his vision.'

'Heard from who? Linc? It was just part of the story he made up. Like Kun being with him. The truth is that he traded his heritage for the start-up funds he needed.'

'Why does any of this matter?' I asked.

'A key thing about the power is you can only use it once in your life. As Lincoln got older he became obsessed with the idea of dying. You know how he idolised Steve Jobs. Even with all his billions, Jobs still died young – aged fifty-six. Linc feared that he was going to die young too. Almost all his staff, certainly the close ones like Koji and Yahl, are Hamatsa. Vekla is as well. You probably don't even notice the wolf tattoo on their wrists, but that's the sign of those who have the power.' Maq held up his own wrist, showing me a wolf's head inside a circle – the same tattoo I'd seen on Koji.

'Vekla?' I asked. 'Who's that?'

'Yahl's sister. She's been working as Lincoln's chef for the last year or so. Koji likes to keep things in the family as much as possible.'

'It seems like a pretty dumb system, to have all these people around who can save Lincoln, but they don't get to know about his death until more than six hours have passed. Why didn't he have some sort of alert so they'd know if he died in his sleep?'

Maq shrugged. 'You'd need to ask Koji. Maybe he did and it got screwed up when the communications failed last night. I don't know.'

'So what's this got to do with Lincoln wanting to eat your heart?'

'Linc decided it wasn't enough to have Hamatsa near him at all times. He didn't just want people around him who could unwind time if he died. Instead, he wanted his own power back. He discovered a legend that there was a way of restoring the power so that he could use it as many times as he liked.' Maq paused, and looked across at me.

I obliged him. 'How?'

Maq smiled. 'By consuming the beating heart of the chief of the Akaht. That's why he broke me out of jail. He wanted to eat my heart.'

Did I believe any of this? I knew Lincoln could be ruthless. You had to be to do what he'd achieved. But would he really have killed his former friend, his chief, even for such a prize?

But what mattered wasn't whether Lincoln would have done it. What mattered was whether Maq believed it. If he did, that was motive enough for murder.

'So you killed him instead,' I said. 'He told you this and you overpowered him in his office and hit him with the axe.'

'I've said that wasn't me on the stream.' Maq sat back, and folded his arms. 'It must be one of Lincoln's ghosts. I was locked up all night where you found me this morning. You've got this all wrong, El. You need to look somewhere else for your killer.'

19

THE LAWYER

'Here's your coffee,' said Koji.

'Thanks.' I checked my phone: 9:03.

Yahl had taken Maq away and locked him in a guest room. I was troubled by the need to rely on Koji and Yahl for help. Until we caught whoever had killed Lincoln, everyone was a suspect. But I couldn't do it all myself. One option was to lock everyone up until the homicide detectives got to us from Victoria. But who knew when we could get in touch with them, and I'd probably have a riot on my hands if I tried that.

If I had to choose who to trust between Maq and Yahl it wasn't difficult. A lot of what Maq had said sounded true, but it didn't get away from the fact that someone who looked just like him had been seen entering the room where Lincoln had been found dead. The idea that that was his ghost seemed very convenient.

Still, I needed to investigate this properly. The obvious answer isn't always the correct one. If Maq was the killer, why hadn't he been covered in blood? It seemed a fair assumption that whoever had killed Lincoln had done so with the axe. Sharp as it was, that would surely have been messy, particularly removing a heart. Yet there was no trace of blood on Maq.

In fact, oddly, there hadn't been a lot of blood around his office. I didn't know much about forensics, but surely if you hit someone in the chest with an axe and dug out their heart there would be blood everywhere. I needed to go back and have another look.

First, though, there were points to check with Koji.

'Take a seat,' I said to him.

He nodded, and sat opposite me.

'Apart from me, who else stayed here last night?'

He looked down, and started counting off on his fingers. 'There was you, Lincoln obviously. And Mr Kleber and Ms Murray. They each had rooms on the same floor as you, further down the corridor. Yahl and I slept in the staff quarters on the lower level. Then there was Yahl's sister, Vekla, the chef ...' He stopped. 'Actually no, she was the last to leave, just after ten o'clock. Normally she'd have stayed over too, but because the party finished early I let her go home. So she wasn't here by the time Lincoln died.'

'She went home in the storm?' I asked. 'Was that safe?'

Koji looked away. 'I probably should have stopped her. But I had lots of other things going on, and Yahl was happy for her to go, so I left it up to them. Yahl said he'd told her about the ghost being loose in the house, and that had spooked her. She didn't want to stay the night.'

'And what about the serving staff at the party? Did they go home too?'

'They were all ghosts, like the guests. Lincoln thought it was a great idea to hire some fancy catering firm in Vancouver and then have them attend remotely as ghosts. It cost a fortune and we had to pay extra to get them trained as ghosts. I could have just had some of the local kids from the village do it, and no one would have noticed the difference. But you know Lincoln; if there were two ways of doing something, and one of them involved technology, he would always take the more complicated option.'

That was true. I still remembered the day he'd proposed to me. Using a robot.

'We have to come up with some way of restoring communication with Victoria,' I said.

'The satellite dish is completely wrecked, and beyond my skills to patch up. And if you tried to drive to Bamfield today you'd get blown off the cliffs. Maybe someone could walk through the woods, but you know what the trails are like round here in good weather. It's a five- or six-hour hike, and everything will be mud today. If you got stuck out there in the dark you'd be in real trouble. And that's ignoring the fact that thunderstorms were forecast for this morning.'

'What about tomorrow?'

'It was meant to ease, although without a signal I can't say for certain any more. Hopefully by tomorrow morning it'll be possible to get to Bamfield.'

So I was going to have to manage on my own for at least the next twenty-four hours.

'All right.' I paused, mentally checking off the points I needed to cover. 'Who knows that Lincoln is dead?'

He shrugged. 'Pretty much everyone by now, I guess. While you were talking to Maquina I found Mr Kleber, the lawyer, trying to get into Lincoln's office. So I had to tell him. Then Ms Murray turned up, so Mr Kleber told her. She was pretty shaken up by it, as you can imagine. They asked what had happened with the ghost Maquina, so I explained. I hope that was OK.'

'I suppose we'd have to tell them at some point, but ask me first next time. We need to keep a lid on information. I'm going to have to talk to both of them.'

'Kleber was desperate to see you. He wasn't happy that I wouldn't let him into Lincoln's office.' Koji hesitated, then said: 'When I told him you were in charge he called you a jumped-up meter maid.'

'All right. I'll deal with him first.' I stopped for a moment. 'Before I do that, though, I need to ask: where were you and Yahl when Lincoln died?'

'Me? I was in bed by eleven. I told you, Lincoln called off the search around ten, and I went down to the staff bedrooms. I didn't hear a thing. I'd already sent Yahl down by then.'

'Can ... can we see that from the door logs, or camera streams?' I asked.

He thought for a moment. 'No. The staff level is just like the guest rooms, there's no record of the door logs. Well, actually, that's not quite right. The locks are the same, but there's a camera at the end of the guest level corridor. There isn't one on the staff level, though. Lincoln trusted us,' he added pointedly.

'So there's no evidence that ... that Yahl, for instance, didn't leave his room in the night and come back up to Lincoln's office?'

'We know he couldn't have been there when Lincoln was killed; I showed you the stream from outside the office. Only Lincoln and Maquina were seen going in.'

'Someone might have been in the office already,' I said. 'Or gone in later. I'm going to need to look at the full stream for the night to check. First, though, I want to speak to everyone who stayed overnight. I'll deal with the lawyer first. Can you find him and bring him up here. Don't discuss anything with him, though. You can blame me if he asks any questions.'

'Before you speak to Mr Kleber I ought to show you something,' Koji said. 'I don't like betraying confidences, but this could be important.'

'What is it?'

Koji reached for the screen on the table, swiped across it for a few seconds, then handed it to me. 'This is from last night. I told you I spoke to Lincoln before I went to bed, and he asked me to leave a bottle of whisky in the kitchen. He also told me to erase this stream. I didn't get around to looking at it last night, but I did just now while you were talking to Maquina. It could be important.'

The image was of a dimly lit corridor that I didn't immediately recognise. Lincoln and Kleber were facing each other, frozen in mid-conversation. The time stamp said 22:08, so before Lincoln was seen entering his office with Maquina.

'This is the camera on the guest room corridor. I've turned up the audio,' said Koji. 'This time you can hear what's being said since it's further away from external walls than the other one.'

I tapped the screen.

As the figures jerked into life Lincoln appeared to be trying to turn away. Kleber called after him. 'Linc, we've got to talk. I told you earlier we needed to deal with this after the party, and it can't wait. If this goes wrong we're all in the shit.'

Lincoln turned back with a smile. 'Well, you are, Paul. You're the one who has an ethics board that could disbar him. Me, I'm an entrepreneur, so I'm expected to play fast and loose.'

'There's a difference between not following the rules and being complicit in the deaths of two of your workers,' Kleber said, leaning in closer to Lincoln. 'I've covered up a lot of shit for you over the years. This is different. I've got to lodge my affidavit tomorrow, and we need to agree what I'm going to say. I'm telling you now, if I go down you go down.'

Lincoln stared at the lawyer for a long moment. 'Don't threaten me, Paul. There's a lot worse things that could happen to you than spending ten years in a white-collar prison. If this all goes pear-shaped I know the people who'd decide where you end up. And think about your family. Would you like your wife to be playing a foursome with her friends at the Victoria Country Club, or begging her estranged father to take her back when she's penniless? How's William doing at Yale? Not so easy to start his legal career when you can't afford the fees. Hell, he won't even be able to pay his fraternity dues.'

Kleber tensed, and for a moment I thought he was going to punch Lincoln. This was a side to Lincoln I'd never seen before. I'd known he was ruthless and controlling, but this?

Then he took a step back, holding up his hands, and smiled, as though a switch had been flicked. 'Tell you what, Paul, we've both said things we might regret tonight, so let's not fall out over this. Send me the draft affidavit and I'll take a look before I go to bed. Then we'll talk about it in the morning. I'll tell you now, though, my view is that the less we say to the court the better.'

The lawyer didn't look particularly appeased. 'We can't just ignore what they're saying. This is a court, not a press conference. You can't respond to the bits you want to and spin the rest, or switch off the questioner if you don't like what they're asking. We'll have to admit something, the only question is how much.'

He pulled his phone from his pocket, held it to his mouth, and muttered something inaudible.

'I've sent it over to you,' he said. 'We need to talk first thing, and you need to understand this is serious, not something you can just wish away.'

Lincoln nodded. 'Let's both sleep on it. Things often look better in the morning. Goodnight, Paul.'

He turned to leave, then looked up at the ceiling, and laughed. 'Just realised where we are. Remind me to get Koji to scrub this.'

Kleber said nothing. He remained in the corridor, staring after Lincoln as he disappeared from view.

I looked up at Koji. 'Can we access Lincoln's phone, or the server in his office? I need to see what it was that Kleber sent to Lincoln.'

'I can access the servers remotely,' said Koji. He hesitated. 'If you order me to, as part of the investigation.'

'I do,' I said. I wasn't sure I had that power, but surely it was better that I read whatever he'd sent than risk leaving a murderer loose in the house. From what I'd seen already Kleber was pretty high up the list of suspects. 'Just get me in and don't touch anything else. Bear in mind that forensics will be crawling over everything we've done once they get here. Tell Kleber I'll see him now. I'm not going to show him the stream, so don't say anything to him about it. I'd rather see what he has to say first.'

'I'll get him now,' said Koji.

Then a thought struck me. 'Before you go, where are the camera streams stored? I need to make sure they're preserved for the investigation. And later I'll need to look at the full version of the one outside the office.'

'I'll have to check,' said Koji. 'I think they're backed up to Iona Island every few days, but that won't be happening now. I'll look into it once I've got Kleber.'

As he stood to leave the sky lit up behind him. Seconds later the windows shook with the rumble of thunder. The forecast thunderstorm had arrived.

We watched in silence as it rolled in towards us, the sky blackening even further, punctuated by brilliant flashes of light. After a minute or so Koji pulled out his phone.

'What's wrong?' I asked.

'I want to get Yahl to check the broken glass. This might be the final straw. I'm worried that—'

His words were drowned out by another crash of thunder – the loudest yet – which coincided with a flash of lightning directly overhead.

Moments later the lights went off.

'Shit,' said Koji, stabbing at his phone. 'Nothing. The power's gone. I'll need to go and reset it in the basement.'

'You do that,' I said. 'I'll go and find Kleber myself.'

It took me longer than I'd expected to get the lawyer.

He answered the door in a bathrobe, hair wet, complaining that his shower had stopped working. I kicked my heels in the corridor while Koji reset the Manor's electrical system and Kleber was able to rinse off. Once dressed he followed me to the kitchen, where he insisted on making himself a coffee before answering any questions.

Then he settled himself at the table and looked across at me. 'Yes, Dr Manning.'

'Mr Kleber, I am conducting this interview as part of my investigation into the death of your client, Mr Shan. The time is 10:05. The interview is being recorded.'

He sat back, and took a long drink. 'Dr Manning, I don't know what you're playing at, since this is my client who's been killed. Given our lack of communication with the outside world I need to take charge of my client's affairs. If word of his death leaks out in the wrong way, billions will be wiped off the value of Orcus.'

'I rather doubt whether your former client is going to care,' I said.

'Don't get smart with me. I demand access to my client's ... my *former* client's office. I'm entitled to it as his executor, so if you won't give me access I'll get a court order.'

'Mr Kleber,' I said, 'I don't think you appreciate that I am the law here. You are being formally interviewed as part of my investigation into Mr Shan's murder, and I would recommend that you cooperate. And unless you brought a carrier pigeon with you, good luck with getting a court order today.'

'You are the law?' Kleber spat the words out. 'You sound like Wyatt Earp. Except you aren't even allowed to carry a gun. How many murder investigations have you conducted, Sheriff ... sorry, *Special* Constable? I'm willing to bet that the answer begins with Z and ends with a big fat O. By the time you've finished you'll have compromised any chance of a successful prosecution. I'm sure I could run a better investigation myself.'

'I may not have much experience,' I said, 'but I was a naval officer for ten years.'

'Of course,' said Kleber, sitting back. 'That makes all the difference. It was dolphins, wasn't it, that you used to command? Do they commit many murders?'

'Well, actually ...' I began. I'd been about to tell him about a study I'd participated in, showing that dolphins kill baby porpoises for fun. But I realised that was hardly going to improve my homicide credentials in his eyes. Or anyone else's.

'Look, Mr Kleber,' I said flatly, 'you may not like the fact that I'm in charge here, but I am. So suck it up. I'll be more than happy to hand over to Victoria Homicide once they get here. In the meantime I'm doing what I can to gather evidence, and the more difficult you are, the more suspicious it makes me. I'm quite happy to lock you in your bedroom until the real detectives get here – however long that takes.'

He sat back, swallowing hard. Then he leaned forward again,

and smiled weakly. Trying, not very successfully, to change from threat to charm.

'Look, Dr Manning, Constable Manning, I appreciate that this is not a good day for any of us, and we all have our jobs to do. Mine is to act as my client would have wanted, and to deal with his estate. To do that I need to get access to his office.'

'What is it that you are so desperate to see?' I asked. 'There can't be anything that urgent, particularly as we can't communicate with the outside world.'

'There were certain court documents that needed to be lodged today. They were important to the future of Orcus. Obviously I'm not going to be able to lodge them now, but Lincoln was going to work on them last night. I need to see what he did with them, and be ready to lodge them when I can. I'm sorry to sound heartless, Dr ... Constable, but things have to keep on moving. It's my experience that judges are very unsympathetic to missing court deadlines, however good the reason. Today I've lost a client and a friend, but I'll mourn later.'

'There's no chance you are getting into the office,' I said. 'It's a crime scene. And trust me, you don't want to go in there. If we can get remote access to Mr Shan's server I may be prepared to let you identify the document you want, under supervision. I'll let you know.'

He nodded. I could see that he wanted to press the point, but as a lawyer he was no doubt used to cutting deals, and realised that was the best he was going to get out of me. He was presumably trying to work out how he could erase the message he'd sent to Lincoln without me knowing.

'In the meantime,' I said, 'I need to ask you a few questions about last night.'

'All right.'

'At the party Lincoln told me you were cross with him for having Maq there. Did you speak to him about it?'

'Yes. I told him it was foolish, and that he should have asked me before copying Maquina. Of course, at that stage I didn't realise it was the real Maquina, and that Lincoln had broken him out of jail – which was utter madness. I thought having the ghost Maquina was bad enough, and I warned Lincoln that it was likely to be used as grounds for a mistrial application.'

'How could that be, when the real Maq was still safely in his cell? I don't see how bringing a copy of him to the party could affect his guilt or innocence.'

'You don't understand, Constable; the law isn't about guilt or innocence, it's mostly about due process. Defendants have rights, often more than their victims. I wouldn't be allowed to pull the real Maquina out of his cell and parade him at a cocktail party for my friends, and forcing him to attend remotely isn't much better. I'm not saying a judge would necessarily have ordered a retrial, but I'd certainly have given it a go if I'd been defending.' He shrugged. 'Anyway, it's all irrelevant now, as we know it wasn't a ghost, but the real Maquina. God knows what will happen to the trial now, but that's hardly our biggest worry.'

'So how did Lincoln respond when you told him off?'

'I didn't tell him off – he was my client. I gave him my advice, in forceful terms, but he didn't seem to care. He said he wouldn't keep Maquina there for long, and anyway would it be such a bad thing ...' Kleber hesitated, as though weighing up how much to tell me. 'He said that he bore Maquina no ill will and didn't particularly mind if the trial collapsed.'

'Did you agree with him?' I asked.

'Did I bear Maquina ill will?' Kleber said. 'I've never met the man. I was more concerned about the effect his trial might have on Orcus. You need to appreciate that Orcus is my biggest client; in reality my only client. Lincoln was not a man for backing down gracefully, whatever the merits of a case, so he kept me busy in court. But I was worried about the oil rig trial. There was the risk of things being said about Orcus that could have harmed its image and caused significant financial damage.' He paused, and rubbed his nose. 'In truth, after I spoke to Linc I wondered if having Maquina – or rather his ghost – at the party had all been part of some clever plan to derail the trial entirely. Lincoln always came at things from a different angle.'

'After the party did you speak to Lincoln again?'

'I was in his office with you and the others afterwards, although I don't think I said much.' He hesitated. 'There is something about that which may be relevant to Lincoln's death.'

'What?' I asked.

'After leaving the office we – that's Koji, Rebecca Murray and I – were walking towards our bedrooms when we saw you saying goodnight to Lincoln outside your room. We saw him kissing you goodnight, and Ms Murray wasn't at all happy.' He waved a hand as I started to protest. 'I'm sure it was entirely innocent, but that's not how it looked to Ms Murray. Once you'd gone into your room she went up to Lincoln and looked as though she was going to slap him across the face. He grabbed her arm and there was a bit of a tussle. They had quite a row.'

Ouch.

I hadn't seen Rebecca yet. This was going to be awkward. Lincoln had started the kiss, but I shouldn't have let him get close enough to even try. I'd been a bit tipsy by then, and he'd always had the ability to throw me off balance. That was part of the reason I hadn't seen him for more than a year. I'd been fairly sure that him forcing me to get involved in the ghost project had been an attempt to get back together again.

'What did she say?' I asked.

'She called you a whore and told Lincoln you were bad news for him. She said that she'd picked him up last time you'd broken his heart and she wasn't going to do it again. He told her to fuck off. I'd gone to my room by then, but I was watching them through the half-open door. I was concerned when I saw her try to strike him and wanted to make sure things didn't get worse. Were you and Lincoln really getting back together?'

'No, although Lincoln seemed to want to.' I paused. 'Shit. Did Rebecca hear what he said to me?'

Kleber shrugged. 'I'm not sure. What was that?'

'He ... oh, God ... he said that he loved me and that he wanted me back. He even promised to step down as CEO of Orcus and travel the world with me. Did she hear that?'

'I didn't, and she was no closer than me,' said Kleber. 'Did he really say he'd give up Orcus for you? He hadn't said anything to me about that.'

'I think it was spur of the moment. You know what Linc was like. He'd promise the world to get what he wanted. Although he seemed pretty passionate about it.' Despite myself I felt a small twinge of regret. What would have happened if I'd said yes? Would I have let him into my room? Would he still be alive?

I shook my head. I was wasting time and energy thinking about the past.

'What happened after their fight?' I asked.

'Lincoln stormed off in one direction, Ms Murray went to her room.'

'And did you see either of them again that night?'

I could see him thinking before he answered, trying to work out whether to tell me the truth. Then he must have remembered Lincoln's final words about getting Koji to erase the camera stream. He couldn't be sure that had happened, so opted for the truth. Or part of it at least.

'Once Ms Murray's door had closed I went after Lincoln. There was an important business issue we needed to discuss about the oil rig trial. We had a brief discussion then said goodnight. We agreed that we would meet early to discuss things in the morning, but obviously ... obviously that didn't happen.'

I decided to wait until I'd read the affidavit before pressing him about that conversation.

'Thank you, Mr Kleber. Those are all the questions I have at the moment.'

He nodded. He didn't seem to want to go.

'Goodbye, Mr Kleber. We'll speak later.'

Reluctantly he got up and left.

I'd felt my phone buzz while I was questioning Kleber. It was a message from Koji.

I've got access. Come to your study.

20

THE AFFIDAVIT

What had become known as my study was a small room on Level Three of the Manor just down the corridor from Lincoln's bedroom. I'd chosen it because, unlike most of the house, it had felt cosy, and it looked north over the lake towards Bamfield. I was surprised it hadn't been repurposed in the year I'd been gone. Then again, the Manor had many rooms and only one permanent occupant, so Lincoln probably hadn't felt any need for it. Or perhaps he'd just been that confident of getting me back.

Koji was sitting at the desk next to the window, a screen propped up in front of him. He jumped up as I walked in.

'Ella,' he said, 'I've got access to Lincoln's messages. I've found the one from Mr Kleber. It was sent at 22:12 last night, so fits with what we saw. I've opened the document that's attached, but haven't read anything.'

'Thanks,' I said. 'Is there any sign that Lincoln read it, or made any changes? Kleber said that he'd planned to review it.'

'The message hadn't even been opened. Lincoln wouldn't have had time. There can't have been long between him leaving Mr Kleber and going into his office with Maquina.'

'True,' I said. 'I'll probably want to speak to him again after I've read this.' I sighed. 'I also need to speak to Rebecca. I understand she saw Lincoln kiss me goodnight, and wasn't best pleased. Kleber says she tried to hit him and they had a blazing row.'

Koji shuffled uncomfortably, as though he hoped he could get out of the door without having to answer me. 'It wasn't as bad as all that,' he said eventually. 'She was cross. They had a bit of a fight, and a few words. They were both drunk. I've had moments like that with my wife, and we've always made up afterwards. I'm sure they'd have been fine in the morning if ... well, you know.'

'Kleber made it sound worse than that. Maybe he was trying to deflect suspicion away from himself, to suggest that Rebecca had a motive to murder Lincoln.'

Koji shrugged and left.

I sat at the desk and turned to the screen.

The affidavit started with various bits of legalese, saying that it was the first affidavit of 'Mr Paul Ronald Archibald Kleber III' in the matter of 'The Crown v (1) James Sitwell (2) Benjamin Smythe and (3) Noah Diaz (alias Maquina)'. There were then several paragraphs describing Kleber's role as attorney for Orcus, as well as personal attorney for Lincoln. Finally I got to the interesting stuff.

8. I understand that it has been alleged by the defendants Sitwell and Smythe that Mr Lincoln Shan and Orcus (i) were aware in advance of the intended attack on the Orcus II Oil Rig in Cook Inlet in May last year and (ii) were in fact complicit in and funded the attack. I will deal with each of those allegations in turn.

9. As to the first allegation, it is correct that one week before the attack on the oil rig a voice message was left out of hours at the Alaskan office of Orcus Oil, in Anchorage, stating, 'We're going to destroy your rig. Stop fucking the penguins.' A copy of the message has been retained and can be made available to the court if required. Since Orcus Oil owns five oil rigs and leases thirteen others deployed around the world, this was not interpreted as a threat towards the Orcus II rig specifically. Even if it had been, the threat was so vague that it would have been impossible to take any steps to protect against it. Orcus Oil does not own any rigs in areas populated by penguins. To put this in context, in the year preceding the attack on Orcus II, Orcus Oil received 583 different threats [relating to alleged environmental damage].

There was a marginal note saying: 'Linc, this one is laughable. Easy to dismiss, but I've gone into some detail to balance it out. Sooner not include the bit about the environment, but your call. PK.'

I read on.

10. As to the second allegation, I understand that two incidents are alleged.

11. First, that on 23 April last year, an associate at my firm, Henry Jameson, met the defendant Sitwell in an underground car park in Larch Street, Toronto, pretending to be an anonymous supporter of GreenWar. It is said that he offered Sitwell and Smythe $20,000 if they would organise an attack on the Orcus II in an inflatable draped with the GreenWar flag. Second, that on 5 May last year I, pretending to be Mr Jameson's legal adviser, met with the defendant Smythe and told him that we 'wanted to see some blood' and 'didn't give a fuck who got hurt'. It is further alleged that when Smythe told me that they had access to explosives I responded, 'Great, let's fuck the bastards over.'

12. As to the first alleged incident, unfortunately Mr Jameson no longer works for my firm. Three months ago he was dismissed following an internal inquiry into allegations of inappropriate behaviour towards junior female members of staff. I understand that Mr Jameson moved to London, England, and is currently working as a paralegal. Unfortunately we have no power to compel him to give evidence. The alleged offer of money to the defendant Sitwell seems improbable, since neither Mr Jameson nor my firm would have had any reason to make such an offer. It seems most unlikely that Mr Jameson would have been offering

his own money. However, if such an offer was made I can only conclude that it was done at a time when Mr Jameson was (as he subsequently suggested in the firm's internal inquiry) suffering from depression and mental illness. No such offer was authorised by me or the firm.

Again, there was a marginal note, saying: 'Linc, this is potentially dangerous. If anyone can get to Henry he could crucify us if he testifies. The complainants on the harassment allegations won't stand up to scrutiny, and it might come out how much we paid them. But I don't see any other way to play it. PK.'

The affidavit continued:

13. As to the second alleged incident, I can categorically confirm that no such meeting took place, and I did not say what was alleged. Moreover, it is hard to understand why Mr Shan, Orcus or I would have thought it advantageous to Orcus to be complicit in an attack on its own oil rig. I understand that it is alleged that our plan was for the attack to go wrong and result in an oil spill in Cook Inlet, thereby causing severe damage to GreenWar's reputation and its funders withdrawing financial support. That is, I would suggest, a proposition that only needs to be stated for its absurdity to be apparent. If – which was not the case – Orcus saw GreenWar as a threat to its operations, there are many other legitimate means by which it could have cut off GreenWar's funding. Were it not so serious, the suggestion that Orcus would have been complicit in the

deaths of two of its own employees so as to damage GreenWar is so far-fetched as to be laughable.

14. Finally in relation to this allegation I should mention that, as anyone who knows me will attest, the words alleged to have been used by me at the meeting do not sound like me. I am perhaps unusual in that I do not use profanities. I can say with certainty that none of my staff has ever heard me swear.

A marginal note read: 'Linc, this is the one that worries me most. If they persist in this it comes down to who the jury believes – me or Smythe. Given the particularity of what is alleged I'm concerned that Smythe may have recorded it. If he did, we're fucked. Only other option is to admit words but deny meaning. Say didn't know purpose? Let's discuss. PK.'

The affidavit went on for another three pages of what was mostly legal argument rather than evidence. Although I spent a while wading through it, I didn't learn anything new. It mostly seemed to demonstrate the tortuous way in which Kleber's mind worked. He seemed to be trying to argue that even if the court concluded that he had tried to pay GreenWar activists to attack Orcus's oil rig, legally it didn't matter.

I could now understand what had led to the confrontation between Lincoln and Kleber the night before. Kleber had been covering up for Lincoln, who by way of thanks was about to throw him under the bus.

Lincoln had threatened Kleber's wife and son with ruin.

Had those threats driven the lawyer to murder?

21

GLITCHES

I needed to speak to Kleber again. Whether he'd murdered Lincoln was unclear, but I certainly had more than enough to rattle him.

I headed back down to the kitchen. The only person there was Koji, looking damp and dishevelled, his hair blown about.

'You've been outside?' I asked.

'I wanted to check on the roof, to see if the glass is holding. It seems to be, although I'm not planning to walk below it in a hurry. Some of the trees have blown right off the roof.'

'Have you seen any of the others?'

'Maquina's still locked up. Mr Kleber went back to his room, I think. I haven't seen Ms Murray again, but I can find her if you like.'

'Leave it,' I said. 'I'll speak to her later. I need to check some stuff with you.' I was a bit surprised that Koji hadn't asked me anything about the affidavit. He had a distinct lack of curiosity. Or maybe he was just fulfilling what he saw as his role.

'Can you get me the full stream from yesterday evening for

the camera outside Lincoln's office. I need to see who else went in and out before and after Lincoln's death.'

'Of course,' said Koji. He picked up his screen and flicked across it. Then frowned, and stabbed at it harder. 'Give me a minute,' he said. He shook his head. He seemed to be getting more and more frustrated. Eventually he set the screen down. 'There's a problem with the streams. I can't access any of them now. Things have been crazy since the lightning storm and the power outage. I've had to reset all the systems, but they still aren't behaving properly.'

'Shit. The stuff you showed me earlier is gone?'

'Yes, everything. It may all come back again as things settle down. I'll look into it in case I can recover something.'

'No,' I said. 'Leave it. Victoria will be able to bring in some IT specialists who might be able to find it again. If you and I start poking around in there we risk wiping it for good. Are the door logs still working? Can you tell when the door to Lincoln's office was last accessed?'

'Let's see.' Koji picked up his screen again. 'They seem to be OK.' He paused. '22:59 last night, it was unlocked with Lincoln's code. Nothing after that until I unlocked the door at 07:47 this morning.'

So if it was Maq we'd seen on the stream entering Lincoln's office, how did he get out?

'I need to go back and search Lincoln's office properly,' I said. 'Before I do, did he still keep his safe in here, or had he moved it somewhere more sensible?'

'It's still here. I know you thought it was stupid, but he always said no one would look for valuables behind the breakfast cereal.' Koji walked over to one of the cupboards and opened it.

He lifted out several boxes of cereal and some cookies, putting them on the counter.

'Thanks. I'll take it from here. I'll let you know if I need you again.'

He nodded and left.

I used Lincoln's code to open the safe.

I was mostly interested to see if I could find anything else about the oil rig. Lincoln wasn't the sort of person to keep incriminating documents around, but if there were any they'd be in the safe. I also wanted to see if he'd left his will there. He had no children, so it would be useful to know who might benefit financially from his death. I could have just asked Kleber, but I didn't really trust him.

There were only two items in the safe.

The one I recognised immediately. A battered black cardboard box contained a Glock 19X and a box of ammunition. I'd made Lincoln buy it, pointing out that he lived in one of the most remote and expensive houses in British Columbia, with only Koji for protection, who wasn't a real bodyguard at all. Lincoln had said that with the Akaht around he didn't need a bodyguard. But after I'd pestered him enough, he had bought the gun to humour me. Instead of keeping it by his bed, as I'd intended, he'd put it in the safe and forgotten about it. I knew Koji occasionally took it out for a test fire, but I'd never seen Lincoln handle it.

I left the gun where it was. It was no use to Lincoln now.

The other item took me a moment longer to recognise. It was white, about ten centimetres high. At first I thought it was a plastic lunch box, but then I realised what it was. Why was it in Lincoln's safe? I reached in and took it over to the table.

It looked like a miniature version of an early Apple computer, a block of white plastic and a black screen. Except this one had arms and legs. And a suitcase in one hand, with the Apple logo on the lid. I turned it over and folded out the stubby legs that had been tucked underneath. I couldn't help but smile.

Linc and I had been in Montreal a few years earlier when I'd spotted the AppleBot in the window of a junk store. I hadn't said anything, but had gone back and bought it the next day after my morning run, smuggling it back into our hotel room under my hoodie. I'd kept it hidden until his birthday a few months later.

It had been something of a joke against myself. Lincoln had once told me that I lacked 'emotional resonance'. It was probably something Steve Jobs had said we all ought to have. After telling me that I 'analysed instead of reacting' he'd called me 'his little robot'. I hadn't been amused at the time, but my present was partly intended to show that I could take a joke. Even if I couldn't.

I don't think Lincoln looked that deeply. He was thrilled with the gift, saying he hadn't seen one in years – only a few thousand had been made as a one-off to celebrate the fiftieth anniversary of the first Apple computer.

Then he'd starting taking it apart. He'd explained that it was meant to be mechanised, so that it could walk and talk, but the internal circuitry must have broken over time. To me it meant the present was a failure, that I couldn't even give him something that worked. But to Linc that made it even better, because it was something that he could pull apart and improve. Rebuild as he wanted it.

I should have seen the signs then.

Six months later we'd been sitting at Lincoln's favourite table in the Rooftop Club, Vancouver, drinking cocktails as the sun set, when a waitress walked over with a tray. On top was a domed silver lid. I was about to protest that we hadn't ordered anything when she removed the lid, and the AppleBot sat up. It then stood and stepped on to the table.

The robot had walked over to me, clumsily dropped to one knee, lifted its little suitcase up and said, 'Ella ... will you marry me?' The lid of the suitcase popped open, a diamond engagement ring nestled inside.

Of course I'd said 'yes'.

Again, though, I should have seen the signs. Lincoln preferred to program a robot to propose for him than do it himself.

Still, it had seemed cute at the time.

I put the AppleBot down and stared at it. Sure, Lincoln could be a dick, but we'd had some good times together. At one point I'd seen myself spending the rest of my life with him. Before I'd realised what was missing.

I noticed an envelope tucked under one of the AppleBot's arms. I pulled it loose. Printed across the front was: 'TO BE OPENED IN THE EVENT OF MY DEATH'. That sounded promising.

Inside was a single sheet of paper. It was dated 8 December 2044, so a couple of months after we'd split up, and read: 'In the event of my death please return the AppleBot to Dr Ella Manning, Marine Science Centre, Bamfield. Lincoln Shan.'

I looked out of the window trying not to feel anything. It wasn't worth much, but Lincoln's gesture meant a lot to me. I put the note back in the envelope, tucked it under the AppleBot's arm, and replaced it in the safe. I pressed the button to lock the safe, then restocked the cupboard with cereal.

This wasn't getting me any closer to finding Lincoln's killer. It was time to ask Kleber about the affidavit.

22

ACCUSATIONS

I tracked down the lawyer in his bedroom. As I approached the door it opened, and Yahl stepped out. He turned away from me, towards the stairwell.

I knocked and the door was flung open almost immediately.

'We can't—' Kleber began. 'Oh, it's you. What do you want?'

'What was Yahl doing here?'

'I don't see why that's any of your business,' he said. 'If you must know, though, in all the chaos last night I lost a favourite pen of mine at the party, and Yahl has been helping me look for it.'

'Did you find it?'

'No, it's a complete mess up there, and Yahl wouldn't let me near the front half of the room as he said the glass roof might go at any minute. It's all rather unpleasant, with piles of food everywhere, and lots of broken glasses and plates. And when you walk there are little white discs from the ghosts crunching underfoot. I'm annoyed about the pen, though. It was presented to me by the Chief Justice.'

I waved away his concerns. 'There's more important things to discuss. Can you let me in?'

He didn't move. 'Why?'

'I've read your affidavit.'

His eyes narrowed. Then he stepped to one side. 'All right.'

I took a seat in an armchair next to a low table, and set my phone to record. He slumped heavily into the chair opposite.

'Mr Kleber,' I said, 'the time is 12:53. This is our second interview—'

'Yes, I get it.' He waved a hand at me dismissively. 'You're the cop, and you're asking the questions, so let's just get on with it. Then you can give me a fine for parking in the wrong place, or not returning my library book on time, or whatever it is you're in charge of this month.'

I ignored his jibes.

'Mr Kleber, you told me earlier that you had a conversation with Mr Shan before you went to bed. You were the last person to speak to him.'

'Not true,' he said. 'We know Mr Diaz ... Maquina, was in the room with him before he died. I don't know why you're asking me things since it's blindingly obvious who killed Lincoln.'

Had I told him that earlier? I didn't think so. Koji knew, obviously. Had he told Kleber, despite my instruction to keep things to himself? Or had Koji told Yahl, and he'd told Kleber?

'Let's take it in stages,' I said. 'If you answer my questions this will go much faster. I'm sure as an experienced trial lawyer you are used to the need to focus on the questions and give simple yes or no answers. So let's try this again. You had an argument with Mr Shan last night, didn't you?'

He leaned across the table towards me. He'd clearly been expecting this, and was ready for it. 'I assume, Constable, that you've seen the stream of our conversation, so you know the answer to that. We had a discussion about an affidavit I was due to lodge today in some criminal proceedings involving Mr Diaz. I was concerned that Mr Shan was expecting me to be less than frank in what I said to the court. Obviously that was not going to happen, because I understand my ethical duties, as well as my oath to the court. However, Mr Shan was my client and I was willing to let him know in advance what I was proposing to say. It wasn't going to change my evidence, though, since I was intending to tell the truth. Nothing more and nothing less.' He sat back, and breathed out sharply, having given what was clearly a speech he'd prepared since our last interview. He fixed me with a stare.

'You seemed to be concerned about going to prison,' I said.

'I recognised that that would be the consequence of committing perjury, which was a further reason why I would only have told the truth in the affidavit, and in court if it had come to it. I made it clear to Mr Shan that I was not prepared to lie in order to protect him, or Orcus.'

'That wasn't my reading of the conversation,' I said. 'You seemed to be concerned that if the truth was known about your activities in relation to Orcus's oil rig, you could end up going to prison. You seemed to think that you and Mr Shan might be implicated in the deaths of his two workers on that rig.'

'In which case you have misinterpreted what was said. You

do realise, Constable, that that stream will have no evidential value in any investigation or hearing? It was taken secretly on private property without my prior knowledge or consent. Moreover, once I was made aware of it I was assured that it would be erased. It is inadmissible.'

I wasn't going to tell him that I had a bigger problem, since the stream might no longer exist. If all that we had was Koji's and my recollection of what we'd seen, and Kleber arguing about the interpretation of it, the question of admissibility would hardly matter.

'This isn't something I'm going to waste time debating with you. But even if you're right I'm sure your board of ethics would be interested in it.'

'Precisely the same rules apply,' he said dismissively. 'It's a matter of due process. You can't adduce evidence that's been obtained illegally. It doesn't matter what the forum is.'

'Let's park that for the moment and talk about your affidavit,' I said. 'I've retrieved your message to Mr Shan from his server, and it makes interesting reading. I can now understand why you were so concerned to get it back. It appears that you were worried that if your former associate, Mr Jameson, gave evidence, he would contradict what you were saying on oath.'

'That's not true at all,' Kleber said. 'First, let me make clear again that this affidavit has been improperly obtained by you without any warrant. A real detective would know that, and would have sought a court order, but no judge would have issued one. I can tell you that it's a confidential lawyer-client communication, as such is privileged, and you will not be allowed to use it in your investigation, in court, or' – he smiled at me – 'in any ethics hearing. Second, it does not in any event bear the meaning that you ascribe to it. As I make clear in my affidavit, Mr Jameson had been dismissed for sexually harassing some of our junior employees. His career was in ruins, and I was concerned that if he was called to give evidence he would lie.'

'Again,' I said, 'let's leave aside your legal points on admissibility. In the affidavit you refer to a conversation that you had with Mr Smythe, saying that you fear he may have recorded it, and you tell Mr Shan that "If he did, we're fucked." That's surprisingly earthy language for someone who claims, on oath, never to swear, and it's pretty unambiguous. You were asking Mr Shan whether you should nevertheless risk it and lie, weren't you?'

'After forty years in the law I know that nothing is unambiguous, Constable. I'm not going to sit here and debate the meaning of inadmissible documents with you. This has nothing to do with Lincoln's murder, which is what you ought to be investigating. I'd suggest you leave and get on with your job.'

'I'll decide when I leave,' I said. 'I'm quite happy to arrest you if I have to, and you can argue the legality of that later.'

'Arrest me? For what? All I'm trying to do is stop you wasting time screwing up the investigation into Lincoln's death. He was a friend as well as a client, and I would like to see his killer brought to justice.'

'It seems to me that this has everything to do with Mr Shan's murder,' I said. 'You've been very keen to blame Maquina for that. But you had just as much reason to kill Mr Shan, maybe more. When you spoke to him last night he threatened you with prison, and your wife and son with financial ruin. You must have known that he was ruthless enough to carry out his threat. He was perfectly happy to leave you to carry the can. If he did that you'd be disbarred and lose everything. But if you got rid of Mr Shan you were free to blame him for what had happened. So after your argument you followed him back to his office and killed him.'

Kleber was staring at me, open-mouthed. For the first time he seemed lost for words, albeit only briefly. 'Me, murder Lincoln? You're crazy. All you've got is some inadmissible evidence that doesn't amount to a hill of beans anyway. Hell, you haven't even got a single bean.' He smiled at his own joke. 'And if you seriously thought I'd killed Lincoln why the fuck are you interviewing me here alone? Do you have any idea about police procedure?'

'Is that a threat?' I asked.

'I'm just pointing out that you don't seem to have a clue what you're doing. Coming in here and making false allegations against me doesn't bring you any closer to finding Lincoln's killer.'

I stood up. 'You can hide behind legal niceties as much as you like, but you haven't actually answered any of my points properly. You might want to think some more about what answers you're going to give to the homicide detectives when they get here.'

I picked up my phone and left.

23

THE BODY

A stillness had settled over Lincoln's office, his presence gone.

The body dominated the room but I knew it wasn't going to tell me much. Although I'd cut open plenty of animals in my time I'd never even attended a human autopsy.

I needed to conduct a proper search of the room, though. I'd found some latex gloves in the kitchen and plastic bags for evidence.

I started by walking round taking photographs from every angle.

I picked up the raven mask from where I'd dropped it earlier and replaced it over Lincoln's face. To put things back to how they were.

And to say goodbye.

I wanted to disturb as little as possible, though, so I left the chess pieces where they were. I examined the chessboard more closely. It was set up for the start of a game except that the black queen and a white knight were missing.

And one other piece: a black rook.

I scanned the floor around the desk but couldn't see it. And it wasn't under the desk. Where had it gone?

I gently pulled the bloodstained remnants of the jacket away from the body and found the rook nestling inside its folds. Odd.

I took a photo of it but left it where it was.

Where else to search? All that was left was the desk itself.

I started in the top left drawer. It contained what looked like an old circuit board, green with parts soldered on. Nothing useful.

The one below was more interesting as it held a collection of books. The first was *Hamatsa: The Enigma of Cannibalism on the Pacific Northwest Coast*. There was a picture of a bearded academic on the back cover, with the blurb saying that the Hamatsa ceremony was the most secret of all, with spirituality on the island being rooted in ritual cannibalism.

The second book was *The Haunting of Vancouver Island*. Why had Lincoln had it? He was far too rational to believe in ghost stories. Had he been doing research into the history of the Akaht?

There were two other books on cannibalism, but neither looked of great interest. If any of this was important to the investigation I, or more likely someone else, was going to have a lot of reading to do.

At the bottom of the drawer I found a shiny strip of metal about twice the length of my hand. I took it out and turned it over. One end had been sharpened to a point, erasing some of the letters, but the words '... *ride of Whitby*' were still legible. I realised that I'd handled this once before in the mines with Maq, when it had been too crusted with dirt to read. It had come from the lifeboat, so how had it ended up with Lincoln?

I put the books and nameplate back and turned to the drawers on the other side of the desk. The bottom one contained two glasses and a bottle of whisky labelled 'Glenmorangie Pride 1974', the same one we'd seen on the camera stream. The glasses were dirty. Had Lincoln shared a drink with Maq before he died? Again, that made no sense if he'd been in the room with Maq's ghost. Unless he hadn't realised it was a ghost.

In the top drawer were various documents, neatly arranged in folders. For a man who ran a cutting-edge technology company, Lincoln seemed surprisingly fond of paper. As I lifted each out, I photographed them. Most appeared to be financial reports, and none looked particularly interesting at first glance.

There wasn't much else to examine. I walked round the desk, looking again at the body from every angle. On the left wrist, just above where the rope had rubbed it raw, was my birthday present from the previous year: the black-and-white Seiko Chariot watch. Although, oddly, the time was set to four thirty. I was certain it had said two o'clock the night before, because I'd commented on the watch being broken. I wondered if it had started working again, but the second hand was still.

Which was strange, but I couldn't immediately see the significance. Why would Lincoln's killer have bothered to change the time on a broken watch?

There was one thing left to do. If the Maq I'd seen on the camera stream was a ghost, and the door logs showed he'd never left the office, then I ought to find a white disc somewhere on the floor. I got down on my hands and knees, trying to avoid the bloodier bits of the carpet, working my way from the desk towards the wall where the mask had been.

My search wasn't helped by the heavy pile of the carpet. It

would have been easy for a disc to slip unnoticed between the threads.

I was nearing the wall when I sensed a stir in the air behind me as though a cold breeze had passed over my neck.

A soft voice whispered in my ear: 'Are you looking for me?'

1804

24

HOPE

5 DECEMBER 1804, PACHENA BAY CAVE

Captain Ross was invigorated – strong and alert for the first time in weeks.

Unlike the bosun, who seemed to have lost any interest in living. He was lying on his side next to the fire, his wheezing breath the only sign that he still lived.

Twice Ross had managed to coax him to eat. Twice he had gagged on Cooper's flesh, thrown it back up, and wept uncontrollably. He seemed to regret what they had done.

Ross had no time for such weakness.

As his strength returned he had prepared to escape. He knew that there were tunnels leading from the rear of the cave. In the early days of their imprisonment he and the bosun had attempted to explore them, but swiftly turned back, fearful of getting lost in the dark, and still hoping to find some other way out.

This time there would be no turning back. He would escape or die in the attempt.

Light was essential. He had made rudimentary torches out of driftwood wrapped in the remains of Cooper's clothing. They were hard to light, and burned weakly, but they were all he had.

He had no means of carrying water, but hoped to find other streams in the tunnels.

As for food, over the past few days he had spent hours cutting flesh from Cooper's body with his increasingly blunt knife, then cooking it. He had enough for several days.

He would wait one more night. He told himself that was because he wanted to be well rested.

In truth, though, he wanted to put off discovering that the tunnels were a dead end.

That there was no way out.

That he had damned his eternal soul for nothing.

2045

25

PURSUIT

At the sound behind me I screamed and jumped up, spinning round and backing away. Not just because I'd thought that I was alone in the room. But because I recognised the voice. It was one I'd never forget. One I'd never thought to hear again.

Lincoln!

My brain told me it couldn't be. That he was lying on the desk, his heart ripped out.

But there he was standing in front of me.

'Linc?' I gasped.

He smiled. Then took a step back, reaching for the axe embedded in the desktop. 'You might want to run,' he said softly.

I hesitated, poised to leap at him. But he was armed and I was not. My scrambled brain opted for flight.

I dashed for the door, conscious of him wrenching the axe loose. As I struggled to input the code I could hear him behind me. I ducked, and the axe slammed into the wood above my head.

213

The door beeped and I pulled it open before he could get the axe free for a second blow. I slipped through, racing down the corridor towards the elevator. I could hear footsteps behind me. I scanned the elevator display as I approached: Level Four – that was no use!

I carried on past, crashing into the door to the stairwell and diving through. I stumbled towards the stairs.

I'd sprinted up two flights before I realised that he was no longer following. I stopped, gasping for breath. Listening. Heart racing.

There was no sound below. Then I heard the whine of a motor in the adjoining elevator shaft.

Was he trying to get above me, to catch me as I emerged from the stairwell?

I was next to the door to Level Five, leading to the guest suites. The elevator motor was still going so it seemed safe enough to risk a glimpse into the corridor.

It was empty.

The elevator display showed it was at Level Three, then Two, still ascending. Perhaps he wasn't trying to catch me at all. Had this all been a trick to get me to unlock the office and let him escape?

I let the door shut and took the stairs up two at a time.

I was panting when I reached Level One and took a moment to calm myself before cautiously opening the door that led to the roof garden.

The wind seized it from my hand, slamming it against the wall. I was blinded by a squall of rain.

As my vision cleared all I could see was chaos. Koji's trees were ruined, most on their sides, pots and soil scattered across the flat roof. In the far corner, beyond the glass roof, were the twisted remains of the satellite dish.

Then I spotted Lincoln. He was picking his way between the debris, almost at the point where the roof met the broken glass. He was no longer carrying the axe. That made me feel a little safer.

'Linc!' I shouted, but he didn't react. I doubted he could hear me over the roar of the wind.

A metal walkway ran along the side of the glass roof, leading to the satellite dish. Lincoln seemed to be heading for that.

I followed, having to lean into the wind to make any progress.

By the time I reached the start of the walkway he was halfway along. He glanced over his shoulder once, but didn't react to my pursuit. It was a dead end, so I wasn't sure what he was hoping to achieve.

I struggled on, clinging to the metal railing to pull myself forward against the wind. I was starting to freeze, my thin clothes no protection against a North Pacific storm.

Lincoln had reached the satellite dish now, and turned to face me. He raised a hand, as though waving goodbye.

Then he vanished.

I thought I saw a white disc swept past in the wind, although I may just have imagined what I expected to see. By now my brain had caught up with me. I knew that Lincoln was dead. I'd known that from the start. So I had to be pursuing a ghost.

It was no surprise that Lincoln had created a copy of himself. And someone else had fired it up to scare me. Or for some other purpose? Since we had no communication with the outside world it had to be someone in the house controlling the ghost. Who?

In truth I'd never been in any danger. I realised now that the ghost couldn't actually have struck me with the axe. The threat had felt real at the time, though.

But why?

I carried on along the walkway to where the ghost had vanished. The satellite dish was a mass of twisted metal and cables, half attached to a metal bracket, half fallen on to the glass roof, shaking in the wind. I could see why Koji wasn't going to be able to fix it.

I looked at the walkway where the ghost had stood before vanishing. I didn't really expect to see a white disc. This spot was slightly sheltered by a low wall, but it was still windy.

There was something else, though. Something heavier than a disc. It was black and gold, a long thin tube, and it took me a moment to recognise it: a fountain pen. I pulled a plastic bag from my pocket and picked it up.

I needed to speak to the lawyer again.

I went to my room for a change of clothes and messaged Koji to bring Kleber to the kitchen.

When I met them there the lawyer was grumpier than ever. 'We've been through all this twice already, Constable. What's your flunky doing dragging me up here again?'

'Sit,' I said. 'Or I will arrest you and lock you in your room. I'm tired of this.'

He glanced across at Koji, then sat slowly. 'What's he doing here?'

I ignored the question. Instead I sat opposite him and passed across the plastic bag containing the pen. 'Do you recognise that?'

He looked at it, then up at me in surprise. 'Yes. It's a Mont Blanc pen. It's mine. Where did you find it?'

'In the roof garden, next to the broken satellite dish,' I said. 'There are two possibilities. Either you dropped it last night, when you were up there messing around with the satellite dish, or you lost it in Lincoln's office last night, and it was being carried by a ghost that ran away from there.'

He stared at me. 'You're crazy! There's no chance I was up on the roof last night, and I've not been in Lincoln's office since we were all there yesterday. I told you, I lost the pen at the party when the roof broke.'

'It seems much more likely that you lost it just before you sliced Lincoln's chest open,' I said.

'Sliced his chest open!' the lawyer exclaimed. 'Gods, is that how Lincoln died?' He swallowed hard and put a hand to his mouth. 'How did they do it?'

'With the axe that Lincoln had on the wall in his study.'

Kleber shook his head. 'The Akaht war axe? Hell, what a way to die. Why would anyone do that?'

I didn't answer him.

'You can't seriously believe I did this,' he said. 'It's crazy. Besides, if that's how Lincoln died I can prove it wasn't me.'

'How?' I asked.

He glanced across at Koji. 'I'm not telling you in front of him. He shouldn't be here anyway.'

'Tough,' I said. 'If you want to tell me why you can't have been the one to kill Lincoln then do it now.'

He looked again at Koji, then back at me. 'All right. I'm only telling you this so you'll stop this stupid nonsense and get on with locking up the real killer, Maquina. I can promise you there's no chance of me lifting that axe, let alone using it on someone.' He rested his elbows on the table, holding out his hands towards me. He half-closed them, curled into fists, his fingers trembling. He grimaced. 'Look, I keep this a secret, because it's never good to show weakness to anyone. But I suffer from chronic rheumatoid arthritis. I have for more than twenty years, and I can't even close my fingers properly to write. Or type more than a couple of words. I'm known in court as the man who never takes any notes. I'm renowned for it, and everyone thinks it's because I have such a command of the case that I don't need to. That's not the real reason, which is that I don't want to be seen taking half a minute to scrawl one word. You can check with my doctor easily enough. Hell, you can come down to my room and I'll show you the medicine I have to take every morning just to be able to hold my toothbrush.'

Fuck!

'Hang on,' I said. 'If you can't write why do you have a pen which you seem to care so much about?'

'I told you it was a gift from Chief Justice Reynolds years ago, when I used to clerk for him. I keep it for sentimental reasons, and for show. As a trial lawyer you need to present yourself in a certain way. Why do you think I wear a hundred-thousand-dollar Rolex when my phone tells me the time? It's all part of the image.'

Maybe he was lying, but it sounded real. If it was a lie it wasn't one that would hold up for long.

I heard a buzzing in Kleber's pocket. He pulled out his phone and glanced at it, seemingly distracted by something.

'What's up?' I asked.

He shook his head. 'It's Yahl calling. What does he want?'

'Leave it,' I said.

But he'd already answered. 'Yes ... no ...' He glanced up at me. 'No ... All right. Do it then.'

'What's that about?' I asked.

'Nothing important.' He shoved the phone back in his pocket.

'I'm not just taking your word for all this,' I said. 'Let's go down to your room, and see if those drugs you were talking about actually exist.'

I knew Kleber was a bully and I didn't trust him at all. Given his job I shouldn't have been surprised that he had answers to all my points. He was no doubt used to picking holes in what looked like a compelling case.

He hesitated. Had he not expected me to call his bluff? This wasn't over yet.

Then he got to his feet. 'Fine,' he said. He looked at Koji. 'Bring him if you want. As far as I'm concerned the more people who see you making a fool of yourself the better. Then we can get on and find who really killed Lincoln.'

Koji shook his head. 'I'm staying out of this. The weather isn't letting up, so I've got to go and do something about the glass roof. We're going to need to try to rig up a tarpaulin or something.'

I left him to it and led Kleber out of the kitchen.

As I opened the door I stumbled, the walls seeming to fade,

and I thought I heard a soft voice echoing down the corridor. It sounded like someone whispering a word: '*Kuwitap.*'

And the wolf ate time.

1804

26

THE GUIDE

This was the first night that the captain saw the wolf.

As on previous nights he heard a howling as he slept, echoing through the tunnels and his dreams.

This time he woke to something different.

He could hear the bosun's wheezing breath nearby.

And something else. Something walking on the shingle by the water, then a snuffling sound near Cooper's body.

The fire was almost out, only a few embers left. Ross grabbed one of his torches and shoved the cloth-covered end into the coals. It took a few moments to catch.

The wolf appeared out of the darkness.

It had been standing over Cooper's body, but moved towards Ross as the torch flared into life. It seemed untroubled by the flames.

The wolf was pure black. It advanced to an arm's length from Ross, then stopped, staring at him with burning orange eyes that flickered in the light of the torch.

Ross felt around him for the knife he had fashioned from the boat's nameplate, then realised he had left it by Cooper's body.

But he did not feel that he was in danger. The wolf merely stared at him for a long moment, then turned away, padding softly towards the rear of the cave.

Ross knew that he was meant to follow.

He stood stiffly and gathered his bundle of torches. His food was already in the pocket of his coat.

Ross needed to hurry. The wolf was almost out of the circle of light now. It paused, looking back at him, as though checking that he understood.

He glanced briefly at the sleeping bosun, then shook his head. The bosun was weak and would hold them back. Better to leave him.

Ross took a last look around the cave that had been his prison for longer now than he could recall. He knew this was his chance to escape.

His last chance to live.

2045

27

THE GIRL FROM BARLANARK

'Here's your coffee,' said Koji.

'Thanks.' I checked my phone: 9:03.

I paused, looking around. Everything seemed normal, but I felt disorientated. I'd had something I wanted to say to Koji, but it seemed to have slipped my mind.

He gave me a sidelong glance. 'Are you feeling all right?'

I put a hand to my forehead. It felt as though I was getting a headache. I rubbed my face.

'I'm fine, thanks. I think I must have drunk too much last night. I don't recall having much, but maybe your people were a bit too efficient at refilling the champagne glasses.' I gestured to the chair across the table. 'Have a seat.'

I sipped my coffee while I composed my thoughts.

'Have you seen any of the other guests this morning?' I asked. 'Has anyone told Rebecca or Kleber about Lincoln's death?'

'They both know,' he said. 'I found Kleber trying to get into

Lincoln's office. And then Ms Murray came along as well, looking for him. So I had to tell them both. I also told them we've
got the real Maquina in the house. I hope that was OK.'

'All right, I need to speak to them,' I said. 'Can you go and
find Rebecca? Tell her I want to ask her some questions.'

Koji made to stand, then stopped. 'I don't want to tell tales,
but there's something you ought to know about Ms Murray
before you speak to her.'

'What?' I asked.

'You know she and Lincoln had been seeing each other, and
she was up here quite often. She always had her own room in the
house. You'll recall that Lincoln was quite old-fashioned in that
way; he liked his privacy. After we all left his office last night
I walked to the guest level with her and Mr Kleber. She was
pretty cross with Lincoln for not telling her about Maquina,
and something about her father. Mr Kleber told her to be quiet,
as he clearly didn't think she should be bad-mouthing Lincoln
in front of me. Then ...' He hesitated. 'Then, as we turned the
corner into the corridor with her room, just down from yours,
we saw you saying goodnight to him.'

Oh shit.

'She saw ... she saw him kiss you.' He shook his head. 'I don't
know what was going on, but as you can imagine she wasn't
happy. After you went in she walked up to him and made to
slap him on the face. I don't know whether she actually would
have, but he caught her wrist, and then she started swearing at
him, saying he'd hurt her. It was quite a fight but I guess you
didn't hear it.'

With the rain beating against the house I wasn't surprised.

And it was probably better that I hadn't stepped out to join them.

'So what happened?' I asked.

'She ...' He looked away. 'She called you a ... a slut and a whore, and other things. Something I think was Scottish that I didn't understand. Then she called him a bastard for chasing after you all night, and said she knew he'd never really loved her. I didn't hear much more because Lincoln took her arm and led her away, but they were still arguing. I said goodnight to Mr Kleber, and went back the other way to check the streams to see where Maquina had gone. That was my job, not trying to get in the middle of an argument between Lincoln and Ms Murray. I didn't see her again until this morning. I'm sorry to have to tell you this, but you can see why it might be important.'

'Thanks,' I said. 'There was nothing going on between us, although Lincoln would have liked there to have been.' I thought back to what had happened outside my door. 'Oh God, I hope she didn't hear what he said to me.'

'What was that?'

I hesitated. 'He said ... he told me he still loved me, that he wanted me back. He even said he'd leave Orcus for me. He wanted us to travel the world together. If Rebecca heard that, on top of everything else, who knows how she'd have reacted?' This was going to make for an awkward interview with her.

'I didn't hear anything like that,' said Koji. 'Mostly he was defending himself – she was pretty wound up.'

'All right,' I said. 'I need to speak to her. Go and get her please.'

*

'Ms Murray, Rebecca,' I said. 'I am interviewing you in my capacity as a constable in the RCMP. I will be recording the interview. Do you understand?'

She nodded. I had expected some hostility after Koji's account of events the night before. But she seemed cowed, subdued by what had happened. Her hazel eyes had lost their sparkle. They looked puffy and bloodshot, and she was sniffing every few seconds.

I'd had to ask Koji to leave while I spoke to her. He'd seemed reluctant, as though disappointed I didn't trust him, but he needed to appreciate that until we worked out who had killed Lincoln everyone in the house was a suspect.

'I realise that there may be personal issues between us, because of Lincoln,' I said. 'However, we need, for his sake, to conduct this interview in a professional manner. So that we have the best chance of finding out what happened to him.'

I paused, and she nodded. So far she hadn't said anything since sitting down. Perhaps she was waiting to see where I was going with this, to decide how to react. Or she was in too much shock to be capable of reacting.

'All right,' I said. 'The interview commences at 09:33. I'd like to begin by asking you something about the ghost dancers, for the record. Then we'll move on to anything relevant that you might have seen last night.'

'I didn't see anything,' she said softly. 'I can't help you with what happened to Linc.'

'We'll come back to that.'

The obvious solution to Lincoln's murder was that the Maq seen entering Lincoln's office with him at 22:59 was the same

Maq who was found in a storeroom the next morning. The real one. But if – as Koji's door logs indicated – the real Maq was in the storeroom all night, then the person seen entering Lincoln's office must have been a ghost.

'Once you've scanned someone to create a ghost is there any reason why you can't create multiple copies of that person?' I asked. 'Could there be a ghost Maq in jail in Vancouver, and another ghost here being run remotely?'

'In principle, yes, but it raises all sorts of ethical issues.'

'Let's assume whoever was doing this wasn't too troubled by ethics,' I said. 'So, in theory at least, the real Maq could have been sitting in a storeroom downstairs while a ghost Maq hit Lincoln with an axe?'

'No,' said Rebecca. 'That impossible. You're forgetting about the "no harm" constraint. You saw Lincoln's demonstration with the champagne bottle last night. That was real, it wasn't just a set-up with the journalist, so there's no chance anyone controlling a ghost could use it to hit someone, let alone kill them. And that stuff Lincoln came out with last night about an AI ghost without constraints was complete crap. He made that up because he didn't want us to know that he had the real Maquina here.'

'I understand that, but surely there's got to be a way around the constraint? I've never heard of a piece of programming that couldn't be hacked.'

'This is hardwired into the discs, by federal mandate. I know I couldn't switch if off, and if I couldn't then I'm sure no one else could.'

In which case the Maq I'd seen going into Lincoln's office

with him must have been the real Maq, because no one else had been there when Lincoln died. And I was back to my original problem of how he'd got out of the storeroom and back again. And why wasn't he covered with blood when I found him?

But Rebecca couldn't help me with any of that.

'Let's move on,' I said. 'I want to ask you about last night.'

She nodded.

'I understand that you and Mr Shan were in a relationship.'

'Yes.'

'Since when?'

'He flew me up here about three months ago, supposedly to talk about the ghosts and AI. In fact he said I was going to meet you, but then made up some excuse about you being stuck out at sea. We ended up having a candle-lit dinner on the roof, and champagne. And ...' She glanced down at my phone. 'Well, one thing led to another, and I thought all my dreams had finally come true. We tried to keep it quiet at work, but there's only so many times you can fly up for a working weekend with your boss before tongues start to wag.'

'Last night, you were cross with him. You had an argument.'

'You know why. It was lots of things. I'd thought I was going to get a tender tribute to my dad, instead of which we got bloody Maq in a cage. And then he told me he'd gone behind my back again, putting AI in Maq.'

'What do you mean by "again"?' I asked. 'He'd done that before?'

She hesitated before answering. 'Well, not exactly.'

'What then?'

'You know what Linc was like, he always focused on the out-come, and wasn't too troubled how he got to it. A few months ago I discovered that one of my team had been reporting directly to Lincoln in relation to some trials that I knew nothing about, and where the proper protocols hadn't been followed. It was soon after that that I got flown up here for what turned into dinner on the rooftop. Having seen the way he was chasing after you last night I was starting to wonder if he ever had any feelings for me, or if it was just a way to stop me complaining.'

'So you got into a massive fight outside my room, and you tried to hit him?'

She looked away. I could see her wondering just how much I knew.

'It sounds awful now,' she said. 'It *was* awful. Unforgivable. But he'd just kissed you, for fuck's sake. I was cross and I'd had too much to drink. That kiss was the final straw. I felt humiliated and I'm sorry, I said some awful things about you, but I didn't mean them. I was just cross, and hurt, and I loved Linc, and for the first time I think I realised he didn't really love me at all. The bastard was just using me.' She put her head in her hands, her shoulders shaking. 'Still,' she sobbed, 'I can't believe that my last words to him were so hurtful.'

'Let's take a moment,' I said. I went to the sink and got her a glass of water.

She took a brief sip, then dabbed at her eyes.

As I waited for her to compose herself the sky behind her lit up, followed seconds later by a roll of thunder. Then another – closer – and the windows rattled.

'Let's rewind—' I began, but was interrupted by a flash of lightning directly overhead, and a booming roar.

Rebecca jumped and looked over her shoulder.

233

The lights flickered, went out for a moment, and came back on again.

I waited for another lightning flash, but the worst seemed to have passed over us. 'Rewinding slightly, you left Lincoln's office just after me, with Koji and the lawyer?'

'Yes. We were just behind you.'

'Did you speak to any of the others again, after your fight with Lincoln?'

'No. He dragged me down the corridor so that we weren't seen to be fighting in front of them.' She rubbed her arm. 'He hurt me. Then ... then he told me I could fuck off back to Glasgow as far as he was concerned, and I should talk to him when I was sober. He stormed off and I went back to my room, and cried myself to sleep. I'm not proud of my behaviour, but you know what he was like.'

'Did anyone see you go back to your room?' I asked.

'I guess not. I don't remember seeing anyone.'

So she had no alibi for the time of the murder.

'Finally, can we go back to the party again? You said last night that instead of using Maq and *The Cage*, Lincoln should have used the chess set, and I noticed there was a chessboard in the office, which was new. What was that about?'

I was hoping she might be able to shed some light on why two of the chess pieces had been next to Lincoln's body, covered in blood, but I wasn't going to tell her about that.

'It was something I'd been working on,' she said. 'I started it in memory of my father, but I actually think it has great commercial implications. Twenty years ago hard light was just a novelty act that a few scientists were playing around with. No one really saw any practical use for it, mostly because of the tremendous energy cost. Dad was one of the first people to try to commercialise it. He built a chess set as a prototype. It was pretty basic and it required a massive projector underneath to make the pieces work. But it was where Lincoln first saw hard light – where I met him, in fact. That's where Lincoln's ghosts came from. Recently, with more modern technology, I've been developing something much better than what Dad was able to. Let me show you.'

She reached into her pocket and pulled out one of the white discs, which she placed on the table between us. Then she took out her phone. 'I just need to link to the disc. This works differently than the ghosts. It's a smaller version of the chess set in Lincoln's office but it functions in broadly the same way.'

After a moment a chessboard appeared where the disc had been. 'Load last game,' Rebecca said.

Pieces appeared on the board. It was near the endgame, with black close to winning.

Rebecca swallowed. 'This was the last game I played with Linc. He was white. He was a crap player when I met him, and he never got much better. It'll do, though, to show you how it works.'

She picked up the black queen and moved it across the board, putting it down next to a white bishop.

The queen pulled a curved sword from her belt and sliced the bishop's head from his shoulders. The head rolled across the board, and then it and the bishop's body vanished. The queen stepped on to the square that the bishop had occupied, and sheathed her sword.

'Clever,' I said. 'So are these just small ghosts with AI?'

'It's the same technology, but they're not like ghosts. There's no one controlling them, and no AI being used. It's just a chess game, with pre-programmed actions when you capture someone. Instead of seeing it on a screen you see it in hard light. Try it for yourself.'

As white, I didn't have a lot of options since most of my pieces were gone. I picked up a knight and took one of the black pawns. The pawn was a small figure of a man, with a war hammer which he raised to defend himself, but the knight knocked it aside with his shield, and then cut him in half with a broadsword.

The pawn disappeared and the knight took its place.

It was impressive, although I did wonder if it would become tiresome after a while. But maybe for occasional players it would seem like fun.

'It's neat,' I said. 'I can see why people might want it. You say that the one in Lincoln's office works in the same way?'

'Yes, it's just bigger. It has a solid board, which houses the projector for the pieces, so they can be larger, and more detailed. Both versions of the chess set went online last night at the same time as the ghosts. I know it's a niche product, but our research showed that it's a strong market, as chess players tend to be obsessive and fairly well off. I don't know why Linc didn't use it last night instead of Maq in a cage, which was just a publicity stunt.'

Rebecca didn't seem to realise how effective that stunt had been with the party guests. Far more so, I suspected, that showing off a fancy chess set that might appeal to a few geeks.

But it didn't really matter whether Lincoln or Rebecca had been right. It was just one of several reasons why she had been cross with him, all of which had converged in a perfect storm last night. She had more than enough motive to kill Lincoln. And I only had her word that the fight outside my door had been the end of the matter. She had no alibi for the time of Lincoln's murder. Had the fight continued? Had she gone to his office with him, tied him to the desk, and then hit him with the axe?

And there was another piece of evidence that pointed to Rebecca's involvement.

Why had there been blood-covered chess pieces next to Lincoln's body?

28

THE CHILD

Staring at the chess pieces a second time didn't provide me with an answer.

I'd sent Rebecca back to her room, then returned to Lincoln's office to carry out a more careful search.

The first thing I'd done was replace the raven mask. It helped a little. Then I carefully circled the room, taking photographs from every angle.

Apart from the body there were four things that struck me as odd: the mask, the axe, the chess pieces and the heart. Inspecting each in turn provided one further mystery. A black rook was missing from the chessboard. I couldn't see it anywhere. Had the killer taken it with them?

I walked around the desk, inspecting the body but not touching anything. On the left wrist was the watch that had been my last birthday gift to Lincoln. It was showing a time of quarter past eleven. Yet I was certain that the previous day, when I'd arrived at the Manor, it had been showing two o'clock. I'd commented on it, saying the watch was broken.

Quarter past eleven was when Lincoln had died. Was that a coincidence? Had his killer reset the watch to match his time of death? But if so, why?

I turned my attention to the desk itself.

There wasn't much. One drawer contained a few bits of electronics. Another several books, including some on cannibalism. I'd need to look at those later. Then a drawer full of slim folders, each neatly labelled. There was only one that interested me. It was labelled 'RM', and I almost passed over it before realising: 'Rebecca Murray'. Did Lincoln keep a folder about all his lovers? Was there one somewhere on me? I flicked through the rest but there wasn't one labelled 'EM'.

The final drawer contained a bottle of whisky and two glasses, which were dirty. Had Lincoln and Maq been drinking together? Which didn't make a lot of sense, but even less if what I'd seen on the stream was really Maq's ghost.

That was it for the drawers. Where else to search? There were no bookshelves, and no filing cabinets. Lincoln hadn't liked clutter.

There was one more thing that I needed to know. I got down on my hands and knees, and meticulously searched the floor from end to end. I'd almost given up when I found it, hidden on its edge in the pile of the thick carpet: a small white disc. I picked it up and dropped it into a plastic bag, putting it in my pocket. I needed to confirm that it had been Maq's ghost, but I was pretty sure.

That at least made sense. But nothing else did.

*

I headed back up to the kitchen, which was deserted. I still hadn't seen Kleber, although Koji had said he was around. I needed to speak to him at some point to get his version of events from the night before.

I checked the time: 10:57. But late as it was, I couldn't face eating. The presence of the body had robbed me of my appetite.

Instead I made myself a cup of tea, and sat down to read the folder on Rebecca.

It was disappointingly sparse, containing only one document, a Vancouver Police report from the Domestic Violence division. The address of the incident was listed as: 'Penthouse Apartment, Orcus Towers, Iona Island'. That was Lincoln's apartment in Vancouver. He tended to live there during the week, and come back to Black Lake Manor for weekends. The date of the report was blanked out, as were some parts of it:

I attended at the above address, at 12:05 a.m., and separately interviewed Mr Lincoln Shan (39) and [REDACTED] (34). It was evident that both were seriously intoxicated. I observed two champagne bottles and a bottle of vodka on the floor, all empty. Mr Shan had bruising to his left cheekbone and around his left eye. His collar was torn. I interviewed Mr Shan first. He said that he had dialled 911 by mistake and no longer required assistance. He said that he wished to withdraw any complaint. I asked him if his partner had struck him, as he had reported, and he said no. He said that he was intoxicated and had fallen. He asked me to leave. I refused, and went to speak to [REDACTED]. She was tearful, and admitted striking the victim. She said that the argument related to another woman. Before I could complete my questioning I received a telephone call from Assistant Commissioner [REDACTED] who instructed me to conclude my inquiry. I left the premises at 12:22 a.m.

Did this show that last night's fight in the corridor outside my room was not a one-off, that they had a history of violent arguments with Rebecca as the aggressor? Perhaps she had finally been tipped over the edge, lured him to the office with the promise of some kinky game, and then hit him with the axe when he was helplessly tied down.

But if so, why cut out his heart? A crime of passion I could just about understand. Cutting out the heart felt like something different.

My thoughts were interrupted by the kitchen door opening. I looked around.

A young girl stood in the doorway. She was wearing an ankle-length green dress and had red pigtails down to her shoulders. I wasn't a good judge of these things, but I guessed she couldn't be older than ten.

She stood holding the door open, staring at me. Silent.

Koji had told me that there were six of us left in the Manor – all adults. So where had she come from?

'Hello, who are you?' I asked.

She continued to stare without saying anything. Unblinking.

I tried again. 'How did you get here?'

She shook her head. Then raised a hand and beckoned to me with one finger.

Her lips moved. The word was so faint that I could barely hear it over the sound of the storm outside. 'Come.'

She stepped backwards into the corridor, letting the door shut.

What the hell?

I pushed back my chair, jumped up and ran across to the door. I flung it open to see the girl walking away down the corridor. She looked over her shoulder, quickened her pace, then disappeared into the stairwell.

I ran after her.

As I reached the top of the stairs I could hear footsteps below me, faster now. She was running.

I raced down. I couldn't see her, but I heard a door slam shut on the floor below.

Level Six – Lincoln's office.

I dropped to that level and stepped into the corridor to see the girl standing outside the office. She looked at me, then opened the door and went in.

I hesitated for a moment, then typed in Lincoln's code and opened the door.

She was standing on the far side of the desk behind the body.

'Don't touch anything!' I shouted. 'We need to get out of here.'

Then I realised that I was too late. She was holding the white knight and the black queen in her hands, like a child playing with blood-soaked dolls.

She held them facing one another and started singing to herself in a high-pitched voice: '*The Queen of Tarts, she stole some hearts, and fried them up to eat. Then someone died, but no one cried, and he learned not to cheat.*'

She looked up at me, giggling.

As I took a step towards her she placed the queen on the body's chest.

And the queen moved.

She unsheathed the scimitar at her hip and put the point in the hollow of the body's throat. Then she started walking backwards towards the navel, slicing into the skin alongside the existing cut.

For a moment I was too stunned to move. It seemed unreal.

The girl placed the knight where the queen had been. '*He's lost his horse, he's dead of course,*' she said, giggling again.

The knight swung his serrated broadsword down from where it rested on his shoulder and inserted it into the cut made by the queen. He started to saw at the bone beneath. A rasping sound filled the room.

I had to stop this.

I took a step forward, grabbed the knight, and pulled him loose. The broadsword came out with a popping sound. I threw him to one side. The queen remained where she was, but her sword hand twitched.

Then the chess pieces left on the board stirred to life, turning towards me. I was suddenly conscious of the number of weapons I faced: longswords, war hammers, broadswords, bows and arrows. True, the pieces were small, but was I in danger? Surely they wouldn't attack me. I had no idea how they were programmed, and they might perceive me as a threat now that I'd attacked the knight.

And what about the girl?

'Get away!' I shouted at her, wrenching the axe free from the desktop, and stepping round the desk. I was taking no chances. Before the pieces could move, I smashed the axe into the centre of the board where I knew the projector must be. The wood splintered and the chess pieces vanished.

So much for preserving the integrity of the crime scene.

I looked around. Any immediate danger seemed to have passed. Not only had the pieces on the board disappeared, but also the queen and the knight that had been attacking the body.

The girl was also gone.

Had she slipped out while I was destroying the chess set? Or had she been a ghost? Although I couldn't see a disc on the floor anywhere.

More importantly, whatever she was, what had she done to make the chess pieces come alive?

I needed to speak to the maker of the chess set. She was now my prime suspect.

29

THE REDHEAD AND
THE ROUGHNECK

'The time is 11:32. I am resuming my interview with Ms Rebecca Murray.'

Rebecca was across the table from me again.

'Ms Murray,' I said, 'I want to start by showing you a police report.'

I'd found some plastic bags in one of the drawers, and put the report in one. It was readable, but hopefully any trace evidence would be preserved.

'For the record, I am handing Ms Murray a copy of a police report of a domestic violence incident in Mr Shan's Vancouver apartment at Iona Island. It records that an unidentified female partner of Mr Shan's, aged thirty-four, admitted to striking him while intoxicated. How old are you, Ms Murray?'

Rebecca was staring at me, shaking her head. 'I'm ... I'm thirty-four,' she admitted.

'Please read it,' I said.

She scanned it, all the while shaking her head, then looked up at me, wide-eyed. 'This isn't me. This never happened. If this is genuine, it's talking about someone else. It doesn't have my name on it.'

'It was found in Lincoln's office, in a folder marked with your initials.'

'It wasn't me,' she said desperately. 'Yes, things got a bit rough with Linc yesterday, but it was the first time.'

'You said at one point last night that you might push him off the roof. And that was before things escalated.'

She glared at me. 'That was a joke; I never meant it seriously. I thought it was a joke between friends.'

'It will be easy enough to establish whether that police report relates to you. Let's put it aside for the moment; I want to ask you about something else. Earlier you showed me the chess set that you had built using hard light figures. As I understand it that was a personal project that you were doing, in honour of your father.'

'Yes.'

'You said it's not AI in the chess pieces.'

'No. It's basically the same as playing a game of chess on your phone, but here the pieces are solid, projected by the disc or the board. The decision-making is the same as any chess computer, it's just a bit more showy. When a piece is captured, or at the end of the game, there is a pre-programmed show.'

'So there's no chance of a piece going crazy, as we were thinking might have happened to Maq's ghost last night?'

'The chess pieces?' Rebecca looked at me as though I was the one who had gone mad. 'Not a chance, and we know now that AI stuff was all crap from Linc anyway.'

'If the pieces are programmed,' I said, 'then presumably you could change them to do something else if you wanted? Say, instead of cutting off an opponent's head, you could program a piece to do a victory dance – or walk off the table?'

'I suppose so, but I'm not sure why you'd want to. If you're asking whether the pieces need to stay fixed on the board, the answer is no. They need to stay within range of the disc or board that's projecting them, but that's the only limit. In some versions of the game when pieces were captured they were dragged to the side of the board and thrown off it instead of disappearing. For the rest of the game they would lie in a heap next to it. Linc quite liked the idea but we scrapped it in the end as too gory. We were hoping parents would buy sets for their children.'

'So who at Orcus was involved in this project of yours?' I asked. 'Was it just you, or were there others programming the pieces?'

'It was my pet project,' Rebecca said. 'I was mostly doing it in my spare time, in memory of my dad.'

'So it was only you who could program it?' I asked.

'Yes.' She hesitated. 'Actually, that's not quite right. Lincoln was very interested, particularly in the larger version that we created for his office. He got involved in the design of the pieces for that. So he knew a bit about how it worked.' She paused. 'Oh, and Yahl, of course. A few months ago Linc asked me to find him something to do as a favour to Koji. I'm guessing you know Yahl from growing up here?'

I shook my head. 'Not really. He was just a kid when I left and I've only seen him a couple of times since I got back.'

'He seems to have had a pretty rough time of it from what

Linc told me. But I'm not sure Koji was doing his grandson any favours by letting him drift from one Orcus company to another. Apparently he'd decided he had an interest in robotics, and seemed to think that was what we did in the Intelligence Department. It's not, but I still ended up lumbered with him to keep Linc happy. He's rough around the edges, but he's actually pretty bright. I couldn't offload him on anyone else, so mostly he sat with me. He helped out on the design of the pieces. And he played around with the animation sequences, testing them. I doubt whether he had much understanding of the programming, though.'

It didn't sound promising, but I decided I ought to speak to him, to close off that line of inquiry.

'Lincoln talked yesterday about the constraints that are hardwired into the ghosts. Would it be the same for the chess pieces?'

Rebecca frowned. 'No, why would you need that? They're just playing a game of chess. The pieces don't have any autonomy.'

So the chess pieces could potentially have killed Lincoln. And I'd seen them slicing open his body. Had I found the murder weapon? In which case Lincoln's killer was whoever had programmed the chess pieces. Rebecca?

But if so, why had she admitted all this so freely?

I had one final question for her. It was a hunch, but it felt right. 'This may sound odd, but can you show me a photo of yourself as a kid, say around ten?'

She stared at me, open-mouthed. But she didn't look puzzled. She looked shocked. She shook her head, and tears started to form in her eyes again.

'How did you know?' she asked.

'Know what?'

'Linc asked me the same question last week.'

'Did he say why?'

'No,' she said. 'He told me it was a surprise. I gave him this one of me with my dad.' She passed over her phone.

The photo was of a couple standing in front of a castle. The man was middle-aged with grey hair, dressed in a black suit. Standing in front of him, his hands on her shoulders, was a young girl with red pigtails. She was wearing an ankle-length green dress.

'Did you find the photo somewhere?' Rebecca asked.

'No,' I said. 'Did you get scanned at Iona Island? Is there a ghost of you somewhere in Orcus's systems?'

'Of course. We all did. The best way of testing the ghosts was to use them ourselves. What's this got to do with anything?'

'It doesn't matter. That's all I need to know for now.' I messaged Koji to come back and collect Rebecca, and return her to her room.

'What's this all about?' Rebecca asked. 'Why did you want to see the photo? Do you know why Lincoln wanted it?'

'I can't tell you that.'

Koji knocked on the door and came in.

'Once you've shown Ms Murray to her room can you get me Yahl,' I asked. 'I haven't spoken to him yet.'

He nodded.

So now I was faced with another puzzle. Lincoln must have used the photo and scan of Rebecca to create a version of her as a child. For what purpose I couldn't begin to fathom. I hadn't found the photo of Rebecca as a child.

Instead I'd met the real thing.

Yahl was a study in contrasts. One moment he would stare at me aggressively, as though challenging me to ask him anything; the next he would drop his head, unable to look me in the eye. I knew the feeling. He was in his mid-twenties, and I'd been much the same at that age. I'd felt that people could look straight into my soul through my eyes, seeing all my fears and insecurities. It had taken me years to learn to hide that.

'The time is 13:43, and I am interviewing Mr Yahl ...' I realised that I didn't actually know Yahl's surname. 'For the record, can you state your full name?'

He leaned forward, and spoke into the phone. 'Yahl de Aguayo.'

It seemed that like many on the island he had Spanish blood mixed in with Akaht. The missionary priests had been less than diligent in observing their vows of chastity, and sometimes the names had stuck.

'I'm interviewing Mr de Aguayo about the death of Mr Lincoln Shan. Can you start by explaining your position at the Manor.'

He looked confused. 'My position?'

'What did you do exactly for Mr Shan?'

'Well, I don't really have a position here. As you know, Naniq-Koj, my grandfather – you call him Koji – works here. He always has, as long as I can remember, so I've been here a lot, helping out where I can. I remember when they were building it, I was a kid, but I used to come and watch. It seemed incredible at the time. Now, though, you have to wonder why.' He looked up, as though daring me to disagree.

'You didn't approve of what Mr Shan was doing?'

'Well ...' He looked away awkwardly. 'Don't get me wrong, Mr Shan has done a lot for us, but me ... well, me and lots of others, those of us who were too young to have any part in it, think he tore the heart out of our village. Now it feels as though we're just a showpiece for his rich friends, as though the elders sold out to him.'

'Still, he found you a job on one of his oil rigs.'

'That was Naniq-Koj really. I was going through a tough time and wanted to get away from here.'

'But it didn't work out for you, did it?'

He looked up again. 'Who told you that?' Then didn't wait for a reply, but glanced over his shoulder at the rain battering the house. 'You think this weather is bad, but it was grim as hell on the rigs, with none of the luxuries you have here. And the men were hard as nails. You don't get to be a roughneck if you're not. They're tough on new boys, and there's not much to do for fun.'

'So you got into a lot of fights, and got thrown off the rig?'

'I was different, being Akaht, so they picked on me a lot. Things could get heated, and they'd call me names. If I didn't stand up for myself they'd have walked all over me. The ... the last time we were on a bar crawl in Anchorage, one of the rougher parts, about ten of us. It was early evening, and we'd been drinking since breakfast. It was just before Halloween, and we went past some shop selling costumes. One of the boys went inside, and came out wearing a Native American headdress. It was nothing to do with us here, I think it was Navajo. But he started dancing round me and pretending to make war cries.

I'd had enough of their shit so I hit him hard, knocked him out cold, and then his friends jumped me. I'd just taken a kick in the face when the cops waded in. That's when this happened.' He grinned at me, showing a missing front tooth.

'And you lost your job because of that?'

'Yes, but I wasn't going back anyway. I'd had enough of those bastards. Naniq-Koj flew up with Vekla – my sister – to bail me out, but then the charges were dropped. Apparently they were worried about the racist overtones, and that it had been ten against one. And Orcus is a big employer in Anchorage, which probably helped.'

'So Koji got you a job in Vancouver?' I asked.

'Not straight away. I came back to help here for a while. I worked with Vekla in the kitchens for a couple of months, and did odd jobs round the Manor with Naniq-Koj. I guess Mr Shan noticed me hanging around a lot. He talked to me sometimes, said I ought to be doing something to better myself, so he got me a job with Ms Murray, in Vancouver. I didn't think I could say no, but it was actually pretty cool, seeing what she's doing there.'

'She said you helped her with the chess set she was building.'

'Yeah.' He grinned at the memory. 'That was pretty neat, and she let me give her ideas for how some of the pieces should look. Mr Shan got involved as well, and I even got invited up to his penthouse to talk about it. He had lots of books with men and women in armour, old books, and he was trying to choose which ones to use. He asked for my help. But then ...' He trailed off, and looked away again. 'We'd all had a lot to drink as the evening went on. Mr Shan went to take a call, and when he came back, Rebecca ... Ms Murray and I were sitting on the couch together, looking through one of the books. Mr Shan seemed to get the wrong idea. He called her a slut ... and ... and other names. He threw a glass of whisky against the wall.'

'Then what happened?' I asked.

'I dunno.' He shrugged. 'Ms Murray said I should get out, so I did. I didn't like leaving her there, though, with him. It didn't feel safe.'

'You felt protective towards her?'

'I what?'

'You wanted to look after her? Were you worried she was in danger?'

'A bit,' he said. 'But I worked for Mr Shan, and so did Naniq-Koj, so there wasn't much I could do. When I saw Ms Murray the next day she apologised for what had happened, said that Mr Shan was under a lot of stress, and the next time I saw him he acted as though it hadn't happened at all. Maybe he'd forgotten, he was pretty drunk. I didn't get invited back to the penthouse again, though.'

'Were you cross with the way he treated her?'

Yahl looked up. 'Cross? It wasn't my place to be cross with Mr Shan. It was up to them to sort things out. I liked her, though. I still do. She was kind to me.' He looked down, blushing suddenly.

It seemed as though Yahl had a bit of a crush on Rebecca. Harmless under normal circumstances, but did that mean that he might have killed Lincoln out of misguided chauvinism? Or helped Rebecca if she'd finally had enough of Lincoln?

'You were cross with Mr Shan last night, though, for what he was doing to Maquina.'

He didn't answer, looking down at his hands.

'I saw you and Koji arguing about it,' I said. 'He told me you and some of the younger Akaht wouldn't be happy about what Lincoln was doing.'

'That ... that's true,' he admitted. 'I don't really know Maquina, he's never been around, but he's our chief. Mr Shan shouldn't have done that to him. It was humiliating to all of us.'

'Did you confront Mr Shan about it?'

'Confront him?'

'Did you have a fight about it?'

'No, I didn't see Mr Shan again after that. Naniq-Koj sent me away to go and help Vekla clean up the kitchen. I think he just wanted me out of the room.'

'Vekla did the catering for last night?' I asked. 'Koji told me he sent her home.'

'Yeah, I helped her till about ten, then she went back to the village.' He paused, looking confused. 'No, actually it was a bit later than that.' He ran a hand through his hair, as though that might help him think. I caught a flash of black on the inside of his wrist, half-hidden by his sleeve. That confirmed what Maq had told me about Yahl being one of the Hamatsa.

'So Vekla went home?' I prompted.

'Yeah, I think it must have been just after ten. I didn't think it was safe, and I offered to go with her, but she said she was fine. Naniq-Koj wanted her out of here. She was grumpy with Mr Shan too, although for other reasons. While we were cleaning up I told her how the guests were ghost dancers, and the nice foods she'd prepared were just scattered around the room when they disappeared. She wasn't happy about having wasted her time making all that fancy stuff for no reason.'

I paused to think. I'd got a bit more insight into the relationship between Lincoln and Rebecca, which confirmed some of what I knew already. But this wasn't actually why I'd wanted to talk to Yahl.

'Can you tell me a bit more about what you did for Ms Murray. You obviously got roped in to help out on the launch last night.'

Yahl grinned up at me. 'That was pretty cool. It was Mr Shan's idea to jump off the roof as a ghost. He wanted to do it himself originally, but I think Rebecca … Ms Murray persuaded him it didn't look good for the boss to die – even for a few minutes. She suggested me instead, which is the reason I was here for the party. We practised it a few times up there. The plan was to have the party on the roof, and I was meant to walk through the guests as Mr Shan told his story about the African king, and then I'd jump off right in front of everyone. Obviously that didn't work with the weather we had last night, and getting the ghost to walk on the glass roof in the storm was a pain. But I still think it looked cool.'

'Were you involved in the programming side at all?' I asked.

'Programming?' He looked at me blankly. 'What do you mean?'

'Telling the ghosts what to do,' I explained. 'Or the chess set?'

'Me, doing that?' He laughed. 'Not a chance. Ms Murray tried to show me bits of it, but it really didn't mean much to me. No, telling them what to do – that was all down to Ms Murray.'

I let him go. He'd provided me with new information which confirmed much of what I already suspected.

But there was something odd about Yahl. He was clearly intelligent – Rebecca had said as much – yet he didn't seem to understand some simple questions, and at times he'd come across as naïve. It almost felt as though I'd been talking to two different people. Had he been playing me? Was there more to his relationship with Rebecca than either had been letting on?

1805

30

HAMATSA

Captain Ross picked his way carefully through the figures sleeping on the floor of the longhouse. It was hard to see much as the central fire seemed to be providing more smoke than light.

He stifled a cough as he pushed aside the beaver-fur curtain protecting the entrance. It was cold outside, but at least the air was clear.

He paused, glancing up at the stars. He might never get on a ship again, but old habits died hard. Even with the moon he could see the North Star and the Great Bear, and they told him it was late – well past midnight.

A voice startled him.

'Where are you going, Ross?'

A man was leaning against the wall of the longhouse next to the entrance, smoking.

John Jewitt, the chief's other tame white man.

'Taking a piss,' said Ross. 'What's it to you?'

Jewitt laughed. 'I thought maybe you were trying to run away from your new bride. Are you enjoying my cast-off?'

Ross spat at Jewitt's feet. 'Piss off. Unlike you, I'm happy to have someone to share my life with here. You need to accept that we're never going home. Eustee is a fine woman, and better than you deserved.'

'Of course you're happy to stay here.' Jewitt pushed himself off the wall and stepped up to Ross until their noses were inches apart. 'You'll never be allowed back to London. Cannibal!' He spat the last word.

'I did what I had to. You're no better. You live here at Maquina's whim. The rest of your crew died while you crawled on the floor and begged to live. At least they fought to survive. As did I.'

Ross regretted some of what he had told the Mowachaht when he had staggered into their village months earlier, following the black wolf that had led him through the tunnels. They had found the package containing Cooper's flesh in his pocket, and recognised it for what it was. It had been hard to offer any answer but the truth. Although he hadn't been entirely honest as to how Cooper had died.

Jewitt, who had been translating while Ross told his story, had turned away in disgust.

The reaction of the Mowachaht had been different. Instead of condemning him, they had said that he had become Hamatsa through eating another's flesh, that the spirit of the wolf had recognised him as one of their own. Yet the more the Mowachaht honoured him, the more Jewitt resented him.

'I didn't eat anyone to live,' said Jewitt. 'I can still go home if I want to.'

'No you can't. Don't think Maquina will ever let you go. When he decides that he only needs one of us who do you think will end up floating in the ocean? The man who rejected his native bride? Or the man the tribe have honoured as Hamatsa?'

Ross stepped around Jewitt. 'Now leave me alone, unless you want to come and hold it for me.'

2045

31

THE REPORT

I didn't feel like eating, but I chewed on a piece of bread while I thought about what I'd learned.

I'd already dictated a summary of events on to my phone, to add to the interview recordings: the discovery of Lincoln's body; what Maq had told me; the camera streams and the door logs; my interviews with Rebecca; the child who had turned out to be a ghost of Rebecca; the strange events in the office, and what I'd found there; and finally my interview with Yahl.

I still hadn't decided what to do about the second part of my interview with Maq, where he talked about turning back time. I'd have to take a view on that later.

First to draw everything together. I picked up my phone again.

'The evidence points to Ms Murray. The police report I found in Mr Shan's office suggests that she and he had a violent relationship, and she had struck him in the past. There is some support for that in what Mr de Aguayo told me about the argument he witnessed at the penthouse. Ms Murray was clearly cross with Lincoln shortly before he died, for several reasons, all of which may have come together. There are witnesses to another violent, at times physical, argument between them last night. The fact that Mr Shan was found tied to his desk would suggest that he was with someone he trusted – indeed, probably someone with whom he had a sexual relationship.

'Perhaps the most compelling evidence against Ms Murray is the apparent role of the chess pieces in the removal of his heart. The mechanics of it are not entirely clear. It will require an autopsy and a forensic examination of the chess set to determine precisely how Mr Shan died. However, it seems clear that the chess pieces had a role in his death, and the principal designer and programmer of the chess set was, by her own admission, Ms Murray.

'Quite what the reason was for removing Mr Shan's heart is unclear. It does not appear to have formed part of any Akaht ceremony, since he was not their chief. Perhaps it was symbolic – Ms Murray's way of saying to the world that he was heartless. The rhyme being sung by the girl in the office might suggest someone aggrieved with an act of infidelity. The fact that she was a younger version of Ms Murray might have been intended to cast suspicion on her. Or might it be a double-bluff? Without knowing who was controlling the ghost it is hard to determine the significance, if any, of the song, or her appearance.' I wasn't going to put this in the report, but I wondered if the 'Queen of Tarts' was meant to be a reference to me, and the 'cheat' was Lincoln.

'So it appears that Ms Murray had both the motive and the means to kill Mr Shan. It seems most likely that she is the one who did.' I paused to think.

'However, there are some difficulties with that conclusion. First, the use of the chess pieces would indicate some degree of pre-meditation, whereas the incidents that might have motivated Ms Murray to kill Mr Shan all occurred last night at the party. I don't know if it would have been possible for her to have programmed the chess pieces in the time between the fight that she had with him in the corridor and his death. Presumably an IT specialist will be able to determine when they were programmed.' Assuming, of course, that that was still possible after I'd destroyed the board with an axe. 'They may well be able to determine who programmed the pieces, which would be the clearest indicator of guilt.'

'There is a second uncertainty, namely whether the police report found in Mr Shan's office relates to Ms Murray. For some reason it has been redacted. If it does not relate to her, then the history of violent behaviour largely falls away. True, they had an argument last night, but that could have been a one-off. It will be easy enough to check the original of the report once we have communication with Vancouver.

'Third, there is the question of how Ms Murray might have got into Mr Shan's office to kill him. The only evidence of anyone entering the office before 23:15 was of Mr Shan and what appears to have been Maquina's ghost doing so at 22:59. It is possible that Ms Murray programmed the chess pieces remotely, and perhaps the ghost Maquina was the one who tied Mr Shan to the desk, but it's hard to see how he could have done that in light of the "no harm" constraint.'

I thought about that for a moment. Could the ghost of Maq have persuaded Lincoln to be tied up on the promise that Rebecca was on her way? That probably wouldn't have offended the 'no harm' constraint. Yet it seemed so implausible that I wasn't going to say it out loud.

'In conclusion, it seems to me that until we have communication with the outside world it is impossible to reach a firm conclusion as to Ms Murray's guilt or innocence. As I have explained, some critical points of evidence will become certain one way or another once communication is restored. The most I can conclude at the moment is that Ms Murray is clearly the prime suspect in the murder of Lincoln Shan.'

Was there anything more to say?

I pressed pause.

Then I heard footsteps behind me. I hadn't heard the door open, or realised anyone else was in the room. The rain and wind must have masked their entry. Had the red-headed girl come back? As I turned to see who it was, I heard a low murmur of voices.

'Do it now!' someone hissed.

Then another voice, more softly: '*Kuwitap.*'

And the wolf ate time.

1805

32

A KILLING

Jewitt watched as Ross followed the path into the darkness of the forest.

The captain had wormed his way into the affections of the Mowachaht with his vile tales of eating human flesh. They had honoured him and made him Hamatsa. If Maquina had to choose, which of them would he favour?

Jewitt was conscious that he had argued with Maquina on many occasions, most fiercely about Maquina's insistence that he take a native bride. Eventually Jewitt had given in and married the daughter of another chief. On more than one occasion, though, Maquina had threatened to have him killed for disobedience.

The only good thing about the arrival of Ross was that it had enabled Jewitt to pass on his bride without any loss of face to her family.

But that had also had the effect of tying Ross even closer to the natives. It showed that – unlike Jewitt – he had no plans to escape when he could.

It was time to act.

He looked around for a weapon. A row of rocks lined either side of the path that Ross had taken. Jewitt picked one up, weighing it in his hand.

Perfect.

He followed Ross into the forest.

The captain had not gone far. He was standing on the edge of the path, half-hidden in the shadows, his back to Jewitt. It was the trickle of water that gave away his presence. Then that stopped, and Jewitt knew that he was about to lose his chance.

He took a step forward, bringing down the rock with all his strength.

The crack of stone against bone echoed through the forest.

Ross fell to the ground.

There were two witnesses to the captain's murder.

Jewitt himself.

And a black shape watching from the darkness, its orange eyes reflecting the moonlight. It growled softly as Jewitt made his way back to the longhouse.

2045

33

THE MOUNTIE

'Here's your coffee,' said Koji.

'Thanks.' I checked my phone: 9:03.

What had I been drinking last night? I thought I'd been fairly restrained, and the party had broken up earlier than planned, but my head was throbbing. I'd not felt this bad in ages.

'Any chance of some painkillers?' I asked. 'I'm not feeling great. Maybe it's the shock finally hitting me.' I'd been avoiding thinking about the body tied to a desk two levels down, its heart in a skull cup next to it.

Koji went over to a cupboard, stirred some powder into a glass of water, and brought it back to me.

I gulped it down in one.

The door opened and Yahl stuck his head round. 'Naniq-Koj, can I have a word? Some of the plants on the roof are moving. I'm worried about the glass breaking.'

Koji nodded. 'Excuse me.'

I was happy to see him go. I put my head in my hands, trying to get my thoughts straight.

At some point I needed to get back down to Lincoln's office to search it properly. Although everything pointed to Maq having killed him, as a scientist I'd been taught never to accept the obvious. And there was the problem of how Maq had done it if he was locked up all night. And if it wasn't Maq then there was a murderer roaming free somewhere in the Manor.

With my head as it was I couldn't face going down there for a while, though. Odds were I'd throw up.

I'd been sitting for a good ten minutes, feeling sorry for myself, when the door to the kitchen was flung open, and someone stamped across the floor towards me.

'There you are.' It was Paul Kleber, Lincoln's lawyer. He stopped too close, looming over me. He seemed to be waiting for me to say something, as though I'd know why he was there.

I looked up wearily and gestured to the chair opposite. 'Please sit. It's hurting my neck talking to you like this. How can I help?'

He sat, leaning across the table towards me. 'You can help by letting me have access to my client's files. I tried to get into his office and your jumped-up little corporal, Koji, said I needed your permission.'

'You can't go in there,' I said. 'It's a crime scene. As the only law enforcement officer within fifty kilometres of here I'm securing it until we can get a forensics team in. That probably won't be till tomorrow, at the earliest. Besides, you really don't want to see what happened in there.'

'Is it true that he was killed in some Akaht ritual?' asked Kleber.

'I really can't comment,' I said.

'Koji said he was wearing an Akaht mask.'

'Why do you need to get into the office so badly?' I asked.

'I can't tell you that. It's covered by attorney–client privilege, and confidential to Lincoln.'

'You do realise that your client is dead? Murdered. Anything you know that might help in finding his killer is my business.'

He snorted. 'Even you must see that the solution to this one is obvious. I understand that Diaz ... Maquina was seen going into the room with Lincoln's body. He's already on trial for conspiracy to murder. What other suspect do you need? It must be obvious even to you.'

'You ought to know better than most that he's innocent until proven guilty,' I said. 'I'm keeping an open mind, making sure we gather in and review all the evidence.'

'You sound like a bureaucrat, not a detective,' sneered Kleber. 'The homicide guys in Victoria would have had this done and dusted by now.'

I smiled. The painkillers were beginning to kick in, and his attitude was starting to get to me. 'Well, maybe I'm a bit less intuitive than your "homicide guys". If there's anything particular you want from Lincoln's office tell me what it is and you might be able to look at it, under supervision. But you're not getting in there.'

He pushed back his chair and stood. 'Fine, *Constable*. I can see you're struggling with this investigation, which is no surprise. If you aren't happy with Maquina as the killer then I suggest you look at the next most obvious suspect. If you knew anything about murder investigations, you'd know that it comes down to means, motive and opportunity, and there's one person here who has a better motive than anyone.'

'Who?' I asked.

'The person named in Lincoln's will as inheriting Orcus after his death. Eight billion dollars is a pretty good motive for murder, isn't it?'

'Who?' I asked again, hoping he might actually have something useful to contribute.

He smiled down at me. 'That would be you, Constable.'

Lincoln had spent his life trying to buy me one way or another. When I was seventeen he'd offered to pay for me to go round Europe with him for a year. I knew what he was hoping for, and it had made me feel cheap. A few years later he'd tried to give me a job at a salary far higher than my marine biology degree and lack of experience justified. Most recently he'd been pestering me to join Orcus and let him get me a research position at the university.

Now, with his death, he was trying to entirely fuck up my life with his money.

Kleber had thought the inheritance was a motive for murder. Anyone who knew me, as Lincoln did, would have realised the opposite. If I'd been told about this I'd have been praying for Lincoln to live for ever. Hell, I'd have been offering to carve out Maq's heart and fry it up for dinner myself if that helped.

I needed to find out what he'd actually left me. Lincoln couldn't just have given me his company. That would be crazy. I had to be able to give it away if I wanted to. Maybe I could disclaim the gift in favour of someone more suitable, whoever that might be.

More importantly, I needed to get on investigating his death. So far I'd got nowhere – except being named by Kleber as prime suspect.

My head was finally starting to feel better when the thunderstorm that Koji had mentioned rolled in. The crashing of the thunder did me no good at all. It didn't last more than five minutes, though. There was a final flash of lightning overhead, which caused the lights briefly to flicker, and then it passed on.

I needed to get on with things. Where to start? As Kleber had pointed out, Maq was the most obvious killer. He'd hated what Lincoln was doing to the planet, wasn't afraid of using violence, and had been seen going into the room where Lincoln died. Why had he made himself more of a suspect by telling me that Lincoln had brought him here to eat his heart? Was he hoping to set up some sort of self-defence argument? Surely if that was his plan he would have told me straight away. There'd have been some story about him struggling with Lincoln, fighting over the axe, and managing to seize it and kill Lincoln in the heat of the moment.

But no jury was going to believe that when Lincoln was found tied to the desk in what looked like some sort of ritualistic Akaht killing. Maq had been seen walking to Lincoln's office with him shortly before he died. There was screaming, and the next morning Lincoln was found dead. Although Maq had also been locked up in the basement when Lincoln died.

Thinking wasn't getting me anywhere. I needed to go and search Lincoln's office.

I was halfway to my feet when the door to the kitchen crashed open. I spun around, my head regretting it. Koji was standing there, gasping.

'Ms Murray wants to—' he began, then was pushed aside.

Rebecca looked a mess. Her hair was tangled, her eyes bloodshot.

She strode across the room towards me. 'You bitch!'

Her face was inches from mine, eyes blazing. Even I could read her anger. She made as though to slap me, and I staggered back, clinging on to a chair.

'You whore,' she shouted, coming towards me again. I slipped backwards, ending up half sitting on the chair as she leaned over me. 'What did you do to him?'

I was too shocked to react.

Then hands grabbed her from behind, pulling her away. It was Koji.

'Ms Murray,' he said, 'you need to stop this.'

I sat up. What the hell was going on?

'She was chasing after him all night, and then she killed him,' Rebecca spat out.

'For fuck's sake, give it a rest!' I said. 'I've no idea what you're talking about. I'm investigating Lincoln's death and this isn't helping.' I tapped my thumb against my forefinger eight times. I needed to restore some calm. 'Take a seat and we can discuss this properly.'

Koji guided her into a chair, then cautiously let go, staying behind her. I was glad he was there.

'I can guess what happened,' Rebecca said. 'Lincoln barely spoke to me all night, and Paul says he was trying to tempt you to Vancouver with a job offer.'

I swallowed. I was glad she didn't know what else he'd offered me. What was it he'd said about her? 'Rebecca's fun, but she's not you.' He'd have dumped her in an instant if I'd said yes.

'Then,' Rebecca said, 'I saw what happened outside your bedroom. You kissed him.'

Oh, shit. Now this was beginning to make sense.

'Look, Rebecca, it wasn't like that. It—'

'Did you meet him later in his office? He told me you were into stuff that I didn't like doing. Paul says he was found tied to the desk, half-naked. Was it an accident, or did you do it deliberately, frightened he was going to take you out of his will?'

For God's sake, what had happened to the attorney–client confidentiality Kleber had been banging on about? Soon everyone was going to think that I had a motive to want Lincoln dead. And how had Kleber known about Lincoln being tied to the desk? Had Koji been talking?

'I can't believe you think you're investigating this,' said Rebecca. 'It's a joke.'

She sat back, seeming finally to have run out of steam.

How to handle her?

Make it less personal. I pulled out my phone, set it to record, and placed it on the table. Put on my best poker face.

'Ms Murray,' I said, 'the time is 09:57. I am interviewing you as a constable in the RCMP, investigating the murder of Mr Lincoln Shan. Do you understand?'

'Whom you killed,' she spat out.

'Ms Murray, I would advise you not to make wild accusations of that sort. You have my condolences on the death of your partner.'

She glowered at me.

'I'm sorry to hear that you felt ignored by Mr Shan at the party last night, but that was not my doing. I'm sorry that you misinterpreted what you saw when Mr Shan and I said goodnight. He and I had, as you know, been engaged, and there was nothing untoward in what you saw.' I winced inside. Like hell there wasn't. 'I did not arrange to meet Mr Shan. I did not see him again yesterday evening. I went to my room and slept. I had nothing to do with the death of Mr Shan.'

I paused. As was my intention, the matter-of-fact way in which I was presenting things seemed to be having some effect on Rebecca. Inside I felt anything but calm. How had I allowed myself to be compromised in this way? To be seen kissing Lincoln just before he died.

'Ms Murray,' I went on, 'your behaviour towards me this morning does mean that I need to ask you some questions about your contact with Mr Shan, in my official capacity. Do you understand?'

She nodded. She glanced behind her at Koji.

'You were cross with Mr Shan last night, weren't you? Did you see him again after ... after you saw him say goodnight to me?'

She sat back, blinking, not answering.

'Did you?'

She looked behind her at Koji again. Was she wondering whether he'd told me about her fight with Lincoln?

'I did,' she said. 'Lincoln and I had an argument and he ... he told me to fuck off back to Scotland. That was the last time I spoke to him. Koji and Paul both saw it, they can tell you I left him and went straight to bed. This is nothing to do with me.'

'How did you discover that Mr Shan had been killed?'

'I was trying to find him this morning. I didn't sleep well. He wasn't in his room. It hadn't been slept in. I thought ... I thought he must have been with you all night. I tried your door, but there was no answer when I banged on it, so I went up to Lincoln's study, and Paul and Koji were outside. They told me.'

'Ms Murray,' I said, 'I had nothing to do with Lincoln's death. I do, however, have a job to do. We have no communication outside the Manor, and it is unlikely that homicide officers will be able to get here until tomorrow at the earliest. Until then I am in charge of this investigation. I will need to speak to you again. Koji, could you please escort Ms Murray to her room?'

Rebecca went with him reluctantly. Halfway to the door she turned back to me. 'Don't think all this "I'm the investigator" crap makes things any better. I know what you did to Lincoln, and I will prove it.'

34

DISCOVERIES

After my confrontations with Kleber and Rebecca I wanted some time alone. And I wanted to take a proper look at Lincoln's office.

I took the elevator down to Level Six.

I started by replacing the raven mask. It felt symbolic. Saying goodbye.

Then I walked round, photographing the room and its contents from every angle.

I looked again at the body. It was hard to understand why the heart had been removed. Even if Maq's story about eating the heart of the chief was true it didn't make any sense. Unless it was intended as a warning. If so, from whom, and to whom?

The only thing of interest was that the time on the Seiko Chariot watch had been changed to four thirty. I was certain it had been two o'clock when I'd seen it previously, because I'd remarked on it. Had it started working again? No – the second hand was still. Someone, presumably Lincoln's killer, must have altered the time. Why? What message was that and the heart sending?

I was sure that I was missing something.

I turned my attention to the desk drawers.

The first contained some electronics. Nothing helpful.

The second was filled with books. Several were devoted to cannibalism, which bore out Maq's story about Lincoln having researched that. In fact one was titled *Hamatsa*, which was the secret society Maq had told me about. I set it aside to read later.

At the bottom of the drawer was a thin book of no more than fifty pages or so. It didn't look to have been professionally published. As I grabbed it something metal fell out, clanging on to the bottom of the drawer. I jumped, then picked it up.

I'd seen it before, many years earlier, although it hadn't looked as good then. It was a strip of metal, sharpened to a point at one end, with '...*ride of Whitby*' embossed on one side. That was the name of the ship that Maq had told me about. The last time I'd seen this had been more than twenty years earlier when he'd handed it to me in the cave. I put it with the *Hamatsa* book, and looked at the booklet.

It was titled *The Tsonoqua Ceremony of the Akaht: Primitive Rohypnol?*, and had been written by Dr Julia Winston, an anthropology professor at the University of Victoria. I was curious to know why Lincoln had been reading this booklet, and I added it to my pile. Could it be something to do with the Akaht heart-eating ceremony that Maq had told me about?

One of the right-hand drawers contained a collection of folders. I flicked through them, pulling out two. The first was labelled 'Last Will & Testament'. I needed to see that, to check whether Kleber had been telling me the truth. The second was labelled 'EM', and I almost went past it. Then I noticed the first page. A credit report dated November 2045, and headed 'Dr Ella Manning'. Had Linc been spying on me after we broke up?

The final drawer contained a bottle of whisky and two glasses, both dirty.

There was one last thing I needed to search for, to see if my theory about Maq was correct. I started at one end of the office, on hands and knees, carefully scanning the floor. I wasn't helped by the depth of the carpet pile. Lincoln had always gone for the best.

I'd almost given up when I spotted it, edge up, lodged in a corner of the room. A white plastic disc about the size of a quarter. Yes! I carefully put it in my pocket.

I picked up the books, the nameplate and the folders, and backed out of the room, making sure it locked behind me.

I needed to find somewhere out of the way to do some reading.

First, though, I needed to get hold of a tactile kit to be able to access the disc. Where would I find one? Rebecca was the obvious person, but I didn't want to ask her. Then I remembered Yahl from the night before. He'd been carrying a kit after the stunt where he jumped off the roof, but I didn't think he'd had it on when I'd seen him arguing with Koji later. So odds were he'd left it in the reception room.

I took the elevator up to Level Two, emerging into chaos. The floor was sticky, covered with the remains of undigested canapés, champagne and scattered glasses. The glass roof was opaque with cracks and was sagging, with water pooling in the middle. It looked as though it could break at any moment; I kept away from that side of the room.

I remembered that I'd seen Koji and Yahl near the elevator after Lincoln had revealed Maq in *The Cage*. There was a low counter there, which had been stocked with glasses and bottles of champagne. I spotted the gloves almost immediately, tucked behind the bottles, the goggles stuffed inside one glove.

I picked them up and headed back down.

35

TSONOQUA

In the days when I'd been a regular visitor to the Manor I'd appropriated a small study down the corridor from Lincoln's bedroom. I'd liked it because it looked north, out over the lake towards Bamfield and the Broken Islands. It was somewhat less bleak than staring out across the endless expanse of the North Pacific.

It seemed largely untouched since I'd last been there.

There was a desk next to the window, with a screen on top that lit up when I tapped it. I dropped the books on the desk and sat down.

The nameplate I put to one side. Also the *Hamatsa* book. It was going to take a while to get through that.

I started with the disc. I put it on the desk, and slipped on the goggles and gloves. I didn't need fully to fire up the ghost to check who it was – just link to it. Yahl's name popped up on one lens. The tactile kit was presumably still connected to a disc somewhere in the reception room. I flicked across, erasing it.

Then I looked down at the disc I'd found in Lincoln's office. It flashed up a long serial number in red, and the option to connect. I confirmed the connection.

'*Noah Diaz*' appeared in green on the lens. '*Enable?*' I disconnected. That was all I'd wanted to know. I'd been right. The Maq in Lincoln's office the previous night had been a ghost. The obvious inference was that someone had used him to kill Lincoln, then switched him off.

Which made perfect sense apart from one thing: Lincoln had said the ghosts were unable to harm humans. Was that true, or was it just another one of Lincoln's lies, in answer to an inconvenient question from a journalist? Had the scene with the champagne bottle all been staged?

Lincoln had said that the 'no harm' rule was hardwired into the ghosts because the regulators required it, which had the ring of truth. Without such a constraint Lincoln's ghosts would be perfect murderers. You could use them to kill someone from a distance, leaving no trace of your presence, and then simply turn them off.

I'd need to check with Rebecca whether there was any way round the 'no harm' constraint, but for now I was going to assume that Lincoln had been telling the truth about that.

So that meant that a real person must have been in the room with Lincoln when he died. Who?

Searching for an answer, I looked at the documents I'd taken from the office. I started with the will – Kleber was right that money is a powerful motive. And I wanted to know if what he had said about me was true.

I was used to reading scientific papers where the authors hid their insecurities and ignorance behind long words and technical phrases that no one else could understand. Lawyers seemed to have taken that to new heights. The document was lengthy, and full of 'wherefores' and 'hereinafters' and 'aforesaids', all of which seemed to detract from ease of reading rather than add to it. After half an hour of flicking between the pages, rubbing my temples periodically, and making notes on my phone, I had got the gist of it.

It had been signed ten months earlier, so presumably before Lincoln and Rebecca had started going out, but after Lincoln and I had split up.

Essentially it boiled down to three points.

First, there was a list of minor personal gifts. Many of the names were unknown to me. Some I'd never met, some I recognised from the Vancouver gossip columns. One was a model that he'd been linked to for a while, although they'd never confirmed the relationship publicly. There were gifts to various staff members, including Koji and Yahl.

Buried in the middle of the list was a gift to 'Dr Ella Manning, of Bamfield Marine Science Centre, her alter ego in my safe at Black Lake Manor'. That seemed cryptic. What was it that he had left me?

Second, there was a charitable trust of the Manor and its surrounding lands, together with two hundred million dollars, for the preservation of Black Lake and the Akaht heritage, the trustees being various named members of the band, including Koji, together with the chief of the Akaht.

Third, the balance of Lincoln's estate was left upon charitable trust for the benefit of the people, culture and land of British Columbia. The trust was to be controlled by a board of trustees with me as chair, and I had the power of appointment of the remainder of the board. That was a relief. It wasn't nearly as bad as Kleber had made out. Apart from whatever was in his safe Lincoln hadn't left me anything personally. Hopefully I could just appoint a board of trustees and walk away.

Lincoln's will did also mean, of course, that Koji, Yahl and the rest of the Akaht had as good an incentive as I did to see him dead. Perhaps even better: two hundred million dollars was a lot of money.

Then I discovered a catch. At the back of the will was a two-page codicil, signed three months earlier, which changed the terms of the gift to the Akaht. The gift was now conditional on 'Maquina (aka Noah Diaz) not being the aforesaid chief of the Akaht at the time of Mr Shan's death, or disclaiming his position as said chief (and Trustee) within thirty (30) days of Mr Shan's death, or not surviving that period'.

So Lincoln hadn't been prepared to leave the Akaht anything if Maq was chief. Had Lincoln changed his will after failing to get Maq to join Orcus as an environmental adviser? Or after Maq had been arrested for the attack on the oil rig? Whatever the reason, it complicated things. Maq had never shown much interest in the Akaht, but now that he was back on the scene, and with two hundred million dollars to play for, would he want to stick around?

I put the will to one side and turned to the folder about me. It was, in some ways, disappointingly short, consisting of only two documents.

The first was a credit report from a year earlier. It confirmed what I already knew, that I had a modest income, limited capital and a small pension fund. It must have looked shockingly inadequate to Lincoln's eyes. I was grateful that despite having seen this he had not left me any money in his will. He knew how much I hated being patronised by him.

The second was a grant proposal that I had put forward a year before on behalf of the Marine Centre, seeking a contribution towards our funding for the next five years. These were the funds that Orcus had provided to us, and then threatened to pull if I refused to assist in Lincoln's ghost project.

Together the documents suggested that Lincoln had been looking at what buttons to push to get me working with him. I had been suspicious when Orcus offered the funding, wondering what strings were attached. It hadn't taken me long to find out.

I turned to the booklet next. The copyright page stated that it was a reissue of an article first published as part of a doctoral thesis in 2001. I read the introduction:

> In 1962 Austrian chemist Leo Sternbach, whilst working for the pharmaceutical giant Hoffmann-La Roche, filed a patent for a new benzodiazepine drug named Flunitrazepam, later sold under the brand name Rohypnol. The drug could cause impairment of balance and speech, sedation and anterograde amnesia, leading to a partial or complete inability to recall recent events. It quickly became a popular recreational drug, often used voluntarily in conjunction

with other drugs or alcohol to enhance their effect. It also became – at least anecdotally – a drug associated with date rape.

In this paper I consider whether the Akaht First Nations band of Vancouver Island had developed their own version of Rohypnol some two hundred years earlier.

I conclude that they did.

My research focuses primarily upon recently discovered evidence – through examination of oral traditions and interviews with elders – of the Tsonoqua Ceremony of the Akaht. The Tsonoqua were believed to live in the woods surrounding the Akaht village, and were described as forest witches. They were thought to be strong enough to tear down trees, and so noisy that lightning engulfed their canoes when they shouted. The Akaht retain to this day several cups which are plainly the upper half of a human skull, which they believe to have been made from dead Tsonoqua. I was permitted to see and hold some of these cups, which are unusually large for a human, particularly if female. Mothers believed that babies who drank from the cups would grow up to be unusually strong.

The cups form a central part of the Tsonoqua Ceremony, which is a mandatory ritual for Akaht children who reach the age of eighteen unmarried. In the year when they turn eighteen, all unmarried Akaht must attend a three-day ceremony in the longhouse, which is cleared of adults. The ceremony commences, on the first morning, with the lighting of a fire into which certain plants are thrown, and over which a large pot of water is boiled. Various herbs and berries native to the island are added to the pot. These include nettles, huckleberries, salmonberries and garlic mustard.

There was a footnote at this point:

In conducting my research I became convinced of the potency of the Tsonoqua drink, as described below. Given the risk that it might, like Rohypnol, be used for purposes for which it was not intended, I am not prepared publicly to list all ingredients of the drink, in particular those which I believe to have narcotic and hallucinatory effects. Serious academic researchers who seek to confirm or duplicate my research can contact me to obtain such information.

The paper continued:

On the first morning the eighteen-year-olds sit across from one another in the longhouse, men on one side, women on the other. The women wear masks modelled on the Hoxhok bird, so are in theory at least anonymous. The men do not wear masks.

As the fire burns, smoke and incense begin to fill the longhouse.

Placed around the fire are the Tsonoqua skull cups. The ceremony starts in earnest when one of the women walks to the fire, takes a cup, and fills it from the pot. She then walks over to the man of her choice, and hands it to him. Both drink from it. Then she sits before him. He takes a mixture of dandelion and chickweed flowers from a pouch at his belt and sprinkles it over her. She takes his hand, and leads him to one of the curtained-off 'rooms' at each end of the longhouse.

And so the ceremony continues until all have drunk from a Tsonoqua cup, and all are paired off.

As noted, the ceremony lasts for three days, and couples may change partners as many times as they wish over that time. After the first day, their inhibitions overcome, the Tsonoqua 'tea' is no longer used. At the end of the three days the expectation is that each person will have found a partner whom they will in due course marry.

Although everyone to whom I spoke maintained that the Tsonoqua Ceremony is now no more than historic, in several one-on-one interviews older members of the Akaht told me that they had participated in the ceremony.

It is evident that the Tsonoqua 'tea' is used in the same way as Rohypnol was originally (and still is by many): i.e., as a recreational drug. Hence the title of this paper. The Tsonoqua 'tea' undoubtedly has hallucinatory effects and causes memory loss, but there is no evidence of it being used by the Akaht for any untoward purposes. Those who participated in the ceremony did so voluntarily, albeit under cultural pressure to do so (they told me that their only alternative was to leave the Akaht village), the 'tea' being seen as lowering inhibitions early on and enabling partnerships that would otherwise not have occurred.

The Tsonoqua Ceremony is perhaps best likened to some of the drug-induced festivals that took place among the hippie counterculture of the late 1960s.

I'd been interested in the reference to the skulls of the Tsonoqua, since that sounded very much like the vessel in which I'd found Lincoln's heart. Disappointingly, however, nothing in the Tsonoqua Ceremony seemed to relate to the removal of a human heart, or explained the role of the skull cup in Lincoln's death.

I flicked through the rest of the booklet, but didn't have time to read the whole thing. I did notice that at the back of the booklet were Professor Winston's contact details, which some-one had circled in red. Had Lincoln been in touch with her to procure the recipe for the Tsonoqua 'tea'? Or was it still known among the Akaht elders?

But this rang a distant bell with me. What was it? My mind ran free as I watched the waves crashing into the base of the cliffs below the Bamfield road, the rain lashing against the window. I wanted to be out there, experiencing the force of nature, away from everyone, not cooped up in a glass box trying to work out who might have carved my ex-fiancé's heart out of his chest. There was a reason that I did a job that took me into some of the roughest seas in the world.

My mind bounced around, and then settled on a dim memory.

I picked up my phone. Did I still have it? I'm a pack-rat when it comes to saving things, always worried I'll lose something I might need later, so by default I tend to store things sent to me. Even without network access I might be able to find this. I did a quick search of my saved files and found an article I'd been sent several years ago.

SHAN–BAILEY SPLIT

Tech entrepreneur Lincoln Shan (controversial owner of tech company Orcus) has always modelled himself on Apple CEO Steve Jobs. Well, now he can add one more link to his idol: alleged sex pest (for Jobs's daughter's biography, see here). Shan's short-lived romance with up-and-coming Toronto actress Jennifer Leanne Bailey (best known for her steamy nude scenes in *Killer Clowns of Texas*, see here) ended Thursday morning following a visit by Vancouver PD officers to Shan's Iona Island penthouse. A police source revealed that Bailey claimed to have no memory of the previous evening after drinking champagne in Shan's penthouse and threatening to leave him. Bailey was said to have suffered unspecified 'injuries'. The source confirmed that Bailey tested negative for any drugs, and that no charges would be brought against Shan. His representative declined to comment.

Surely not? I'd dismissed it at the time as a girlfriend regretting the night before after too much alcohol. And maybe trying to generate a bit of publicity out of her association with Lincoln. If so, it hadn't worked, since as far as I was aware Bailey had sunk without trace after that.

I found it hard to believe that Lincoln could have used some form of hallucinatory drug on his girlfriend. Yes, he was ruthless, manipulative even. But it was a long way from that to drugging people.

Although this seemed of peripheral relevance to Lincoln's death, I wanted to chase it down, if only to satisfy myself that there was nothing in it.

I needed to speak to Maq again.

The guest rooms in the Manor were more like high-end hotel suites. There was a bedroom, a separate sitting area and en-suite bathroom.

Maq was seated in one of the armchairs, looking relaxed. I sat across from him.

'So, have you come to tell me that you've proved I'm innocent?' he asked.

'No,' I said. 'I'm keeping an open mind. But I haven't proved that you're guilty. Yet. I need to ask you about a couple of things.'

I showed him the nameplate from the lifeboat.

'Do you have any idea how Lincoln ended up with this?'

Maq leaned forward and took it from me, turning it over in his hands.

'Where did you find it?'

'It was in Lincoln's office. Do you know where he got it?'

'I brought it back from the caves with me and cleaned it up. It confirmed that the lifeboat we found came from the *Pride of Whitby*, but I knew that anyway. I wasn't sure what to do with the information. I couldn't tell Linc. The only person I could have told was my father, but we were barely speaking at the time. He was sick and knew I wanted to leave Black Lake. Also, I was worried that maybe we'd violated some sacred place and I'd get in trouble. I did scout the cliffs a bit, trying to find the way the Royal Marines got in, but it was impossible. I wasn't going to go back through the tunnels again. I kept the nameplate as a paperweight for a while. When I left Black Lake a couple of years later I gave Linc a box of my things. I can't recall now, but I guess the nameplate was part of that.'

'Strange that he kept it close,' I said.

Maq shrugged. 'If he'd looked up the name there might have been some record of the *Whitby* sinking off Pachena Point. Maybe he thought it was a cool artefact to have around.'

I took it back.

'OK, second question. Have you heard of the Tsonoqua?'

Maquina snorted. 'The witches who live in the forest? What about them?'

'Did you ever see a cup made from their skulls?'

'The one that makes the super-babies? Let them drink from the Tsonoqua cup and they get super strength? I don't think it was real, and I certainly never saw one of the cups.'

'What about the Tsonoqua Ceremony? It was a coming-of-age ritual among the Akaht.'

'As far as I know we stopped doing it a long time ago. You'd need to speak to some of the older Akaht if you want to know more, but why does it matter?'

'Linc had been reading a book about it and I'm curious to know why.'

'It's the sort of thing boys would giggle about, and then forget. Maybe the girls giggled about it too. I'm surprised there's a book about it, though, and I don't know why Linc would have had a copy. I'm sure he and I talked about it when we were kids. You'd see some girl, and one boy would say to the other, "I'd like to do the Tsonoqua with her." Stupid stuff like that.'

'It sounds a bit sick,' I said.

He shrugged. 'I'm not going to try apologising for the past.'

I couldn't see how this had anything to do with Lincoln's murder.

Other than the fact that his heart seemed to have ended up inside a Tsonoqua skull.

36

THE CODE

Kleber was in the corridor outside Maq's room. He seemed agitated.

'There you are,' he said. 'Can I get access to Lincoln's messages now? There are some that are urgent.'

'Really?' I asked. 'Even with your client dead they can't wait?'

'There are things I need to deal with for the estate.'

'Aren't I your client now?'

'Not until after probate. Until then I'm acting for the estate, not you.'

'Anyway,' I said, 'you didn't tell me the full story. I found a copy of the will, and I don't inherit eight billion dollars. I get to be the chair of a charity holding Orcus's assets.'

'Are you disappointed?' he asked. 'Do you realise now that you killed Lincoln for nothing?'

'You don't seriously think that, do you?'

'I was merely pointing out to you earlier that if you don't

like Maquina as your prime suspect then you'd be high on the list. The fact that you don't actually have the money to spend on yourself is irrelevant. You'd be running one of the largest charitable foundations in the world, getting invitations to the White House and Buckingham Palace. And you'd be astonished how many first-class flights you can charge to "charitable expenses". If I took your position and auctioned it there would be people bidding fifty, maybe a hundred million dollars for the right to control Orcus, so don't tell me it isn't a motive for murder.'

'Well, it wasn't,' I said. 'I don't want it. You might as well accuse Koji and Yahl of murdering Lincoln. They get two hundred million dollars out of this, provided Maq resigns as chief. Is that even legal?'

'I drafted it, so of course it is. Lincoln wasn't going to give money to the Akaht if they were being controlled by Maquina. We were worried he'd run off and spend it on his environmental battles. I don't know if you noticed that the condition was a late addition to the will?'

I nodded. 'I saw it was in a codicil.'

'We added it recently, when Maquina reappeared and got interested in the Akaht again. They have a choice. They make Maquina resign as chief or they get nothing. He's hardly served them well over the past twenty years, going off and fighting other people's battles, and he may well be in prison for the next twenty.'

I turned to leave, and he put a hand gently on my arm.

I pulled away.

'Please,' he said. 'I really need access to Lincoln's server. Just five minutes will do. I woke up with the headache from hell, and since then the day's just got worse.'

'I'll see, but any access will be under supervision, and you'll need to show me what you're looking at.'

I messaged Koji to meet me in the kitchen.

I was making myself a herbal tea when he arrived five minutes later.

We sat at the table, the fumes of ginger and lemongrass making me feel a little better. I hadn't had a hangover this bad since I'd been a student. I really didn't think I'd drunk much.

'I want to get to the bottom of Maq's movements last night,' I said. 'And to see who else had access to the office. Can you set up the stream of the corridor outside the office from, say, ten o'clock last night through to eight this morning, so I can go through it.' My head wasn't going to thank me, but it needed to be done. And much as I trusted Koji, I needed to do this myself. Everyone in the house was a suspect.

'Sure.' He picked up his screen and flicked across it. Then frowned, and stabbed at it harder. 'There's a problem, let me try something else.' He fiddled with the screen for several minutes, then shook his head. He sighed. 'I can't see any of the streams. We've been having issues ever since the power went out with the lightning storm earlier. It seems to have screwed up the systems.'

Shit. This wasn't going to help any case against Maq. Koji and I could testify that we'd seen a stream of him entering the office with Lincoln, and heard screaming afterwards, but without the stream we risked being taken apart by a good defence lawyer.

'All of them?' I asked.

'I think so.' Koji was fiddling with the screen again. 'We've still got the door logs,' he said. 'Here we go. Starting at 22:00 last night, Lincoln's office was unlocked at 22:16, and then again at 22:59. That was when Lincoln went in with Maquina, we saw that on the stream. Then unlocked again at 23:18. After that nothing until this morning, when I went in at 07:47.' He looked up at me. 'I'll send the log over to you.'

'The stream you showed me last night. I didn't watch the whole thing, but you said the screaming stopped after a minute or so?'

'Yes, perhaps a bit more than that, but no more than three minutes in total, I'd say. Although it hardly felt short listening to it.'

'And then someone leaves the office at 23:18. So that could have been Maq, if he was the one we saw on the stream, not a ghost. He kills Lincoln, then leaves. That makes more sense.' I hadn't shared with Koji my finding of the disc in Lincoln's office. I wasn't sure where it fitted in.

'It's possible.'

'And we know the door was opened earlier, at 22:16. Could that have been Lincoln?'

'I don't see how,' said Koji. 'If that was someone going in they didn't leave before Lincoln and Maquina entered at 22:59.'

'Could it have been someone leaving? Did Lincoln go in again after the party?' I asked.

Koji looked down at the screen again. 'No. We can't tell from the door logs whether someone was entering the room or leaving. All they show is when the door was unlocked, and not whether it was from inside or outside. But we can work it out from the order of the entries. There's one at 21:28 last night, which must have been all of us going to Lincoln's office after the party. The next entry is 21:40 – so that must be all of us leaving, when Lincoln showed you to your room. I was right behind you with Rebecca and the lawyer. I know there was no one left in the room, as I was the last out. The next one is 22:16, which can't have been anyone leaving the room, because we know there was no one inside. It must mean that someone entered the office then, and was waiting for Lincoln when he and Maquina entered.'

'True,' I said. 'That means that there was a third person in the room with Lincoln and Maq – or his ghost – between 22:59 and 23:18. Someone who was there when Lincoln was murdered. We find out who that is and we've got our killer.'

Koji was looking down at his screen again, frowning.

'That can't be right,' he said.

'What do you mean?' I asked.

'Both times the door was unlocked it was with Lincoln's code. We know he can't have entered the office at 22:16, because he was outside it at 22:59. If he'd gone in and come out again there'd be another log entry between those times. And we're pretty certain he was dead by 23:18, so he can't be the one who opened the door then.'

'You said his phone unlocked the door. Could someone have used that to trigger it?' I asked.

'No. The phone was linked to his biosigns. It wouldn't have worked for anyone else at 22:16, and it definitely wouldn't have worked after he was dead.'

'So someone must have typed his code into the door,' I said.

'No one else had it,' said Koji. 'Except ...' He looked up at me.

Oh, fuck.

Was Koji thinking what I was thinking? Remembering me typing in the code to Lincoln's office earlier that morning.

'Well, it wasn't me,' I said. 'I was in my room by ten last night. Until this morning I'd forgotten I even knew Lincoln's code. Who else had it?'

'No one,' said Koji.

'What about Rebecca? Could he have done the same for her?'

'No. I set her up with her own code without waiting for Lincoln to ask me to, so she wouldn't have needed his.'

Had he misread the logs? I pulled out my phone and opened the file he'd sent me, labelled 'Office Door Log'. It contained a list of dates and times.

'How do I follow this?' I asked.

'It shows unlock times for each of the doors we monitor,' he said. 'I've only sent you the log for Lincoln's office.'

I scanned down it:

10/04/45
21:18 - LS
21:40 - LS
22:16 - LS
22:59 - LS
23:18 - LS
10/05/45
07:47 – HoS
07:48 – HoS
07:51 – LS
07:57 – LS

'HoS is you – Head of Security?' I asked.

'Yes.'

'OK. So this morning we've got you going in and finding Lincoln's body, then leaving. And three minutes later me coming back with you and using Lincoln's code to get in. And last night we've got Lincoln's code being used to unlock the door at 22:16 and 23:18, probably by the killer, and being used by Lincoln at 22:59.'

'That's right,' said Koji.

'Is it possible Lincoln walked up to the door at 22:16, but changed his mind about going in? Could his phone have triggered the lock, but then he didn't go through, so it locked again?'

'I'm not sure that's possible,' said Koji. 'But that could only explain the 22:16 entry, not the one at 23:18. Lincoln was dead by then.'

True. There was only one other explanation I could see. Rebecca had been pretty cross with Lincoln. Could she have been in the room when he died? Had her anger towards me all been a pretence?

I needed to test that theory. 'Can you go and find Ms Murray? Say I want to meet her outside Lincoln's office in ten minutes, that there's something I need her help with. I want to get some stuff first.'

Koji nodded. 'All right.'

I went back to my study. If we knew who else had access to Lincoln's code we could identify who'd killed him. Had he been more careless with it than Koji knew? Could he have given it to his lawyer? No – Kleber had been trying to get into the office all day.

He was desperate to for some reason. If he knew the code, the fact that it was a crime scene wouldn't stop him. So it had to be Rebecca.

The books were where I'd left them on the desk. I grabbed them and the folder. I needed something else, to make it look convincing, so I picked up Yahl's tactile kit as well, shoving the goggles inside a glove, and balancing it on top of the books.

Then I waited another five minutes. I wanted to make sure that Rebecca was there before me, and that she'd be anxious. On the way back down I stopped to grab another cup of tea from the kitchen.

Rebecca was waiting in the corridor outside Lincoln's office.

'What is it?' she asked. 'What do you need me for?'

She seemed more docile than the last time I'd seen her. And more nervous. No doubt at the thought of seeing Lincoln's body.

'Sorry to take you in there,' I said as I approached. 'I need your help to look for something.'

'What?'

'Hang on,' I said. I had the books and tactile kit in one hand, and the mug of tea in the other.

Rebecca looked at the steaming cup. 'Should you be taking that in there? Won't it contaminate things?'

'It's fine,' I said. 'Can you get the door? I've got my hands full.'

She turned to it and tapped the screen to bring it to life.

Yes! I was right.

She typed in a few numbers.

Nothing happened, so she tried again. Then stepped back, and gave me a puzzled look.

'My code isn't working. I've never actually tried it on Linc's office. This was his space; I never went in without him. Maybe it needs a special code or something. Or maybe Koji's locked it.'

Fuck.

She looked relieved that we couldn't get inside. That she wouldn't have to see the body.

'Don't you have Lincoln's code?' I asked.

'No. Only my own.'

Maybe she was bluffing. I still wanted to see how she reacted to the body.

'Hold these.' I handed her the books and put the tea on the floor next to the wall. She was right. It had been a prop, and I definitely shouldn't be taking it into a crime scene.

I unlocked the door and stepped inside, holding it open for her.

She didn't follow me. Instead, she took a step back down the corridor.

'I'm ... I'm sorry,' she said. 'I can't see him. What did you want me for?'

'We think maybe there was a ghost in here with Lincoln when he died. I wanted your help to see if we could find a disc anywhere.'

'You don't need me for that,' she said. 'You're looking for a white plastic disc the size of a quarter. Here, take these.'

I stepped back outside and took the books.

She dug in a pocket and handed me a disc. 'This is all they are. I'd have thought you were pretty familiar with them.'

'Thanks.'

She turned away and practically ran down the corridor.

She was right that she hadn't needed to show me what the discs looked like. That hadn't been the point of the exercise.

I'd just proved that only Lincoln and I had known his code.

And he'd been dead the last time it was used.

I left the books and the tactile kit in the corridor. I didn't want to contaminate the crime scene any more than I had already.

But there was one thing that was still nagging at me.

I went back into the office and walked over to the desk, looking again at the watch. Why had the time been changed from when I'd first seen it? Had the killer set the time, or had the hands simply got moved during Lincoln's final struggles?

Gingerly, trying to avoid touching cold flesh, I reached for the crown that adjusted the hands, to see how easily it moved. It spun freely, and the hands moved back. As they did so something twitched in the ruined folds of the jacket.

Shit! What was that? Had vermin got in and started chewing at the body?

I pulled the remains of the jacket away from the body, dried blood cracking. A black chess rook tumbled on to the desktop.

It was a strange piece, a tower with a flat roof mounted on a spiralling, twisted column. I set it upright on the desk.

The watch now read three minutes past one. I turned the crown again, moving the time further back.

Nothing.

Maybe I'd imagined the movement earlier. I ought to leave the watch as I found it, so I turned the crown the other way, to get back to four thirty. As the hands turned the rook wobbled, then went still again.

Odd. I looked at the time on the watch: one forty-five. I turned it the other way again, going backwards, more slowly this time. As I passed one forty the rook moved again, then stopped.

I pulled out my phone to check the time: one forty.

I set the watch to that time.

This time the rook moved and didn't stop. It seemed to be shrinking. The spiral column of the tower was twisting, and the tower itself was getting shorter.

And other things were happening. The queen, standing on the far side of the body, had drawn her scimitar from the sheath at her waist. She was holding it above her head.

I could hear something moving on the floor behind the desk. The knight?

Somehow the old watch that I had given Lincoln was controlling the chess set that Rebecca had built. What was going on?

I spun the time forward again. The rook and the queen froze in place.

I had to stop this, but I wasn't sure how. It seemed that when the time on the watch matched the actual time the chess pieces were programmed to move. I didn't want that happening again, particularly when I wasn't there.

I undid the strap on the watch and shoved it into my pocket.

Then I backed out of the room, eyes fixed on the chess pieces. They remained still.

37

SIX SUSPECTS

I needed to think. I was a scientist by training, and it was time to apply some logic to this investigation.

I went back to my bedroom, dumped the various props I'd taken to the office with me, and took a seat looking out at the ocean. My brain was at its quietest when I was underwater. This was the closest I could get at the moment.

I needed to organise my thoughts. I picked up a screen and drew a rough grid, four columns across, the second, third and fourth headed 'Motive', 'Means' and 'Opportunity'.

I started by writing 'Maquina' in the first row. He had more than enough motive. Distaste for what Lincoln was doing to the environment. Then throw in the fact that Lincoln had kidnapped him to eat his heart. I put a 'yes' in that column. Means? Hit him with an axe. Seemed simple enough. So that would be another 'yes'.

But was it really that simple? What was the business with the

312

chess pieces? If the chess set had something to do with Lincoln's death then it was hard to see how Maq had been involved. I added a question mark to the 'yes'.

It was the opportunity column which was most difficult for Maq. If what I'd seen on the stream outside Lincoln's office had been Maq then he'd been in the office with Lincoln at 22:59 and had the perfect opportunity to kill him. But there it all started to unravel. In two ways. First, we had found Maq the next morning in the basement, in a locked storeroom. How had he got from the basement to Lincoln's office, and then back again after killing him? Second, someone had gone into the office at 22:16 and left at 23:18, using Lincoln's code. I couldn't conceive of a circumstance in which Lincoln would have given Maq his door code.

So, a question mark in the third column for Maq. At the moment it didn't stack up.

Who next? In light of the weird business with the chess set, I wrote down 'Rebecca'. Motive? Some, although perhaps not as strong as Maq. She'd been angry with Lincoln for a variety of reasons, but did that really add up to killing him? Perhaps everything had come together last night and pushed her over the edge. So a question mark in the first column. Means? She was probably strong enough to chop open a man's chest with an axe. And if the chess set had something to do with it, then she was by far the most obvious candidate, as she had built it. Either way that was a 'yes' in the second column for Rebecca.

Opportunity? Was she the one who entered the room at 22:16, and left at 23:18, using Lincoln's codes? He had given me his code, so why not her? If she'd been faking not knowing his code then she could have been waiting in the office for him, and left once he was dead. And maybe used his codes this morning to delete the camera streams. Maybe that hadn't been a glitch caused by the storm. It made sense, so I'd call that a 'yes'. With a question mark, as she hadn't fallen for my door trick earlier, so I couldn't prove she knew Lincoln's code.

I wrote 'Kleber' in the next row. Motive? I was drawing a blank there. Lincoln was his biggest client, so why kill the golden goose? Kleber seemed pretty unpleasant and aggressive, but then so were most lawyers I'd ever met. I couldn't just assume that every trial lawyer was a closet sociopath who was prepared to commit murder. So that was a 'no'.

Means? He seemed pretty old, so less likely than Rebecca to be able to wield an axe. And I didn't see how he had anything to do with the chess set. Another 'no'. Opportunity? The same as Rebecca, really. Unless he'd had Lincoln's codes it was hard to see how he could have done it. Another 'no'.

So Kleber didn't look a likely suspect. But that was mostly because I didn't know enough about him. I couldn't eliminate him yet, so I went back and added question marks.

Who else?

What about Yahl? He probably had motive enough. He'd been cross with Lincoln over what had happened to Maq, and from what Lincoln had told me he had some history of violence. But cross enough to kill Lincoln? Doubtful. Means? No question he could have used the axe, and he'd had some involvement with the chess set. Opportunity? All the same issues as with Maq, but worse, because at least a version of Maq had been seen going into the office.

There were only two other people who had been in the house.

Koji? What would his motive be? He was fiercely loyal to the Akaht, and if Lincoln died they got Black Lake and two hundred million dollars. If Koji had had to choose between Lincoln and the Akaht, I had no doubt he'd choose his people. But had he actually known about the terms of Lincoln's will? Means? For his age Koji was as fit as anyone, and he could easily have killed Lincoln with the axe. I doubted he could have had anything to do with the chess set, though. Opportunity? All the same issues as the others. Yes, he had access to Lincoln's office, but there was no evidence he'd gone near it when Lincoln was killed.

I was avoiding the obvious, though. The most compelling piece of evidence was that someone had let themselves into the office at 22:16, and left at 23:18, using Lincoln's codes. Reluctantly, I added 'Ella' to the first column.

Motive? Control of eight billion dollars. As Kleber had pointed out, most people would regard that as more than sufficient motive. So viewed objectively, a reluctant 'yes'. Means? Could I have killed Lincoln with a swing of an axe? Almost certainly. I spent my life in and out of the North Pacific, wrestling with its currents. I was lean and tough from my time outdoors. Although where did the chess pieces come into it? Because of them I added a question mark.

Opportunity? Someone had entered Lincoln's office at 22:16 the previous night using his code. It hadn't been Lincoln, and I had the code. Someone had left the office at 23:18 using the same code. And by then Lincoln was tied to a desk with his heart at his side. So that definitely wasn't him. A third reluctant 'yes'.

I looked down at the table I had produced:

	Motive	Means	Opportunity
Maquina	Y	Y ?	?
Rebecca	?	Y	Y ?
Kleber	N ?	N ?	N ?
Yahl	?	Y	?
Koji	?	Y	?
Ella	Y	Y ?	Y

There was only one person with a 'yes' to each. The single question mark gave me little comfort.

Fuck.

Except I knew I hadn't done it. As I'd told Rebecca, I'd been in my room when Lincoln died. This was madness.

So it came down to Maq or Rebecca. And of the two Rebecca now seemed the more likely. Particularly after the weird incident with the chess set.

I checked the time: 14:30. Somehow I was going to have to turn this into a report. And somehow I was going to have to avoid making it apparent that to any independent observer I was the most obvious suspect.

Then a message from Koji popped up on my phone: *Could you meet me in the kitchen ASAP. Important development.*

On my way, I replied.

What now?

38

THE KANGAROO COURT

Koji wasn't alone in the kitchen.

There were five of them sitting in a U-shape at one end of the table. Rebecca and Maq were on the far side, their backs to the ocean. Koji and Yahl opposite them. Kleber was between them, at the head of the table.

Yahl was in my usual seat.

'What's Maq doing here?' I said. 'Who let him out?'

'I did,' said Koji. 'We need to discuss things with all of us here.'

'We'll discuss things when I say we need to,' I said. 'I'm conducting this investigation. I represent the law here.'

'This isn't the OK Corral,' scoffed Kleber. 'We are all concerned that you have a conflict of interest.'

'Of course I do,' I said. 'The body of my ex-fiancé is lying dead downstairs with his heart ripped out. In normal circumstances there's no way I'd be allowed anywhere near the case.

But nothing here is normal. I can promise you that the moment Victoria Homicide get here I'll step aside.'

'That's not the conflict that concerns us,' said Kleber. He indicated the single chair at the foot of the table, opposite him. 'Please, sit down.'

'Why?' I asked.

'You may be the law in name,' said Kleber. 'However, we are entirely out of contact with anyone in authority. There are five of us and one of you, and you aren't even armed.'

'Are you threatening me?'

Kleber gestured to the chair again. 'Of course not, *Constable*. But as sensible people surely we can all sit down and have a conversation? Let's do that.'

I wasn't sure how they'd react if I walked out. I knew that Yahl at least was armed, but would he try to stop me? I looked to Koji for help, but he was staring down at his lap.

I still didn't know which one of them had killed Lincoln. Kleber's job was argument and reason. Perhaps it did make sense to talk things through with them.

Unless they had started to put together the pieces of the jigsaw in the same way I had.

Reluctantly I sat, uncomfortable in the wrong seat. 'What is it that you want to discuss?'

'I'll start,' said Kleber. 'It seems to us that you are facing a difficulty in your investigation. Realistically one of us in this room must have killed Lincoln.' He looked from left to right, then back at me. 'That's an uncomfortable thing to say, but it must be true. I know it wasn't me. But, of course, we can all say that. Maquina – Mr Diaz here – is the most obvious suspect.'

Maq straightened up, as though about to interrupt. Kleber held up a hand towards him.

'However,' he continued, 'there is a real difficulty with Maquina being the killer. Koji has explained where Maquina was found this morning – the wrong side of a locked door – and he's also shown us the door logs for Lincoln's office. Someone else was in the office when Lincoln went in last night, and was there when he was killed. Who? I had no reason to want Lincoln dead – quite the opposite. I wasn't in his office last night, and I've never had his door code. The same is true of Koji and Yahl here. And what motive did they have?'

'Two hundred million dollars,' I interjected. 'We both know the Akaht will get that on Lincoln's death, plus Black Lake. Provided, of course, that Maq resigns as chief.'

I was watching Koji and Yahl as I said this. They didn't react to the mention of two hundred million dollars, so they'd known about it. But Koji's heard jerked up and he looked across at Yahl when I mentioned the condition. The recent codicil seemed to be news to them.

Kleber waved a hand dismissively. 'Look around you. The Akaht were doing very nicely out of Lincoln while he remained alive, so it doesn't seem much of a motive. Who else might have wanted him dead? Rebecca perhaps? She certainly had a good motive after the shabby way Lincoln treated her last night. She was humiliated. But again we have a problem.' He paused and looked across at Rebecca. 'The locked door. How did Rebecca get into the office, or out again, last night? She was puzzled by the little game you played downstairs just now, trying to get her to unlock the door to Lincoln's office. But now it makes sense, and it was quite clever actually. You were hoping that she'd show that she knew Lincoln's codes. But she didn't.'

Rebecca glared at me, shaking her head.

'So that brings us to the one person we know did have Lincoln's codes,' Kleber said. 'You, Dr Manning. You could have let yourself into Lincoln's office at 22:16 last night, been waiting for him, and let yourself out again at 23:18.'

'I—' I began.

He held up a hand. 'Wait, let me show you one more thing first, then you can respond.' He turned to his left.

Koji reached under the table and produced a white plastic box. Then he turned it round, placing it on top. It took me a moment to realise what it was.

AppleBot. I hadn't seen him in years.

'What's this got to do with anything?' I asked.

'A good question,' said Kleber. 'Once we realised that we had the same suspicions, Koji and I searched your bedroom. We found this hidden in a wardrobe.'

'You had no right to search my room,' I said. 'Koji shouldn't have let you in.'

Koji was looking down at his lap again. 'I'm sorry,' he muttered. 'Mr Kleber insisted, and I didn't think we'd find anything.'

'There wasn't anything to find,' I said. 'I didn't put it there.'

Kleber jumped back in. 'You say that having control of eight billion dollars isn't a motive for murder. Personally I disagree, but let's give you the benefit of the doubt on that one. Maybe this is the real motive.'

I stared. 'What? You think I killed Lincoln to get hold of

a cheap plastic toy that cost me two hundred dollars in a junk shop in Montreal? You're crazy.'

'No,' said Kleber.

Koji fiddled around with the back of the AppleBot until it started to move.

'*No!*' I shouted. 'Don't do that.' I remembered the last time I'd seen this. The rooftop with Lincoln, on the day he proposed – or rather, it proposed for him. The last thing I wanted to do now was relive that moment.

It started walking across the table towards me, swinging from side to side on its jerky legs.

Then it stopped in front of me, swaying as it dropped to one knee.

'No!'

I shut my eyes. I didn't want to watch this. I'd managed to put my memories of Lincoln to the back of my mind while I investigated his death. I didn't want that calm disturbed.

'*Ella … will you marry me?*' said the AppleBot in its tinny voice.

I heard a whining noise as the bot's arm swung around. Then a click as the little suitcase opened. Then silence.

'Would you care to explain that?' Kleber asked.

I opened my eyes.

My engagement ring was nestled inside the suitcase, resting on a red velvet liner.

All five of them were staring at me. Yahl and Kleber were impassive. I struggled to read Koji – was that disappointment? Rebecca was shaking her head. I couldn't tell if it was pity or hatred I could see in her eyes. Maq was sitting back, head tilted, smiling slightly.

'I can see why you didn't want us to know what the robot was hiding,' said Kleber. 'I seem to recall, when you got engaged, that the media speculated that that ring was worth over one million dollars. No doubt you regretted giving it back to Mr Shan when you walked out on him last year. It's not a bad haul for someone whose net worth is' – he produced a document from on his lap – '$6,187.23.' So they had found my credit report.

'Where did you get that?' I asked.

He ignored my question. 'We found one other thing of interest.' He nodded to Koji again, who reached behind him and pulled my red pantsuit out of a bag.

'Can you confirm that this was the suit you were wearing to the party last night?' asked Kleber.

I nodded.

'Care to look at the sleeves?'

Koji passed it to me.

'Note the stains,' said Kleber. 'It's the sort of pattern you might get if you attacked someone with an axe.'

I turned it over. It was true that the sleeves and the front of the suit were spattered with dark stains. But they could have been anything.

'How the fuck would I know what those are?' I said. 'This is nuts! I arrived here in a storm, and stuff spilled everywhere when the satellite dish went down. I'm sure your Fifth Avenue suit is looking worse for wear this morning. Besides, we don't even know Lincoln was killed with the axe. There was some weird crap going on with the chess set earlier.'

Kleber seemed uninterested in that, maybe because it didn't fit his theory. 'Even without the jacket stains you've got to

322

admit that it's not looking good, is it, Constable? Put on your Stetson, look around you, and ask which one of us in this room you'd arrest?' He grinned. 'Actually, do they even let you wear the hat, or do they save that for the *real* Mounties?'

He sat back, a satisfied smile on his face, prosecuting counsel having finished his closing submissions. And I had to admit that they sounded pretty persuasive to me.

But this was ridiculous. However things looked, they were wrong.

'It's just not right,' I said. 'I can't explain it all, but that's not what happened. Nothing went on between Lincoln and me last night. He kissed me goodnight – that's what you saw. But I pushed him away, I rejected him. I didn't see him again – at least not alive. And whatever you think, I didn't want the engagement ring. I knew what it was worth when I gave it back to him last year.'

'I've gone along with this charade of you investigating my client's death,' said Kleber. 'I've let you play your part, thinking you couldn't make too much of a mess of it. But now I'm beginning to think that maybe you're not just incompetent when it comes to homicide investigation. Perhaps you're deliberately doing a bad job to make it harder for the real detectives when they get here.' He looked at the others on either side of him. 'Maybe you'd like to tell everyone how you got your job with the Mounties. Why it was that you left the navy.'

How the fuck did he know that? No one knew that. Not even the press had discovered it when I'd been going out with Lincoln.

'When you got engaged to my client I did some digging,' he

said. 'I have a lot of contacts. No one was prepared to speak on the record, but I got the story.'

'That's got nothing to do with Lincoln's death,' I said.

'Do you want to tell it, or shall I?'

I took a deep breath. 'I agreed to resign from the navy because I punched some entitled dickhead on the nose. He deserved it.'

'A dickhead who, unfortunately for you, was a rear admiral in the United States Navy,' said Kleber.

'As I said, he deserved it. If you want the full story, I'd been seconded by the Canadian Navy to the US Navy's Marine Mammal Program, and we were doing a training exercise off San Diego. A bunch of senior officers had come on board to observe for the day, and my dolphins were demonstrating how to locate mines. By evening we'd got them all back except one. Sometimes they'd get distracted and be late, and needed some encouragement. So I got suited up, and was ready to dive in, when I got a message that the admiral was pulling us out, abandoning the last dolphin. I couldn't believe it. I marched up to the bridge in my scuba gear, and explained that the dolphin was muzzled for the demonstration. We did that to stop them getting distracted by foraging when they were working. But it meant that if we didn't get her back she would slowly starve to death. The admiral just shrugged and said he needed to get to port for a dinner. I pleaded with him, but he grabbed my arm to push me away. So I punched him. I accept that with hindsight it was ill-judged, but I don't like being touched, and he deserved it.'

'And that was the end of your naval career,' said Kleber. 'Which died along with your dolphin.'

'I was given the option of resigning my commission, to

keep it quiet. The admiral didn't want it known that he'd been floored by a girl, apparently. And the US Navy didn't want to damage its relations with Canada.'

'So you did a quiet deal with the Canadian Navy,' said Kleber, 'who agreed to bury the incident so you could get a job up here. They probably didn't think that there was much damage you could do in this backwater.'

'All of that's true,' I said, 'but it's got nothing to do with Lincoln's murder.'

'I'm not sure I agree,' said Kleber. 'What was it the navy report concluded: "She has a propensity for violence?" Was that it?'

'I don't recall,' I said. 'I was the innocent party. And it's got nothing to do with this. It did say in mitigation that I had an unusual empathy for animals.'

'And none for humans,' said Kleber. 'That's right, isn't it? No one has seen you shed a single tear for Lincoln since you found him dead.'

I stayed silent. They wouldn't understand. I couldn't bring Lincoln back to life by crying, but I was going to honour his memory by finding out who had killed him.

'Let me suggest what happened,' said Kleber, leaning forward again, staring at me. 'We all saw how Lincoln seemed more interested in you than Rebecca last night. Why did he choose to escort you to your bedroom instead of her? Probably so that he could set up a meeting with you later in the one place where he knew Rebecca could never get in – his office. But, conveniently, you could. So you go there to wait, slipping in at 22:16, using Lincoln's code. He knows that Maquina is locked in the basement, so no need to worry about finding him till morning. He doesn't want to find him quite yet, because he's arranged to meet you, so he tells Koji to go to bed. Koji was puzzled by that, but it all makes sense if Lincoln has something more enticing on offer from you. Quite why he fires up a ghost of Maquina and takes him to the office we can only speculate. I know you three were close when younger. Maybe you and Lincoln fancied a threesome to relive your teenage years. Maybe that journalist last night who asked about ghost lovers wasn't so far from the mark after all.'

'For fuck's sake,' I said, 'that never happened. This is complete fantasy. I wasn't even looking to get back with Lincoln. I told you, I rejected him.'

'Really?' said Maq. 'He kissed you goodnight, told you he loved you, said he'd give up running Orcus to have you back—'

'He what?' Rebecca interrupted. 'He said that? The bastard! Why—'

Kleber talked over her. 'I'm sure he didn't mean it – it's certainly news to me. But none of this matters. Whatever the reason, she was waiting inside the office for him. Things started getting interesting and she and Maquina – the ghost Maquina – tied Lincoln to the desk.' He glanced across at Koji. 'I understand that Lincoln had quite an extensive ... ah, set of toys in his bedroom.'

Koji looked down at his lap, not meeting my eye.

I shrugged. I've never been interested in other people's sex lives, and I didn't see why they should be interested in mine.

'Perhaps Lincoln liked being the sub,' said Kleber. 'Then he provoked you in some way. We all know he could be a complete

326

prick. He made all of us mad enough to want to kill him at some point. And we know you have quite a temper when provoked. You were still slightly drunk, emotional, so you grabbed the axe from the wall, took a swing, and that was it. Then you decided to try to cover it up by putting the raven mask over his face, to make it look like some Akaht ceremony. You switched off the ghost Maquina, cleaned up as best you could, and went to bed. Either Lincoln had brought the robot and ring to show you, to tempt you back, or you stopped in to get them out of the safe on the way to your room. You knew it was all about to go down, and you wanted to have some reward for what you'd put up with over the years from Lincoln.'

'This is all bullshit,' I said. 'We get a forensics team in here and they'll show you that whatever's on my suit isn't blood, and certainly not Lincoln's blood. None of what you said will fit with the evidence.'

'Really?' asked Kleber. 'You've been in and out of that office all day. Taking over the investigation so you could screw it up was a touch of genius. I'll bet your DNA is all over the axe, and you'll just say it happened during your investigations.'

'You're wrong,' I protested. 'Besides, as I said, he may not even have been killed with the axe. There's something going on with the chess set. It seems to be controlled by his watch. Look.' I dug in my pocket and pulled out the Seiko Chariot I'd removed earlier, dropping it on the desk. 'When I changed the time the chess pieces moved.'

'Wasn't Lincoln wearing that?' said Rebecca.

'Yes, I had to remove it,' I said.

'And this is exactly what I mean,' said Kleber. 'What the hell were you doing removing something from the victim's body? Do you have any idea how to conduct a murder investigation? Or was this something else you fancied having, like the ring, so you just stuck it in your pocket? Another thing you gave to him and wanted back.' He shook his head. 'Christ, what a mess.'

'That's not what happened,' I said. 'I had absolutely nothing to do with Lincoln's death. I said goodnight to him and went to sleep. You all saw that. The next thing I remember is waking up this morning.'

They all stared at me in silence. Disbelieving. Even Koji, whom I'd have thought might support me.

But help came from an unexpected quarter.

Maq glanced at Kleber, then sat forward. 'She may be telling the truth,' he said.

Five heads turned to him in surprise, including mine.

'What?' said Kleber.

'I'm not saying Ella didn't kill Lincoln,' said Maq. 'I'm saying she might be telling the truth about not remembering it. Earlier today Ella came to see me, to ask about an ancient Akaht ceremony. She said that Linc had been reading a book about it, a book which Koji found in her room.' He looked across, and Koji passed the book down to him. 'It's called *The Tsonoqua Ceremony of the Akaht: Primitive Rohypnol*? I assume we're all familiar with Rohypnol. It's not as popular as it used to be, but it was once the date rape drug of choice. Slip it into someone's drink at the bar, and the next thing they know they're waking up naked in the morning thinking they drank too much and made some bad choices. It's not an entirely fair comparison. The Tsonoqua Ceremony was more of a drug-induced orgy, with everyone being consenting adults, but the details don't really matter. It's the fact that it involved an hallucinatory drink that caused memory loss. Why was Lincoln reading about it? We'd all heard things about him that people were afraid to say in public, too worried of being sued.'

He looked across at Kleber. The lawyer nodded. 'There was that story in the press about an actress a few years ago. It got hushed up with a payment and a non-disclosure agreement. Nothing was ever proved, though.'

'So how about this?' said Maquina. 'The scenario is pretty much as you said, but with a slight twist. Lincoln knows that Ella isn't just going to jump into bed with him again, after all that's gone on between them. He knows she'll have some respect for Rebecca here. Maybe she's telling the truth when she says she rejected him initially. But we know when Lincoln set his mind on something he got it. So he decides to stack the odds in his favour, and he conjures up this Tsonoqua brew. Who knows, perhaps he even has one of their skull cups hidden away somewhere. It wouldn't surprise me.'

My eyes must have widened at that point, or I gave something away, because Maq paused. 'I'm right: he does, doesn't he? That's the reason you were asking me about it earlier.'

'Possibly,' I answered reluctantly. 'Lincoln's heart was next to his body in what looks like a cup made from half a human skull. It looked old.'

'I remember that,' said Koji. 'It was four or five years ago, Lincoln told me he was doing some research into Akaht traditions, and asked if I could get hold of a Tsonoqua skull cup. I wasn't even sure what it was, but I asked the elders, and they eventually found one. I never saw it again, though, so I don't know what he did with it.'

'See, it fits together perfectly,' Maq said. 'Earlier in the evening, when he was alive, it obviously didn't contain Lincoln's heart. So he brews the Tsonoqua tea and gives it to Ella in the skull. Maybe he leaves it for her in the office, so she's had it by the time he gets there with the ghost. Then if things go well, great. If they don't he can still have his bit of fun and Ella here will be none the wiser. After that things pan out pretty much as you said, Paul. Lincoln acts like a dick, or Ella discovers she's being drugged, or maybe both. Maybe he boasts to her about it. She decides to get her revenge before she passes out, then staggers back to her room. This morning she recalls nothing – other than waking up with a very sore head – and starts playing the part of Constable Manning. How does that sound?'

Rebecca was staring at me, blinking. They were all staring at me.

'It's possible,' Rebecca said. 'Surely it could be proved one way or another with a blood test?'

'That won't work,' I said, before I could stop myself. Then I realised I was buying into this madness of theirs. But the presence of the Tsonoqua skull had shaken me.

'What do you mean?' Rebecca asked.

It was too late to go back, and could hardly make things worse. 'The actress who accused Linc of assault, she was tested for drugs, and nothing showed up. Presumably because this Tsonoqua thing isn't a recognised drug.' I found the article I'd read earlier on my phone, and passed it over to Rebecca.

She read it, then looked up at me. 'How did you feel when

you woke up? How was your head? Did you remember anything?' She sounded concerned, which was surprising given that she seemed to believe I'd killed her boyfriend, the man she'd wanted for most of her adult life.

'I remember going to bed,' I said. 'I was surprised how well I'd slept after everything, but I just thought I was tired. I felt a bit fuzzy-headed when I woke, but not too bad. I assumed it was the alcohol, although I didn't think I'd actually had much to drink. And then it seemed to get worse. I had a splitting headache by mid-morning, and had to take some painkillers. I've not felt great all day.'

'Give me the pantsuit,' said Maq, holding out his hand.

'Why?' I asked.

'Just do it.'

I passed it down the table. He sniffed at it, then scraped his fingernails across the cloth. He rubbed his thumb and fingers together, and a delicate powder fell on to the surface of the table. Green and white, flecked with yellow.

'It's part of the Tsonoqua Ceremony,' Maq said. 'If you look in the book it says the man sprinkles a mixture of dandelion and chickweed flowers over the woman. That's what this is. At some point last night Ella had it sprinkled over her. It's hard to see why Lincoln bothered with that bit, but maybe he did believe in some of that mystical crap. This confirms El took part in the Tsonoqua Ceremony.'

'How would this play out in court?' Rebecca asked Kleber. 'Is it a defence?'

'Hard to say.' He stroked his chin. 'If I was prosecuting I'd be saying none of this mattered – it was done intentionally, to get the ring. But if the jury could be persuaded to swallow the story that Lincoln drugged her, it might work. Automatism can be a defence. The only witness who knows what happened is dead. It doesn't help that he was tied to the desk, helpless, and cutting out the heart wouldn't go down very well with a jury.' He shook his head. 'It would be a toss-up. It might work.'

'But I don't remember anything,' I said weakly.

'That doesn't mean it didn't happen,' said Kleber.

He sat back. Case closed.

1805

39

THE WOLF
EATS TIME

It was the howling of the wolf that woke Eustee. She tried to shut it out, to go back to sleep, but as she rolled over she realised something was wrong. Her new husband – the white captain – was gone.

The wolf howled again, as though calling to her.

She sat up and pulled aside the curtain that offered some slight privacy in the longhouse. It was still dark, the fire low, the others sleeping.

She stood, sliding on her shoes, and picked her way to the entrance.

The black wolf was sitting outside, staring at her. She recognised it at once. There were no black wolves on the island. This was the spirit that had brought the captain to them.

It turned away and trotted slowly towards the treeline, turning once to ensure that she was following.

It traced a twisting course between the dark cedars until it stopped and turned to her, barely visible apart from its orange

335

eyes. There was a dark shape in the grass at its feet. The wolf put its head down, and nuzzled at what was hidden in the shadows.

Eustee took only a moment to realise that the shape was a man; and barely any longer to realise that it was the captain. She could tell by his distinctive clothing.

He was lying on his back, sightless eyes staring up at the stars through the branches. He wasn't moving, or breathing. Eustee ran a hand over his skull and felt bones shift under the skin.

He was dead.

She sat back on her heels.

What to do?

She looked around for the wolf, but it had disappeared into the darkness.

If she was found with the captain's body would they think that she had killed him? Would anyone even care? He might be Hamatsa but he was not one of them.

She wasn't troubled by his death. She had been with him for only a month. True, he was kinder than the other one, Jewitt, who had insisted that she learn his language in the year they had been together. Who had also taught her to fear. And who had eventually rejected her.

She should go to the chief and tell him that the white captain was dead. Would he insist that Jewitt take her back? Or would he return her to her own people? Neither choice appealed.

She heard a rustling in the trees behind her. The wolf was back. It was carrying something in its mouth, which it dropped in front of her.

She picked it up, and then recoiled. She knew what this was.

A blackened, dried arm, skin shrivelled, fingers curled tight. She had seen it before in the longhouse. It was used in the Hamatsa Ceremony. The initiates would take bites from the arm, swallow some dried flesh. She knew that she should not be touching it.

The wolf whined and pushed it towards her.

She shifted back on her heels, shaking her head.

The wolf looked down at the arm, then back at her, licking its lips and snarling to show its teeth. It picked up the arm and offered it to her again.

'No!' She hit out, knocking the arm from the wolf's mouth.

It cocked its head, golden eyes staring at her, as though trying to make her understand. Then it put a paw on the arm and used its teeth to tear a strip of dried flesh away. It offered this to her. She hesitated. Not because the thought of eating human flesh troubled her. But because only Hamatsa initiates were meant to do so. And all Hamatsa initiates were male.

But the wolf was a spirit. A god.

What harm could it do?

She reached out and took the strip of meat, placing it in her mouth. It was tough and chewy. Dry. But, in fairness, she had eaten worse.

As she swallowed she felt a power pass through her. A breeze rattled the branches overhead.

The wolf stepped closer, fixing her with its eyes. It placed a paw on the inside of her right wrist.

A sound seemed to echo through the forest: '*Kuwitap*' – open the door.

And the wolf ate time.

337

2045

40

REVELATION

I chose to retain what little dignity I had left by agreeing to stay in my room until the homicide detectives arrived from Victoria. Koji and Yahl escorted me down, and Koji told me, apologetically, that the only code that would work on my door was his.

I'd thought he was looking bad earlier, after finding Lincoln's body, but he seemed to have got worse since. Even I could read the pain in his eyes. 'I'm sorry, Ella,' he said. 'I'm sorry it had to come to this.'

He seemed to want to say more, but Yahl grabbed him by the elbow and hustled him out of the room. Koji gave me a last look as the door closed.

So much for him helping me.

I sat in one of the leather armchairs, staring out unseeing at the ocean. The weather had eased somewhat, the beating of the wind against the windows having died down. I checked the time: 15:12. They'd left me my phone. Without external communication there wasn't much I could do with it, and who was I going to call for help anyway?

Hopefully by the morning someone could get to Bamfield and make contact with Victoria, get some proper detectives up to sort out the mess. Surely once we got a forensics team into Lincoln's office they would be able to show that I'd had nothing to do with his death?

But would it all be too late by then? Having convinced themselves that I'd killed Lincoln, the others would be off guard. The real killer could be going round destroying evidence while I was locked away. Or worse. And I was still no closer to knowing who the killer was.

I was trying to piece together the last twenty-four hours of my life. My memory felt disjointed. I remembered going to bed, but then nothing until morning. I'd thought at the time I'd slept unusually well. Was it more than that? Was it possible that Maq was right? I hadn't had that much to drink, but my headache seemed to have got worse as the day went on. Was there more than just alcohol working its way out of my system?

And if Maq was right, was it my fault? Kleber had said that I had a propensity for violence and a lack of empathy. If it had been me with Linc when he died it had been me that had done it, even if I couldn't remember anything now.

But how did the chess set fit into this? I hadn't allowed it to run its course, but clearly the pieces had been programmed to do something when the actual time matched that set on the watch. That couldn't have been anything to do with me even if I'd been stoned on Tsonoqua tea. Programming the chess set indicated premeditation. I wished now that I'd let them play out whatever it was that they were meant to do. Then I could have understood exactly what role, if any, they had in Lincoln's murder.

Was there anything more I could do to try to show that the others' suspicions – and my fears – were false?

They hadn't left me much to work with. Most of what I'd found during my investigation was gone. They had taken the books and the folder about me, as well as the copy of Lincoln's will. All I had left was the *Pride of Whitby* nameplate and Yahl's tactile kit which I'd thrown on the bed earlier.

I picked up the nameplate and tossed it from hand to hand, enjoying the feel of its weight. There was something about it that troubled me, but I couldn't quite grasp what.

I set it down and picked up my phone. What could I do with that? The internal network was still working, for what it was worth. Lincoln's code was universal, so I could still access the server. But what good was that to me?

I found my way to the streams that Koji and I had looked at earlier. As he had said, everything was gone. Where else could I look? The door lock logs had been working. Could I get anything from those?

Leaving aside the chess set, the one part of Kleber's theory that didn't make much sense was why Lincoln and Maq's ghost had entered the office together at 22:59. True, I'd found the disc from Maq's ghost on the office floor. Kleber had suggested we'd planned a threesome with the ghost. That was not only distasteful, but unthinkable. Lincoln had been jealous of Maq's relationship with me when we were teenagers. There was no chance he'd have wanted to share me with Maq. There had to be another explanation.

Koji had only sent me part of the door logs for Lincoln's office. Maybe if I looked at a wider range I might learn something more, see who had gone in and out earlier in the day. I pulled up the logs.

From what Koji had told me, they only showed when the door had been unlocked, so I could expect to see a matched pair of entries. The first for someone going into the office, the second for when they left. That seemed generally to hold true.

The door had been unlocked at 21:28 on 4 October, using Lincoln's 'LS' code, and then again twelve minutes later, at 21:40. That first one was the group of us entering with Lincoln after the party, and the second one was us leaving to go to bed. Just before the kiss.

Again, there were matched entries at 07:47 and 07:48 on 5 October, using Koji's code. That was Koji finding Lincoln's body, then rushing off to call me. That was followed by entries at 07:51 and 07:57, using Lincoln's code: me entering and leaving the office.

The only break in the pattern was Lincoln's code being used at 22:59 on 4 October, when he entered with Maq. There was no matching exit. Which made sense if Maq was a ghost and was switched off remotely. Whoever had been controlling him hadn't needed to use the door. Nor had Lincoln, because he was dead. But how had Lincoln died during that period if Maq was a ghost who was unable to hurt him?

Then it struck me that there were two things that didn't make any sense.

First, the logs showed the 'HoS' code being used at 09:46 on 5 October, and again at 09:51. What had Koji been doing going into the office two hours after we had found Lincoln's body, staying for five minutes, and then leaving? He knew it was off-limits. Or someone using Koji's code. Could Kleber have got hold of it? He'd been desperate to get into the office, and five minutes might be about right for finding what files or documents he was after.

Second, what had happened to the log records showing that Lincoln's code had been used to unlock his office door at 22:16 and 23:18 the previous evening? There should have been records for '22:16, LS' and '23:18, LS', but they were gone. I flicked back to the door log file that Koji had sent me in the kitchen. Both entries remained there.

And those two entries were the entire reason the others thought that I'd been in the office with Lincoln, and killed him. It was because no one else had Lincoln's codes that it must have been me, whether I remembered it or not. Take away those entries and I was tucked up in bed asleep at that time.

How could they be in the document Koji had sent me but not in the underlying logs on the Manor's server? Nothing else looked odd in the logs. Everything else fitted with what I knew.

There was only one possible answer. The door log file that Koji had shown me in the kitchen was false. It had been produced to convince everyone, including me, that I had been in Lincoln's office when he died.

I sat back. Stunned. A wave of relief rushing through me.

Relief followed quickly by anger. I was being set up, and I'd almost fallen for it.

So who was behind this?

Kleber had led the charge, but had that just been the lawyer in him following the evidence? Which, as I'd been forced to admit, was compelling.

No. Much as I didn't like the guy, it didn't feel like him.

It was someone who'd been able to falsify the entries in the door log file. Who'd been able to delete the camera streams from outside Lincoln's office. Because if the streams had been working the door logs were irrelevant. The streams would have shown who'd gone in and out. Someone who knew where to find the AppleBot and had the opportunity to plant it in my room. And someone who knew enough about Akaht traditions to be able to give Maq the idea that I'd killed Lincoln while drugged and then forgotten about it.

Someone who the logs showed had gone back into Lincoln's office again that morning, despite my orders to keep it sealed. Planting evidence for me to find? Or removing it?

I'd thought before that the door log file was the most compelling evidence as to who killed Lincoln. It still was, just not in the way that I'd expected.

The person who had created the fake file must be Lincoln's killer. And there was only one possible candidate for that.

Koji.

1805

41

EXILE

It was to Captain Ross's advantage that Jewitt valued his privacy and had secured an alcove in the top corner of the longhouse, as far away from others as it was possible to be.

Ross carefully slid through the curtain that shielded the alcove, and stood over the sleeping man. He was lying on his back, snoring loudly.

Perfect.

Ross still wasn't certain what had happened the day before. At first he had thought he must have dreamed that Jewitt had followed him into the forest and killed him. But Eustee had had the same dream. And the black wolf had reappeared.

Whatever had happened in the forest, Ross was certain that Jewitt would try again. He intended to act first.

He slipped the knife from his pocket and leaned over the sleeping man. The chest was too hard. The knife might break on bone. It needed one swift blow to the throat. He recalled how Seaman Cooper had screamed and gurgled. That needed to be avoided.

Ross raised his arm to strike.

As his arm fell someone seized him round the throat from behind. Another hand batted the knife away, and it clattered into the darkness.

As Jewitt sat up the curtain was torn to the ground.

Ross struggled and was twisted round.

To face Maquina.

The chief's face was grim. 'Why do you try to kill my metal-worker?' he asked.

'He killed ... he tried to kill me!' Ross shouted.

'I did not!' protested Jewitt, who was standing now beside his bed.

'He won't remember,' said Ross. 'Ask Eustee. She was there, and so was the wolf.'

Maquina looked from Ross to Jewitt. 'It would be easiest to have you both killed, to avoid this trouble; and the girl too. But I let Jewitt live for a reason, he has value to me. You' – he looked the captain up and down – 'you have no value.'

Ross tensed against the man who held him, ready to try to fight his way out. He didn't intend to meekly let them butcher him.

'But you are Hamatsa,' Maquina continued. 'And the spirit of the wolf saved you for a reason. And if I kill Upquesta's daughter we will have war. No. You have till sunrise to leave the village. If you are found here after that my warriors will be free to kill you. And take the girl if she wants to go with you.'

'Where will we go?' protested Ross. 'It's winter, I have no food, no shelter. You are just killing us more slowly.'

'Would you prefer to die quickly?' asked Maquina. 'Stay here till sunrise and you will.'

2045

42

ESCAPE

The knowledge that Koji had been lying to me was perplexing.

Perplexing and devastating.

Koji-Na. Uncle Koji. He had been my rock. The one person I trusted.

And he'd screwed me over.

When my mother had abandoned me and gone back to her life in Toronto, Koji had been there for me. As my father had become increasingly distant, and his trips away grown ever longer, Koji had looked after me. He had become the parent that they were not.

Yet not only had he lied to me, he must also have killed Lincoln. Otherwise why try to blame me?

I sat on the edge of the bed, staring out at the rain beating against the window, trying to make sense of it.

What could possibly have driven Koji to this?

I knew that he valued the Akaht above all else. Lincoln's

speech at the party about loyalty could have been written for Koji. He wouldn't have jumped off a cliff for Lincoln, but he might have for the Akaht.

I needed to clear my head. Going back over the past wasn't helping.

I leaned forward, putting the palms of my hands against the window, closing my eyes. I could feel my connection to the water running down the glass, to the ocean below, to the creatures within it.

To Scarlett in her tank.

You can tell what an octopus is thinking. It can't lie. Its colour tells you its mood. Black, sulky. Red, excited. White, calm. I pictured Scarlett's arms on the other side of the glass, held up to mine. White. Calm spreading through the glass to the palms of my hands, up my arms, throughout my body.

I stayed like that for a minute, then sat back blinking.

I knew what I had to do.

The realisation that Koji must be behind Lincoln's death, and the attempt to frame me, led me to two other realisations.

First, I must be at risk myself. Koji had never been as close to Lincoln as to me, at least not when we'd been growing up, but they had worked together for almost twenty years. For Koji to have been willing to sacrifice Lincoln, and in such brutal fashion, the stakes must be high. Koji had cleverly dangled a superficially compelling case against me before Kleber and Maq, and they had pieced it together, but that was all it was – superficial. I couldn't believe it would stand up to careful scrutiny. But if by the time the homicide detectives got to Black Lake I was dead, perhaps having left some suitable final confession, any investigation would be cursory. Was I being paranoid? Or was the plan for my bedroom window to be found open, and my body on the rocks below?

Second, Maq was in equal danger, and I'd been the one to put him there. I'd seen Koji's reaction, and the looks that he and Yahl had exchanged, when I'd mentioned the codicil to the will. And I'd never heard of an Akaht chief resigning. Maq had always hated the burden of being chief, so surely he'd have resigned long ago if he could. Which meant that Maq's death was worth over two hundred million dollars to the Akaht. If that was what had led them to kill Lincoln – and I could think of nothing else – then it would also lead them to kill Maq.

I needed to do two things: get out of my room, and speak to Maq.

How to achieve them?

The windows opened, but it was a sheer drop of a hundred metres or more to the rocks below. Tying the bedsheets together and lowering myself down would merely bring about a faster death. And going up was no better. The windows were smooth, and wet for good measure. I wasn't going to be climbing free.

The door was solid oak, and barely moved when I pulled on the handle. It opened inwards, so there was no chance of kicking it down. Not that I thought it possible anyway.

The only other option was to wait for them to come and fight them off. Which sounded hopeless. I wasn't armed, and I knew that Yahl was. There was also Lincoln's Glock in the safe, which Koji knew about.

What did I have to defend myself?

My gaze passed over the bed.

The *Whitby* nameplate wasn't sharp enough to be of much use. But figuring it might be better than nothing if it came to a fight, I shoved it into a pocket.

Yahl's gloves and googles from the tactile kit were even more useless.

I lifted the corner of the mattress to see if there were wooden slats underneath that could be removed, but the base was solid.

As I dropped the mattress back into place one of the gloves slid off the bed, and I caught it one-handed.

And a thought struck me.

Hang on. That might work.

I grabbed the gloves and sat down in the armchair. I unfolded the googles and put them on, together with the gloves.

Was I still connected through the house network?

'*Noah Diaz*' appeared in green on the lens. '*Enable?*'

Yes!

There was a moment of disorientation as I emerged at a strange angle. Then I realised that I – or rather Maq's ghost – was standing on top of the desk in my study where I'd left the disc from the office.

I jumped down, looked left, then right, up and down, and wiggled my fingers in front of me. I had to admire Lincoln's vision, to have created something so immersive. It truly felt as though I was no longer in my bedroom, but standing two levels up in the middle of the study.

I didn't know how long I had.

Although I felt that I ought to be moving furtively, avoiding being seen, in fact the opposite was the case. I needed to act as though I was Maq. Which might work as long as I didn't bump into the *real* Maq.

The first thing I needed was a weapon, and there was only one place I knew to find one in the Manor.

I took the stairs down one level, then along the corridor, and cautiously opened the door to the kitchen. It was empty. I opened the cereal cupboard, pushed the boxes aside, and typed in Lincoln's code. The panel at the back of the cupboard slid down. I grabbed the box containing the Glock, and checked that it was loaded. The ghost couldn't actually shoot anyone, but a warning shot might be necessary.

I closed the safe, then rooted round in the drawers. Even Lincoln had one filled with the usual sort of accumulated junk, including two flashlights. I didn't know how long they'd been there, but they turned on. A vague plan was forming, so I put them in my pocket.

I found an old backpack in one of the cupboards, which I filled with some bread, cheese and fruit, and a couple of flasks of water. I wasn't sure how long we might need to wait.

The corridor outside was empty, and I took the stairs down another level to the guest rooms. When I reached my door I pondered trying to kick it open. It would be easier from the outside. But there was no guarantee the ghost could do that, and anyway the noise would draw attention. Better if I waited for them to come to me.

Just down the corridor from my room was a storage closet where the cleaning staff kept their materials, spare sheets and towels. I opened the door and slipped inside, leaving it fractionally ajar so that I could see down the corridor. I stowed the backpack and settled the ghost down to wait.

Inside the bedroom I slipped the googles up my head for a moment, to give my tired eyes a break. Then I retreated to the bathroom, perching on the edge of the bath. I didn't want to be in view when someone opened the door. If they did. What if I was wrong about all this? I could be waiting for ever.

I pulled the googles down and scanned the corridor again. Nothing. How much longer were they going to be? I needed to speak to Maq. What if they went to him first?

My musings were interrupted by movement in the corridor. Someone was heading my way. I checked the time: 16:27. Things were about to heat up.

It was Yahl. He was walking quickly, and had his right hand buried in his jacket pocket. I was pretty sure that I knew what he had in there.

Inside the room I reached out with one hand and turned on the shower. I pushed the bathroom door almost shut.

Outside the room I eased open the storeroom door slightly. Yahl's back was to me as he keyed in the code to my room.

The Glock 19 nestled comfortably in my hand.

From within the bathroom I heard my bedroom door click open.

From the corridor I watched as Yahl stepped inside. Then I took two quick strides across, following him into the bedroom. I made sure that one foot held the door open.

Yahl paused, then evidently heard the shower running, and relaxed.

He took a step towards the bathroom.

Then froze as Maq's ghost lightly touched the muzzle of the Glock to the back of his neck and whispered: 'Don't move, don't turn round, drop the gun or I fire.'

For a moment he seemed about to resist, his arm tensed, and he drew the gun from his pocket.

'Who is that?' he asked.

'Quiet,' the ghost hissed in his ear. 'Drop it now – last chance.'

If he resisted I was in big trouble. Maq's ghost wouldn't actually be able to hurt him. And if he moved the ghost couldn't follow. I needed it to hold the door open. That had been the whole point of this exercise. If I let it shut there was no guarantee I could get Yahl to unlock it again.

After a brief hesitation Yahl's shoulders sagged, and he dropped the gun on the floor.

I was still in danger, though. If I emerged from the bathroom wearing the tactile kit Yahl would realise what was going on. And he was closer to both guns than I was.

'Lie on the bed, face down,' said the ghost.

For a moment Yahl refused to move, but he had made his decision when he dropped the gun. He stepped forward and lowered himself on to the bed, burying his face in the duvet.

I dashed from the bathroom, pushing the goggles away from my eyes, and grabbed Yahl's gun from the floor. Then I snatched the Glock from the ghost, which had frozen in place when I removed the goggles.

Yahl half turned, and saw me. I raised the Glock. 'Stay right there.'

I wondered whether to stop and try to question him, but I feared we could be getting more company at any moment. Koji might be on his way. Or Yahl might be meant to take me to him, in which case we would be missed very soon. And Koji had an entire Akaht village to draw on. I just had Maq's ghost, which couldn't actually hurt anyone.

I stepped out into the corridor, pulling the goggles down and making the ghost follow me. I couldn't lock the door as Yahl had the code to it. I considered wrecking the mechanism by shooting it, but that might not work, and the noise would presumably bring Koji running. I had a better plan. I shut the door, and then made the ghost hold the handle from the outside, while bracing its legs on either side of the doorframe. Then I snatched off the goggles and gloves, freezing it in place. It might not hold Yahl for long, but it should be enough for my purposes.

I stepped across to the laundry closet, picking up the backpack that the ghost had stowed there, then ran two doors further down the corridor, and used Lincoln's code to unlock it.

Maq was dozing in an armchair. He sat up sharply when he saw me, his eyes widening as they went to the gun in my hand. 'El, what the—' he began.

'We don't have time to discuss this,' I said. 'I've just trapped Yahl in my room. He was coming to shoot me, and you were next on the list. Come with me and I'll explain later. Or stay here and die.'

He hesitated, and I waved the gun at him.

'Now!' I shouted.

He made his decision, and jumped to his feet.

'Get to the elevator,' I said.

I hesitated over whether to give Maq Yahl's gun. It might be useful if they came after us, but it felt safer if I was the only one armed. Instead, I ran to the window, opened it, and threw the gun out. Then I followed Maq down the corridor.

The elevator doors were opening as I got there, Maq stepping inside. 'Level Eight,' I shouted. As the doors closed I could hear feet pounding on the nearby stairwell. Had Yahl been cleverer than I'd expected, and called Koji instead of wasting time trying to break out?

We started descending.

Maq turned to me. 'What is all this?'

'I'll explain soon. We need to get to somewhere safe first, though.'

'Where are we going?' he asked.

'The one place no one can follow us.'

The elevator had stopped, and the doors opened.

The basement of the Manor was very different from the glamour of the upper floors. The walls were bare concrete, with stark overhead lighting that flicked on as we passed. It was cold, the smell of damp hanging in the air.

We walked down a long corridor with metal doors off to the left. Eventually we came to the one I wanted, marked *Ventilation*. I opened it and gestured Maq through.

I had no doubt Koji would be able to track where we had gone, which doors we had opened, but that wouldn't matter soon.

We were in a long narrow room full of machinery, with the sound of air being driven through fans.

'Where are we going?' Maq asked again.

'Where we'll be safe,' I said. 'Back to the mines.'

43

THE MINES

I'd like to say that it was good to be back in my childhood haunts, but it wasn't.

Twenty years earlier I'd never have come down into the mines after so much rain. The tunnel walls were dripping and I could hear the distant roar of water. I knew from past experience that there were several underground streams, and some of the caverns filled up in the rainy season.

We had no choice, though. Last time Maq and I had been fleeing for our lives when we left the mines. This time we were doing the same, but heading back in.

I was troubled that we only had one light source each, breaking my first rule of caving. Flashlights had improved a lot in the last twenty years, and we wouldn't need to keep swapping out battery packs, but it still made me nervous.

We were walking quickly. Although we'd entered the mines in an unusual place I knew roughly where we were, and I was pretty comfortable it would all come back to me as we got deeper in.

'Why did Linc connect his house to the mines?' asked Maq.

He hadn't spoken since leaving the ventilation room, and it seemed an odd first question, but perhaps he was avoiding the more difficult ones.

'It was all part of the eco-resort thing,' I said. 'It meant he could draw cool air from underground for his air conditioning and get the house certified as zero-energy. Ignoring the fact that they'd had to tunnel through a hundred metres of bedrock to get here, and that he owned fifteen oil rigs. You know what Linc was like, it was all about image. He could boast to his friends that the whole of the Black Lake resort was carbon neutral.'

Maq snorted. 'I know we don't speak ill of the dead, but what a piece of shit. I've given up half my life for the environment, risked prison to make people see what matters. And here Lincoln was with his billions, someone who could really make a difference, and all he did was pretend.'

I didn't bother to answer. I was more interested in whether we were being followed.

'You know he—' Maq began.

I held up a hand. 'Quiet. We can talk once we're deeper into the mines. Noise travels down here, even when it's muffled by the water. If you must speak keep it down. I'd like to know if there's anyone behind us.'

Maq seemed about to protest but I waved the gun in his direction and he shut up.

I was glad when we got to the first of the tunnel junctions. Every junction gave anyone pursuing us a fifty-fifty shot of losing us, with the odds getting better for us each time.

I didn't actually recognise where we were so I chose the one that descended. It was a gamble. The lower tunnels cut through bedrock, so were less likely to have collapsed. But there was a greater risk of them being flooded. If we had to backtrack we could run headlong into any pursuers.

After almost an hour of walking I was beginning to feel more confident. We'd gone through three more junctions, and the sound of water was receding.

'Let's stop for a moment,' I said softly. 'Turn off your light and see if anyone is behind us.'

We stood in silence in the darkness for several minutes. I was just about to say something to Maq, fairly sure that we were alone, when I heard the soft scrape of a shoe on rock further up the tunnel from the way we'd come. I raised the gun. I found it hard to believe that anyone could have tracked us that far, particularly without showing any light.

Then I realised they hadn't.

I switched on my flashlight and the beam caught Maq ten metres up the tunnel, one hand trailing along the wall.

He froze.

'What the fuck do you think you're doing?' I said.

'What do you expect?' he answered. 'I only came with you this far because you had a gun on me. Why would I want to stay here with you?'

'Because if you don't you'll be dead, one way or another. Either Koji and Yahl will catch you and kill you or you'll get lost and never find your way out. Even I'm not sure where we are at the moment. Come back.'

He turned, and walked slowly back to me.

'I thought we were hiding,' he said.

'I'm pretty sure we're alone. We need to carry on.'

'Now's the time to explain,' said Maq. 'Why do you think Koji and Yahl are going to try and kill me.'

'Because they're the ones who killed Linc.'

'Seriously? What makes you think that?'

'I'll explain when we stop. First, though, we need to get further into the mines, to places I know, where I'm sure they can't find us.'

'How do I know you haven't brought me down here to kill me?'

'If you prefer I can point the gun at you again to keep you moving.'

He shook his head, and started walking.

Thirty minutes on I was sure I knew where we were. We were back in the passages I'd usually come to from the entrance by the beach. Still, I made us press on until the tunnel opened out into a small cavern, with rocks where we could sit.

'We'll stop here for a while,' I said.

'You need to tell me what's going on,' said Maq. 'Why should I believe that Koji and Yahl killed Lincoln? Or that they wanted to kill me? Do you really think that you've solved Lincoln's murder?'

'We eat first, then we talk,' I said, opening the backpack to dig out the food that the ghost had packed.

I tore off some bread and cheese and passed them to Maq, together with an apple and a flask of water.

We ate in silence.

When we were done I said: 'So, what is it you want to know?'

'What makes you think Koji and Yahl killed Lincoln?' he asked.

'It's the only thing that makes sense,' I said. 'Everyone seemed to have a motive to kill Linc. But I know now that Koji was the one who set me up, and Yahl came to visit me with a gun just before I broke you out. That proves he and Koji were working together. I'm guessing the plan wasn't to shoot me unless they had to. Maybe they hoped to chuck me out of the window, or off the roof. You were all convinced I'd killed Lincoln, and with me having killed myself through grief there would have been an easy solution offered. Two deaths solved in one.'

'Why would they have come after me?'

'Koji knew that the Akaht would get two hundred million when Linc died. When I told you all that neither he nor Yahl reacted. But when I said that it was a condition of the will that you aren't chief any more, Koji flinched. They didn't know that bit. I guess Lincoln was hoping that you'd be made to resign by the Akaht. But I don't think resignation is what Koji has in mind.'

'You can't resign as chief. What the hell's going on? First Lincoln wants to kill me for my heart. And now you tell me Koji wants to kill me to get Lincoln's money. What did I do to either of them?'

'Koji knew it was the only way for the Akaht to get their cash. You have to die in the next thirty days. I guess it wouldn't have just been me feeling remorse and jumping off the roof. Maybe both of us, or maybe a murder-suicide. They've been pretty imaginative so far, so I'm sure they'd have come up with something.'

'Why are you sure it was Koji? Why would he have done this to you of all people?'

'What was the one bit of evidence that made everyone think I was to blame for Lincoln's death?' I asked. 'Hell, it almost convinced me too. Koji's door log file which showed someone using Lincoln's code to get into the office at 22:16, and then leaving after the killing at 23:18. You all thought it could only be me because no one else had Lincoln's code. But that file doesn't match the underlying data. It's a fake. Looking back, I think he probably also deleted the camera streams. He must have known I'd want to look at all of them, and used the thunderstorm this morning to pretend they had glitched. That way I couldn't check who'd gone in or out of the office.'

'Surely it would have been easier to just change the underlying logs. How did he know you wouldn't check?'

'He knew that I trusted him. Which was stupid of me. My guess is he couldn't amend the underlying data so he'd probably have deleted it later, the same as the camera streams. But he could hardly do that at the same time as he gave me the door log file. He'd have done it before the police arrived and then all that would have been left were his fake entries which proved my guilt.'

'So they murdered Lincoln for the money,' Maq said.

'With Lincoln dead Black Lake belongs to the Akaht for ever. We both know he was fickle. Now they never have to worry about him finding some shiny new toy to play with and letting this place die.'

'This is going to tear the Akaht apart,' said Maq.

'It doesn't have to. It's your chance to step up and be the chief they want. They need you.'

'First we've got to get out of here,' said Maq. 'How are you planning to do that?'

'I haven't thought that far yet. Koji can't just hide at the Manor for ever, though. Once the storm is past people will want to know what happened. Either Koji calls the police and tries to pin Lincoln's murder on me or he makes a run for it. Either way, we wait till it's safe to come out. I'm happy enough to take my chances with the police now that I know the truth.'

Maq looked around. 'And what do we do in the meantime? This place is freezing and half-flooded.'

'I know somewhere better. It's a bit of a hike, but it's higher up and usually dry, with a couple of ledges we can lie on.'

We packed up, and trudged on.

The cavern wasn't as cosy as I'd hoped, but it was at least dry. We finished off the last of the food, then sat in silence, lost in our thoughts. My mind drifted back to the last time I'd been in the mines, twenty years before. I'd been with Maq then too, although he'd still been Noah. And we'd had Kun with us. And only two of us had left the mines.

Then Maq spoke: 'What time is it? I feel as though we've been walking for hours.'

I reached for my pocket – then stopped myself. 'I don't want to run my phone down. If the flashlights die it's all we've got left. Last time I checked it was some time after seven. We ought to turn off our lights as we've no idea how long they'd been sitting in Lincoln's drawer.'

I did so and put mine in my pocket. Maq did the same and suddenly my world shrank to nothing.

I doubted I would get to sleep, and now that the immediate danger had passed my mind was starting to wander.

'What's gone wrong since you and I were last down here?' I asked. 'Everyone seems to want to kill someone else. Lincoln wanted to kill you. Koji and Yahl killed Lincoln, and then tried to kill us. It seems like you and I are the only two left.'

'Maybe it's not so surprising. We Akaht were born out of murder after all.'

'What do you mean?'

He paused. 'I suppose there's no harm in telling you now. You know half the story already. We're going to be down here a while, so tell you what – I'll trade you a story. In return I want to know why you dumped Linc.'

I considered that. 'All right, but you go first.'

'You remember when we found the lifeboat and you asked me what happened to the seventh man, the one whose skeleton wasn't in the cave. He's actually the most important part of the story. He was the captain of the *Pride of Whitby*. Of the seven men who escaped the ship most died quickly in the cave, but three of them were trapped and slowly starving. They only had one food source left.'

Maq let that thought hang in the air.

'You mean the bodies?' I said.

'Exactly. It's not clear precisely what happened. By the end the captain was the only survivor and he was pretty hazy on the details. He said they drew lots to see who would die. Two of them killed the third and ate him. But only the captain escaped from the cave. He said he was visited by a giant black wolf, which led him to safety, and he ended up in the Mowachaht village.'

'The Mowachaht, not the Akaht?' I asked.

'There were no Akaht then,' Maq said. 'The chief of the Mowachaht was Maquina – the original Maquina, whose name I took. The captain had thought that he would be reviled, that they might even put him to death. But Maquina recognised him for what he was, a man who had been visited by a spirit and eaten of the flesh of men. He was Hamatsa. He even married one of their women, the daughter of a neighbouring chief.'

'So where did the Akaht come from?'

'The captain invented them. Maquina already had an Englishman living with him, a man called John Jewitt, who resented the arrival of the captain. No one knows exactly what happened, but Jewitt got the captain expelled from the village. A few of the Mowachaht went with him, including his bride, and they settled here in Pachena Bay. There were too few of them to survive, so whenever an English or Spanish ship visited to trade with the Mowachaht the captain would go and meet them. There were always a few sailors, and sometimes families, tired of the harsh conditions on board. In the summer at least Vancouver Island would seem like a paradise in comparison. So he tempted foreigners to desert. Not all stayed, and many died, but that's how the Akaht were founded.'

'So you're telling me that the Akaht aren't really a First Nations band at all? They're basically a bunch of colonists who've adopted local customs.'

'I'd prefer to say that we've assimilated. It's true, though, that the blood of the Mowachaht runs pretty thinly through our veins these days. Have you never wondered why we, among all the First Nations bands, cling so strongly to their customs?

Look at our names. Lincoln Shan – did he ever tell you why he was called that?'

'He was proud of it,' I said. 'He said Lincoln was a corruption of Hlit-kun, the goose. And Shan was a killer whale. That's why he called his company Orcus.'

'And Koji means wolf. Yahl is the raven. We preserved those names, but the other bands laugh at us behind our backs. Look at the First Nations Council of Elders: Bob, Lisa, Brian, Cole. You won't find any wild animals amongst them.'

'So why were you called Noah?' I asked.

'I never asked, but I guess my parents decided to go with the European side of their heritage.' He laughed. 'But look, even then I ended up going back to an Akaht name – Maquina. This pretence draws us all in. We've clung to the traditions because we need them for our identity, but they aren't really ours at all. Of course, we do have one ability that is unique to us, that the captain acquired when he became Hamatsa: the power to call the wolf. Over time the Akaht realised that those who were descended from the captain and who were Hamatsa had inherited that power.'

'So that's what you meant by the Akaht being born out of murder,' I said. 'Your founder killed his own crew and ate them. Maybe it's no surprise that killing runs through you all so strongly.'

'Maybe. Or maybe it's just that deep down Lincoln and Koji and Yahl are bad people.' He paused. 'Anyway, that's my story, now it's your turn. Why did you dump Linc? What did he do that was so terrible?'

I sighed. 'He didn't do anything. It was me.'

2044

44

DISENGAGEMENT

Municipal regulations limit the height of skyscrapers in Vancouver to two hundred metres. In typical fashion Lincoln had managed to avoid that rule by building just outside the city limits, on Iona Island, so that from his penthouse he could look down on everyone else.

I preferred the view he had over Black Lake. There were fewer people.

For once I was buzzing. Usually I was the one trying to decide how early we could leave a party without looking rude, dragging Lincoln home as soon as I could. But this time it had been the other way round. This time my demons had stayed away.

I'd had fun. I'd been charming and witty. I'd floated from one group to the next, not fearing what they were thinking of me or that they might reject me. I'd found the eye of the storm and stayed within it all evening.

And I'd no idea why. I didn't know what it was that had set me free that night. Settled my brain. I doubted I'd recapture it again in a hurry.

It had helped having Lincoln there. He acted like a magnet, drawing people to him, taking attention away from me. I could flit around the periphery, observing, choosing who to speak to.

Yet he hadn't been himself. Sure, he'd gone through the motions, effortlessly turned on the charm, but he'd seemed distracted. He'd wanted to leave early, saying that we needed to get up to Black Lake in the morning.

Eventually I'd let him drag me from my unaccustomed place on the dance floor and into a car.

Still, I hadn't wanted the evening to end. On our return to the penthouse I'd insisted on a final bottle of champagne in the swing chair overlooking the lights of the city. I'd kicked off my heels and curled up next to him, head resting on his shoulder.

For once I was content.

He was stroking my hair with his free hand. 'You were on good form tonight, El.'

'I felt free,' I said. 'Tonight I wasn't trying to understand people, or worrying if they were thinking I was odd. I just let go and it was such fun. And you're part of it. Having you there makes it easier.'

He said nothing, just breathed out heavily.

I turned to look at him. 'What is it? You've been in a funny mood all night.'

'You actually noticed? Sometimes I think you aren't interested in what I do or what I'm thinking, as long as I'm there when you need me.'

My heart sank. Were we about to have one of those difficult conversations where Lincoln tried to get us to share our feelings? How to get through this as quickly as possible?

'You know I care about you,' I said. 'You're the one who's married to your company.'

'That's not what I mean, and don't try to deflect this on to me. I'm not saying we don't see each other enough, but when you're here I feel as though it's only part of you. I've known you longer than almost anyone but I still feel as though you're keeping something back. I'd thought things would change now we're engaged, but nothing has.'

'I don't understand,' I said. 'I'm not hiding anything. I treat you as I'd like you to treat me.'

'That's exactly it!' Lincoln said fiercely. 'You behave to me as you'd like me to behave to you, and you think that's OK. But it's not, because we're different.' He shifted away, turning side on to me. 'I'd like to know what's here.' He touched his hand to the side of my head, then let it rest just above my heart. 'And here. Sometimes I feel I don't know you at all and I'm not sure I can live like that.'

Fuck!

How to shut this down?

'I don't get it,' I said. 'I don't need to know every emotion you feel, and I don't want to burden you with mine.'

'Why should it be a burden? That's what couples do. They share their lives and their feelings. You don't seem to want to, and there's a part of you that you want to keep locked up for ever.'

I shook my head. 'There's nothing I'm hiding, Linc. I don't know what more there is that you want me to tell you.'

He sighed and shook his head. 'We're getting nowhere and I'm tired, and I don't think you'll ever change. I'm going to bed.'

I let him go, sadness mixed with frustration.

*

So that was it.

There was no dramatic scene in which I threw Lincoln's engagement ring in his face. No angry words were exchanged. Contrary to what everyone thought, I didn't dump Lincoln because he cheated on me. In fairness to him, he never tried to correct that view.

Instead it was all over in a couple of minutes.

At least in my mind. It was all suddenly very clear.

I sat toying with my empty champagne glass as I went back over our conversation. Eventually, when I was sure he must be asleep, I ordered a car.

I took off my engagement ring and left it on a side table. He'd find it in the morning.

I got his birthday present from my bag and left it next to the ring. Would he still want it? I didn't know anyone else who might like a Seiko Chariot watch, and it might provide him with some comfort.

I hesitated at the door.

Logically it was the only sensible decision. True, Lincoln could be good for me. He helped me find that place of calm that was so hard to inhabit for long. He made me more than just content sometimes. Happy even.

But what was I giving in return? Not enough.

He wanted an emotional bond, and he thought I was holding something back from him.

He might get that with someone else, but not with me. If that was what he needed he deserved the chance to find it.

I wasn't holding anything back, because in truth I knew there was nothing there. Whatever it was that he was looking for I just didn't have.

It was better for him to know that now, before I hurt him more.

2045

45

KUN

19:15, 5 OCTOBER 2045, BLACK LAKE MINES

'That's not what I'd expected at all,' said Maq. 'I thought he'd been cheating on you. I think everyone thought that.'

'He didn't seem to care about correcting that impression. Maybe he preferred it to the truth. But I know I made the right decision that night. I was never going to make Linc happy because I was taking what I needed but couldn't give him what he wanted.'

'I don't think he saw it that way,' said Maq. 'We know he wanted you back.'

I sighed. Would Lincoln still have been alive if I'd agreed? But it was pointless worrying about the past.

We settled into silence in the darkness. It was surprisingly peaceful. After all that we'd been through it was good to have some calm.

I shifted to a more comfortable position and something in my pocket dug into my leg. I'd forgotten about the nameplate that I'd stuck in there as a potential weapon, hours ago now. I pulled it out, contemplating throwing it away. Perhaps it was best left underground where we had found it. But I hesitated. It was the only thing that had survived our visit to the cave all those years ago.

Which I realised didn't make sense. Something had been bothering me about the nameplate ever since I'd found it in Lincoln's office.

Suddenly I knew what it was. If Maq had told me the truth back then, how could I be holding the nameplate?

I stopped. I shook my head. That couldn't be right. But it was.

I stared through the darkness to where I knew Maq was sitting. Unsuspecting.

'Maq,' I called.

'Yeah? What is it? Can you hear someone?'

I ignored his questions. I pulled out my flashlight again and flicked it on, shining it over the nameplate. 'How did you get this?'

'You were there. I found it in the cave, took it back and cleaned it up. I told you before, Lincoln must have got it in my things after I left Black Lake. Why does any of that matter now?'

'Don't lie to me, Maq,' I said. I shook my head. 'You bastard.'

'What's wrong, El?' His flashlight came on, shining towards me. 'Are you all right?'

'Perhaps I should just leave you in the mines, after all,' I said.

'What? Why?' He looked around. 'What's going on with you?'

'It isn't far,' I said. 'Stay here if you like. Or come with me. I'm not sure I care any more.'

I headed back up the tunnel we'd come down, but at the first junction took a right, towards the older parts of the mines.

I could hear Maq stumbling along behind me. 'El, wait!' he called once.

I ignored him.

I stopped when I came to a pile of rock half blocking the tunnel. I shone my flashlight at the ceiling. Part of it had fallen in.

Twenty years earlier.

This was the place.

Maq caught up with me. He was out of breath, panting.

'Talk to me, El,' he said. 'What's got into you?'

'You lied to me, Maq.'

'What ... what about?'

'Last time we were down here. You lied to me. Don't deny it.'

'Twenty years ago?' he said. It was odd, but he almost sounded relieved at the accusation.

'Don't pretend it didn't happen.'

'I've no idea what you're talking about,' he said. 'I seem to recall that last time we were down here I saved your life.'

'So you say.'

'What do you mean? I've always been the one helping you out, while you try to push me away. Like this afternoon, when the others were blaming you for Lincoln's death, I tried to help.'

'You didn't really believe any of that Tsonoqua crap, did you?' I asked.

He didn't respond.

'Look,' I said, 'if you're going to deny it, you can either give me a hand or watch. Your choice.'

I found a ledge on the wall to rest my flashlight, and started pulling some of the bigger rocks off the top of the pile. Eventually Maq joined me.

'Is this meant to keep us warm?' he asked.

'Don't you remember this place?'

'No,' Maquina said. 'Should I?'

This time I was the one who didn't answer.

By the time we found him I was sweating. At first I thought it was just another damp rock. Then I noticed the teeth. A row of pointed premolars. As we uncovered more the high cheekbones and empty eye socket became visible, and his short terrier nose.

'Enough,' said Maq. He walked away and squatted next to the wall, in the shadows, breathing hard. 'I see where we are now, and you've made your point.'

'Why did you do it?' I asked. 'Why did you pretend that you'd saved my life by turning back time?'

He answered my question with another. 'How did you know?'

I reached into my pocket and threw him the nameplate. 'This was the first clue. I've had a lot of time sitting upstairs to think about things and this kept bothering me. When we got back here I realised why. What was troubling me wasn't how Linc had ended up with it, but how you had it in the first place. You told me that you'd turned back time after the rockfall, that you'd saved my life, and we'd ended up back before finding the cave. You said that I remembered the cave as though it was real because I'd died, which made some sort of sense at the time.

When I asked why I still had a bump on my head you made up some crap about dropping me when the earthquake happened again. If my brain hadn't been rattled I'd never have believed that.

'If you'd really turned back time to save me then our discovery of the cave never happened, and it existed only in our memories. Linc's first words to us when we crawled out of the mine were that we stank like dead whales. Which was true. We stank of rotten seaweed from uncovering the lifeboat. But if you'd turned back time then in Lincoln's reality we'd never found the lifeboat. And the nameplate is the clincher. How could Lincoln have it in his drawer if in his reality we'd never gone to the cave? It would have vanished from your backpack when you turned back time, and only we would have remembered. You told me you never went back to the cave. So it was impossible for him to have the nameplate if what you'd told me was true.'

I looked down at the skeleton at my feet. 'This just confirms it. Kun didn't run away. Why would he? He always stayed close to the light. He didn't run away because he was dead. When you stood here, paralysed with fear, Kun waited for you. He was killed by the rockfall that knocked me out. And he never came back to life again because you didn't turn back time at all. You just dragged me round unconscious for a while hoping I'd wake up to save you.'

I crouched down, touching Kun lightly on the forehead. 'Just leave me alone.'

This time at least I could say goodbye. It was better to know that he hadn't died running round lost in the mines, wondering why I didn't come back. At least it had been quick. I wished

I'd known then, though. I started stacking rocks back over him again. He was long gone, and this was as good a place as any for him to be buried.

When I'd finished I went over to where Maq was sitting. I slumped down opposite him. 'Why did you lie to me? What was the point?'

'You were being a complete bitch,' Maq said. 'You told me I was pathetic. Linc had called me your lapdog and I realised he was right. The only reason I ever came into the mines was to be with you, but you still thought I was a coward. Lincoln wouldn't even come in and you liked him more than me. I wanted you to owe me something, so I said it without thinking, and I could hardly tell you the truth later, could I?' He paused. 'Not that it made any fucking difference. Even when you thought I'd saved your life you didn't want me, you still ended up with Lincoln.'

'What a crappy thing to do to someone.'

He shrugged. 'Linc did much worse. He's been destroying our planet for twenty years and you forgave him. And despite the way you treated him he still wanted you. The two of you deserved each other.'

I didn't have an answer to that. This discussion seemed a waste of time. I knew that I was on my own again. Pretty much everyone I'd ever thought was a friend had betrayed me.

Maq looked around. 'God, I hate this place. What time is it?'

I didn't answer him because something he'd said had triggered a thought.

'What did you mean?' I asked. 'That he still wanted me?'

'You know he was still crazy about you, even with Rebecca

on the scene. There's no one else he'd have given up his company for.'

'What?'

'What he told you last night, that he'd dump Rebecca, step down from Orcus and travel the world with you. He wouldn't have done that for anyone else.'

'True,' I muttered.

But my mind was spinning. Maq had said that before when defending me to the others in the kitchen. With everything else going on I'd missed the significance then. He had repeated what Lincoln had said to me the previous night, when we'd kissed outside my bedroom door. But no one else had been close enough to hear. And I hadn't told anyone.

'What time is it?' he asked again.

'For fuck's sake, Maq,' I said, 'why are you so fussed about the time? We'll be here all night.'

It was easy to lose track of time in the mines, but why did he care so much?

Time.

I knew I hadn't told anyone what Linc had said to me.

Time.

Not that I remembered.

'How did you know what Linc said?' I asked.

He looked at me blankly. 'You must have told me. Or Rebecca did.'

'No she didn't. When you said it earlier in the kitchen she was shocked. She called him a bastard. And I know I didn't tell anyone. So how did you know?'

'Maybe Kleber told me. Why does it matter so much?'

'Kleber said he didn't know, and he couldn't have. There was no one else there last night, it was just Linc and me.'

What was going on? My world felt as though it was shifting again.

I'd woken feeling a bit rough, but halfway through the morning it had turned into a splitting headache. Hangovers usually got better, not worse.

And Maq knew things I'd never told anyone. Things that he simply couldn't have known.

Not in this reality at least.

I slid my hand into the pocket containing the gun.

Maq. Who'd lied to me twenty years before. Who kept asking me what the time was.

I scrambled to my feet, pulling the gun from my pocket and pointing it at him.

'What the fuck, El! I told you I was sorry. You're not going to shoot me for a lie I told you twenty years ago.'

'It's not that lie that matters,' I said. 'What have you bastards been doing to me? Twenty years ago you lied to me about turning back time when you hadn't. This time you've done it and not told me, haven't you?'

He stared at me. Silent.

'There's only two possibilities,' I said. 'Either Lincoln told you what he said to me last night or I did. But he wouldn't have told anyone and I know I didn't. And you were locked in the basement until he died so it's impossible for you to have overheard it.'

He stayed silent.

'I'm right, aren't I?' I said. 'There's another timeline in which

I told you – or someone. Admit it or you'll never get out of the mines alive. Without me you're stuck here.'

Maq shrugged. 'Actually, I'm not. I don't need you to get out.' He pulled up the sleeve of his right arm, exposing the black wolf tattoo. 'It doesn't really matter what I admit or deny, does it? Whatever I tell you now, you'll just forget it all again.'

Was he bluffing? If he still had his power then he didn't need me to escape. Worse. I'd be back to where I was six hours earlier with no memory of anything. Where had I been? In the kitchen, facing down the others? Or locked in my room? It didn't really matter. Everyone else would be convinced of my guilt, and this time I was sure Maq wouldn't delay in sending Yahl to my room. There would be no chance for me to find the truth and use Maq's ghost to rescue myself.

'What time is it?' Maq asked again.

Suddenly it was starting to make sense.

I glanced at my phone. 'It's just gone nine thirty.'

He smiled. 'That late? I didn't realise we'd been down here so long. Good.' He paused. 'Before we do this, do you want to know what really happened to Lincoln?'

46

THE SECOND MURDER

Maquina walked down the corridor towards Lincoln's office, Lincoln a pace behind him.

'Good to have you back, Maq,' he said. 'I told you I'd get you out, and I did.'

'Thanks,' said Maquina over his shoulder. 'It was neatly done.'

The door clicked open as they approached, and Lincoln gestured for Maquina to go first.

'Have a seat,' he said, pointing to one of the comfortable leather chairs in front of the desk. He reached into a drawer and produced two glasses, then opened the bottle he'd been carrying. 'Glenmorangie Pride 1974. The most expensive malt they've ever produced. You were the one guest at the party who never got a drink so join me to celebrate your release.' He poured two generous measures, then walked round the desk and handed one to Maquina. Lincoln sat in the other armchair, removed his cufflinks, and rolled up his sleeves. 'It's been a long night, and although it didn't go quite as planned, I'm sure we can still make this work.'

Maquina took a drink. 'Why are you wearing that battered old watch. It hardly suits your image.'

'El gave it to me last year. It's a Seiko Chariot, as worn by Steve Jobs.'

'That must have cost her.'

'It's not the original,' said Lincoln. 'I tried to buy that a few years ago. Apple had got it at auction for $252,000. I offered them a million and they refused to sell, saying that they had "ethical concerns" about my owning it. They're so up themselves. I guess this is probably the closest I'll ever get to it. There aren't many of them left, so it'll still have cost Ella a fair chunk of cash.' He looked down at his wrist admiringly. 'I've modified it a bit.'

'Sorry I didn't manage to bring you a present,' said Maquina. 'The gift shop in the jail has a limited range.' He sipped his drink.

'Not to worry,' said Lincoln. 'You did, you just don't know it yet. A bit more difficult to get the wrapping off, but a present nonetheless.'

'What do you mean?'

'I haven't been entirely honest with you about my intentions. I didn't actually bring you here to help you escape.'

'Really?'

'You know that I summoned the wolf twenty years ago. I earned the money to start Orcus, and the rest is history. Turning forty, though, it makes you think. Steve Jobs died at fifty-six. I've always got Yahl or Koji or Vekla or one of the others on hand, plenty of people who can do for me what I did for the duke all those years ago – the day I met Rebecca. Even so, I'd feel safer if I could summon the wolf myself. When we use our power we say "*Kuwitap*" – "open the door" – because we're opening a door to the past. Why can we only open that door once? What if we could walk through as many times as we wanted?'

'We know that's impossible,' said Maquina.

'Is it, though? I've been doing a lot of research, talking to the Hamatsa and the Akaht elders. Early on it came as a shock to people to know that the power had gone after one use, and they were looking for ways to get it back. I came across a legend that there is a way, and that it's been used once, and it gave one Hamatsa the power to unwind time as often as he wanted. But the price was too high for anyone else to try.'

He paused, and Maquina obliged him. 'What was the price?'

'It involves a sacrifice,' said Lincoln. 'You have to pluck the beating heart from the chest of the Akaht chief and eat it.'

'Really?' said Maquina. He seemed surprisingly untroubled. 'You'd get blood all over your expensive carpet. Cream was a poor colour choice if you're going to indulge in that kind of thing.'

Lincoln frowned but said nothing. He walked over to where Maquina sat, taking the empty glass from his hand, then went back behind the desk, replacing the bottle and glasses in the drawer. He withdrew a rough-shaped grey bowl, which he cradled in his hands.

'My old Tsonoqua skull,' he said. 'I thought it fitting to put it to a new use today.' He placed the skull carefully on the desk. 'I'm afraid your glass had a little something extra. You should be beginning to feel the effects already. It's a crime to ruin such a great malt with the addition of Baclofen, but I was worried you might fight back otherwise. It's a muscle relaxant, and you'll be feeling dizzy, unable to stand properly, loss of coordination. It really shouldn't be mixed with alcohol, but that won't be what kills you.'

Lincoln paused, and looked down at his wrist. He fiddled with the watch for a moment, changing the time. 'I'd thought we were going to be doing this later, after all the guests had gone. But now we've started we do need to get on with things.'

He walked across to the chessboard on the side of the room and picked up three pieces: the black queen, a white knight and a black rook. He placed them in a line on the edge of the desk.

Maquina inclined his head. 'I'm not sure your drug is working.' He stood up.

Lincoln looked puzzled. 'What? Stay there?' He took a step backwards, then stumbled sideways as his right leg buckled. He grabbed the desk to steady himself. 'What the fuck?'

Maquina grinned. 'Enjoy your whisky?'

Lincoln stared at the bottle, then staggered across the room, crashing into the wall below the war axe. He grabbed at it, pulling the axe free. But it slipped from his grasp. Then his legs collapsed beneath him. He fell to the floor, twitching, face down on the carpet. He tried to reach for the axe, but his arms wouldn't move.

Maquina walked over to him. 'The axe won't do you any good,' he said. 'I'm afraid you won't find a heart in this version of me. Also, it's not susceptible to the effects of Baclofen.'

Lincoln managed to twist his head to look up at Maquina.

'Help me!' Lincoln screamed. His lips felt thick, his words starting to slur.

Maquina looked at him for a moment. 'Of course. That's something I can do.' He grabbed Lincoln under the armpits, dragged him towards the desk, and swung him up on to it, lying him on his back.

Then he opened one of the desk drawers, withdrawing several coils of rope. He walked around the desk, methodically tying Lincoln's wrists and ankles to the legs of the desk.

'Help me,' Lincoln whispered hoarsely.

'There's no one left to help you. Koji and Yahl know what happened. Koji was the one who spiked the bottle.'

He walked over and picked up the war axe, slamming the blade into the desktop next to Lincoln.

Lincoln no longer seemed able to move his neck, but his eyes rolled towards the axe, wide and staring. Helpless.

Maquina leaned over the desk, tearing open Lincoln's jacket and shirt. Lincoln's chest was heaving, a sheen of sweat coating it.

Maquina looked around. He removed the wooden raven mask from where it hung on the wall, and placed it over Lincoln's desperate eyes.

'Get it off me, please,' Lincoln gasped, barely audible through the mask. 'Take it off me. I'll give you anything.'

Maquina shook his head. 'It's time.'

Lincoln managed to swallow and his voice came back, high-pitched. 'You want him!' he screamed. 'He's Maquina. He's the chief. Not me!'

'They can't hear you,' said Maquina. 'Goodbye, Lincoln.'

Then he blinked out of existence, a white plastic disc spinning through the air, to land edge up in the pile of the carpet.

Lincoln heard something moving on the desk next to him, then felt it pulling at his jacket as though climbing up him. Something heavy landed on his chest. Then a cold sharp point touched the base of his throat.

The queen's scimitar.

He knew what was coming.

He managed to force his muscles into a final scream.

47

THE COWARD

I stared at Maq.

'I don't care what he had planned for you,' I said. 'There was no need to kill Lincoln. He was our friend once.'

Maq shrugged. 'I prefer to think that Lincoln killed himself. Besides, every day more than ten thousand people die from the use of fossil fuels, so why do we count his death as worth more than theirs? And if it takes one death to make the world aware of what rich people like Lincoln are doing to the environment it's a price worth paying.'

'That's nonsense,' I said. 'You weren't trying to claim Lincoln's death as part of GreenWar's campaign. You were trying to blame me for it. You're not a martyr, you're a coward. I still don't understand why you unwound time, though.' And then I realised. I remembered Koji's attempt to apologise as he'd locked me in my room. What had he said? That he was sorry it had come to this. 'Of course, that's why Koji couldn't even look me in the eye. He wouldn't have wanted to blame me unless you had no option. Unless you'd tried to frame someone else and failed. That's what happened, isn't it?'

'Why so many questions?' asked Maq. 'You do realise none of this matters? I wouldn't have told you anything if it did. Five minutes from now you'll forget everything I've told you, everything you've worked out in the last few hours, and you'll be locked back in your room. It was stupid of Koji to let you access the door logs, but this time I'll make sure he gets rid of them. So it really doesn't matter what I tell you now, since you'll only forget it again.'

I took a surreptitious glance at my phone. I needed to spin this out for a few more minutes.

'If I'll forget it then there's no harm in telling me,' I said. 'I'm right, aren't I? We've done this before.'

He hesitated, then shrugged again. 'This was the third time through. We were improvising, but I thought I'd create a smokescreen. Get you to fuck up the investigation, so no one would ever work out what really happened. The first scenario seemed perfect, using Lincoln's corrupt lawyer, who was terrified he was going to be used as a scapegoat on the oil rig trial. We dropped clues in front of you like confetti, and you lapped them all up. We even fired up a Lincoln ghost to spook you and drop the last clue. We didn't know about Kleber's medical condition, which was about to lead you to rule him out as a suspect. Once you'd done that you'd have been asking who'd given you all the evidence that pointed to his guilt. And that was Koji. And Koji would have led you to me. So Koji had to summon the wolf.

'The second time round we decided to make use of what had really happened. We wanted to make sure you knew that the chess set was involved, so we used Rebecca's ghost to get you into the office, and replayed the death scene. And from there it was an easy step to suspecting Rebecca. But we tried a bit too hard. Koji doctored a police report to make you think it was about Rebecca. But he hadn't thought it through properly. Once the real police got here the truth would have come out. And we realised that once they worked out who'd programmed the chess pieces Rebecca was no better a suspect that anyone else. So strike two, and Yahl had to call the wolf.'

Maquina grimaced. 'It's a real mindfuck, though. Yahl was the only one who remembered what had happened that time round. So he had to get Koji away from you and explain it to him, and me. The third time round was the best. I was having to think things up in a hurry, and we were running out of viable suspects. I decided to use your own insecurities to drive you to the obvious conclusion. It was perfect, and it will be perfect again. Because we're going to replay the last part of this scenario, and this time it will stick. You'll be back in your bedroom, with the door locked, and everyone convinced you killed Lincoln while drugged. Paul and Rebecca believe it, and they'll tell the police that. Hell, you'll probably believe it again.'

I sneaked a glance at my phone again. Two more minutes ought to do it.

'Did Koji …?' I hesitated, not sure I wanted to know the answer. 'Did Koji send Yahl to my room?'

'You still don't want to believe anything bad of Koji-Na, do you?' said Maq. 'He's the one who set you up. It may be tearing him apart, but for him the Akaht come before everything.' He paused. 'Actually, he wanted to leave it to the police; he said we'd sown enough confusion that no one will ever suspect us whatever they do with you, or Kleber, or Rebecca. But he's wrong. It's all very messy, and there are too many ways this can be unpicked. It needs finality. There needs to be a clear end to the story – an admission of guilt from someone who can't be asked any questions. That makes it easy for the police to tick the boxes and go home.' He looked up at me. 'I'm sorry, El, but there's no other way.'

'There is,' I said, raising the gun.

Maq shook his head. 'I know you, you're not going to shoot me in cold blood, whatever I've done. You think you're clever enough to work this out a second time and catch me all over again.'

He looked down at the wolf tattoo on his wrist.

I smiled. 'You're right, I'm not going to shoot you.'

'What time is it?' he said.

'Stop asking me that.'

I crouched down, placed my phone on the floor, picked up a rock from Kun's grave, and smashed the phone into several pieces.

'What the fuck, El!'

'You're right, Maq,' I said. 'I do think I can solve this again. I know you too well. I realise now that you always hated it down here in the mines, and you were only here to impress me. For all your talk you're too much of a coward to die here just to spite me. Bear in mind that you don't have long. Without my phone you've no idea what time it is. You're cutting it fine already, and if you leave it too long you'll come back stuck in the mines again, and you'll die down here.'

'You aren't going to remember any of this.'

'Yes I am,' I said.

'What do you mean?' he asked. 'No! You can't be—'

He stared at me as I placed the barrel of the gun under my chin, and took a deep breath.

'Wait—'

I saw his fingers twitch, about to touch the wolf tattoo. His lips began to form a word.

I pulled the trigger.

48

RETRIAL

So I lied to Maq. When I told him it was nine thirty it was actually just after eight. It's easy to lose track of time in the mines.

I'd needed to come back before they locked me up alone in my bedroom. Second time round Maq would have sent Yahl in straight away. I'd have had no chance to escape.

Had I been stupid to trust my life to one man's cowardice? Perhaps. But I'd known Maq well. He wasn't willing to wait, and risk coming back lost in the mines.

Besides, in the alternative scenario I probably died anyway. It was the door logs that had made me realise that Koji was behind everything, and Maq had told me that second time round he'd make sure they were deleted. So if I'd come back with no memory of the previous six hours I'd never have discovered the truth in time.

I'd had no choice.

My real gamble had been as to whether the story about the power of the wolf was real. The only clear evidence I'd ever had of it was what had happened in the mines twenty years earlier. And Maq had just told me that was a lie.

But I'd grown up with it as accepted truth. And Koji had told me it was true, twenty years earlier, at a time when he'd had no reason to lie to me.

And most important, it was the only explanation for Maq knowing what Linc had said to me outside my room. It had to be true.

So it had seemed a risk worth taking.

And I'd been right.

Without knowing the time, Maq hadn't dared to delay.

I'd known he'd panic and do it straight away.

I'd timed it perfectly.

I walked through the door to the kitchen, typing on my phone. Then looked up at the five people assembled at one end of the table.

The kangaroo court. Ready to convict me for a second time. Not that they knew it. Kleber in the centre. Koji and Yahl to his left. Rebecca on his right.

And Maq. Staring at me. Blinking. Realising he'd been shafted. I winked at him.

'So, what is this, a family conference?' I said, pulling up the only empty chair. This time I didn't care that Yahl was in my usual seat. I'd done this once already. 'You all look terribly serious.'

'We are,' said Kleber. 'My client is dead, and we're concerned you're screwing up the investigation.'

'So what are you proposing as an alternative?' I asked. 'Investigation by consensus? We have a show of hands round the room

404

and whichever one of us gets the most votes is the winner? First prize is twenty-five years in Kent Maximum Security Prison?'

'So you accept it could be you?' he said.

'Or you,' I said. 'It seems as though everyone in this room had some reason for wanting Lincoln dead.'

'Excuse me,' said Maq. 'Perhaps—'

Kleber raised a hand towards him. 'Not now, Mr Diaz. You are here under sufferance only, as you remain a key suspect in this case. You will have your chance to speak later.'

For once Kleber's bullying nature was serving me well. Maq was desperate to shut the conversation down in some way, to get the chance to talk to Koji and Yahl alone, but he couldn't without causing suspicion. He sat back, muttering something under his breath.

Kleber turned to me. 'I can assure you, Constable, that I had no reason to kill Lincoln. He was my principal client.'

'Really?' I said. 'You were worried Lincoln was going to use you as a scapegoat on the oil rig trial. That seems like motive enough.'

He sat back, frowning.

I was hoping he didn't ask for details, as I had no real idea of why he might have wanted to murder Lincoln. I was just repeating what Maq had said to me in the mines.

I continued quickly: 'So that's your reason for killing Lincoln. Koji and Yahl here – with Lincoln dead the Akaht stood to take control of Black Lake and get two hundred million dollars.' Koji started to protest, but I continued. 'Rebecca? Lincoln treated her like shit last night and would have dumped her in a moment to get back with me. After she'd pined after him for most of her life. Maybe I'd have put an axe through his chest if he'd treated me like that. Maq? He hated what Lincoln was doing to the environment, and then got tricked into coming here so Lincoln could eat his heart. Again, sounds like a decent motive to me.'

Kleber and Rebecca stared at me when I mentioned the heart-eating.

'And then there's me,' I said. 'On Lincoln's death I get to control eight billion dollars. I can see how some might think that's a motive to murder him, although I can promise you it's not. The last thing I want is that sort of burden, but I can see why some might disagree.'

I paused for breath, and Kleber jumped in.

'That's not all,' he said quickly. 'It seems you had a far more immediate motive to kill Lincoln.'

He nodded to Koji, who lifted the AppleBot on to the table, pressed a button on the back, and it started to walk towards me. I raised an eyebrow to Maq as it made its jerky progress. It was a shame I hadn't managed to get back earlier in time, when I could have found the AppleBot in my room and swapped the engagement ring for something else. It would have been amusing to see their faces when the suitcase opened. But it would have given Maq time to talk to Koji and Yahl and stop this whole charade. Being in the room with everyone was what was keeping me alive.

I could see Maq regarding me quizzically, no doubt wondering how I was going to get out of this one.

The AppleBot dropped to one knee. '*Ella ... will you marry me?*' it asked. Then its arm swung round towards me, holding out the suitcase.

I reached forward and held the lid shut. After a moment it stopped trying.

'I'd rather it didn't throw a million-dollar engagement ring halfway across the room,' I said, cautiously releasing it. The lid stayed closed.

Kleber stared at me. 'So you admit there's a valuable ring in there?'

'Of course,' I said. 'And when I opened the case in my room earlier it fell out. I ended up having to scramble under the bed to find it.'

Koji frowned. He knew I was lying, because he'd only just planted the AppleBot in my room.

Kleber didn't. 'So you accept,' said the lawyer, 'that you had taken a million-dollar engagement ring that belonged to Mr Shan and hidden it in your room?'

'I admit that I was concerned about a valuable ring being left in a safe to which various members of staff might have access, one of whom might be guilty of murder.' I looked across at Koji. 'So, in my capacity as investigating officer I took it into my custody, leaving it in my locked room, and logging it in the case file as being in my custody.' I held up my phone. 'You can check if you want. I can't change what I've logged, and the moment we have communication again the full file will be uploaded to Victoria PD. There was never any question of my trying to hide the fact that I had the ring.'

I might not know much about police work, but I'm an expert on logging evidence in case files. I'd spent two weeks in a windowless basement in Victoria doing nothing but logging exhibits on cold cases.

No one said anything.

I tried not to look too smug.

Kleber seemed thrown. Then he looked down at the papers on the desk in front of him. 'I can see why you needed money,' he said. 'You only have $6,187.23 to your name.'

'Since I wasn't taking the ring for myself I'm not sure how that's relevant. In any event, I live within my means. I don't have any debts, as you'll have seen from that credit report. I'm not driven by money. I could have a better job in Victoria or Vancouver if I wanted. Lincoln offered me jobs on several occasions, including last night. I always turned him down.'

Kleber sat back, seemingly deflated, looking left and right for someone else to help. His cross-examination wasn't going well.

Koji looked at him. 'There's the door logs,' he muttered.

'Of course.' Kleber leaned forward again.

Maq shook his head. He just wanted this to end.

'You, Constable, are the only person who had Lincoln's master code,' said Kleber. 'That's right, isn't it?'

'I don't know that for certain,' I said. 'But I'm happy to assume it for the moment.'

'Yes, you tried a little game with Ms Murray earlier, outside Lincoln's office, to see if she had the code, but she evidently didn't.'

Rebecca scowled at me.

Kleber continued. 'So do you accept that you entered Mr Shan's office at' – he glanced down at a printout in front of him – 'at 22:16 last night, and left at 23:18? As the logs show.'

'No,' I said. 'That would mean that I was in the office when Lincoln was murdered. I wasn't.' I held up a hand as Kleber made to interrupt, pushing his printout towards me. 'Let's look at the original door logs. As Koji told me earlier, unfortunately the storm has caused glitches in the system. I think the entries that you are referring to may be evidence of just that.'

There was a screen on the counter behind me. I twisted round to pick it up, and caught Koji's expression as I turned back. He was motionless, staring straight ahead. He knew what was coming.

'One of the advantages of having Lincoln's master code is that I can access the original door logs,' I said, as I tapped on the screen. I made a pretence of scanning down the numbers, then passed the screen across the table to Kleber, looking puzzled. 'There does appear to have been a glitch of some sort. You'll notice that, unlike your printout, there is no entry for 22:16 or 23:18.'

Kleber studied them for a moment, then dropped the screen angrily on the table. He looked across at Koji, who shrugged.

Kleber turned back to me, brow furrowed. 'You seem, Constable, to be remarkably well prepared to deal with all these points. Suspiciously so.'

'As I'm sure you've told many judges, Counsellor, the truth will shine through.' Although I very much doubted whether Kleber had more than a passing acquaintance with the truth.

'There's more,' said Kleber. To his credit, he didn't give up easily. I was wondering what it was going to be. The suit, or the reason I was fired from the navy? Sensibly, he decided to drop the suit. It was hardly his best point. 'Can you remind us why you left the Canadian Navy?'

'Because I punched an admiral on the nose who thoroughly deserved it. He'd killed one of my dolphins because he wanted to get back to base in time for dinner. What possible relevance has that got to Lincoln's killing? Can you really imagine how this would play out in front of a jury? People like animals. No one's going to turn some entitled dickhead's sore nose into me slicing Lincoln open with an axe.'

I sat back. I felt that someone ought to be cheering at my

performance, but they were all just staring at me, seemingly unsure where to go next.

'Nothing else you want to ask me?' I said. I looked across at Maq. 'We were chatting about the Tsonoqua earlier today. Nothing more to discuss about that?'

He shook his head.

Don't get cocky, I told myself. *Stop now*. I'd got them on the run. Now I needed to work out my exit strategy. I needed to drive a wedge between Maq and the other two.

'I'm sure this has been helpful to my investigation in eliminating some false leads,' I said. 'Before we adjourn there is one other topic I'd like to explore. Mr Kleber, the gift to the Akaht in Lincoln's will. I'm right in understanding that it comes with a condition, doesn't it?'

'Ah ... I'm not sure I'm comfortable discussing probate matters in this forum,' he said.

'No one had much compunction about discussing my private matters,' I said. 'It's relevant to my investigation. If you're too coy let me tell you my understanding of the will, and you can correct me if I'm wrong. On Lincoln's death the Akaht inherit title to the entirety of Black Lake village and the Manor, plus a sum of two hundred million dollars. That's right, isn't it?'

Kleber nodded reluctantly. Koji, Yahl and Maq had their eyes fixed on me, waiting to see where I was going with this. Rebecca looked puzzled by it all.

'But that gift was altered by a codicil that Lincoln signed in the last few months. It is now conditional on Maq not being chief of the Akaht. If he remains chief thirty days after Lincoln's death then the gift is entirely ineffective.' As I'd expected, Koji looked surprised and glanced at Yahl, then across at Maq, then back at me.

'It's quite a problem, isn't it?' I said. 'Because we all know that you can't resign as chief. Death is the only way out. It seems Lincoln didn't know that – or he wanted to leave chaos behind him.'

I stood and picked up the AppleBot.

'Perhaps you're right,' I said to Kleber. 'Maybe it would be better to leave this in the safe after all.'

Yahl was watching me closely, then leaned in towards Koji, muttering something I couldn't hear. Koji whispered back.

I opened the cupboard, pushed various cereal boxes to one side, and typed in Lincoln's code. I replaced the AppleBot and slid the Glock out of its box.

As I turned back to the room everyone's eyes went to the weapon in my hand.

Maq was the first to speak. 'I'm not sure how you think this is going to play out. Are you hoping to shoot all three of us? I can tell you that only Yahl is armed.'

'Keep quiet,' hissed Koji. Yahl shifted in his chair. Was he reaching for his gun?

Maq ignored Koji. 'You seem to have got me boxed into a corner. I don't see any way out. That was a nice lie you told me down in the mines.' The others looked at him in confusion. For them there had never been an escape to the mines, and there never would be. Only he and I remembered it. 'The problem I have is that the moment I leave this room my life is in danger. You've just ensured that, by telling Yahl and Koji about the condition in the will. They have no loyalty to me. They've come so far now they're not going to let me stand between them and the future of the Akaht. So I'm inviting you to take me into protective custody, Constable. In fact, I think it's your duty to do so.'

He sat back, a slight smile on his face. Maq, for all his talk, was always looking to preserve his own skin.

It was Koji, not Yahl, who lurched to his feet, gun in hand. When he'd shifted in his seat Yahl must have been passing him the gun.

Koji pointed it at Maq, then swung round to point it at me. His hand was shaking, his face screwed up as though in pain.

I hesitated.

The barrel of Koji's gun was bouncing around. I remembered what my navy instructors had told me about the inaccuracy of pistols. Even at that range I doubted if he could hit me.

Would I stake my life on it?

'Drop the gun!' I shouted, my finger tightening on the trigger.

'No!' he screamed, turning again towards Maq, who shrank back in his chair.

They eyeballed each other for a long moment.

Then Koji threw the gun down on the table. 'I can't!' he screamed.

Yahl reached towards the gun.

'Don't!' I shouted, taking two quick steps towards Yahl. For the second time that day I touched the back of his neck with the barrel of the Glock. Only this time it wasn't a bluff.

He froze, hand halfway across the table.

And Koji turned and ran. He knocked over his chair and raced for the door.

I knew that if I fired at him, by the time I turned back to Yahl he would have Koji's gun. Or was that just an excuse for letting Koji go?

I kept my gun on Yahl as the kitchen door slammed shut behind Koji.

'Rebecca, get the gun,' I said. She hesitated. 'Now,' I said more firmly. If Maq got his hands on it his loyalties would shift again quickly. He wouldn't be seeking protective custody any more.

Rebecca reached across the table and took the gun. She was holding it loosely at arm's length, and didn't look much more competent with it than Koji had been.

'Point it at the floor,' I said. 'Or at Maq. I don't care if you shoot him by accident.'

She went with the second option. Maq shrank even further into his chair.

'Paul,' I said.

Kleber looked up at me.

'I need you to find some rope or cable ties or something. Dig around in the drawers. Go that way.' I gestured to the left with my gun, past Maq. I still didn't trust Yahl. And while I wouldn't particularly have cared about Kleber being taken hostage, it could get messy.

Kleber got slowly to his feet and made his way round the table. I could hear him rooting around behind me.

My heart rate and breathing were beginning to return to normal.

'Are these good enough?' asked Kleber.

I wasn't going to turn to look. 'What are they?' I asked.

He walked back towards Maq, showing me black cable ties.

'Perfect,' I said. 'Start with Maquina. Tie him to the chair.'

He didn't resist as Kleber, somewhat clumsily, fastened his wrists to the frame of his chair. I kept my eyes on Yahl.

'Rebecca, check the ties,' I said. 'Then bring me your gun.'

Maq winced as she pulled them tighter. I took Koji's gun from her and put it on the counter behind me.

'Now Yahl,' I said. 'Be careful.'

He struggled more than Maq.

'Is there another gun in the Manor?' I asked him. 'Where will Koji have gone?'

Yahl shrugged and said nothing.

'Stay here,' I said to Rebecca and Kleber. 'Don't let them loose whatever they say. And if they try to escape shoot them. I'm going after Koji.'

I stepped cautiously out into the corridor, but it was empty. The elevator display showed that it was at Level Eight – the basement.

Perhaps it was a bluff, but it was the logical route for him to take to escape from the Manor.

I used the stairs. When I reached the basement I pushed the door open a fraction and peered through. There was no sign of Koji.

I started by checking the funicular as that was the quickest way of getting to the Akaht village, which was where he'd go first for help. The carriage was at the top station so it didn't look as though he'd used it.

Could he be hiding somewhere in the basement, waiting for the weather to improve before trying to get to Bamfield?

I moved slowly down the corridor, gun at the ready. I paused at each door, listening.

Nothing.

I was halfway down the corridor when I noticed that one of the doors was ajar. It could have been a bluff by Koji. But then I realised which door it was, and began to suspect that he was beyond trying to bluff me. I knew where he was going, and I could guess why.

It was the same door that Maq and I had used a few hours earlier. Or would use in a few hours. In a different reality at least. In this reality none of that would ever happen.

The door was marked *Ventilation*, and led to the mines.

I pushed it fully open. The passage beyond was empty, the only sound the rush of air being drawn into the Manor.

I walked to the far end, to the entrance to the mines. The door was shut, but on the floor in front of it was a phone.

Koji's.

I knew that it had been left as a message for me. It confirmed what I had guessed already. He didn't want me to follow him.

I picked it up and checked the display to see if he had written anything. An apology perhaps? There was nothing.

What could he possibly have said to me to make things better?

I put the phone in my pocket and stood to one side of the door, angling my gun at the lock. I fired three shots in quick succession, then tried to open it. The lock was wrecked, jammed shut. Koji's override code was not going to work on this door.

I turned away.

Koji was gone.

49

A DEAL

'You never did let me finish what I was telling you in the mine,' said Maq. 'It was a neat move, shooting yourself so you'd remember. I'd never have had the guts.'

'That's what I was counting on,' I said.

We were back in the storeroom where we'd found Maq that morning. Although it seemed much longer ago. And this time Yahl was locked up next door. I'd removed their phones, and unlike the guest rooms there was no inbuilt communication. The last thing I wanted was them contacting other Akaht in Black Lake village, and finding myself having to replay the whole scenario over again. Not that I would remember, of course.

If Maq had to spend another night asleep on a concrete floor that was his problem. 'I came here because we need to talk,' I said. 'You'll be going on trial for Lincoln's murder, as well as what you're currently facing. If you and Yahl try to run a defence based on turning back time you'll be laughed out of court. And

416

if I say what really happened they'll suspend me and send for a shrink. I'm willing to testify that Lincoln broke you out of jail against your will and brought you here to sacrifice you in some Akaht ceremony. I won't be saying why. My testimony might help you, although tying him to the desk and carving out his heart doesn't look great.'

'That wasn't me,' said Maq.

I shrugged. 'I'll leave the lawyers to argue about that one. You left him helpless. If we start talking about time travel and multiple timelines this is all going to fall apart very fast, to no one's benefit. I'm willing to keep quiet about Akaht secrets, as long as you and Yahl are.'

'If you'd let me finish instead of shooting yourself you'd have realised it's not as simple as you think,' said Maquina.

'What do you mean?'

'I told you I didn't kill Lincoln,' said Maq. 'It was his own fault he died. And besides, it was self-defence. Sort of.'

50

THE FORGOTTEN MURDER

Maquina walked down the corridor towards Lincoln's office, Lincoln a pace behind him.

'Good to have you back, Maq,' he said. 'I told you I'd get you out, and I did.'

'Thanks,' said Maquina over his shoulder. 'Neatly done.'

The door clicked open as they approached, and Lincoln gestured for Maquina to go first.

'Have a seat,' he said, pointing to one of the comfortable leather chairs in front of the desk. He put the bottle of whisky he was carrying on the desk. 'Let me get you a drink. You were the only person at the party who didn't have one.'

He walked round the desk, reached into a drawer, and pulled out two glasses. 'Glenmorangie Pride 74. You've not been one for the finer things in life, Maq. You don't know what you've missed.'

Maquina shrugged. 'You never did think of anyone other

418

than yourself, Linc. I could tell you what the carbon footprint is of that bottle, but I won't. It's been a rough night.'

Lincoln poured two healthy measures, and handed one to Maquina, who downed it in one.

Lincoln winced. 'You're meant to savour it. Always the philistine.'

He sat in the other armchair, and looked across at Maquina. 'How are you feeling?'

'Fine, although I think that's gone straight to my head. I'm feeling a bit woozy.'

'You weren't meant to gulp it down like that,' said Lincoln. 'You know, I haven't been entirely honest as to why I brought you here, I'm afraid. It wasn't to help you escape. Turning forty, I've been thinking a lot about mortality. You know I used up my power a long time ago, as did you. Whereas you wasted yours trying to get El into bed, I used mine to start Orcus. But as I got older I began to want that power back. It turns out that there is a way: it plays to our oldest Hamatsa traditions, and requires a blood sacrifice.' He paused, and grinned at Maquina. 'You have to eat the heart of your chief.'

Lincoln sat back, chuckling to himself.

'Wha ... what?' Maquina was slurring his words, his throat closing up.

'That'll be the Baclofen. It's a muscle relaxant.' Lincoln shook his head. 'If only you'd drunk it slower we'd have had more time to talk.'

Maquina was struggling to swallow. He pushed himself up on the arms of the chair, then collapsed forward on to the carpet, legs kicking helplessly as he tried to get up. His hands

419

were twitching, trying to bring them together, to touch the wolf tattoo on his right wrist. But he had lost control of his muscles, and he could no longer speak.

His eyes followed Lincoln as his oldest friend stood up and walked behind the desk, opening a drawer. He took out some ropes, then grabbed Maquina by the front of his shirt, tearing it open and lifting him on to the desk.

He tied Maquina to the desk, then removed the watch that he was wearing. 'Bit earlier than I intended,' he said, adjusting the time. He fastened the watch to Maquina's wrist.

Lincoln looked around the room. 'What else?'

He walked over to the chess set, studying the pieces for a moment, and then selecting the black queen, a white knight and a black rook. He placed them on the desktop next to Maquina.

Maquina gave a strangled gasp. 'Wha—'

'They're programmed to identify their ... ah ... patient as the one wearing the watch. And to start operating at the time set.' Lincoln reached into the drawer where the whisky bottle was, and took out a bowl made from a skull. 'They'll be needing this.'

Lincoln cast one last look around the room, then headed towards the door. 'I'll be back shortly. Sorry, old friend, but we need to get on with this. And I don't want to be here for the really nasty bits.'

The door shut behind him.

Maquina could no longer move his head, and his eyes seemed locked on the ceiling. He sensed a black figure moving at the periphery of his vision.

Something clawed at his shoulder, climbing up.

He watched in horror as the black queen stood on his chest,

drew her curved scimitar and rested the point just below the hollow of his throat.

She pressed down, slicing through skin.

Maquina was numb and could no longer feel pain. But he could sense the pressure of the sword as it cut through to his breastbone. As she moved lower down his chest she vanished from sight, but he could still feel the pressure of the sword as it traced a path across his stomach, then stopped at his navel.

For a moment everything went still.

Then the white knight appeared in place of the queen. He swung the serrated broadsword down from his shoulder, forced it into the gap that the queen had opened, and started to saw through bone.

It was at that point that Maquina passed out.

Mercifully, he did not have to witness the final stages of the murder that all but he would forget.

51

A TEST OF LOYALTY

Koji was woken by the sound of hammering on his bedroom door. Someone was shouting his name.

He struggled out of bed and opened the door.

Lincoln was outside, leaning against the doorpost, a bottle of whisky in one hand. It was almost empty. His shirt was spattered with blood. There seemed to be blood around his mouth.

'They fucking lied, Koji,' said Lincoln. He seemed on the verge of tears. 'They fucking lied to me.'

'Who did?' Koji asked, brushing a hand through his hair.

'The fucking elders. They told me if I ate his heart I'd get my power back. For ever, and as many times as I want. They said it had been done before, but they lied. It doesn't work. I tried.' He held up the empty bottle. 'I had to drink all this before I could bring myself to eat it.'

Koji wasn't sure what was happening. He'd never seen his boss this drunk. Maybe once. The week that Ella had broken off their engagement. Lincoln had come up to the Manor and drunk himself into a stupor.

Koji took him by the arm. 'I don't understand. Come and sit down, and tell me what's going on.'

The staff bedrooms were not to the same standard as the guest suites. There were no plush leather armchairs, so Lincoln perched on the edge of the bed, and Koji crouched next to him.

'What happened, boss? Has someone died?' he asked.

Lincoln nodded. 'Noah's dead. I killed him for no reason, just because of these stupid fucking stories. I killed my oldest friend for no fucking reason.'

'You mean you destroyed Maquina's ghost?' asked Koji, confused. 'So what? Good job done. Did you catch him and turn him off?'

'You don't understand,' said Lincoln. 'That wasn't a ghost in *The Cage*. It was Maq. I broke him out and brought him here, to eat his heart. What a waste of time.'

He paused, then lurched forward and grabbed Koji by his collar, his eyes desperate, pulling him closer. 'Maybe the heart wasn't fresh enough. The legend said you had to eat the beating heart of the chief. Maybe I left it too long, getting them to kill him while I wasn't there. I should have been braver. Maybe I need to do it with my own hands.' Suddenly he looked excited. 'We could try again. Who's the heir? Who's the next chief? It would still work with them. You'd help me, wouldn't you, Koji? You always help me.'

Lincoln released his grip on Koji and took a final swig from the whisky bottle, then threw it into the corner, and collapsed on to his side. He curled up in a ball on the bed.

'Go up to my office and tidy it up. Do whatever you need to. Sort it out for me. I'm going to sleep.'

Just when Koji thought things couldn't get any worse, there was a loud banging on his door: 'Naniq-Koj,' came a voice. 'What's all the noise? What's going on in there?'

It was Yahl.

52

CHOICES

Koji and Yahl stood in the doorway to Lincoln's office.

Koji shook his head. He'd fixed some messes in his time working for Orcus, but nothing like this.

There was blood everywhere.

Maquina lay on the desk, tied down, a long red gash running from his throat to his navel.

The room stank of blood and whisky.

A skull-shaped cup was upturned on the floor, next to a bloodstained white chess knight.

'What the fuck!' Yahl exclaimed. 'What happened here?'

'I don't know exactly,' said Koji. 'Lincoln told me he'd killed the chief and eaten his heart, but he didn't say how.' Koji's eyes flicked to the war axe hanging on the wall next to the desk. Its blade was clean. If Lincoln had used that, why was it the only thing in the room that he'd bothered to clean up?

'Where do we even start?' said Koji. 'We could get him down

to the bay. The ocean has swallowed enough bodies over the years, it won't notice one more.'

'They died on the ocean, in shipwrecks,' said Yahl. 'Not like this. How do we get him out of the house without anyone noticing? There are too many people staying: the lawyer, Dr Manning, Rebecca, someone would notice. And even if we get him out, how do we clean up this mess with no one seeing?'

'Lincoln will be sober enough by morning,' said Koji. 'He can keep them out of the way. We get rid of the chief, and we tell the others that he escaped from the house in the night, and disappeared. They think he's just a ghost, they're not going to care what happened to him.'

'Really?' said Yahl. 'They're not stupid. If we've got the real chief – or had him – then the one in jail must be a ghost. From what you said he'll be found out soon enough. When that happens, do you really think Dr Manning, or Rebecca, or the lawyer, aren't going to realise that we had the real chief here? You told me Dr Manning spoke to him. She'll work it out.'

Koji went silent for a moment. 'True. If they get the police up here there's no way we can hide this mess from them, however well we clean up.'

'Why are we even thinking of doing this?' asked Yahl. 'We've done nothing wrong. Lincoln has killed our chief, and wants us to cover for him. Maquina may not have been good to us, but he's still our chief. If I have to choose between him and Lincoln, it's an easy choice.'

'Are you saying you won't help?'

'Why do you want to help him when you owe him nothing?

If he gets caught we sink with him. We've tied ourselves so tightly to him that we don't even own our land any more.'

'So what do we do?' asked Koji.

'We summon the wolf and get the chief back. Do we know when he died?'

'It can't have been before ten o'clock, as I saw Lincoln then. That was when he sent me downstairs, saying we'd deal with Maquina in the morning. Now I know why.'

'We bring him back.'

'And then what?' asked Koji. 'Lincoln won't remember, so he'll just try again. You know what he's like. He won't believe us if we say that the heart-eating is a lie. He was saying some terrible things to me just now. He said he'd try again with the next chief, because maybe the heart hadn't been fresh enough when he ate it. He's obsessed with this. Whatever we do, it isn't going to end here.'

'We could end it,' said Yahl. 'We get ourselves away from Lincoln for ever.'

'How?'

'You told me that if Lincoln dies the Akaht inherit Black Lake and enough money to live on for ever. And from what you tell me, this is never going to end while Lincoln is around.'

'What are you suggesting?' asked Koji.

'We swap Lincoln for the chief. There's a justice to it. This is our one chance, and we need to act now before Lincoln does something worse. He has no respect for the Akaht any more.'

Koji said nothing. He checked the time: 03:52.

'Lincoln deserves to die, after what he's done,' said Yahl. 'It would be right.'

427

Koji was silent still, staring at Maquina's body.

'You know I'm right, Naniq-Koj. We need to be bold, and we need to do this for our people. If we are too timid we may lose everything.'

Eventually Koji nodded. 'If we do this,' he said, 'we'd need someone to blame. We can't hide Lincoln's death, he's too well known to just disappear. We don't have much time. We need to speak to Maquina, and find out what terrible things happened in this room.'

'So who will summon the wolf, Naniq-Koj?' asked Yahl. 'You or me?'

'No,' said Koji. 'We may still need our power. Besides, I want no one else here for what is to happen. We get Vekla to do it, and then she leaves. I want your sister out of this. It makes it a little more complicated, but it will still work. The most important thing is that Maquina will remember.'

Koji headed back down to the staff bedrooms, Yahl following.

He knocked on a door, and after a minute a young woman opened it, running a hand through her tousled hair.

'What time—' she began.

Koji interrupted her. 'We've got to move fast. I need you to summon the wolf. No time to explain, but when it is done you need to find me, and take me to Maquina. He'll be reliving some very unpleasant memories, but I need to speak to him immediately.'

The woman shook her head and blinked. 'What's this about? Why?'

'Time's tight,' said Koji. 'The chief is dead and Lincoln killed him. We need to bring him back.'

Vekla's eyes widened. 'What the fuck! Why?'

'I'll explain later,' Koji said urgently. 'Please, you just need to do it. Now!'

She looked over his shoulder at Yahl, who nodded.

'Right now?' she asked.

'Yes. Before you do it,' Koji said, 'I need you to remember three things, and you must repeat them back to me when you see me next, because you will remember them and I won't. First, Lincoln killed Maquina and ate his heart. Second, Lincoln must die for the Akaht to survive. Third, the Akaht cannot be blamed for Lincoln's death – find a suspect. Can you remember that?'

Vekla stared at him, then looked at Yahl. She seemed about to ask something, but stopped herself. Finally she took a deep breath, and nodded.

'Good, do it now,' said Koji. 'Then find me, tell me those three things, and take me to Maquina.'

Vekla touched the fingers of her left hand to the wolf tattoo on her right wrist, and whispered softly: '*Kuwitap.*'

And the wolf ate time.

2046

53

FRANKENSTEIN

Prosecuting counsel leaned forward, peering at me over his
half-moon glasses.

'I want to be absolutely clear about your evidence, Constable
Manning.' He glanced sideway at the jurors, for emphasis. 'You
say that the defendant, Mr Diaz, deliberately left Mr Shan to be
killed. To have his heart cut out?'

The judge coughed. 'Perhaps, Sir Charles, if you let the witness – your witness – give her own evidence that would assist
the jury more. Besides, I'm not sure that Constable Manning
is in any way qualified to speculate as to the defendant's intentions. I do have to keep in mind that Mr Diaz and Mr de Aguayo
are unrepresented.'

'Of course, my lord.' The lawyer reddened slightly, and
turned back to me. 'Constable, could you explain to the jury
your understanding of how Mr Shan died.'

'Obviously I wasn't there to see it,' I said. 'When I found Mr Shan on the morning of 5 October he had evidently been dead for some time. He was tied to the desk in his office, and it appeared that his heart had been removed. Subsequently Maquina ... the defendant, Mr Diaz, told me ...' I hesitated, and looked up at the judge. 'Am I allowed to say what I was told?'

The judge nodded. 'I have already ruled on that in the absence of the jury. Although you didn't caution Mr Diaz before interviewing him, I have determined that what he said was volunteered by him outside a formal interview, and is therefore admissible.'

I swallowed, and nodded. 'Mr Diaz told me that on the evening of 4 October Mr Shan took him to his office, and offered him a glass of whisky. Mr Shan then claimed to have drugged the whisky with a muscle relaxant. In fact, it appears that Mr Shan had, inadvertently, and fatally for him, muddled up the drinks. So Mr Shan got the drugged one, and Mr Diaz the other. Mr Shan told Mr Diaz that he had broken him out of jail so that he could take part in an Akaht ceremony, which apparently involved cutting out the chief ... Mr Diaz's heart.' I looked round the court. There were several members of the Akaht in the public gallery.

'I should say, in fairness to the Akaht,' I added, 'that I could find no record of any such ceremony, and I've subsequently been told by them that it doesn't—'

The judge interrupted me. 'Constable, on this occasion I am going to stop you. If this is relevant to the case against the defendants, no doubt the prosecution will call a witness who has actual knowledge of it.'

'Sorry,' I said. 'Anyway, for whatever reason, Mr Shan said that he wanted to remove Mr Diaz's heart. He had apparently adapted some surgical procedures he was working on with Victoria General Hospital to achieve that.'

'Let's take this in stages,' said the prosecutor. 'First, he intended to drug Mr Diaz?'

'That's right.'

'And then he was going to have his heart removed, but he wasn't going to do that himself?'

'No, he was planning to use some new technology he'd developed for micro-surgery. Although,' I added, 'it was hidden in a chess set designed by Mr Shan's girlfriend.'

'Did he say why he'd gone to these elaborate lengths to remove Mr Diaz's heart?'

'Not exactly, but knowing Lincoln there were probably three reasons. First, he loved technology, and he would use it even when it made things more complicated than necessary.'

'Can you give us any examples of that?'

'There are two that immediately come to mind,' I said. 'A few years ago, when he proposed to me, he programmed a robot to propose instead of doing it himself. And the night that he died he insisted on all the waiters at the party being ghost dancers and attending remotely from Vancouver. It would have been much simpler, and far cheaper, to have used local staff attending in person. But Lincoln adored using technology.'

'And what were the other reasons why he used the chess pieces?'

'Well, second, he had a strange sense of humour. I suspect he found it amusing to hide his surgical tools – his murder weapons – in plain sight in his office. And the third reason is that he probably thought it the most efficient way of achieving what he wanted: the removal of Mr Diaz's heart. I understand that from a surgical point of view it's not that easy, and would have been difficult to do with an axe, which is what I initially thought had been used.'

The prosecutor held up a hand. 'I'll stop you there, Constable. The jury is going to hear next from the surgeon at Victoria General Hospital whose work Mr Shan adapted to create the chess pieces. Now let's move on to what you can give evidence about. Were you aware of how the chess piece surgeons were controlled?'

'Yes. I saw direct evidence of that when I was in the Manor. Mr Shan had programmed them to start working when the time on the watch that he was wearing matched the actual time. And he apparently told Mr Diaz that they were designed to operate on the person wearing the watch.'

'But Mr Shan was the one wearing the watch, so that seems a mite foolish.'

'Mr Diaz said that he assumed Mr Shan would have put the watch on him if the drug in the whisky had worked. I guess Mr Shan wanted some failsafe mechanism for them to identify the person to be killed, and then it backfired on him.'

'Please don't guess,' said the barrister. 'Just tell us what you know.'

'That's my understanding.'

'So, after Mr Shan collapsed in his office, what happened?'

'Mr Diaz told me that Mr Shan called for help, and he lifted him on to the desk.'

'Most admirable,' muttered the lawyer. 'And yet he then tied Mr Shan to the desk. Why did he say he did that?'

'Mr Diaz told me that he feared that Mr Shan would attack him, or try to escape. He thought maybe Mr Shan was faking a reaction to the drug. I'm not sure I believed Mr Diaz, though.'

The judge coughed. 'Your belief is not what matters, Constable Manning. I will instruct the jury to ignore the last part of that answer.'

'And then what happened?' asked the prosecutor.

'Mr Diaz said that he left the room. Well, I say "left" but he was never actually in the room. He was there remotely, as a ghost dancer. But he turned off the link.'

'Again, the jury will hear more about the workings of the ghost dancers in due course, from a technical expert,' the prosecutor said. 'Very well.' He looked down at his notes, then turned to have a muffled conversation with the lawyer behind him. 'I've no further questions, my lord.'

The judge leaned forward, looking at Maq and Yahl. 'Mr Diaz, the evidence of the witness seems clear, but if you have any questions for Constable Manning, now is your time to ask them.'

Maq stood up. 'Just a couple, your honour.'

He turned to me. 'El ... Constable Manning, from your evidence, I am not the person who cut Lincoln's heart from his chest?'

'No.'

'I am not the person who killed him?'

'No.'

'And nor was Yahl ... Mr de Aguayo?'

'Not that I'm aware.'

'Mr de Aguayo wasn't even in the room when Lincoln died, was he?'

'No.'

'In fact, it's right, isn't it, that Mr Shan was killed by his own creations, which he had programmed to remove the heart of the person wearing his watch?'

'I believe so, yes. But—'

'And if—'

The judge interrupted him. 'Mr Diaz, I don't think that the witness had finished her answer. It will help us all if you let her do so.' He smiled at me. 'Was there more you wanted to say?'

'Yes. I was going to add, that although Mr Diaz didn't kill Lincoln, he could have removed the watch from Lincoln's wrist, and stopped him being killed.'

'But then,' said Maq, 'I'd have been the one left holding the watch, and the ghosts would have attacked me.'

The judge interrupted again. 'Mr Diaz, I won't stop this line of questioning, as you are unrepresented, although this seems to me to be a matter for argument, not evidence. But if the witness has anything to say on this, I will let her answer.'

'We don't know for sure what would have happened if Mr Diaz had removed the watch,' I said. 'I understand however, that the RCMP IT team have determined that if Mr Diaz had removed the watch from Mr Shan, and thrown it on the floor, the chess pieces would have stopped working. They depended on the watch to identify their target.'

The prosecutor jumped to his feet. 'My lord, in fairness to the defendants I should say that I recognise that Constable

Manning has no relevant expertise on this point, and cannot give that evidence. However, I will be adducing expert evidence in due course to confirm what she has just told the court.'

The judge nodded. 'Thank you, Sir Charles.'

Maq continued, 'Of course, I didn't know that at the time?'

'Not that I'm aware,' I said.

'And I didn't actually know that the pieces were programmed to operate on the person wearing the watch?'

I hesitated before answering. As Maq and I were well aware, he'd been told that in clear terms by Lincoln, and then seen a practical demonstration of it first hand when the black queen sliced open his chest. But that had happened the first time they had been in the office, when Maq had died, before Yahl's sister, Vekla, had unwound time. It wasn't something I could start talking about if I wanted to retain any credibility with the jury.

'I ... I don't know,' I answered. 'But it doesn't matter, because you were never at any risk, because you weren't actually in the room. It was just a ghost you were controlling.'

'But a very realistic ghost,' said Maq, 'designed to make me believe that it was real. That was the whole point of the technology and I was caught up in the moment.'

The judge coughed. 'I really don't see how the witness can answer that, Mr Diaz.'

Maq nodded, and glanced at Yahl, who shook his head. 'I've no other questions, your honour.'

'Thank you, Mr Diaz,' said the judge. 'Any re-examination, Sir Charles?'

'No, my lord. May Constable Manning be released as a witness?'

'Of course. Thank you for your evidence, Constable. You are free to leave.'

As I left the witness box the prosecutor turned back to the judge. 'With your lordship's permission I will call my next witness, Surgeon Regina Latham, from Victoria General Hospital.'

I took a seat at the back of the courtroom, as I was interested to hear what the surgeon had to say. After she had been sworn in and confirmed her name and qualifications, the prosecutor asked: 'Can you tell the court about the interactions you had with Mr Lincoln Shan before his death?'

'Certainly. Mr Shan approached the hospital early last year to say that he was working on new technology which he thought might be of interest to us. I attended a presentation with one of my colleagues at Iona Island, the headquarters of Mr Shan's company. We were made to sign a fairly onerous confidentiality agreement as he said that the technology was top secret. What he showed us was a form of portable hard light that he had developed. Of course I'd heard of hard light, but it had never occurred to me that it might usefully be applied in my field.'

'And what did he propose to you?' asked the prosecutor.

'His initial suggestion was that we could develop human-sized surgeons from what he called his ghost dancers, that could be fitted with artificial intelligence and used to carry out operations. It seemed to us that that was a non-starter. AI technology is nowhere near advanced enough to safely permit that. But we did see a potential use for hard light, and over the next few months we developed something different: surgical tools made from hard light.'

She paused, and looked around the court. 'Perhaps if I could demonstrate?'

'Of course,' said the prosecutor, nodding to the court usher.

The usher walked over to the witness box and handed the surgeon a metal suitcase, which she opened. She angled it so that the jury could see the contents, a grey foam inlay holding what looked like surgical instruments.

'These are the tools we developed with Mr Shan,' she said. 'We already use robots in our operating theatres, essentially programmable instruments mounted on movable arms that perform some tasks for us. What was so revolutionary about Mr Shan's technology was that we could create a set of miniature hard light tools, each of which was programmed to carry out a single function. It would be of limited use in a hospital such as ours, but the possibilities out in the field were enormous, as were the implications for hospitals without our resources, particularly in the developing world. Despite what happened with Mr Shan, and how he twisted this technology, we are continuing to work on it with Orcus. It has an extraordinary potential to save lives.'

'But, as you say, Mr Shan twisted the technology?'

'Yes. My speciality is heart surgery, which with hindsight is perhaps why Mr Shan wanted me involved. Some of the tools we had developed were intended to assist with that, to cut open the chest, saw through the sternum, and hold it open while the surgery takes place. Mr Shan evidently saw a way of using those tools for his purposes.'

'You have examined the chess pieces that Mr Shan created?'

'I have,' continued the surgeon. 'They were essentially

modified versions of our tools disguised as chess pieces. The queen was a mobile scalpel, used to slice open the skin, and later to cut the blood vessels leading to the heart. The knight had been given a serrated broadsword that operated like a sternal saw – which we use to cut through the sternum, the breastbone. The rook was effectively a rib-spreader – what we use for holding the ribs apart during surgery. It was a clever adaptation, two spiral tubes, one inside the other, which would get longer or shorter as the spirals turned.'

'So these chess pieces – these adapted surgical tools – were what killed Mr Shan?'

The surgeon hesitated. 'Well, I think that's really a matter for the pathologist to tell the court. What I can say is that the pieces were programmed to remove a human heart. In my experience that usually results in death.'

The judge looked up. 'Except in lawyers, perhaps.'

The row of barristers dutifully laughed.

'Very droll, my lord,' said the prosecutor. 'I've no further questions.'

'Mr Diaz?' said the judge. 'Do you have any questions for the witness?'

Maq shook his head.

The judge turned back to the prosecutor. 'The witness may be released. Sir Charles, in light of the evidence we've heard this morning it seems to me that there is a legal issue that I need to resolve, namely whether Mr Diaz owed a duty to try to save Mr Shan's life by removing the watch, and whether he is culpable if he failed to comply with that duty. And different consider-ations will apply to Mr Aguayo. I will need your assistance, Sir

Charles, on what may not be entirely straightforward issues of law.'

'Certainly, my lord. If the jury was to retire early before the short adjournment, perhaps we could decide then how, and when, to deal with these issues. In the meantime, I will call my next witness, Inspector Francis du Pont from the RCMP.'

I left them to it. I had no desire to live through the events of that day yet again.

A week later, after legal argument, the judge directed the jury to acquit Maq and Yahl of the single charge of murder that they faced. He said that legally Maq had owed no duty to prevent Lincoln being killed, and Lincoln was to blame for his own death. It was, concluded the judge, 'a case of Frankenstein being killed by his own monster'.

He described the case against Yahl as 'flimsy in the extreme'.

If only he'd known what had actually happened over those two days in Black Lake. Perhaps Maq was not legally to blame for Lincoln's death, but he had known perfectly well what was going to happen when he left Lincoln tied to the desk and wearing the watch. Maq had lived through it himself and could easily have stopped the killing.

And later he and Yahl had intended to murder me in my room, which certainly deserved punishment. But that had all happened in a time that Maq had unwound. It was a reality which only he and I could remember. Even Yahl would know nothing of it.

Nevertheless, perhaps the law had unknowingly achieved

a fair outcome. After all, in another reality Lincoln had had Maq tied to his desk, had his heart cut out, and eaten it. I could understand how someone might overreact a little to that sort of behaviour.

I was unlikely ever to see Maq again. But I had no doubt that there would be nights when he would wake up screaming, helpless as the black queen sliced his skin from throat to navel. Knowing that what was to come was worse.

Those were memories that no wolf could erase. Perhaps that would be punishment enough.

There were three other sets of legal proceedings that followed the events at Black Lake Manor.

In the first, Paul Kleber did a deal with the prosecutors. Ever the lawyer, he'd seen the writing on the wall, and decided to cut his losses. He pleaded guilty to colluding in GreenWar's attack on Orcus's oil rig, blaming everything on Lincoln who wasn't there to defend himself. Kleber was serving five years in a white-collar prison and had been disbarred.

Not that he had any clients left anyway. I'd fired him as Orcus's lawyer at the first opportunity. I'd then got some proper advice as to what I could and couldn't do with Lincoln's fortune. I was proposing to set up the charity, appoint a decent board of directors, and step away. Handling that sort of money wasn't within my skill set. Not that it was eight billion dollars any more. With Lincoln dead the value of Orcus's stock had fallen sharply. And then, once it became known how he'd died, the market for ghost dancers had vanished. In the public's eyes the chess pieces and the ghost dancers were one and the same.

After Maq was acquitted of Lincoln's murder the prosecutors quietly dropped the case against him in relation to the oil rig murders. They said they couldn't prove that he had ordered the attack.

There was a second set of proceedings involving the Akaht. With Maq still alive the codicil to Lincoln's will meant that they wouldn't get their two hundred million dollars. They were challenging that, arguing that a condition in a will that incited people to murder was illegal. In return, the Attorney General of British Columbia was arguing that they shouldn't inherit anyway, because it was Akaht members who had killed Lincoln. The Akaht case had presumably been helped by the acquittal of Maq and Yahl. I rather hoped they won: they deserved to control their own destiny again.

The third set of proceedings hadn't lasted long. I'd had to appear in front of an RCMP tribunal inquiring into the circumstances of Koji's escape. I'd been commended for my actions. The tribunal said that in the circumstances I'd been right not to shoot.

It gave me no comfort.

54

KOJI

14 APRIL 2046, PACHENA BAY

The Akaht burial ground is on a spit of land high on the cliffs overlooking Pachena Bay.

It wasn't easy to find Koji's grave as there are no headstones. But I knew that the carved wooden wolf was his namesake, howling at the stars where the Akaht believed that he now dwelt.

Lincoln's grave was in Victoria, a much grander affair made out of marble. I suspected he would have preferred to be buried in Pachena Bay, but the Akaht wanted nothing more to do with him.

I knelt next to the wolf, my knees sinking into the damp grass, and asked Koji to forgive me. I knew he'd lied to me. Yet still he was Koji-Na. And what he had done had not been for himself, but for the Akaht. His loyalties had torn him apart.

I was probably the one person who could have found him.

But I hadn't offered to help. I was pretty sure he'd gone into the mines to die. For Koji, a lifetime spent inside a prison cell would have been worse than death. And I couldn't see him trying to flee through the mines. Even if he could have found a way out, where would he have gone? His life was with the Akaht at Black Lake.

So I told the police where he was, although I didn't expect them to find him. Not alive at least. They tried. They flew in specialist underground teams and divers, and spent days exploring the mineshafts.

And found nothing. I liked to think that he'd managed to get to the cave with the lifeboat and the skeletons. That he'd died where the story of the Akaht had begun.

It seemed unlikely, though. I'd never told him about the cave. But maybe Maq had. Or maybe a black wolf had appeared to guide him through the tunnels, reversing the journey on which it had led the captain so many years before.

Whatever the truth, Koji's body had not been found. So his grave was a memorial rather than a burial site.

It was my first visit, and would also be my last.

I was leaving Bamfield. I'd resigned my position at the Marine Centre and my post as special constable.

There was nothing left for me at Black Lake. Like Maq, I had memories I couldn't erase. All I could do was try to outrun them.

I reached into my pocket and took out the nameplate from the lifeboat. I ran my fingers along the raised black letters. It hadn't been relevant to the case against Maq and Yahl, so it had never made it into any evidence log. I had intended to leave it on Koji's grave, my tribute to him. But I realised now that it had little to do with Koji. It was part of a different story.

Down on the reef at the end of the bay was where it had all begun when the *Pride of Whitby* sank almost two hundred and fifty years earlier. Maquina – the original Maquina – had stood somewhere nearby and watched her crew drown.

I rested my hand on the head of the wooden wolf, stroking it. Then I stood, and turned my back on Koji-Na for the last time.

I walked to the edge of the cliff looking out over the bay. Today the sea was calm, and somewhere beneath it was all that remained of the *Pride of Whitby*. I threw the nameplate as far out as I could, watching it disappear into the water.

Then I took the footpath back through the woods towards Bamfield.

I hadn't decided where I was going. Probably somewhere warmer. Lincoln had been right about one thing – I was getting too old to be jumping into the North Pacific chasing octopuses. Rebecca was fleeing her memories too, and had returned to her native Scotland. Perhaps I would take up her invitation to visit.

With his gift to me of our engagement ring Lincoln had given me the opportunity to go where I wanted, to do something for myself.

He had given me freedom.

55

SCARLETT

I had one last duty to perform before I could leave.

I borrowed a boat from the Marine Centre to get to a small island off the coast of Bamfield.

I anchored about fifty metres from the shore, above a reef, then unstrapped the barrel that I'd carefully stowed aboard. I lowered it over the side, still tied on.

I checked my tank and regulator, pulled down my mask, and slipped backwards into the water.

Strictly speaking, for safety, I should have had a second person in the boat with me. But I wanted this moment to myself. I didn't want to have to share it with anyone.

I swam up to the barrel and unscrewed the lid.

Scarlett shot out, diving for the dark rocks below.

I replaced the lid and followed more slowly.

Part of me feared that she would find a cave to hide in and not come out until I'd gone. But after a few minutes she reappeared, her mantle bright red, excited and curious about her new environment, arms moving rapidly across the surface of the reef. Fish darted out of the way.

I floated nearer, trying not to spook her.

I knew she'd seen me, but whether she would recognise me like this was another matter.

As I drifted closer she stopped moving, regarding me out of one eye. Then she cautiously reached out an arm, running her suckers across the bare skin of my hand, tasting me. Another arm followed, pulling me towards her. Then another. Her skin turned white.

Behind my mask I was crying.

I stayed with Scarlett until my air was almost gone, swimming, touching, losing each other round the reef, then finding each other again.

Eventually, however, I had to prise myself loose from a final embrace. I headed for the surface, leaving her where she belonged.

Not looking back.

There was a risk to Scarlett with her missing arm. I hoped that despite the scars she bore from past battles she would survive her freedom.

I had the same hope for myself.

ACKNOWLEDGEMENTS

My mother recently asked why *Black Lake Manor* had become more gory with each successive draft. My answer was two words: Miranda Jewess.

Her editorial notes include advice to take the killing more slowly because otherwise '*it removes all the fun*'; and that to extract a heart from a living human '*you'd be better off ripping it out with your bare hands*'. She also had helpful views on which parts of the body to eat first: '*always start with the buttocks*'.

Miranda's extensive and detailed knowledge in these matters was as useful as it was disturbing. Once again, I owe her my heartfelt thanks for turning my original 80,000-word manuscript (of which perhaps half survives) into a published novel.

In writing *Black Lake Manor* I had the input of two brilliant editors. When Miranda went off to build her own tiny human (presumably from spare parts kept in the basement), Therese Keating stepped in. I recognise that I didn't make her job easy by having four separate timelines, one of which is repeatedly rewound. My thanks to Therese for making sure that all the pieces fit together properly, and for helping translate my 'lawyerspeak' into human dialogue.

Thanks also to everyone at Viper and Profile Books for their hard work and support, in particular: Graeme Hall, Flora Willis, Drew Jerrison, Claire Beaumont, Siân Gibson, Alex Elam and Niamh Murray. And for her meticulous copy edit, my thanks to Alison Tulett.

As ever, my agent, Max Edwards, provided excellent support and ideas along the way. I am particularly grateful to him for making me see what I couldn't: the need to deal with Ella's internal turmoil and how she coped with it through her relationship with Scarlett. That insight was invaluable. My thanks to all at Aevitas Creative Management for their continued support, including, behind the scenes, Sydney James and Tom Lloyd-Williams.

My wife, Julie, has – as before – borne much of the burden of my writing. I do appreciate that there are times when I disappear down the rabbit hole and become even more difficult to live with than normal. Perhaps the low point was when I told her the story about the Person from Porlock. I appreciate that I am no Samuel Taylor Coleridge – but in my defence there had been an awful lot of knocks on my study door that day.

Julie was also the first reader of – and enthusiast for – *Black Lake Manor*. My thanks to her, and also to Geoff Steward, Charlotte Peach and Mimi Steward for their comments on early drafts. Particular thanks to Taryn Tomlinson, not only for reading several drafts, but also for her intimate knowledge of Vancouver Island. She gave me the location of Black Lake, and told me the haunting story of the wreck of the *Valencia* near Pachena Bay in 1906, elements of which appear in the (fictional) wreck of the *Pride of Whitby* a hundred years earlier.

I not only visited Vancouver Island, but also read numerous books about the island and its people. Most useful were *Hamatsa: The Enigma of Cannibalism on the Pacific Northwest Coast* by Jim McDowell; *The Haunting of Vancouver Island* by Shanon Sinn; and *The Adventures of John Jewitt* by John Jewitt and Robert Brown. The story of Jewitt and Maquina is broadly true, although Captain Ross is fictional – as are the Akaht. The Tsonoqua Ceremony – and the booklet that Ella finds describing it – exist only in my imagination.

In relation to Scarlett my main source of inspiration was the excellent *The Soul of an Octopus* by Sy Montgomery.

Finally, I should thank my family – Julie, Elliot and Caden – for their time, thoughts, ideas and love.

ABOUT THE AUTHOR

Guy Morpuss worked as a barrister in London for thirty years, on cases featuring drug-taking cyclists, dead Formula 1 champions and aspiring cemetery owners. His favourite books involve taking a twist on reality and playing with the consequences, which led to his debut novel, *Five Minds*, about five people stuck in one body, trying to kill one another. He is currently working on his third novel. Guy lives near Farnham with his wife and two sons. When not writing he can usually be found walking or running in the Surrey Hills. Find him on Twitter @guymorpuss